BEHIND THE LIES

BEHIND THE LIES

To: Stuart Cohn
From: Jim Tribbett for your years of friendship. This author was a high school classmate who has written one of the most timely and effective books and should soon be a best seller

Joe Smiga *Joe Smiga*

Copyright © 2009 by Joe Smiga.

Library of Congress Control Number: 2009900250
ISBN: Hardcover   978-1-4415-0286-5
           Softcover   978-1-4415-0285-8

All rights reserved. No part of this book may be reproduced or transmitted in any form or by any means, electronic or mechanical, including photocopying, recording, or by any information storage and retrieval system, without permission in writing from the copyright owner.

This is a work of fiction. Names, characters, places and incidents either are the product of the author's imagination or are used fictitiously, and any resemblance to any actual persons, living or dead, events, or locales is entirely coincidental.

This book was printed in the United States of America.

For an author signed copy go to: **www.joesmiga.com**

To order additional copies of this book, contact:
Xlibris Corporation
1-888-795-4274
www.Xlibris.com
Orders@Xlibris.com
50061

Contents

Acknowledgements		11
Prologue:	April 2010	13
Chapter One:	Washington, DC Same Time, Seven Zones to the West	17
Chapter Two:	Next Day in Iran	21
Chapter Three:	Oval Office: CIA Presentation	25
Chapter Four:	Late at Night	30
Chapter Five:	A Week Later	34
Chapter Six:	Beginning of May	37
Chapter Seven:	Mossad Proposes	41
Chapter Eight:	Joint Presentation	44
Chapter Nine:	Feedback	49
Chapter Ten:	Middle of May	52
Chapter Eleven:	Following the Training	58
Chapter Twelve:	End of May	63
Chapter Thirteen:	First Week of June	69
Chapter Fourteen:	The Same Week	72
Chapter Fifteen:	One Week Later	76
Chapter Sixteen:	First Trip to Russia	81
Chapter Seventeen:	Meeting with Top Military Leaders	85
Chapter Eighteen:	Third Week of June	92
Chapter Nineteen:	After Their Trip	98
Chapter Twenty:	Authorized Mission	102
Chapter Twenty-One:	July Departure	107

Chapter Twenty-Two:	Meeting the Mafiya	115
Chapter Twenty-Three:	Engineering Challenges	119
Chapter Twenty-Four:	August Insertion	122
Chapter Twenty-Five:	Same Night Off Iran	128
Chapter Twenty-Six:	NSA Tracking Capabilities	131
Chapter Twenty-Seven:	Second Guessing	134
Chapter Twenty-Eight:	Executive Power	139
Chapter Twenty-Nine:	Second Week in August	142
Chapter Thirty:	Radioactive Readings	147
Chapter Thirty-One:	Working a Deal	151
Chapter Thirty-Two:	End of the Second Week	155
Chapter Thirty-Three:	Fourth Week in August	157
Chapter Thirty-Four:	Second Site	160
Chapter Thirty-Five:	Leaving No Traces	168
Chapter Thirty-Six:	After Labor Day	172
Chapter Thirty-Seven:	Two Days Later	175
Chapter Thirty-Eight:	Second Week of September	179
Chapter Thirty-Nine:	End of September	182
Chapter Forty:	Seventy-Two Hours Later	187
Chapter Forty-One:	Pushing for a Sample	191
Chapter Forty-Two:	Succession Matters	194
Chapter Forty-Three:	Early October	197
Chapter Forty-Four:	Successful	203
Chapter Forty-Five:	End of October	208
Chapter Forty-Six:	Middle of November	211
Chapter Forty-Seven:	Same Time in November	215
Chapter Forty-Eight:	Arranging a Return	220
Chapter Forty-Nine:	End of November	224
Chapter Fifty:	After Thanksgiving	230
Chapter Fifty-One:	Early December	237
Chapter Fifty-Two:	Packing the Goods	242
Chapter Fifty-Three:	Reporting to the Guardian Council	246
Chapter Fifty-Four:	In the Prime Minister's Office	249
Chapter Fifty-Five:	Transporting Purchases	251

Chapter Fifty-Six:	Do We or Don't We?	255
Chapter Fifty-Seven:	Middle of December	258
Chapter Fifty-Eight:	Before the Holidays	262
Chapter Fifty-Nine:	January 2011	265
Chapter Sixty:	Council Pressure	269
Chapter Sixty-One:	Bringing the Navy Aboard	272
Chapter Sixty-Two:	Creating Fear	275
Chapter Sixty-Three:	Assassination	277
Chapter Sixty-Four:	Early February	281
Chapter Sixty-Five:	The Same Week	285
Chapter Sixty-Six:	Middle of February	291
Chapter Sixty-Seven:	End of February	294
Chapter Sixty-Eight:	Early March	298
Chapter Sixty-Nine:	Last Week of April	304
Chapter Seventy:	End of May	307
Chapter Seventy-One:	Middle of June	310
Chapter Seventy-Two:	End of July	314
Chapter Seventy-Three:	Tuesday After Labor Day	317
Chapter Seventy-Four:	That Same Day	321
Chapter Seventy-Five:	Thursday That Week	324
Chapter Seventy-Six:	Jibril Atwan's Death	328
Chapter Seventy-Seven:	Same Week	330
Chapter Seventy-Eight:	Tracking Melanie Jacobs	336
Chapter Seventy-Nine:	Top Secret Orders	339
Chapter Eighty:	Second Week of September	341
Chapter Eighty-One:	NSA's Nightmare	344
Chapter Eighty-Two:	Feeling Blind	347
Chapter Eighty-Three:	Second Week of October	351
Chapter Eighty-Four:	Halfway Through the Mediterranean	354
Chapter Eighty-Five:	The Same Week in October	357
Chapter Eighty-Six:	Third Week in October	360
Chapter Eighty-Seven:	Same Day	367
Chapter Eighty-Eight:	Changing Tactics	371
Chapter Eighty-Nine:	The First of the Four Days	375

Chapter Ninety:	Convincing Evidence	377
Chapter Ninety-One:	Plans Set in Motion	381
Chapter Ninety-Two:	End of October	385
Chapter Ninety-Three:	Same Day in D.C.	390
Chapter Ninety-Four:	Dealing with the Vice President	395
Chapter Ninety-Five:	Third Night of the Uprisings	404
Chapter Ninety-Six:	Iran Ablaze	410
Chapter Ninety-Seven:	Mission Accomplished	414
Chapter Ninety-Eight:	Kilos Arrive	418
Chapter Ninety-Nine:	Missiles Airborne	425
Chapter One Hundred:	Missile Mishap	430
Chapter One Hundred One:	Three Down—One To Go	435
Chapter One Hundred Two:	The President Addresses The Nation	439
Chapter One Hundred Three:	Aftermath of Destruction	444
Chapter One Hundred Four:	At the United Nations	450
Chapter One Hundred Five:	Epilog	455

DEDICATION

To Our Children: Joe, Sharon, Jake, Seth and Dina.

I hope the future holds a better picture for you than everyone who is pictured in this novel.

Acknowledgements

Please read this page to share my warmest thanks to those who helped make this book possible.

To my wife, Linda H. Feinberg, who encouraged me to take an English composition course, in order to properly express my many ideas. She is my greatest supporter. Linda also supplied the photo of me for the covers.

To the seven members of my writer's group, they thought that "Behind the Lies" had possibilities beginning with the very first chapter. Two of the women even think this should become a movie. Thank you John, Neil, Rodger, Dennis, Marilyn, June and Marilyn.

To my dynamic editor, Nancy Grossman of Back Channel Press in Portsmouth, NH, who took a good book and turned it into a great book.

To my very talented graphic artist and hunting buddy, Mark Langlois of Langlois Design and Photography, who created the covers for both the softcover edition and the hardcover edition of this book.

To my publisher Xlibris, a division of Random House, and all of their staff whom I have had the pleasure to work with.

Last but not least the many people who encouraged me and guided me in my searches for editing and publishing to bring you the reader the finished copy.

I sincerely hope that you will enjoy this novel as much as I have had the pleasure in creating it.

Prologue

April 2010

The room is fifty feet below ground level to avoid electronic listening devices. Maps of the Middle East hang on all four walls. Each map is pock-marked with various colored pins and flags designating armies, suspected terrorists camps and civilian locations.

Three men sit at a round teakwood table built for four, their faces close enough to smell each other's breath. Sweat pours off them even though the air conditioning is running on high. The room is a miasma of cigarette smoke laced with the aroma of strong coffee.

One of the men is young, green, wet behind the ears; what wisdom he has acquired has come from the three years of training he has recently concluded. The two others are older. How much older is hard to say. Their hard, fit bodies give no clue. Theirs is the kind of aging that comes with the acquisition of wisdom from the streets, the desert, the sea, the air. The kind of wisdom that comes from making too many life-and-death decisions, too frequently, too fast. The three share one common feature, that being that they are all what most people, untrained in surveillance, would define as 'nondescript.'

After a long pause in the conversation, Avi Singer, the youngster, pushes back from the table and heaves a sigh. "Well, all I can say is, it feels like déjà vu to me." He throws his head back, perhaps just a bit too dramatically.

Oh, great, thinks Shlomo Herzl, who has been assigned as Singer's mentor. *They think I am Strasberg? They send me Peter Falk?* Singer, in fact, does look like a young but taller Peter Falk, looks like he sleeps in his clothes, looks like he's been chewing on the unlit cigar in his mouth for days. He will make a good 'katsa,' a good field agent, Herzl knows—some day. A perfectionist, Singer soaks up languages like a sponge. He's no zealot, and he's not in it for the money, that's for sure. His motivation is an unquestionable love of Israel. His acting abilities will hold him in good stead—some day.

Herzl's eyes swing to those of Yosef Bergman. Bergman, who had once mentored Herzl as Herzl now mentors Singer. Though Herzl had been older at the time—he hadn't joined Mossad until he was almost thirty. Herzl and Bergman eyeball each other in silence for a few seconds. Bergman barely nods. His nod clearly communicates, *he's your responsibility,* and *you speak for the both of us.* So Herzl turns to the younger man.

"Avi." He pauses, waiting him out, his eyes locked on those of his protégé. Singer finally gets the message and pulls his chair back to the table. "Avi," Herzl starts again, "how can it feel déjà? You were not even born in '81." His aggravation shows.

"I didn't have to be there to know what we had to do in '81," Singer replies evenly, "to protect ourselves from Iraq. Operation Opera." Singer, a student who had been consistently top of his class from the first day he ever entered a classroom, struggles to keep from rolling his eyes. "But it does appear that we do find ourselves in the same situation all over again, do we not? Same problem, just a different country." *How long is it gonna take for these guys to start taking me seriously?*

Same shit, just a different day, thinks Herzl to himself. "It has always been like this, Avi," Herzl says aloud, taking off a pair of rimless glasses and rubbing the bridge of his nose. Sprawling back in his chair, he runs a hand over his graying military brush cut. "It has been like this for over two thousand years. Why should it change now." This last is not a question. *Where have you been, young man?*

"So, you tell me—what can we do about it?" asks Singer, no longer coming across so smug, now actually asking.

Bergman interrupts, speaking heavily. "Our job is to make certain that our intelligence is correct. After we confirm what we believe, we provide the prime minister with the facts. No hearsay, only the facts as we know them. From that point on, it will be out of our hands." Singer squirms with frustration.

"Avi, we have lost three experienced agents over the last year on this project alone," Bergman continues patiently. "We have to assume that security on those sites is extraordinarily tight. Trust me, those agents were very good at what they did. We must be dead certain that Iran is only months from being able to deploy nuclear warheads." He looks across at Herzl, who grasps the edge of the table, about to stand—at least his body has decided to stand. His mind still works the problem. Again the two older men confer, eye-to-eye, silently.

Singer sits back, crosses his arms in exasperation, and looks up to the ceiling. *I am sure they would much prefer that I were not in the room.*

Herzl stands, then walks to the counter for his fourth cup of coffee. "This should have some good scotch in it instead of milk," he says sourly.

Just then, the three men hear faintly the sound of a siren. The day is April 11. Yom HaSho'ah, the day set aside to remember the Holocaust.

"It must be sundown," Herzl says quietly, then sits down with his coffee. After the three observe two minutes of silence, each in his own way ruminating on the meaning of the day, the realities of which all Israelis live with every day of their lives, Herzl sighs and says, "Okay, Yosef, where do you want us to begin? We can't just sit here and sweat. This gets us nowhere. We need to find an inside source, one who can confirm what we already believe."

Bergman sits forward, wraps his arms around his skinny frame, then starts to finger his heavy black beard. "Shlomo. You know we have no inside sources in Iran we can trust for anything as critical as this. We have never been able to penetrate the Iranians to this level of confidence. Starting now, even if we could, it would take years. We do not have the luxury of time," says Bergman.

"So what do you propose we do?" Singer explodes.

"I am aware," Bergman responds calmly, impervious to Singer's outburst, "of two very good ex-elite force members who might be exactly what we are looking for." Now he has both men's undivided attention. "They have lived in the desert for months at a time as a surveillance team. If we can put them in position to see first-hand what's going into and out of these particular sites that concern us, then—possibly—we'll have our answers."

How like Yosef to play his trump card after hours of discussion, Herzl groans inwardly. *We wrack our brains, when he's had the answer all along.*

Singer's mouth falls open and both hands fly into the air. "What! Am I hearing this correctly. Put two Jews on Iranian soil!" Singer explodes. *Now I've heard everything!* "What if they are captured? That's enough for a declaration of war. Then where do we stand? And—" he changes gears, "—why did it take you so long to bring up these two 'very good ex-elite force members' of yours? We've been steeping in this hell hole for hours."

"Avi," Bergman answers the young man with his own sigh, "we didn't ask for this shit. The president of Iran has said publicly that Israel should be wiped off the map. Isn't that a declaration of war? The world knows this."

Bergman turns, lowers his head and stares at Singer over his glasses, his eyelids half closed. *I know they all have to start as greenhorns, but you'd think they might at least know more of their own history.* He would like to ask the youngster what they are teaching in school these days. Instead, he simply says, "Avi, if you don't want to be part of the decision-making process, just say so."

Herzl turns to Singer. "I know that what Yosef proposes is risky, my boy, but as risky as I know it is, I have to agree that it is our only choice, because of the time factor," he explains as clearly as he can. "God help us to find out what's really happening," he says to both men. "We need to make the right choices. Millions of Jews and innocent Muslims must not be destroyed through carelessness and ego. Yosef, I vote that we take your idea to the prime minister. Avi, are you with us—or not?"

"That's not much of a choice—I'm already out-voted anyway," observes Singer with a fatalistic shrug, "so I might as well make it unanimous."

Yes, always put on a united front, Herzl thinks despondently, *even if it is not true.*

Chapter One

Washington, DC
Same Time, Seven Zones to the West

Janet White shakes back her long auburn hair, a predictable, unconscious habit, as she stops what she's doing to pick up the phone and bring it to her ear. "Good afternoon. The president's secretary speaking."

"Janet, this is Allison McDonald," comes a crisp, no-nonsense woman's voice on the other end. Allison McDonald is the director of the CIA. "Please put me through to the president. It's imperative that I speak with him, immediately."

"One moment."

Sounds urgent—and I could use a stretch. Janet puts the director of the CIA on hold, gets up, works out a kink in her neck, crosses the office and takes the liberty of knocking on the door of the Oval Office, knowing the president is alone. If he were not, she would of course use the intercom.

She hears the words "Come in," opens the door quietly and pokes her head around it. "Mr. President, the director if the CIA is on line one. She says it is imperative that she speak with you. It sounds urgent."

"Thank you, Janet. I'll take it," says William Egan, America's first black president, reaching his long, lanky frame for the phone. "Allison, how are you?" he says into the receiver. His deep, smooth delivery carries a hint of the orator who honed his skills at Harvard.

"I'm fine, sir," she replies. "Thank you for asking."

"Janet tells me she sensed urgency when she answered your call. Has something critical come up?"

"Yes, sir, it has." *This president is so ready to face facts. What a difference a change of administration makes.*

Egan had promoted Allison McDonald to CIA director from within the ranks upon his taking office, and has been entirely pleased with her performance in the two years since. She'd served as assistant director for five years prior. A petite brunette, five-foot-five, she has a figure of which she's oblivious but which makes most men drool. Her ability to analyze and lead the CIA is second to none. As director, she has yet to overreact to a situation.

"Sources are telling us, Mr. President, that there's imminent danger—*nuclear* danger—from Iran. I feel that you and your staff need to be brought up to speed. Quickly. I can make myself available for a meeting any time you choose."

The president stands up, then begins to pace, as he usually does when taking calls that require his complete attention. He thinks best on his feet. "Allison, I thought that the IAEA reported finding no smoking guns in Iran in terms of a nuclear arms program—wasn't that just a month ago?"

"Yes, sir, they did, or so they say. However, we're talking the same agency that completely failed to detect Iran's undeclared nuclear program for close to two decades."

"Do you have hard evidence regarding this concern, or are we dealing with perceived terrorism?" *This I do not need. It's time to start gearing up for re-election.*

"Mr. President, I can only give you the facts that our sources provide and our analysts decipher." *Com'on, Bill, don't let me down here.*

"Don't worry, Allison—I know you wouldn't have called if you didn't feel it was of the utmost importance. I'll check with Janet to see what my schedule looks like. She'll advise you of the time and date. And I'll have her let you know who all will be in attendance. Allison, thank you for calling," he says rather stiffly, hangs up, then turns to stare out the window.

*

President William Egan was elected as a peacemaker, and peace he made, in less time than he'd even promised on the campaign trail. He had big plans for peace. Peace was what he wanted, and he sure as hell doesn't want a nuclear threat derailing his agenda. *I'll face it if I have to,* he thinks to himself, *but I'd much prefer to face things like the underfunding of domestic needs, maintenance of infrastructure and simplifying tax codes, universal health insurance, education, and all the rest of the unsexy day-to-day necessities of running this country of ours. All the necessities that always have to end up taking a back seat to international crises.*

Turning back to his desk, Egan picks up his phone, rings Janet and asks her to come in and bring his calendar with her.

Janet White had been Senator William Egan's personal secretary for eight years. She'd come to Washington with him, and had become a president's personal secretary the day he took office. Over the years, she has developed an instinct for knowing what her boss wants and how to handle it for him.

She has already started to sit before the president half-motions for her to take the armchair before him at the desk. Wearing her favorite dark navy blue suit with a new white lace blouse, she perches on the edge of the chair, her steno pad at the ready, knowing she appears both professional—and feminine. She knows by experience, however, that the president is pretty much tone-deaf when it comes to taking notice of femininity. She doesn't care. Being secretary to the most powerful man on earth gives her life a real sense of purpose, as she readily tells anyone who asks.

As she sits in front of the president's large mahogany desk (*a gift from Queen Victoria in 1880,* she can never help remembering), she asks, "Sir, I assume you want to schedule a meeting with the CIA director. Would that be today, or will tomorrow do? I can re-arrange some of today's schedule if you'll tell me how much time you require."

President Egan says, "No, I'll want the vice president, the chief of staff, the secretary of defense and the national security advisor at this meeting, too, as well as CIA. Are they all in town today?"

Janet notes his wishes as she answers, "Everyone but defense," she says without looking up from what she's writing. "He's due back from Paris tonight. I know they're all available tomorrow." She checks his agenda. "Tomorrow's schedule could handle a one-hour meeting between three and four p.m. Will that be time enough?"

"Set it up for three. This will probably be the first of many such meetings, but I believe we can accomplish our first objective in an hour. Please go ahead and notify everyone. And when you speak with Allison, give her the list of those who'll be attending, but"—he pauses, thinking as he speaks—"I don't want anyone else to know that she'll be there. I don't want any preconceived notions coming into this meeting. In fact, we'll meet here in the Oval Office. That should let some air out of their tires."

Sitting back in his chair, he closed his eyes for a moment. "What do I have next? I need some time to think."

"You have Senators Larch and Maxwell in five minutes. I could hold them. How long would you like."

"I could really use fifteen minutes."

"Fifteen minutes you've got, sir," she replies. *Damn, I love this job*, she thinks.

As Janet rises and leaves, the president stands up, stretches and wanders over to the furthest window, the one by the grandfather clock, and looks out over the rose garden. But at this moment, he does not see roses. He sees a mushroom cloud. *Dear God, don't let this be true. A fanatical nation with nuclear arms could be the beginning of the end of the civilized world.*

Bill Egan turns to prayer as he contemplates the White House from this angle. In the two years in which it has been his return address, he has come to think of it very much as home. But after his brief conversation with Allison McDonald, he suddenly sees it quite differently.

This could be Ground Zero. I could be standing at Ground Zero, right here. This could be only one of who knows how many Ground Zeroes across the United States, around the world, for that matter—potential targets for rogue nuclear bombs. Millions of people could die.

Chapter Two

Next Day in Iran

Morning prayers at the Rajab Ali mosque in the Darkhangah district of Tehran draw to a close. Three men stand at various points around the edge of the large assemblage of worshippers. Acknowledging each other's presence by fleeting eye contact only, one nods and, one by one, they proceed to leave the mosque by different exits.

Each has been instructed that he will be picked up individually by a black Mercedes limousine. One of the men will be picked up directly in front of the mosque on Mostafa Khomeini Street. The second will walk three blocks to the right of the stairs at the front entrance. The third has been directed to make his way around the rear of the mosque and proceed four blocks to the right. Muhammad Abdullah, Kamil Hussein, and Hamid Dakham each wait as inconspicuously as possible at their appointed places according to the instructions each received late last night.

Muhammad Abdullah, twenty-six, is an engineer, his skills such that he honestly believes he can fix anything. A short, slim, confident man, his complexion is dark but ruddy, his eyes deep brown. He wears western dress, a plaid cotton shirt, a pair of khakis and sneakers. A tracery of black beard outlines his chin. A friend of Hussein and Dakham, he's waiting as he was directed to but with no idea why.

Kamil Hussein and Hamid Dakham are both Iranian Secret Service operatives, both in their mid-twenties and single. Both believe that Iran will take its rightful place as leader of the Middle East and will one day fulfill its destiny, to conquer the West.

Hussein, fair complected for an Iranian, stands almost six feet tall, with dark brown eyes and short black hair. He's clean shaven, and wears an embroidered tunic over loose grey pants. More than anything, Hussein waits for his opportunity to be a hero within the Islamic revolution. A passionate and fearless man, analytical thinking often takes a backseat to his emotions. In spite of this, the Iranian Secret Service considers him a valuable asset.

Dakham wears a white kufi hat over thick black hair that continues on into a shaggy full beard and mustache. Shorter and a bit stouter than Hussein, he's dressed in an elongated black linen jacket, buttoned to the neck, over white pants. He is of deep olive complexion and he wears heavily-framed black glasses. Though he tends to follow rather than lead, he's the clearer thinker of the two.

*

Muhammad Abdullah sees the black Mercedes limo approach and pull to the curb in front of him. Entering the vehicle, he slides across to the far side and settles in on the comfortable rear seat facing the vehicle's only other passenger. Moments later he's joined by Kamil Hussein, who slides over next to him when Hamid Dakham enters. None looks at the others. The eyes of all three are locked on those of the man sitting before them. None of them ever expected to find himself sitting across from Jibril Atwan, a close advisor to the Ayatollah Fadil Ahmajid, the Supreme Leader of Iran.

Jibril Atwan is well known as a rebel within the ranks of Iran's militants, and in this respect has the trust and confidence of the Supreme Leader. Widowed, he's a large-framed, overweight, highly suspicious man.

"You gentlemen look like the cat that just swallowed the master's pet canary," says Atwan dryly. "Are you surprised to receive this kind of treatment? Don't be. You will earn it."

Jibril Atwan easily instills fear in those he chooses to manipulate. As an advisor to the Supreme Leader, this man has the power to shorten a person's lifespan with the shake of a head, should he choose to. Jibril is named for Gabriel, the archangel God sent as a messenger to the prophets, revealing their obligations. His face is lined with both scars and age.

Abdullah, Hussein and Dakham can each read the panther-like gleam in Atwan's eyes at his sense of control over individuals—at the moment, over them.

*

Atwan turns to speak to the driver over his shoulder, instructing him to proceed north through the steaming streets of Tehran and into the mountains, then tells him to close the privacy panel between himself and his passengers.

Atwan is silent as they pass out of the populated area. Once free of the possibility of listening devices picking up their conversation, but before the limousine reaches the foothill of the Arborz Mountains, he says, "The three of you have been chosen to work on a special project. This project must be operational in eighteen months. Muhammad, you will be working alone. Kamil and Hamid, you will work as a team."

The three look this powerful man square in the eyes, unblinking. However, Abdullah gulps unconsciously, Hussein's facial muscles contract and Dakham sits a bit straighter."

Look as calm as you want, my friends, Atwan takes plenty of time to think. *You cannot disguise your fear of me.* "The three of you have been selected by the Supreme Leader," he finally continues, "because of your skills and your proven dedication to Islam. Are you prepared to commit to Islam and to your country to insure that this project is carried out successfully?"

Simultaneously, Abdullah, Hussein and Dakham nod, without so much as asking what the project might be, with what it could be connected, or what their individual roles might be. Their sense of duty, religious beliefs, loyalty to their government and their massive egos combine to guarantee that none of them would ever think of questioning a higher authority. *Besides,* they are all thinking, *to do so would be a serious mistake.* Dakham carries the thought to its logical conclusion: *Call it what it would be—suicide.*

Atwan holds each man's eye in turn, finally nods and then proceeds. "In two weeks, each of you will begin special training. Muhammad, with your particular scientific skills and your engineering background, your assignment will keep you within the borders of Iran."

"Kamil and Hamid, both of you have been chosen to operate as a team. You will be working outside of Iran until we achieve the goals we have established. You have been selected for this project based on your skills as intelligence operators." Both men acknowledged this honor with slight nods.

"What's vital to this project is its complete secrecy," continues Atwan. "None of you are married. You are living apart from your families. The only thing you will be allowed to tell others close to you is that you're going on a planned vacation. Yes, even you, Muhammad," he said in response to a quizzical look that crosses Abdullah's face. "You will be living in special quarters until your part in the project is completed."

Atwan settles back in his seat. Apparently his presentation is over. A few minutes later, he taps on the window behind him, then turns to them again. "We now return to Tehran. Each of you will be dropped off in the city at a different location. As of this moment, Muhammad, you will have no further contact with Kamil and Hamid. Likewise, for the two of you, Muhammad does not exist." Again, the men merely nod. None of them has uttered a word the entire time.

Atwan picks up the phone next to him, keys the intercom to the driver and gives him the cross streets for the three different locations where the men are to be dropped. Then, sitting back in his seat again, he retreats within himself, staring out the window at what can already be seen of the Milad tower, now ahead of them, the tallest landmark in Tehran. It is as if he's traveling alone.

*

As the limo glides up to each of the three designated drop-offs, Atwan comes out of his reverie momentarily and nods, first to Hussein, then to Abdullah, then to Dakham, indicating that this is where each man is to get out. All debark as directed, each location an area far from their respective districts. They are all on their own to seek out transportation to their homes.

After Dakham is left off, Atwan picks up his phone and calls his office. "Are the tails on the three in place?"

"Yes," is the reply.

"Good. If our choices are correct we'll find no need to eliminate any one of them. If we find that we made any wrong choices, then we'll know before their training begins."

Chapter Three

Oval Office: CIA Presentation

Vice President Patrick Devonshire, Chief of Staff Maria Sterling, Secretary of Defense John Anderson and National Security Advisor John Walker chat quietly about what the reason behind such an abruptly convened meeting could possibly be as they congregate in the sitting area just outside the Oval Office, waiting to be called into the three p.m. meeting with the president.

A full five minutes before three, Allison McDonald, wearing one of her seemingly limitless wardrobe of black pant suits, comes striding into the sitting room to join them. She finds the winces on the faces of those already waiting rather amusing. McDonald smiles, then merely offers them all a group hello.

Hey, nobody told me CIA was going to be here, the vice president groans inwardly. *What the hell's going on? Why am I never in the loop here?* He's not alone in his aggravation.

Precisely at three o'clock, Janet White comes out from behind her desk and ushers the group in to join the president in the Oval Office.

Once inside, they each move directly to their usual spot, within the usual pecking order for this particular group. The vice president and chief of staff take seats on the couch to the president's left, while defense, national security and CIA take the three seats on the couch to his right. Allison McDonald perches in the catbird seat closest to President Egan. Once everyone is settled, he eyes each participant individually. His usual courteous, "Thank you all for attending on such short notice" is greeted by nods all around.

"The reason I've called you all here this afternoon," the president goes on, "is that Allison feels we all need to be brought up to speed on a critical situation she sees developing in Iran. A nuclear threat. Allison, the floor is yours." *And this better be good, my dear.*

"Thank you, sir," McDonald says, then gets right into the meat of her presentation with little preamble. "We are all aware of the rhetoric that the president of Iran has been putting out over Iran's right to have nuclear capabilities for domestic use. This is nothing new. However, Iran's recently elected president has an advantage that past presidents have not had. Iran is beginning to sit quite comfortably on a major influx of money because of the skyrocketing price of oil. And they appear to be using a great deal of that money for major expansion of their nuclear program."

John Anderson, with short, thick grey hair, a receding hairline and a bulldog jaw, puts his elbows on the attaché case that sits across his lap. Locking his hands and dropping his chin upon them, he looks up at McDonald, consciously working to keep from appearing irritated. "Excuse me. Hasn't the IAEA given Iran a clean bill of health, nuclear-wise?" he asks her pointedly. "The president of Iran's toeing the line." *I've had it with you Central Intelligence types crying wolf.*

McDonald has gotten used to John Anderson's attitude when it comes to the CIA. She continues unrattled. "You're right, John. But may I point out that the IAEA is the same agency that failed to detect Iran's hidden nuclear program for over twenty years. So, are we to sit back and believe the IAEA, or do we look at the level of intelligence we're gathering to make decisions in the best interest of the United States?"

"Whaddya got here, new information, or merely a comb-through of old intel?" John Walker interrupts. *My people aren't tellin' me this,* thinks the national security advisor, a burly, cantankerous, white-haired man who both speaks and thinks in the pronounced southern accent of a boy born and bred in southwest Georgia.

"Intelligence reports indicate that Iran has several nuclear development sites, as you know, John," McDonald says with a slightly exaggerated politeness. "That, of course, is not new. However we now know that Iran has over four hundred fifty nuclear experts on their payroll, and that is new information." Walker may look mollified, but he's far from it.

"I certainly don't have to remind any of you," she goes on, looking around at all of them, "that their secret nuclear weapons program is being supervised by both the military and their Supreme Leader. The president is merely a mouthpiece. The Supreme Leader has all the control, the Supreme Leader and the mullahs he has chosen to serve as his Guardian Council."

Of course he's a mouthpiece. Now you've managed to insult every one of us, Maria Sterling notes, uncrossing and recrossing her best assets, a pair of spectacularly long legs in an equally spectacular pair of strappy red heels. She has never been much of a fan of Allison McDonald. *Damn this bitch, always trying to make headlines with the president.* With a smirk, Sterling asks, "What evidence—what conclusive evidence do you have that makes you think Iran wants to build nuclear weapons instead of simply utilizing nuclear power for internal purposes?"

Ignoring the smirk and the attitude she knows accompanies it, McDonald responds without emotion. "I'm glad you asked that question, Maria. Mahmoud Khasanjani's rhetoric suggests that his goal is to become the regional superpower. With Iraq on the sidelines, now that they no longer have Saddam Hussein calling the shots, nor our protection, Iran would like nothing more than to become the leader of the fundamentalist Islamic world."

Poker-faced, the vice president asks, "Allison, can't we get U.N. sanctions against Iran, to force them to toe the mark?" A small man with a compact build, a youthful face and blond hair, he wears glasses and well tailored, trim dark suits with bold, striped ties.

"Pat, I wish I could feel confident doing that, but you and I both know that China and Russia will never agree. They'll veto any sanctions we might ask for. They have too much riding on Iran, financially. The CIA is open to any competing viewpoint to compare with our intelligence," she said, looking pointedly at John Walker again. "Besides, as I'm sure you've noticed in the media,"—*which you evidently haven't*—"Iran is withdrawing its assets from foreign banks so that they can't be frozen. Iran is also toying with the idea of getting OPEC to drop the amount of oil shipped world-wide if they agree to do likewise. Iran is playing hardball. There's no bluffing going on here."

Showing his discomfort, John Walker squirms in his chair and asks, "Allison, I understan' the threat that Israel and all of Europe may be facin'. What do y'all see affectin' the United States?" *What else does CIA know that NSA doesn't?*

"John, Israel and all of Europe are within range of Iran's Shahab-3 missile, which has recently passed its performance tests satisfactorily. If they can load a nuclear warhead into that missile, then they hold the European continent and Israel at gunpoint. We're getting reports that Iran is seeking ways to fire that same missile from the four Kilo-class submarines they recently purchased from Russia. If that happens, cities in the United States could also be in jeopardy." She let that thought sink in before summing up.

"Mr. President, I'm through for the moment. The responsibility of the CIA is to report on its analysis of the data we receive from our agents and other sources. We see Iran as a rogue tiger at this point, a sleeping giant with plans to become the supreme fundamentalist power in the Middle East. This could have very serious repercussions, on the United States and on the economy worldwide."

The president says, "Thank you, Allison." *Not too bad. Actually better than I expected.* "You've given all of us some serious information to consider. I'd like each of you to give me your opinion based on what you've just heard and what your own resources have given you. Pat, as vice president, let's start with you." The vice president, whose attention has been riveted on McDonald, shifts in his seat to better face the entire group.

"Mr. President, there are compelling facts and strong intuitions to build such a case as Allison's presenting today. Personally, I feel that we should try to continue some sort of negotiations with Iran. However, we should also have a military pre-empt in place, should we need to shift gears in a hurry." *I assume that's what you'd want me to say.* Patrick Devonshire constantly refers to himself as a consensus builder, to the point that some members of the cabinet refer to him, behind his back, as the 'Census Taker.'

"Maria, your thoughts?" the president prompts his chief of staff.

"Well, Mr. President, I've heard so many assumptions and conjectures that I don't feel remotely comfortable reaching a conclusion without far more information. Information based on verifiable fact." *I can't believe she's pulling this crap.*

"Mr. Secretary?" the president cues Anderson.

"Mr. President, speaking for the Department of Defense, I feel that Allison has presented some serious intelligence that we must consider for the safety of the United States." *Oh, God, does that ever sound lame.* Anderson starts to add to this thought, but the president has already moved on to his national security advisor.

"Mr. Walker."

"Mr. Pres'dent, NSA's seen some information similar to Allison's, which could lend credence to what she's presentin'. Howevah, she's also presented some information that we are not aware of. Now, if we could pool our information, I'm sure our agencies could come up with a much clearer picture which, I'm sure y'all'd agree, would lead to a much bettah decision." *Ask me, this is gonna develop into one serious nightmare—a serious political nightmare.*

*

Once everyone has had their say, President Egan gets up, then pauses for a few moments, pulling his thoughts together. When he does speak, he speaks firmly and succinctly. "My first reaction is to try and reason with Iran. Yet, my gut warns me against wasting precious time. John, Allison, I'd like you both to meet over the next week and pull together a presentation, based on *all* the information you have at your combined fingertips. We need to stop playing games as to who comes in with the best information and wins the gold ring." McDonald and Walker's eyes meet.

"I'll be the first to admit," continues the president, "that I would much prefer to see this go away quietly. However, I believe I'd only be fooling myself. Ladies and gentlemen, we'll meet in two weeks, at the same time, unless something major comes up. I'll also be asking representatives of the military to that meeting to assist us in clarifying our military options. I suggest you allow three hours on your schedules. Thank you all for coming."

Chapter Four

Late at Night

Yosef Bergman is the last one to leave the meeting; Avi Singer and Shlomo Herzl have each gone their separate ways. It being very late, he decides not to phone the director of Mossad tonight. Rather, he will meet with him in his office first thing in the morning. Heading home allows him time to think, before he approaches the director with the idea the three of them have agreed upon.

Yosef Bergman is forty-five years of age, though he looks thirty. His six-foot height, broad shoulders, dark complexion and jet black hair all serve to reinforce his role as a leader within the organization. Bergman is a sabra, a native born Israeli.

In the Yom Kippur War, he saw the Arab armies' treachery and ruthlessness first hand and made a promise to himself that he would dedicate his life to protecting his country's security. He did not anticipate that his dedication would consume his whole life, leaving very little time for anything remotely resembling a personal life.

Tonight the pressures of leadership weigh heavily upon his mind. Israel must know what's really happening inside of Iran. *Can we pull it off by sending a couple of desert rats in search of evidence? Can these two obtain the factual proof that Israel must have? Or am I just sending two more Israelis to the slaughter, and probably causing another international incident in the attempt?*

In spite of his serious mood, Bergman walks through the streets of Tel Aviv smiling, knowing that even with the constant threat of terrorism, he's probably safer here than anywhere else in the world. He reaches the door of his apartment, enters, deactivates the security system, turns on the lights and throws his keys on the dining room table. Opening the refrigerator, he takes out a cold beer.

Oh, this tastes so good! In fact, I believe tonight will be a two-beer night. He pulls a second from the refrigerator, then heads across the living room and out onto the balcony. He finishes both standing in the darkness, overlooking the city he loves. *Cities look spectacular at night with their lights on,* he reflects. *Tonight seems particularly special. Perhaps it's knowing how easily we could lose all of this that makes Tel Aviv, Israel, life itself, feel so extraordinary tonight.*

Bergman knows that before making any decisions, he must get some sleep. Ideas to propose will come easier and clearer with a good night's rest. At least he hopes he can sleep with all that's churning in his mind.

*

A good night's sleep does not come easily and Yosef Bergman awakes as he always does, at five a.m. After a hot shower and shave, he begins to feel a bit more human. He eats a quick breakfast of eggs and toast, and downs a mug of strong Arabian coffee. *You have to give them credit—the Arabs do know how to make great-tasting coffee,* he thinks as he swallows the last of it, then returns to the balcony to fine-tune the thoughts he will present this morning.

Walking the mile to Mossad's headquarters gives him even more time to think about what he needs to include in his discussion with the director. Entering headquarters, he goes at once to the director's office and presents himself to the director's secretary, asking to be placed on his morning agenda.

"He can see you in about thirty minutes, after he finishes with his morning briefing," she says crisply.

"I will be in my office until he is free," Bergman tells her.

Ariel Wattenberg, director of Mossad, is not known to be big on formalities. He picks up the phone after his meeting ends and calls Bergman directly. "I have time for you now, Yosef," he says. "Come down to my office." Bergman gets up from his desk, takes a deep breath and heads down the hall.

Bergman steps into Wattenberg's office. Unlike the offices of top executives around the world, corporate or military, the director's office looks Spartan, more like an interrogation cell than the office of the head of one of the world's top-ranked intelligence services. A tremendous satellite photo map of the Middle East provides the only visual distraction. The room boasts one large metal desk. Behind the desk is the director's only extravagance, a black leather executive office chair. Four metal folding chairs are lined up in front of the desk. Like every other office in this building, this office has no windows.

"So tell me what happened at your meeting last evening," asks Wattenberg, sitting forward, his hands clasped in front of him. Ariel Wattenberg is a man with no patience for small talk. Bergman delivers his recap with this in mind.

"Shlomo, Avi and I spent five hours going over everything, our reports on what our agents suspect is going on in Iran, what we hear from intelligence from around the world. Our conclusion: we believe that it is almost a certainty that Iran will have nuclear warhead capability within two years. And perhaps far sooner."

"You could have put that in a written report," Wattenberg observes tersely. "Why the request for a meeting this morning?"

"The 'perhaps far sooner' part scares the hell out of us," Bergman says vehemently. "We are requesting that we place a team inside Iran to monitor what's really happening, on the ground. If what we suspect is true, then we must act accordingly. I don't need to tell you that we've lost good agents trying to penetrate Iranian circles. We need to try something different."

"What kind of team do you have in mind?"

"We are aware of two very highly trained special ops people who are capable of living in the desert for long periods of time." *Make this sound like this is coming from the group,* Bergman coaches himself. "These are high-tech specialists. With the right equipment, we know they could monitor conversations, movements of materials and people, gas emissions, any number of pieces of the puzzle to which we have no access at this time. IDF has released the two from active duty. They have set up a business of their own—doing corporate intelligence, security, hazardous conditions training, that kind of thing. We know this would come with a price tag, but doesn't everything?" Bergman passes this last remark off with a shrug.

Wattenberg sits back and looks across his desk at Bergman somberly. Ariel Wattenberg is a man who has built his reputation on facing worst-case scenarios head-on. "And these two men, this 'team,' as you say. If they get caught?" He lets the thought hang in the air a moment. "What are the consequences for Israel?"

"Ariel, you know I cannot give you a one hundred percent guarantee that they will not, yet I can tell you that they are exceptionally good at what they do. They have never been captured in the field." Bergman's answer comes out in a rush.

"Yet *you* can tell me . . . hmm. This has all the markings of a Yosef Bergman plan. How did you get Shlomo and Avi to agree with this?"

Shit, I walked into that one. "Shlomo agrees we are desperate for time. Avi agrees because, well that's Avi—he likes things to be unanimous." Another shrug.

"And I suppose these two characters of yours are just dying to volunteer for a job like this." Wattenberg's is the face of a poker player. Bergman has no idea how his plan is going over.

Perched on one of the small folding chairs, Bergman leans forward and grips the edges of Wattenberg's desk. *It's time to close this deal.* "Sir, I would never contact them without your approval. Security alone dictates that. However, I seriously doubt they would be interested in 'volunteering' for this job, as you put it. I would need to know what kind of offer we could make them financially, how we could provide the equipment they would need, what kind of a cover story if they were to be apprehended, what kind of extraction support we would have set up just in case. Ariel, we need to think outside of the box on this. We don't have the luxury of time, the way things seem to be headed."

Wattenberg folds his arms; one hand goes to his chin as he looks away, thinking. Finally he looks back at Bergman and lays that hand on the surface of his desk, fingers splayed. "I like your spirit and your creativity, Yosef. However, this is not just some clever business plan. Major repercussions could develop from this attempt, were it to go sour. I will need to talk with the prime minister about this. If Yaakov buys your idea, then I need to talk with some of our top military people."

"Of course." *We're in!*

"Give me three days to give Yaakov time to consider it without forcing an immediate answer." He stops, looks down, then looks back up at Bergman, square in the eye. "I like it. I like it because, if these two are as good as you say, Iran will never know how we found out whatever these two can get us."

Chapter Five

A Week Later

"So, how do our new recruits look?" Atwan asks the party to whom he speaks on the phone.

"Everything appears to be what we expect it to be. Nothing out of the ordinary. Nor are we are getting any word of them mentioning anything," answers the caller.

"Good. Set their pick-ups in motion. Everything according to plan," says Atwan, the man with the Supreme Leader's ear. "Notify me when they have completed their training sessions, before they officially begin their assignments. I will wish to speak with them again."

The phone rings four times before the sleeping Muhammad Abdullah wakes to answer it.

"Who is calling at this hour?" is all Abdullah can think to ask.

"You need to get used to the unexpected on your new assignment, Muhammad," the caller says. "Tomorrow you must prepare to leave. Be ready to be picked up at 0200 the following morning. Pack enough clothing and toiletries for one week. The rest will be provided for you. A green jeep with a driver and a relief driver will take you to your first assignment," continues the anonymous voice. "Be standing outside of your apartment. Don't make them wait."

"Can I ask where I will be going?"

"No, you cannot. Nor will you know when you arrive. Do not be late for the pick-up." The phone line goes dead.

Relief driver? Where the hell are they taking me?

Within the next fifteen minutes, both Kamil Hussein and Hamid Dakham receive similar phone calls. They are told to be ready at 0400 hours the following night, that a red station wagon will be picking them up, Hussein first, Dakham ten minutes later. The caller emphasizes that they should not be late.

*

At 0200 hours the street outside of Abdullah's apartment is chilly, dark and desolate. Standing just inside of the entrance to his living quarters, Abdullah shivers.

He sees headlights approach, pass him by, then turn around; they belong to a green jeep, he sees when it pulls up in front of his apartment. The passenger on the right side calls out to him across the driver. "Muhammad, we are told you are expecting us. We need to see some identification."

Abdullah hands over his identification and the jeep's passenger says, "This looks like you, yet you look more like a jihad fighter than the engineer we are supposed to pick up." At this he smiles and loosens up a bit. "Throw your gear on the back seat and get in. You might want to get some sleep back there. We have a couple hours of driving. I'm told you will have a very busy first day."

Abdullah climbs into the rear of the jeep, nods, wonders what he has gotten himself into, then tries to sleep.

*

At 0400 Kamil Hussein's ID is being checked, and ten minutes later, Dakham goes through the same routine as his associates.

The red station wagon that picks them up speeds out of Tehran for close to an hour, then does something very interesting: it makes a wide turn and heads back into Tehran on a parallel road to the one which they had taken out of town. Hussein and Dakham look at each other. They both appear to be asking each other, *what the hell is going on?*

Both the red station wagon and Abdullah's jeep stop for morning prayers.

Joe Smiga

*

Just around 0600 Hussein and Dakham arrive in front of the Iranian Secret Service headquarters. Hussein sends an extra prayer to the heavens. *Oh, Allah, reveal to me what this mission is that you would have us do?*

At roughly the same time, Abdullah arrives at the naval military installation in Bandar Abbas with similar questions of the deity.

Chapter Six

Beginning of May

"Good morning. National Security Agency. This is Ms. Harmon," the receptionist answers the phone.

"Good morning, Jeanine," responds her caller. "This is Allison McDonald, director of Central Intelligence. May I speak with the director?"

"One moment, please."

McDonald, put on hold, will have to endure almost a full sixty seconds of numbingly bland music.

"Janet, this is Jeanine at the switchboard. I have the director of the CIA on the phone wishing to speak with the director. Is he available?"

"Let me check, Jeanine."

Janet calls into the director's office. John Walker informs her that he's 'tied up' at the moment. "Could y'all please tell the director I'll get back to her in fifteen minutes." *I'm not about to jump just because she calls,* Walker tells himself. *Let her wait.*

Janet advised the receptionist, who in turn advises McDonald.

Of course, thinks McDonald, irritated. *The male ego game again. Men at play.*

*

Half an hour later, Walker returns McDonald's call. He apologizes for phoning later than he'd said he would. "I assume y'all were callin' to schedule gittin' together as per the pres'dent's instructions, Allison." Walker prefers the declarative to the interrogative.

"That I am, John. How much time do you think we need, and what's your schedule looking like?" McDonald has no problem asking questions; she knows that Walker will want to set the agenda. She has more than enough experience under her belt to know how to pick—and shape—her battles.

"Well, I'd say let's plan for at leas' two hours," says Walker without hesitation. "And leave 'ditional time in case we need it. After all, we'll be makin' us a majuh presentation next week. We can meet in the NSA conference room, if that suits y'all, Allison."

"Fine with me, John. Is next Wednesday afternoon at two good for you?"

"Two o'clock on Wednesday's fine. Yes, that'll be fine, Allison," Walker confirms. "Oh, and when y'all arrive, I'll have someone downstairs bring y'all up to the fourth-floor conference room. I'll meet y'all there."

Like I don't know what floor your conference room's on, you condescending s.o.b.? fumes McDonald. *This'll be some meeting. Or have I let myself get too sensitive? Am I letting my feminist perspective cloud my judgment?* She gave the subject a split-second's thought before rejecting it with a snort. "Bye, John," she says casually before hanging up.

Wednesday afternoon at one forty-five p.m., McDonald's car pulls up before the National Security Agency's headquarters. Inside, she approaches a guard, M. Malden, according to his ID badge, who dutifully checks his list of expected arrivals, but fails to find her name there.

"I have a two o'clock appointment with the director," she states coldly.

M. Malden goes to check with his fellow guards, then returns to his station and informs her that none of the guards have her on their lists. McDonald feels her blood begin to simmer.

M. Malden picks up the phone at his station and calls the director's office.

"That's odd," Janet says, flustered. John Walker rarely lets her in on his intended insults and manipulations, and she hates getting drawn into one of them. "It must be an oversight. Please tell the director I'll be right down. I'll escort Ms. McDonald to the conference room personally."

M. Malden repeats Janet's words verbatim. *Gee, wonder why I have a bad feeling about how this meeting's going to go,* McDonald's brain mutters darkly.

Janet stays with her in the conference room until her boss arrives. McDonald's brain's mutterings grow darker with every minute she sits ignoring Janet's minute-by-minute apologies for his delay. She finds herself looking at the clock's second hand to see if her apologies actually spaced a minute apart, and smiles to herself when she finds that she's right. *Where do they find these people,* she has to wonder

*

John Walker arrives a full ten apologies late, leaving McDonald to ponder where that puts her in the pecking order of his political priorities.

"Oh, Allison, I'm so sorry. I've been runnin' behin' schedule all day," he says as he feigns rushing into the room. "Somethin' came up and I couldn't get it ended in time."

"Do you keep everyone waiting—or just women?" McDonald asks icily. *Might as well set the tone for this 'collaboration,'* she decides. Getting no response, she gets to the point. "John, as CIA director and former deputy director, I've never once attended a joint meeting of our two agencies. I'm sensing that you probably feel that we've been put in an untenable situation. Regardless, I'm hopeful that our two agencies—that *we*—can provide the president with what he needs, and not let inter-agency pettiness get in our way."

"Allison!" Walker responds in mock astonishment. "I'm surprised to hear y'all make such an allegation! Why, that's practically slandah!" He laughs merrily.

Surprised, my ass. "Okay, John, I'll play along with you. You're surprised," McDonald says, her voice dripping skepticism. "Fine. You do what you want. I'm laying my cards on the table. This is a national security issue we're dealing with. We cannot allow ourselves to present this information in any other way but as a jointly supported proposal." She drags the last three words out, then leaves time for emphasis before moving on.

"Of course . . ." Walker says to buy his own time, scrambling to decide how he can regain the offensive in this conversation.

"We cannot use this forum to grandstand," McDonald continues to steamroll him. "We need to clarify the issues and give our opinions, either as jointly supported or, at the very least, present them as clearly individual viewpoints, if we differ. You don't suddenly come up with something that makes the CIA appear incompetent. I, likewise, refrain from doing that to you and the NSA."

She pauses, but before he can respond, adds one more thought. "Everything we discuss here is for presentation. Should other issues arise before the meeting, we notify the other. Am I making myself clear?"

"As a summer day, my dear," Walker says unhappily. *And this is just the first five minutes.* The session doesn't end until well after seven.

Chapter Seven

Mossad Proposes

Ariel Wattenberg, director of Israel's Institute for Intelligence and Special Operations—Mossad—sits comfortably in the reception area of the prime minister's office. The prime minister's secretary called him two hours ago, asking him to be here for a meeting at 1600 hours.

Wattenberg wonders what's on the prime minister's mind—is it about Yosef Bergman's idea or has something else come up which requires the Mossad's attention? *No matter*, Wattenberg muses, *whatever it is, I plan to enjoy the view. The prime minister must hire his secretaries by making them take the elbow test,* he amuses himself, *the one wherein they're asked to lace their hands behind their necks, then walk towards a wall. If their elbows touch the wall before their nipples, then they most likely won't get the job.* He chuckles inwardly at the distracting notion.

At exactly 1600 hours, Wattenberg is escorted into the prime minister's office.

Entering, Wattenberg sees Prime Minister Yaakov Brumwell sitting in his favorite leather chair. A small man, he actually looks lost in it. Brumwell reminds Wattenberg of Israel's first prime minister, David Ben-Gurion. Ben-Gurion was small of stature, with thinning hair and a stern look on his face most of the time. Regardless, he was a giant of a leader. Brumwell, however, has a way about him with people that Ben-Gurion never had. He listens, and he doesn't jump to conclusions.

"Come in, come in," Brumwell says warmly, another trait in which he and Ben-Gurion would have differed.

"I've given Mossad's proposal of a covert action a great deal of thought," he says, settling back in his chair. "However, we need to iron out some issues before I can make a decision."

Wattenberg sits down in an equally comfortable chair in front of Brumwell's desk, wondering where this conversation is going to go.

"What issues do we need to discuss?" Wattenberg asks noncommittally.

"Well, for one thing, Ariel, how much time do you estimate we'll need for an operation such as you have proposed to bring us positive results?"

"We estimate that it will take us, at minimum, one and possibly as much as three months to get reliable information, Yaakov. Of course, we'll have contact with our team on a schedule that will allow us to make real-time decisions to continue or to withdraw."

"Who will set up the itinerary for your team to follow, or are they going to have carte blanche?"

"Mossad will set up the itinerary. Yosef Bergman will be the team's inside contact."

"Have you invented identities for these two so they don't end up on CNN exposed as Israeli spies?"

"Of course, Yaakov. Yosef and I will meet with them, first to simply see if they believe this plan of ours is really feasible. Right now it is only a brainstorm. We are simply asking for your permission to proceed, to see if this idea can become a reality."

"How much money do you expect this little brainstorm of yours will cost us?" asks Brumwell.

"Will it be cheap? Certainly not," replies Wattenberg. "Is it necessary? I would say very definitely."

Brumwell looks down at his desk, then slowly raises his eyes to meet Wattenberg's again. "What I want you to do, before I can give my final decision, my friend, is to meet with these gentlemen. Have them sign a Mossad secrecy document. Work up what their fees would be for three months, cost of equipment to do the job efficiently, cost of insertion and removal, plus an emergency extraction plan, should that become necessary." The prime minister looks down momentarily, then looks back up at Wattenberg. "I have to tell you, Ariel, this idea of yours intrigues me." Wattenberg dares to look hopeful, but Yaakov Brumwell raises a hand. "And it scares me to death."

"I know," Wattenberg says heavily. "I feel the same way."

"Okay, get moving on it and when you have it put together, we'll meet again. When we do, I want to have Bergman in on that meeting as well. He needs to understand that his ass is on the line, every inch as much as those of the two men in the field."

"Of course," Wattenberg says, nodding grimly.

Wattenberg leaves the prime minister's office, taking one last look at Brumwell's secretary just for good measure. *Dirty old man,* he chastises himself, but just as quickly excuses his behavior. *Oh, please, no—surely I must qualify as a sexy senior citizen by now.*

*

From his office phone, Wattenberg calls Yosef Bergman. He wastes no time on trivialities. "Come down to my office. We need to talk."

"I'll be right there," Bergman says. *Shit, this doesn't sound good. I wonder if the prime minister shot down the idea.*

As Bergman comes through Wattenberg's doorway, Wattenberg looks up at him, his eyes as heavily lidded as those of a crocodile. As much as he would like to, Bergman still cannot pick up any positive vibes coming from his superior. Taking a seat in front of Wattenberg's desk, he waits while his boss makes notes on a legal pad. Finally Wattenberg looks back up at the taller, fitter—*hell, I might as well acknowledge it*—younger man.

"Yosef, go ahead and set up a meeting with this clandestine team of yours." Bergman's relief is palpable. "You and I will be the only Mossad attendees," Wattenberg continues. "If we can reach a mutual agreement, you and I will then meet with the prime minister to explain all the details."

Yosef Bergman's eyes grow wide. *The prime minister wants me in a meeting?*

The two have worked together so long that Wattenberg has no trouble reading Bergman's mind. "Yes, Yosef, both of us."

Chapter Eight

Joint Presentation

President Egan is the last person to enter the Situation Room. His Secret Service detail and two Marine guards remain just outside the heavy steel door. Everyone stands as he enters; he motions for all to resume their seats. Taking the center seat at the center table within the u-shaped tables, he smiles. The u-shaped arrangement makes it possible for everyone to both face each other and see the screen that will be used during the presentation.

Admiral Robert Smith of the Navy, General James Bradley of the Air Force and General Victor Sanford of Special Forces sit together on the left wing of the arrangement. Secretary of Defense John Anderson, CIA director Allison McDonald and National Security Advisor John Walker sit opposite the military team on the right side. President William Egan sits between his vice president, Patrick Devonshire, on his right and Maria Sterling, his chief of staff, on his left.

After pouring himself some water from a nearby pitcher, the president opens the meeting. "Ladies and gentlemen, the directors of NSA and the CIA are going to make a presentation regarding the escalation of Iran's nuclear intentions. When this presentation is completed, I want each and every one of you to comment on three things. Number one: what additional means of dialog can we generate to convince Iran to abide by their previous non-proliferation agreements? Number two, if Iran persists in going ahead with their hard-line tactics on enriching uranium and possibly developing nuclear weapons, what military means can we use to stop them? And lastly, if we are to take a military course of action, what results would you expect? What kind of retaliation do you foresee the Iranians taking?"

He turned to Walker and McDonald. "John, Allison, who wishes to go first?"

"I lost the toss of the coin," McDonald jokes, getting to her feet.

McDonald stands before the group today wearing a particularly stunning black pant suit with a thigh-length jacket, the effect of which she'd softened with a low-cut pink silk blouse. The pink warms her skin tones and brings out the highlights in her brunette hair.

"Let me begin by saying that John and I would like you to feel free to interrupt with questions at any time during this presentation. Needless to say, the materials that we'll be viewing and discussing here today have a top secret classification.

"The CIA sees the following:

"Over the past five years, Iran has been benefiting from high profits in oil. They have made substantial amounts of money which they are investing in further developing their nuclear program. Our agency estimates that their current investment is in the *billions* of dollars, between locations and personnel they have acquired on the open market."

McDonald turns on the overhead projector, then begins a PowerPoint presentation to underline her message. The first image, not surprisingly, is a map of Iran.

One at a time, she locates on the screen the sites CIA has designated as potentially nuclear sites. Karaj, Ab-Ali, Natanz, Arak, and another in Ardekan. "These are the sites they we are sure of," she tells the group. "What we don't know is if there are others. We do know of other sites that are necessary for the enrichment process, but which do not enrich uranium themselves.

"To date we have learned of approximately four hundred and fifty nuclear experts working in Iran who were hired from Russia, China, North Korea and Pakistan. We believe as well, as does the NSA, that Russia is Iran's prime supplier of nuclear materials, know-how, and personnel to Iran. We suspect that Iran has become a major customer of Russia's in arms dealings. Iran is probably Russia's third or fourth largest customer for nuclear arms purchases of some type." She paused to let this thought sink in.

"We know about the creation of Iran's new Shahab-3 missile," McDonald continued, as an image of one appeared on the screen, "and we are getting information that they plan to develop ways to launch it from their Kilo-class submarines, the same way we do cruise missiles. We have good evidence that they have ordered two more Kilo-class subs from Russia which when delivered will give them six that we know of." The image on the screen of a Shahab-3 is replaced by that of a Kilo-class sub.

"Israel and the nations of Europe are already under threat. If Iran can deploy those missiles from submarines, then we have to accept the fact that American cities are no longer safe."

Out of long-standing habit, the tall, trim Admiral Smith rubs a hand unconsciously over his bald head before speaking. His questions are terse and to the point. "Allison, how accurate is your information about Iran attempting to fire missiles from their submarines, and secondly, what's the suspected acquisition time for the next two subs?"

"Admiral, the talk of firing their missiles from submarines first surfaced when they purchased their first Kilo. What we are hearing lately is a more focused discussion on how to accomplish that, which our sources consider an indication of how close they are to nuclear capability. In order for Iran to become the leader in the Muslim world, they need to bring the war to us. Otherwise the scope of their goal is limited. We believe that goal is nothing less than worldwide Muslim domination.

"To answer the second part of your question, Admiral, we hear that the Russians have two remaining Kilos that they want to off-load. We know that both of those vessels have been stripped for spare parts to keep those in the fleet operating. The word that we are getting is that it will take Russia eighteen to twenty-four months to make those vessels seaworthy again.

"Are there any more questions before I turn this meeting over to John?" McDonald asks all assembled. The room is silent. "John it looks like you have the floor."

"Thank you, Allison," says John.

John Walker likes black and today he too is wearing a very sharp black suit, his with a white shirt and a bright red tie. John is a strong believer in power colors—as if his physical size of six-foot six weren't commanding enough.

"Admiral, to continya with the question y'all asked about sub acquisition time, the NSA agrees with the CIA's assumption of one-an'-

a-half to two yeahs. Howevah, we feel it'll also take Russia, at the least, another six months to a yeah to put those refurbished subs through propah sea trials."

Walker turns and addresses his next remarks directly to the president. "The NSA is extremely concerned about Iran's newly acquired high-speed torpeduhs and their stealth anti-aircraft missile systems. They say their tests have proven successful, somethin' we haven't been able to confirm. Our majuh concern is what they plan on *doin'* with these new weapons. Mahmoud Khasanjani is constantly makin' public statements about their continuin' with the enrichin' of uranium. Then he turns around and says Iran is willin' to abide by IAEA guidelines. Next you hear him threatenin' to wipe Israel offa the map. Y'all ask me, this is a deliberate plan to keep us off balance as to what their true intentions are."

"What *does* the NSA feel their true intentions are?" asks the president.

"Well, suh, both the CIA and the NSA feel that Iran is tryin' to expand its geographical boundaries and its sphere of influence within the Muslim world. Which they will, as soon as they feel they've got sufficient nuculer capabilities. NSA is lookin' at three to five yeahs, Mr. Pres'dent. CIA's now sayin' two to three."

"John, what kind of input is the NSA getting from our European allies?" asks John Anderson, the secretary of defense.

"Britain' purty tight-lipped right now," Walker responds. "We think they're layin' low after bein' involved with Iraq for so long. Nor are we gettin' much from France, Germany or the rest of Europe, for that mattah."

"Allison, what's the CIA hearing from Israel these days?" asks the president.

"We aren't receiving much from the Mossad, sir, or from our contacts within Israel. Which leads us to believe they're planning something. However, I have no specifics."

"Planning what, to take out the nuclear enrichments sites?" asks the vice president in alarm. "My God, they could start World War Three if they try what they did in 1981 with Iraq."

"We don't think that's their plan at this moment, not just yet anyway, Pat," replies McDonald. "We sense that something covert is going to go on, but we aren't able to put a finger on it as of now."

Sterling turns to Walker and asks, "John is the CIA and the NSA really on the same wave length with this concept, or are there any disagreements we haven't heard? I find it hard to believe that both of your assessments mesh so easily."

Walker responds slowly, stressing each point. "Maria, Allison and I met as the pres'dent directed us to. We've woven our ideas together to create as clear a picture as possible. Both of our organizations feel that Iran's in a holdin' pattern, 'til they're more confident they can accomplish what they've set out to do. Are you askin' me if we see things differently on Iran? Not really. Allison and I sat hashin' out our ideas and beliefs for five hours, and we *are* pretty much on the same wave length, as you put it. Mattah of fact, the pres'dent's idea of havin' us work together like that was a great step forward for both of our agencies and I think I can say personally, for Allison and myself as well."

"Well, it appears I finally got something right," jokes the president. "Now to the three questions I'd like to address. Is there anyone in particular who would like to begin?"

Chapter Nine

Feedback

As the president raises his question, John Walker takes his seat and notices a very warm smile coming from McDonald. *Guess she liked the way I handled Maria's question,* Walker thinks, pleased, and gives himself a mental pat on the back.

Admiral Smith lifts a finger and speaks first. Again running a hand over his bald dome, as if smoothing out his opinions, he launches right into them. A quick-spoken man, he gets right to the point. "Mr. President, I'm definitely no politician, so I'm going to pass on what we can do to create further dialog with Iran. Given Iran's geography and given the politics of sailing waters to its north and south, the Navy is limited under normal circumstances. Iran has a viable naval force, and that too must be taken into consideration, but that we can handle. As far as retaliation is concerned, I should think that would be based on what Iran had left standing." A chilling thought.

Vice President Patrick Devonshire speaks next. "I feel that we must keep talking. There must certainly be new ideas we can address or old ones we can try again. Iran must realize the seriousness of what they are doing. Personally, I feel that Iran really wants to have dialog but is posturing for the benefit of its neighbors in the Middle East. I think they want to come to the table having shown strength against the United States. I'd leave decisions on military action to our military leaders. But as far as retaliation is concerned, we absolutely must weigh every possible alternative before acting. We could lose millions of Americans."

Chief of Staff Maria Sterling jumps into the silence. "I tend to agree with Pat," she says, with a nod to the vice president. "In the face of war, possibly conducted in the continental United States, we must ask ourselves this question: are our people really ready to deal with that? Iran is certainly not what the Soviet Union was, in terms of capability, but they can still be very deadly. We survived a cold war with the Soviets. By resisting the first strike alternative, World War III was averted. What it boiled down to was that all we had to do was wait for the Soviet economy to fail. Sometimes I get the feeling that Israel would like us to solve their problems for them, and might actually be working to heighten tensions to do so." This thought hangs in the air.

After a few moments, John Anderson joins the conversation. "Speaking for Defense, I don't know how long we should be willing to continue the dialog route. It's already been four years since the United Nations started their discussions. I know dialog is vital, but my gut feeling is that Iran *wants* to drag dialog out until they're good and ready to launch attacks against Israel and the United States. And after that, Europe. Personally, I'd listen to our military leaders, retaliation-wise. I suspect Iran would make good use of some of its free-lance terrorist groups, using them as guns for hire, along with their own forces. I foresee a coordinated conflict, and in the not so distant future. Whether we attack first, or they get the initiative." As Anderson wraps up, the room goes silent again, digesting his thoughts.

General Bradley, commander of the Air Force, speaks. "I'm with the Admiral on dialog. Militarily, the Air Force can play a major role in a conflict with Iran. How much retaliation will be called for will depend on how completely we're allowed to do our job."

General Sanford concurs. "I agree with both the Admiral and General Bradley on dialog," says the commandant of the U.S. Marine Corp, nodding at his peers. "Special Forces are capable of many functions but, like General Bradley said, what will we be allowed to accomplish? If we smack the tiger in the face with a wet noodle, Iran will be able to retaliate. If we really care about American lives and the welfare of this country, we won't worry about world opinion on how to win a war."

John Walker raises a finger. "Mr. Pres'dent, I have nothin' I can add to what's already been said."

"Mr. President," McDonald steps back in, "may I be so bold as to suggest that we deal with this issue jointly with Israel, the country which stands to lose so much—as much if not more than we do. I know it is highly irregular, but nobody's written a text book covering this scenario."

The president summarizes what he's heard, then adds, "It's my opinion that we don't have to make a decision overnight. Maria, I'd like you to have our ambassador to the United Nations come back to Washington for a briefing after I meet with the military once more. McDonald and John, I want daily reports on what you both see happening with Iran. Admiral and both Generals, I'd like each of you to present me with specifics on how you see your forces handling a situation such as we believe we have here. May I suggest that you confer with each other and—create your plans for the worst case scenario. I want you all to take time. I'd like to see a strategy plan from our military leaders in six weeks.

"I will close with my own following thoughts," the president continues after a pause. "I've studied Iran for many years. I don't see them having the same economic problems the Soviet Union had. I also believe that Israel may have averted nuclear war over the last thirty years because of the action they took in 1981. That said, we still need to make careful, rational decisions for the future. Thank you all for coming."

The president rises, nods to each in turn, then leaves the Situation Room.

The rest rise and try to relieve the tension they feel with small talk or by just leaving the room.

The director of the CIA and the National Security Advisor are the last to file out, McDonald bringing up the rear. John Walker stops and graciously signals that she should precede him through the door. "No south'n gen'lman would evah allow a lady to pass through the door behin' him. My mama taught me bettah mannahs than that," he drawls laconically.

Chapter Ten

Middle of May

The morning after he receives permission to set up a meeting with his so-called desert rats, Bergman calls Natan Schwartz. He leaves a message on Schwartz's voice mail asking him for a return call.

Four hours later, Mossad's receptionist calls Bergman, and tells him that a gentleman identifying himself only as 'Natan' is returning his call. "He's on line three," she tells Bergman.

Bergman punches the button and picks up his phone. "Natan," he says. "How are you?"

"I'm fine," a deep voice replies with distrust, "but to whom am I speaking? Do I know you? I'm sorry, but I know a lot of Yosefs."

"It's not your imagination," Bergman agrees. "We have never met personally. However your new business venture has been recommended to me and my boss. We would like to meet with you and your partner. Would it be possible for you to fit us in to your schedule, either this week or next?"

"Do you mind telling me what you have in mind?" asks Schwartz.

"I'd rather that my boss tells you and that both of you hear it from him together. If after hearing about it you have any interest in our project, we can proceed from there, or simply forget about it." Bergman pauses, then adds, "All I'm authorized to tell you is that it would be a full-time project, involving anywhere from thirty to ninety days."

"I will speak with my partner to see what his schedule looks like, and if he thinks we can consider that lengthy a project at this time. I will call you back, in two days time."

"That would be fine. Thank you, Natan."

"Thank you, Yosef," Schwartz replies, then breaks the connection. Schwartz sits looking at the receiver in his hand, mulling this call over, then releases the button he'd been holding down and calls his partner. He too gets an answering machine.

"Mark, Natan here. Call me when you get a moment. I'm in the office. I need to run something by you. Someone seems to have brought some 'bikkurim,' some first fruits, our way. A fitting run up to Shavuot, I would say."

*

Within twenty minutes, the phone rings. "What's up, Natan?"

"I had a call from someone I do not know. He simply said we had been recommended to him and his boss. We have been asked to consider a project that would take thirty to ninety days, full-time. I told him I would get back to him in two days. What do you think? Do we want to tie ourselves up in such a long-term project and risk having to turn other clients away?"

"Well," Mark says, thinking, "we do have to finish up with the Halberstan job. That should not take more than, what, another two weeks? We can do the two surveillance jobs in the midst of it. Then we are open—nothing else had been scheduled yet. Why don't we at least listen to what he has to say? We can always turn it down."

"Okay, I'll call this guy back."

But I think I will wait the full two days. We do not want to appear over-anxious. Something about this one tells me we should proceed cautiously.

*

Schwartz calls Bergman late on the second day.

"My partner and I would like to meet with you. We could meet a week from today."

"That would be good for us, too," Bergman says. "Early in the morning, if that's possible?"

"Say, nine?" Schwartz suggests.

"Excellent," Bergman agrees.

"At our office," Schwartz tells him, and gives him the address, on Eliyahu Street in the Lower City, in close proximity to the port of Haifa.

*

Driving the hour up the coast to meet with Natan Schwartz and Mark Silberberg, Yosef Bergman and Ariel Wattenberg discuss how they should go about presenting this idea. It needs be handled cautiously. If there is no agreement and too much has been said, what the two men have been told could jeopardize the future of the project.

Arriving at the given address, both Bergman and the director of Mossad have to chuckle, reading the sign over the door. Written in both Hebrew and in English is the name of the organization: "Hidden Talents."

"Well, at least they have a sense of humor," says Wattenberg. "That's good to know."

Entering the office they hear chimes going off, signaling the door's having been opened.

Natan Schwartz appears in the entryway. "Can I help you?" the short, bearded, muscular man say politely. From what Bergman knows of Hidden Talents' reputation, any propriety from either of its operatives should be taken, at most, as skin-deep. The man is wearing a black short-sleeved, v-necked tee-shirt and black jeans; his arms and chest are as hairy as his chin and head.

"My name is Yosef. This is my boss, Ariel. We have an appointment with Natan and his partner in fifteen minutes. I know we are a little early. Would you prefer that we wait outside?"

"Nice to meet a face that matches a voice on the phone," says the man, now smiling broadly. "I am Natan Schwartz. Mark will be along in about five minutes. Very nice to meet you, Yosef." He turns to Wattenberg. "And your name is Ariel, you say? What, may I ask, does your company do that you wish to hire Hidden Talents?"

Wattenberg answers slowly and deliberately. "We are in the business of collecting and evaluating . . . special data . . . enabling top decision-makers to make . . . accurate and decisive decisions."

Oh, I think I smell the sweet perfume of a government job, thinks Schwartz.

At that moment, Mark Silberberg walks through the front door, as solidly built a man as his partner, though considerably taller. Schwartz makes the introductions, everyone shakes hands, then the four of them move to the rear of the office into the conference room.

"Would you like something to drink? Coffee, tea, water?" Silberberg asks.

Wattenberg and Bergman both decline. The four sit down around a small square table with very uncomfortable chairs.

Schwartz starts. "So—what's this project you have brought to us?"

Wattenberg answers first by telling the two men what he knows about them. "We understand that both of you were honorably discharged from the IDF about six months ago and have a great deal of electronic intelligence and communication experience, as well as extensive familiarity with working in the desert."

"Just about every member of the Israeli Defense Force has a great deal of desert experience," replies Silberberg, offhandedly. *These people have done their homework.* "Why don't you be more specific and stop playing mind games?"

Wattenberg bridles at the young man's rudeness. "Is it true that both of you have spent long periods of time on covert action in the desert?"

"Well, let's put it this way. We may or may not have," says Schwartz. "If we have, that's confidential military information and not for discussion with you or anyone else."

"Good," states Wattenberg, "Just what I wanted to hear. Gentlemen, what we are about to discuss involves top secret security issues. The government wishes to hire Hidden Talents to perform a covert desert action which could last from, as you have been told, thirty to ninety days. Are you available?"

"Where is this mission to take place, and when?" asks Schwartz.

"When? To be scheduled. Where? Within the borders of Iran," replies Wattenberg quietly.

"You have got to be kidding," laughs Schwartz.

"No, actually, I'm not," Wattenberg replies. "We believe that if we can monitor emissions from various nuclear plant sites, monitor traffic in and out of those plants and do some electronic eavesdropping, we should be able to determine if Iran is continuing with their uranium enrichment program."

"Two Jews are just supposed to go waltzing into the Iranian desert and walk out with all of this 'data,' as you call it," says Schwartz, incredulously.

"Of course not," Wattenberg says. "We have come here with an idea that we believe can work. We are here because you two are the experts we need to tell us if we are out of our minds, or if this could possibly be pulled off." *Don't shy off now. You're the ones we want*, thinks the director of Mossad anxiously.

"Well, for starters," says Silberberg, who has been letting Schwartz do all the talking since offering these potential clients a beverage, "to be successful, this mission would need a great deal of high tech equipment, most of which we don't use. Who would bankroll this undertaking? We would need special clothing, identities from God knows where in case we are captured, weapons from foreign sources, an insertion plan, an extraction plan, an emergency extraction plan. How is this all going to happen?" Silberberg paused for effect, then added, "And that doesn't even take into consideration our fees. We don't work for IDF wages anymore, you know." Silberberg is the detail man, the 'closer.'

"And this project would require very close communications with one or more persons so that no one in the field—either of us—is left high and dry," Schwartz states unequivocally.

"Yosef here would be your contact," Wattenberg tells them. "He has years of experience with teams in the field." Schwartz turns and looks Bergman over, closely, head to toe.

"Yosef, how many Mossad team members have you lost in the field?" Silberberg asks bluntly.

Bergman falters, not knowing what or how much he should say at this point.

"Look Yosef, I want an answer," Silberberg demands. "We can see that you're Mossad. We're not stupid."

If we thought you might be stupid, thinks Wattenberg, irritated, *we wouldn't have come to you in the first place.* He nods to Bergman, okaying an answer.

"I've never lost a team member in the years I've been with Mossad," Bergman replies.

Schwartz rises. "Gentlemen, you have given us much to think about. You have evidently been thinking about this for a while. Don't expect us to give you an answer overnight. We will get back to you in two weeks, to let you know whether or not we are interested."

*

"So what do you think, Yosef?" As they climb back into the new Volvo Wattenberg received as his latest car.

"I think that they are both very intelligent, very cautious individuals," Bergman answers. "I can see why they did not continue as officers in the military. Both of them express a sense of disrespect for authority. Yet, I think they will come back with a proposal. I read their military files, Ariel. These men are not easily frightened. They know what the political situation is with Iran. I imagine they both recognize this as a last-ditch effort to uncover the truth about Iran before the Israeli government reacts. No, they certainly aren't stupid."

Speeding down the highway to Tel Aviv, Wattenberg frowns and asks, "What do you suggest we do if they say no?"

"Ha," snorts Bergman. "You are the director, Ariel. Don't put that one on me."

Wattenberg starts thinking about how he only has five more years to retirement. *Will I have a country left to retire in or will I be living in a giant bomb crater? Will I be living at all?*

Sensing Wattenberg's need to be quiet, Bergman stares out of the car window watching the Mediterranean Sea streak by on his right. *How beautiful and peaceful it all looks,* he muses. *Why couldn't all of life be like this?*

Chapter Eleven

Following the Training

Muhammad Abdullah spends two weeks of intensive training within the close confines of a torpedo room. Most men would experience some degree of claustrophobia, thrown into such a situation. Abdullah, however, is the kind of man who has no trouble adapting to his surroundings, no matter how squalid or lavish, confining or liberating.

Now Abdullah finds himself in a small office awaiting the arrival of Jibril Atwan, advisor to the Supreme Leader, the man who sent him here. Abdullah had a message from him yesterday, telling him that the two of them need to meet upon his arrival at 1000 hours today.

Having more than an hour to wait, Abdullah has plenty of time to let his imagination run away with him. Pacing the small room, for the life of him, he cannot comprehend what this training is meant to prepare him for. His former naval service involved only surface vessels.

He looks around the small room wherein he waits. With its window overlooking the harbor, an old metal desk and two small chairs, it is not the most comfortable place in which to pass the time. Now freed from the close quarters of the torpedo room, he finds himself longing for some sunshine and fresh air.

Just before 1000 hours, Atwan walks in the door. He chooses the seat closest to the window. "Sit down! After two weeks in that submarine you must feel at home here in this little room," he says almost jovially.

Abdullah sits as directed but does not reply.

"Not the most attractive place to spend two weeks—or months—in, unless that was your job. Yet, we get many volunteers for submarine duty. Of course not all of them qualify," Atwan adds.

Abdullah is only further mystified. "So, am I to be assigned to one of the submarines?" he asks. *Anything but that.*

"No," Atwan answers. "No, you were given the training to learn the ins and outs of the torpedo room, to better understand the physical limitations that you will be dealing with."

"Forgive me," Abdullah says earnestly. "I don't understand. If I'm not being assigned to a submarine of what use is such information to me?"

"Muhammad, you have been chosen to lead a team of engineers whose job will be to insure that we'll be able to fire our new Shahab-3 missile from beneath the ocean, just like the Americans launch their cruise missiles."

All Abdullah can say is "Oh?"

"Yes. We want the physical characteristics of the missile and launch capabilities to be operational in ten months. That gives us six to eight months for test launchings." Atwan pauses. "Do you have a problem with this assignment?"

"How many engineers will I be working with?" Atwan likes the prudence of the engineer's question.

"We have four engineers besides you. They, too, have already experienced two weeks in the torpedo room. You are to be the team leader. The success or failure of this project is your responsibility." Atwan smiles thinly. "Of course, we are not expecting you to fail, based on your engineering profile." *Failure is not an option.*

"Who are these engineers? I would need to meet them."

"Of course you would. They are all very qualified for this project. However; we feel the project requires a stronger leader if it is to be completed on schedule. You will meet them this afternoon. Do you have any doubts about the project or your own capabilities?"

"I understand the project. I know my own abilities. Frankly, I work better on my own than as part of a group." *Might as well just say it.*

"We are aware of that." *I like this man,* Atwan thinks, *praise be to Allah.*

"I will do my best to keep an open mind until I meet this team you have selected."

"You doubt our decisions, Muhammad!"

"No, sir, I do not, only I cannot assure you what I can expect of this team, without assessing their abilities myself."

"Fair enough. After you meet with them, I would like a personal opinion report on each of them from you, within twenty-four hours. I also insist on weekly progress reports on the advancement of this project. Money is no object. Your assignment comes directly from President Kahsanjani."

Again, Abdullah could only say "Oh."

"Yes. A special courier will be assigned to you. The courier will bring your correspondence directly to me. Anything you give to the courier must be sealed. I will correspond with you by the same courier and in the same manner. Nothing is to be sent to me by e-mail, is that understood? No phone calls, either."

"Yes, I understand. With whom else am I allowed to discuss this project, beside yourself and the team?"

"No one."

"I expected as much."

*

Unlike the undersized and under furnished room in which Abdullah had met earlier with Jibril Atwan, this conference room, though small as conference rooms go, is spacious enough and quite comfortable. Six leather chairs surround an oval shaped table. Even the windows have drapes on them. The Iranian Secret Police Headquarters Building offers ample room for luxury.

"Your advisors have told me that the two of you are quite the negotiating team," Jibril Atwan says to Kamil Hussein and Hamid Dakham.

"Negotiating is an understatement," Hussein assures him brashly, brimming with youthful confidence. "If what you want is available on the open market, we'll get it for Iran." Hussein, a recent graduate of Amirkabir University of Technology, is a radical revolutionary looking for a cause. He wants nothing more from life than to become a hero for Islam.

"This will not be as easy as buying groceries," Atwan chides him. "Remember the ride you took out of Tehran and then reversed direction to get back here?"

This time Dakham answers. "Yes, we were both confused by that at first. But after our two weeks of training, we understand fully how important it is for us to make ourselves inconspicuous, to be sure that we are not being tailed." Dakham has recently left the elite Quds Force of the *Pásdárán*, the Army of the Guardians of the Islamic Revolution, where he was known as a follower rather than a leader, but while he was following, he was thinking. Clearly. He was often credited with being the brains of a successful operation.

"The moment you set foot outside of this complex, you can assume you are subject to observation by numerous people who would be more than happy to trade information for money or favors. And it will only become worse when you leave Iran. That I can assure you," Atwan stresses.

The two men nod in unison.

Atwan gets down to specifics. "Our current uranium enrichment manufacturing process cannot supply us with all we need. In order to have sufficient quantities on hand, we find we must obtain materials that are available only on the black market. As I said, this is not as easy as a stroll through the Grand Bazaar. This is a matter of finding the sources, identifying the real sellers, insuring the quality of the materials, shipping the goods and settling on a fair market price. Most important of all, Iran must not be traceable as either the buyer or end user of the ore."

"Although generic in nature, our past two weeks have given us a good foundation in what we can expect and what we need to do," Dakham says quietly.

"So, if you two were planning this mission, where would you start?" asks Atwan.

"I would start looking for those sources that have had past access to nuclear materials from within and around the former Soviet Union," Hussein states coolly.

"Hamid, do you agree? Or do you think otherwise?"

"I agree. They are certainly known to be lax in the monitoring of their nuclear storage. And it is a well-known fact that most of their military commanders can be bought for a price."

"What happens when those commanders are caught, or start feeling they have betrayed the motherland?"

Dakham pauses. "I sense you have a more definite proposal, Jibril. How would you approach the problem?" he asks prudently. *No point* in reinventing the wheel, or in this case, a plan for the procurement of uranium ore.

Atwan nods. *Yes, this one is smart,* he smiles to himself. "The former Soviet Union part of it you have correct. We are sending you to Russia, very soon. Your cover will be that you are two Pakistani engineers looking for parts replacements. You will be scheduled to meet three men sometime within a week after you arrive. You are to make contact and it is imperative that you play your roles out well."

"Can you tell us anything about these three men?" Dakham asks.

"All I can tell you is that these men are not what they appear to be. We need to be sure who and what we'll be dealing with. The decision has been made that if everything plays out as planned, we will pay their price, within reason of course. These men are not military commanders, who may have some hidden agendas and no honor. No, this is business. You will be dealing with the Russian mafiya."

Both Hussein and Dakham say the same thing at the same instant, "The mafiya?"

Dakham is the one to ask, "How can we trust them to come through for us?"

"You forget, this is for 'fuluss,' for money," Atwan says, rubbing his thumb slowly up and down against his pointer finger. "You will imply that there is the opportunity for more deals in the future. Screw this up and they never get another chance. Not to mention the fact that any false moves on their part and they will land on our hit list." *And, yes, we all know what that means.*

"Besides, we trust the mafiya." Atwan says, rising to his feet. The meeting, apparently, is over. "They know how to keep their mouths shut. Communications will only be through this building. Contact me after your meetings."

Chapter Twelve

End of May

On the fourteenth day of the promised two weeks, Schwartz calls Bergman.

As his palms begin to sweat, Bergman asks, "So, my friend, what have you and Mark decided?"

"We would like to schedule a second meeting. We think your plan might have merit. There are a number of issues we need to work out together, however. If we can come to a reasonable agreement on the overall operation and costs, then possibly we can come to terms."

"And what are your terms?" Bergman asks reflexively, then kicks himself. He knows the answer before Schwartz can speak the words.

"Yosef, Yosef, this is not something that can be settled over the phone," Schwartz scolds him, but his tone is good-natured. "Have Ariel come with you, if he's the real decision-maker. If he's not, then bring whomever is."

Bergman hangs up and sits staring blankly at his office wall as if a video is playing on it. *My God, maybe this is a good idea after all! If I could only tell Ariel, but he's off in the Negev, out of contact till the day after tomorrow. Ariel will want to set up the meeting. I doubt he'd bring someone above him to play 'decision-maker.' Prime ministers don't just bounce around the countryside whenever someone wants the top dog.*

Bergman leaves word with Wattenberg's secretary to have him call as soon as he returns. In the meantime, he has other concerns to address. *If this mission is to succeed, I must consider how I can most effectively communicate with them. Data and operational messages need to be sent and* received without any possibility of detection. This is becoming downright scary. This may be the most sensitive mission I've ever been involved in.

*

Upon Wattenberg's return, he and Bergman speak. Wattenberg authorizes Bergman to go ahead and schedule a meeting based on what his secretary tells him his schedule can handle.

He reaches Schwartz on his first try. "Hello, Natan. This is Yosef. Ariel and I could meet with you next Thursday, if that's convenient for you and Mark."

"What time next Thursday?"

"Let's say we begin at 1000 hours and see how long it takes to reach a decision."

"All right, 1000 hours it is. Who is coming to this meeting?"

"It will just be Ariel and myself."

That would make this Ariel the director of Mossad, reasons Schwartz. *Good. We can't expect the prime minister to come. However, he will certainly have the final say.*

Bergman hangs up and advises Wattenberg's secretary to hold next Thursday for an all-day meeting in Haifa.

*

The new blue Volvo makes the second trip to the offices of Hidden Talents.

On the way, Wattenberg and Bergman try to figure out what they can expect. Neither has been able to come up with a satisfactory sketch of the operation.

They arrive at 0945 and Silberberg leads them into the same back office where they held the previous meeting. Schwartz picks up on the fact that both Wattenberg and Bergman notice how the room is now outfitted with different chairs from the previous meeting.

"Ah, you notice the chairs," he chuckles. "We intentionally make it uncomfortable for a first meeting, just in case. It prevents it from becoming a long, drawn-out meeting. It is easier to have them leave because they are uncomfortable that for us to impolitely end a meeting early."

"Yeah, and we don't want people to think we're executive types instead of field types," adds Silberberg.

Not only is there more comfortable seating, but a long table has appeared against the back wall, covered with trays of sandwiches, pastries, chips, pickles, and drinks. And this time the drinks included wine and scotch.

"All of the food is kosher, including the wine," says Schwartz. "The scotch I can't vouch for."

"So you expect this to be a long meeting, I see," says Wattenberg approvingly.

"Ariel, if it's not long, you have wasted a trip up here and we have wasted two weeks of thinking about your proposal," says Silberberg.

"Would you like some coffee and possibly a pastry before we start?" asks Schwartz.

Bergman does not hesitate. "I would. I skipped breakfast this morning, and I don't think well on an empty stomach." The ice broken, everyone helps themselves to pastries and coffee.

"Oh, yes, these chairs are a marked improvement, I must say," Bergman smiles as he makes himself comfortable.

"Okay, let's get down to business," Wattenberg says.

"Before we begin, I'm concerned about what conversations can be picked up from this room," says Bergman.

"Yosef, you can rest assure that our conversations are as guarded as any you have at Mossad headquarters," Silberberg replies. "It's one of the things we pride ourselves on, complete client confidentially. The other is not letting anyone know what Natan and I do to protect our own asses. But seriously, trust me. We have equipment you cannot see or hear that will prevent anything on the market today from penetrating our conversations."

Bergman indicates his satisfaction with Silberberg's answer.

Schwartz starts. "Okay. Your plans contain both things we like and things we find a bit fuzzy. Let's start with the idea that the goal is to monitor emissions, possibly monitor communications and report on whatever traffic goes in and out of certain facilities."

"That's what we need to accomplish," says Wattenberg, nodding.

Silberberg takes up the conversation. "What kind of equipment do you have to accomplish these goals, short of someone being right on top of these facilities?"

"We know that the equipment is available on the market," Wattenberg replies. "As yet, I'm not sure Israel has possession of everything we need."

"Okay. I like your honesty," says Silberberg. "If Israel doesn't have it, where is it going to come from?"

"We know of certain high tech companies that can provide us with listening and spotting devices. Companies that are not Israeli. Whatever you use, it cannot have even a smudge of an Israeli fingerprint on it."

"Good, I'm glad that we see eye-to-eye on that issue. Of course, we do not want to leave our bodies as evidence, either," says Schwartz, smiling grimly.

The rest of the morning's conversation concerns sources for equipment and estimates of associated costs.

*

It is now nearly noon and the four break for the lunch spread out before them. After some food and small talk, the conversation returns to the 'what ifs' of the mission.

"Okay, let's say you come up with the necessary equipment, what plans do you have for an insertion?" asks Schwartz.

"Our thoughts are to turn that problem over to our top military people, to have them develop a plan," says Wattenberg.

"Would you consider allowing us to recommend who we would want to make that decision, or if not, then do we have the option of scrubbing the whole project if we think it is unrealistic?" Silberberg asks.

"Based on your military experience and your reputations, we are open to your recommending who should prepare this plan, and implement it as well, if you wish," says Wattenberg. "This goes for insertion, removal and emergency support contingencies, as well."

"After all, this is a totally different type of operation for the Mossad," Schwartz comments, then changes topics. "You say this is a thirty to ninety day project. How the hell did you come up with that figure, if you will excuse me?"

"Well, I can't give you an exact answer on that," Wattenberg replies, unruffled by Schwartz's sudden use of profanity, "but our people believe that it is realistic, that it could take somewhere within that time frame to collect the information we are looking for."

"This is not meant as a put-down, but do either of you realize what a project like this takes from day one to execution, to debriefing?" asks Silberberg.

"You are suggesting . . ." Wattenberg prompts him to elaborate.

"If you truly want this project to succeed, this is what we propose," says Schwartz, slowly, deliberately ticking off their obviously thought-out requests on his fingers. "We recommend the manufacturers of the equipment we need to achieve your goals. We recommend the military decision-makers to make this project happen and keep their mouths shut. We meet jointly with those leaders to develop a plan to achieve your goals and to keep our hides from becoming Persian throw rugs."

"This will take time," Silberberg speaks up, "and your window of one to three months may get thrown out with the bath water. If identities for us are created to our satisfaction and there seems a decent chance that we'll come out of this with our hides, then there is only one thing left to discuss."

"That being?" Bergman asks both of them. Schwartz answers.

"Our fees. Gentlemen, let's speak openly. We are going to be putting our asses on the line for the Jewish state. We both have young families that could possibly be left without financial support. We want them to have the following." Again he starts ticking off requirements, rapidly this time. "Hidden Talents will have three million dollars in U.S. currency deposited in two different Swiss bank accounts. You are to deposit one-half of the total to each account. No taxes to be drawn against this money. The beneficiaries of those accounts we will set up. Your financial dealing with those accounts are for deposit only. You will be unable to withdraw funds."

Wattenberg looks Schwartz in the eye, his demeanor giving no hint of his reaction so far.

"This amount will cover the first ninety days of planning," Schwartz continues, slowing back down for greater emphasis with each new demand, "and possibly executing the project. For each additional month, you will deposit one million dollars, on the first of the month, into these accounts, to be divided equally, until the project is complete, including debriefing and/or any other issues deemed necessary."

"Are you done?" Wattenberg asks after Schwartz finally comes to what appears to be the end of his list.

"Yes."

"So, what? Are you nuts?" Wattenberg explodes. "Where may I ask, among your so-called 'hidden talents,' is your sense of patriotism?"

"Ariel, I'm demonstrating my sense of patriotism by having you back for a second meeting," Schwartz says evenly. "But Mark and I are also realists. It is *our* lives that will be on the line. If we die, it is our families who will suffer. We have calculated roughly how much we could possibly earn, should we, God willing, live to retirement. That's how we came up with this fee. If you are not happy with it, go find someone else to do your dog and pony show."

"This is a decision I cannot make," Wattenberg says. "For that kind of money, I will have to get approval." *And I want you to think that I'm not at all sure I can get it.*

"No shit," Schwartz says without emotion. "So why don't you just call the prime minister and set up a meeting."

"You know, Natan, I really resent your attitude."

"Well, Ariel, get over it. We have to work together. I think what you really resent is having to pay for something that you have seen people throw their lives away for—for nothing. Is that your definition of patriotism, perhaps? Patriotism will not support my wife and children if I'm dead in the deserts of Iran. You look around and tell me how much the Knesset would provide for my family. Mark and I have spent enough time in the IDF. We have many friends there and love them for what they do. But that love doesn't put food on the table. You can choose to accept this proposal, or leave it. The choice is yours. Or I should say, the prime minister's." *I must say, I rather enjoy sticking the needle into you, Ariel. I know your type. And you know mine.*

Wattenberg looks across the table at Bergman and motions with his head that they are leaving. This meeting is over. *Ariel is clearly pissed,* thinks Bergman he hurries after his boss. *He cannot tolerate being set up like this. He's a man who needs control—and right now, he's a man with none. And there goes my project, up in smoke.*

Stony-faced, Wattenberg pushes the outside door open and strides across the small parking lot to the car without saying a word, saying nothing to Bergman.

The minute they are in the car, Bergman cannot contain himself any longer. "So much money! What will the prime minister say?" he asks anxiously

"I think he might go along with it," Wattenberg answers, suddenly cheerful. "You know, Yosef, Natan and Mark are no dummies in what they do. I can see why they created their own business. These are two men with the foresight, plus the brains and brawn to make things happen."

Chapter Thirteen

First Week of June

Ariel Wattenberg puts a call into the prime minister and obtains a meeting date and time two days hence. "Bring this Yosef Bergman with you to this meeting," Yaakov Brumwell instructs him when he returns Wattenberg's call.

*

Wattenberg ushers Bergman into the waiting area of the prime minister's office, allowing Bergman a unimpeded view of the well-endowed receptionist. Gawking, Bergman nearly trips over the threshold. Wattenberg just smiles as the red faced Bergman tries to recoup his composure.

"You could have warned me," Bergman whispers, irritated.

"Why? And ruin my fun?" Wattenberg jokes. "You are not the first to be sent sprawling by the woman, you know. And it's not every day that I can catch one of my staff in a compromising situation."

"Yeah, that was real funny. Ha ha." There is no humor in Bergman's manufactured laugh. *How auspicious a beginning is that*, he rebukes himself.

After a wait of a delicious ten minutes of stolen glances, a phone on the exquisite receptionist's desk rings. She answers it, then turns to Wattenberg and Bergman. "The prime minister will see you now," she says in a throaty contralto, then rises from her chair to escort the two men into the prime minister's office. This time Wattenberg takes the lead, knowing he owes Bergman something for all his embarrassment: the receptionist's hand laid gently on the shoulder of the last to enter, the grazing of a breast against an arm, and the full, luscious smile and slow wink that always accompany it. Yaakov Brumwell's receptionist is nothing if not predictable.

Unfortunately, Bergman can barely appreciate the fleeting moment, the touch, the graze, the smile and the wink, as nervous as he is. He has never spoken directly with the prime minister before.

The prime minister rises and shakes both of their hands. "Have a seat," he says graciously. "Please, make yourselves comfortable. Yosef, I'm hearing some very creative thinking coming out of your group."

Bergman is floored that he's the first to be addressed, and by first name. "Thank you, Mr. Prime Minister," he says, somewhat disconcerted, but hits his stride quickly. "But let's get it off the ground first, and see it to completion. Then you can tell me if it was such a great idea." He smiles sheepishly.

The prime minister raises his eyebrows. "What? What kind of a confidence level is that?" *Have I been misjudging what I've been hearing?*

"The confidence of this being a good idea is there, sir," Bergman says, making an effort to convey greater conviction. "In all honesty, however, I will feel better when we have our people back on Israeli soil and we have the data we require," he adds.

"Good," says Yaakov, nodding. "Over-confidence can lead to lousy planning and disasters." Then he turns to Wattenberg. "So, tell me how your meeting went with our two scouts."

Wattenberg can only shake his head his head in frustration. "Well, Yaakov, as the Americans say, they held us up at the pass."

"Do not speak to me in American slang. What the hell are you trying to say?"

"Sir, they want complete control of this operation," Wattenberg explains. "Starting with ordering equipment, deciding who will handle the insertion and evacuation, supplies—everything."

"So, what's the big deal?" asks the prime minister, a bit perplexed. "That's not out of the ordinary. I would expect it of them."

"They made it perfectly clear that they would decide if the plan is operational or not, and reserve the right to cancel it."

"So?" Yaakov shrugs. "I still don't feel you're getting at what's bugging you, Ariel."

"Their terms. Just to begin this program, they want one million dollars a month, split into two individual Swiss accounts in which we can only make deposits, to cover the first three months. If it takes longer, they want another million a month until the program is completely wrapped up." Rolling his eyes, Wattenberg goes on, "Oh, and did I mention, they want their payment in U.S. dollars, non-taxable and payable on the first of the month."

Yaakov smiles at both Wattenberg and Bergman. "Aside from your feeling that they've got us over a barrel, how do you really feel about this project?"

So American slang is all right for you but not for anyone else, Wattenberg thinks, amused, then answers first. "If this is ever to work, I am well convinced that they are the men to make it happen."

"Yosef, your input?"

"From what I know of these two, I agree with Ariel completely."

"Yosef, I understand that, should we go through with this, you will be entirely responsible for all communication with these two individuals while they are in the field, am I correct?"

"Yes, sir, you are correct. If something caused me not to be able to perform my job, it has already been decided that Ariel himself would take over. We need the utmost in security."

The prime minister has been nodding at all he hears. "Then meet with them again," he tells them, "and have them sign a contract of confidentiality. Then begin the process of getting this off and running. Iran is not sitting around with its hands on its ass."

With that statement Wattenberg and Bergman rise. Relief is evident on both of their faces, but all three men eye each other with equal solemnity. This is serious business they are about to enter upon, and the first step has just been taken. Shaking the prime minister's hand, they leave. *Breathe,* Bergman says to himself. *Breathe.*

Bergman doesn't even notice the receptionist as he exits the outer office.

Chapter Fourteen

The Same Week

President Egan speed dials his secretary.

"Janet, I'd like you to have Admiral Smith, General Bradley and General Sanford phone me tomorrow at noon for a conference call on a secure line."

"Yes, sir, I'll call them immediately," answers Janet. "Is there anything else you'd like?"

"Yes, have the directors of the CIA and NSA call me on a secure line for a conference call this afternoon at five."

"Yes, sir."

Putting her other work aside, Janet promptly places the phone calls to the five individuals. She has to wait for two of them to return her call. As soon as she has everyone confirmed, she will advise the president.

Within fifteen minutes, both phone conferences are coordinated and confirmed, and she rings through to advise the president that everything is scheduled as requested.

"Janet, you never fail to amaze me," he responds warmly.

Which is what keeps me doing this job, Janet smiles to herself. *I love pleasing this man.*

*

Both the director of the CIA and the director of the NSA call in a few minutes before five. Janet has them waiting on a conference call line, then calls into the Oval Office for the president to join them.

"Thank you, Janet." Janet can hear his smile of appreciation.

"Allison, John, how are you?" William Egan says in greeting. "Let me get right to business. I'm calling because I want both of your agencies to arrange for our satellites covering the Middle East to ramp up their focus on all Iranian military units, military movements and traffic going in and out of any known or suspected nuclear facility sites."

John Walker thinks a moment, then responds first. "Suh, how often do y'all want updates on what we're findin'?"

"At this point, John, I want anything you feel is critical included in your daily reports."

"Is there something specific you are looking for?" asks Allison McDonald.

"What I have in mind right now is to observe their daily routines, to get a base line, and to see if any changes start to come about," the president explains. "I suspect they'll be aware that we're watching via our satellites. If changes are made, I have no doubt they will attempt to keep them as invisible as they possibly can. Your analysts will need to be extra observant to spot any differences."

"Currently we're coverin' Iran with three satellites on a daily basis, Mr. Pres'dent. Do y'all want any of our others reprogrammed, to take additional photos?"

"John, only if we start to see something out of the ordinary. I believe you understand what I'm asking for. I'll expect to start seeing whatever you come up with in your regular reports, starting the day after tomorrow. I'm sorry to make a change like this so late in the day, but this is important. You both have a good evening. I have a fund raiser to attend. The president should never be late."

Everyone disconnects from the call. It falls to John Walker and Allison McDonald to spend the evenings at their desk, implementing the president's orders.

*

In the same manner that she handled yesterday's conference call, Janet White waits until the admiral and both generals are on the line before notifying the president. She has observed over the two years she has been working as the president's secretary, and always finds it amusing, that admirals and generals particularly dislike being put on hold while waiting for others. *Even the president of the United* State. She always finds this amazing.

Just before noon she calls into the president and advises him that all three parties are on the line waiting for him to pick up.

"Admiral, generals," he greets them all, "it's three weeks since we met last. I'm looking for an update on your strategy presentations."

Admiral Smith speaks first. "Mr. President, we are looking at your order in two different, and very distinctly different, ways. We are looking at two sets of conditions: a pre-emptive strike and a retaliatory strike. We are also looking at surveillance possibilities which will enable you to reach your executive decision."

My executive decision—what a smart-ass way of saying the buck stops on your end.

"Mr. President, we can be taking satellite pictures and do stealth fly-overs to give you a better idea of what's going on below," the admiral adds.

General Sanford speaks. "Mr. President, I could have insertion teams on the ground within a couple of days. They could be in and out of Iran without anyone knowing otherwise."

All pause while the president briefly considers this thought. "Is three more weeks sufficient time for you to give me the different strategies you'ld propose?" the president asks. They all agree that they could make their recommendations in three weeks.

"Fine, then we'll meet in the Situation Room again. Only this time, gentlemen, it will only be the four of us who are in on this conference call. I want you to come prepared to make compelling arguments for ideas you recommend. I expect that you will have strong feelings about certain issues, and I want to hear them, even if you think you'll offend the president of the United States." President Egan pauses, underlining the importance and seriousness of his request.

"Gentlemen, this is not going to be a cake walk," he continues. "I may get loud. I may get emotional. I welcome all three of you to do the same. Whatever goes on in that room, stays in that room. We have nothing less than the safety and future of our country at stake.

"Okay, then. Your job is to get together and come up with a plan that we could put into action if absolutely necessary. Janet will call all of you and advise a date and time. I'll see you then, though please feel free to call beforehand if you feel the need to. Have a good afternoon, gentlemen."

The phone goes dead in the hands of America's top three military leaders, all of whom are in awe of what the president has just asked of them. Never has any of them been party to a conversation of that nature coming from the Oval Office. If they could see each other's faces, they would observe a new resolve develop in how each of them would approach his plans. *This president will get what he wants.* Of that, there is no doubt.

Chapter Fifteen

One Week Later

"Natan, this is Ariel. It's a go. When can you and Mark meet with us, Yosef and myself?"

"My, my," says Schwartz, surprised that decisions on a project of this scale can be made so quickly within the government. But his mind gets on with business. "Ariel, we would definitely want to continue meeting here. We do not want to be seen walking into Mossad headquarters under any circumstances."

"Certainly. That's understandable," says Wattenberg. "When can we meet in Haifa?"

"Next week. What day is good for you?"

Wattenberg checks his calendar. "Let's make it Wednesday. At 1000 hours?"

"Wednesday, 1000 hours it is."

*

Wattenberg and Bergman pull in and park in front of at Hidden Talents at 1000 hours precisely. Schwartz holds the door for them as they enter, and both Schwartz and Silberberg greet the two warmly as they escort them back into the conference room.

When they all are seated, Schwartz leans forward. "Ariel, I never realized the government could react this swiftly. We had assumed it would be weeks, maybe months before we heard back from you."

"We can when we have to," says Wattenberg dryly.

"They have accepted our proposal without any questions?" Silberberg asks, still incredulous. He won't believe what he's been hearing without convincing.

"Well, let's just say that your friend Yosef here put in a very good word for you," Wattenberg answers. Bergman smiles, nodding.

"First we need to have you sign our standard confidentiality agreements," says Wattenberg, pulling paperwork from his briefcase. "Please, take your time to review them carefully."

Silberberg and Schwartz read through the documents word for word. Once they're both finished, they look up at each other, rolling their eyes as if to say, *These forms are absurd.* Both of them sign and Bergman signs as a witness for each of them.

"Now," says Wattenberg, glad that formality is out of the way, "we need to discuss the first stages of this operation." *At long last.* Up until now, Wattenberg has been in sales mode, carefully weighing each word he utters, until the deal is done. At this point, he shifts into management mode, his expression neutral, words flowing rapidly and dispassionately from his mouth. He sounds like he's reading from and checking off items on a long to-do list, but nothing in writing sits before him on the table.

"The prime minister and Mossad have agreed to set up this operation. Its success relies entirely on your expertise. We do want to be able to call the shots on where you are going and what you will be monitoring." At that he pauses, giving either Silberberg or Schwartz the opportunity to comment, but they both simply nod their agreement.

"Okay. Yosef will be in contact with you on whatever schedule you feel is sufficient to transmit information or any communication you need. The Mossad will provide both of you with identities made up from the country of your choice. Monitoring equipment and weapons, food supplies, desert fatigues, anything you need to purchase, will be handled by our internal Mossad group, though no one will know the identity of the recipients of these items, not even within Mossad. We want you to contact the IDF's chief of staff after we have called him. We will alert him that you will be calling. You have the prime minister's authority to advise the chief of staff as to whom you want to work with concerning your insertion and retrieval. Any questions to this point?"

Schwartz shakes his head, but Silberberg is still suffering from disbelief that they have all the control they want. "So then, you are saying that we get to direct this entire operation?" he asks, then rephrases his question. "You give us our targets and our responsibilities—what we are to observe and report back on, but otherwise, the details are entirely in our hands. I just want to be absolutely sure we are all agreeing to the same thing."

"That's exactly what we are saying, Mark," Wattenberg smiles. "We believe that we can gain a great deal of critical information from this operation. I told the prime minister that if anyone can do this, it would be you two. We agree that it is better for you to choose your support people than for us to. We all find that request entirely appropriate. We realize that you know who would—or would not—be able to manage an operation of this magnitude." Schwartz nods his agreement.

"Using your services allows us to maintain the strictest security," Wattenberg adds, "comfortable in the knowledge that you have the best people working with you."

"I will be rooming at Mossad headquarters during the entire time of this insertion," Bergman tells them. "I will be your regular contact, with no other Mossad responsibilities. Once you start feeding us data, it will be my responsibility to get that material analyzed. Only Wattenberg will substitute for me, if necessary."

"I'm impressed," Schwartz says.

Satisfied, Wattenberg continues with the briefing. "When everything is set up for a launch date, this is where we want you to go." He pulls out a small, well-marked satellite image of Iran. "Our intelligence and U.S. intelligence have identified a number of nuclear sites. But we question another site no one seems to be talking about yet, a facility at Bampur." He points to a spot in a mountainous desert area near the southeast corner of the country.

"Look at all the rectangles. There must be water there. It seems to be broken up into farm land," observes Silberberg.

"Yes, but we know that this rectangle is industrial," says Bergman, pointing to a specific area on the map. "This is your target there."

"Our people think the site has been recommissioned to perform uranium enrichment," Wattenberg says, tapping his finger on Bampur. "We suspect that its out-of-the-way location was chosen so other nations would not even consider it a possible site. We haven't heard as much as a peep about this place yet. We suspect that security here, which appears to be relaxed, may be a ploy. Heightened security is a dead giveaway to anyone watching."

Schwartz nods. *Of course it is,* he thinks. He finds himself chaffing at the feeling of being talked down to. He stifles it, knowing such thinking is not productive.

"Afterwards, we want you to monitor the military installation at Bandar Abbas, on the Straight of Hormuz. Security there, however, will be problematic. We are looking for you to intercept communications there and see what you can learn about their Kilo subs. After that you will be retrieved somewhere south of Bandar Abbas."

"So, just the two targets," Schwartz says. *Three months to execute this? I was looking forward to the overtime.*

"Yes, just the two, but I would suggest you drop the word 'just.' Bandar Abbas will be no cakewalk, gentlemen," he says soberly, then adds, "My only suggestion to you is that you consider going in and coming out by submarine, via the Gulf of Oman."

Only suggestion, Silberberg laughs to himself. *That's rich.* "That's not a problem for us," he replies. "As you know, we have both had submarine experience."

"I'd ask that you wait until tomorrow to call the chief of staff. This will give us time to reach him and advise him of this operation," says Wattenberg.

"And about the financial arrangements that we discussed . . . ?" asks Schwartz.

"Tomorrow each of you will receive, by special courier, an identification to your Swiss bank accounts. These accounts will be handled only by you or someone you designate. I suggest that you designate someone along with yourselves, and also that you create new passwords so that you know your monies are secure. The State of Israel will be listed on the accounts only as a depositor." *You damn well better be pleased,* Wattenberg grimaces silently.

Smiling, Silberberg says, "Gentlemen, it's time for lunch. We always treat our special clients very well here at Hidden Talents. We have a caterer arriving in just a few minutes. Let's loosen up, so we can properly digest our food."

*

Lunch is a goodly spread of falafel, hummus, bagels, lox, cream cheese, onions, vegetables and pita bread for those who might not care for a bagel. This time only non-alcoholic beverages are offered for refreshments.

A tangible closeness is building between these four individuals. This is no longer just a job for Hidden Talents. All are aware of how much is riding on the success of this operation.

After lunch the four agree that all future communication will go through Bergman, starting immediately. Schwartz and Silberberg will put their thoughts and suggestions together and notify Bergman of where they are and how things are proceeding. Schwartz and Silberberg agree that they will no longer solicit clients until this operation is completed. Once the insertion can be given a date, the operation will be given highest priority.

As the four men shake hands, the air crackles with electricity. As they prepare to leave, both Wattenberg and Bergman offer their prayers for the safe return of both men and the success of this mission.

The hour drive back down to Tel Aviv is quiet and subdued for both of them, each of them brainstorming any and every possible pitfall that could develop, all the ways the operation could possibly go wrong—and how to prevent them from happening.

For some reason, for both men, this operation seems like no other they have ever undertaken, maybe because its success or failure is so monumental. Neither can get the image of an atomic explosion out of his mind.

Chapter Sixteen

First Trip to Russia

Kamil Hussein and Hamid Dakham are directed by Jibril Atwan to leave the Iranian security compound at 0200 the next morning. They are told they will be picked up by limousine and taken east to the border of Pakistan. Both of them think this is an ungodly hour to depart, yet recognize the value of darkness. Security comes at a price.

The limousine travels four bumpy, tedious, hours, the driver saying not so much as a single word. At the border crossing, the driver gets out of the vehicle and walks over to the Iranian checkpoint. After conferring with the Iranian soldiers manning it, he proceeds to the Pakistani side and meets with two Pakistani border crossing guards. He hands each Pakistani an envelope. They in turn give him the okay to allow his party to cross over into Pakistan.

The driver returns to the limo, opens the back door, smiles in at them, then says, "You can cross the border. There will be no need to show any identification." Hussein and Dakham climb out, wary. Both are surprised and unnerved a bit not have to show their passports to guards on either side.

Once they are on Pakistani soil, they follow their instructions, proceeding on foot alongside the road. Nearly one hundred meters from the border crossing, a vehicle flashes its lights, the signal they have been told to expect. Regardless, as they hurry in the direction of the lights, they are both anxious that they might yet be arrested by Pakistani border guards, police or security forces.

The vehicle, it turns out, is a beat-up twenty-year-old Nissan SUV. They already miss the luxury of the limousine; this next part of their journey will not be as comfortable as the first.

As soon as they enter the vehicle, the driver turns to them and starts speaking to them in Farsi. They sit and act dumbfounded, then both start speaking rapidly, talking over each other, in Urdu, as if that's their native tongue.

"Good," the driver replies, again in Farsi. "You never know who I might really be. Anyway, you are safe so far. On the floor around your feet, you will each find a carry-on bag to take with you on the plane. Those bags have your passports, your flight tickets, hotel reservations and other important papers and information—who you work for, your reason for entering Russia, those kinds of things. Check the passport photos and make sure you each get the right bag. In the trunk, we have luggage for each of you to check in. You want to appear to be on a prolonged business trip. Any questions?

Are you kidding, thinks Hussein. *My only question is, is this mission important enough to qualify me as a hero of the Islamic revolution?*

"We are headed for the airport at Karachi. As soon as it gets a little lighter, we'll find a place to stop and have breakfast." The driver has evidently made this trip before; he assures them he knows where they will get a good breakfast.

An hour later, he pulls up in front of small green building with a bay window. As they exit the car, he suggests they only speak in short sentences or one word replies. "Don't get into conversations with me, he says. I will not respond with who I am, nor do I want to know anything about either of you." Hussein and Dakham nod. "Nothing personal," the driver adds.

Inside, they choose a table towards the back of the dining area.

A young woman, sporting a lot of cleavage and a small white apron over wide hips, approaches their table. Other than having a pleasant smile, her service leaves a great deal to be desired. "Breakfast?" is literally the only word out of her mouth, as she sets a carafe of coffee and three mugs on the table. Actually, this makes things easier as they don't have to answer any extraneous questions she might have. Dakham orders for the three of them, the same breakfast for everyone: an omelet, patties, a croissant, and some fruit.

The coffee, they all agree with silent nods after their first sips, is good. The waitress, even though her professionalism lacks, is a treat to the eye, they also agree with silent nods as she awkwardly juggles their three plates. The breakfast is tasty. The driver pays the tab as soon as they are finished. They leave without having said so much as ten words. Their thoughts would fill a book.

The remainder of the ride to the Karachi airport is quiet, just like the ride they had in the limousine. Arriving at the airport, the driver leaves them off at the front entrance, and pulls away as soon as they get their luggage from the back, without so much as a wish for a good trip.

Once inside, they check the monitor for their departure time. Their flight to Volgograd, known from 1925 to 1961 as Stalingrad, is on schedule. They check their luggage and proceed through security. Their carry-on bags will go into the racks above their seats. On the way to the gate they stop to browse at a newsstand. Each of them buys a different Pakistani newspaper.

Sitting at the gate, Hussein leans over to Dakham and whispers, "The man standing by the entrance to the newsstand? He was following us around when we were inside. I may be getting paranoid, but I believe we have a tail."

Knowing enough not to look around, Dakham says, "When we board the flight, let's see what he does. It could be airport security. It could also be someone Atwan ordered to follow us. I wouldn't put it past him."

Thirty minutes later both Hussein and Dakham board the plane and take their seats. The man from the newsstand boards as well, taking a seat two rows behind them.

The Airbus 300 handles the two-and-a-half hour flight with ease. The flight is not full, allowing the cabin attendants to easily take care of the needs of all those on board. Surprisingly, the flight lands on time. Hussein and Dakham pick up their luggage and proceed on to customs where an agent checks each of their passports, asks a few questions regarding how long they plan to stay in the Russia.

"And what's the nature of your visit?" each is asked. Their replies of staying at least a month as they look for proper replacement parts for their firm seems to satisfy the custom agent and they are checked on through.

Leaving customs, they proceed out of the airport and hail a taxi which is waiting in line. The driver stays behind the wheel, pops the trunk and yells to them to put their bags inside. As they come around to get in the cab, Hussein whispers to Dakham, "This guy's something else." Once settled in, Hussein directs the driver to take them to the Best Eastern Volgograd Hotel. The driver floors it, taking off like this is an emergency. They quickly understand why. Emerging from the airport, the cab immediately has to take its place amid a sea of slow-moving traffic. *The quarter mile from where he picked us up to the highway is the poor guy's only chance to get up any speed all day*, Hussein imagines.

Both are surprised to see how much traffic ties up Volgograd during the work week. Whether the driver is padding the mileage or not they cannot tell, but it does take him a full forty minutes of fighting that traffic before he pulls up in front of the hotel.

As they prepare to exit the cab, the driver again pops the trunk, turns to tell them not to forget their bags and holds his hand out. When Hussein and Dakham get out without offering him anything, he complains out the window to them, "What, no tip?"

"You'll find it in the trunk," Dakham replies with a clearly annoyed chuckle.

The driver gives them the finger, then speeds away. *Great hospitality so far*, they both think to themselves.

Check-in at the Best Eastern goes smoothly. They are given adjacent rooms with an entrance door between the two. A porter takes their luggage up to their rooms and shows them the amenities. In each room, the bed is small, and the bathroom like a closet. At least they have a television, radio and telephone.

After unpacking their bags, Hussein places an encryption device on his room phone, then calls a number in Pakistan that will ring into the headquarters of the Iranian Secret Police. He leaves the following message for Atwan with Atwan's assistant: "Arrived on time, so far everything according to schedule. Did you send us a partner to travel with? If not, we may have acquired a friend leaving Karachi. Please advise."

Chapter Seventeen

Meeting with Top Military Leaders

President Egan calls Janet White and instructs her to set a date one week from this Friday for him to meet with Admiral Smith and Generals Bradley and Sanford. "Make it for in the Situation Room. It will just be the four of us," he tells her. "We'll start at nine. Tell them to plan to spend all day if necessary. And arrange for Marine guards posted outside."

"I'll contact the admiral and the generals, sir," Janet answers. Two hours later, she confirms the meeting.

"Janet," the president adds, "If anyone needs my attention that day, you are to instruct them I am unavailable unless it is, literally, a national emergency. If absolutely necessary, you, and only you, are to call me in the Situation Room."

"Yes, sir, Mr. President. I'll handle my end." Janet could not keep from smiling at the thought of how the rest of the president's staff will take this. *They're gonna go bonkers*, she thinks with pleasure, *wondering why they weren't included and what's going on.*

*

At eight on the morning of the meeting, the president calls Janet. "When the admiral and the generals arrive, Janet, please have them escorted down to the Situation Room. Make sure there is plenty of coffee and cold water, plus some Danish set out, and let's have a screen available in case any of them has come with a presentation. Let me know when they've all arrived."

"Yes, sir," replies Janet.

*

At 8:50 the president receives the call from Janet. "Sir, the admiral and both generals are on their way down to the Situation Room. Do you plan to leave immediately for the meeting?"

"Yes. You're to follow my previous instructions regarding any interruptions."

"Of course, sir." *You betcha, Mr. President.*

Upon arriving at the door of the Situation Room, President Egan advises his Secret Service detail to remain outside with the Marine guards.

As he enters the room, the admiral and generals rise to their feet. Inside the room, he notices that the smaller tables were set up just as he'd requested, in a square shape, each table with only one chair, so that everyone has no choice but to face each other. "Gentlemen, relax. This is going to be a long day. Let's start with coffee, water, a Danish if you'd like, then get down to work," says the president. "May I also suggest we take off our jackets and ties. It may get a little warm in here. But—" he smiles, "please, don't let me leave this room without putting my tie back on."

Each of the military men returns his smile at the self-effacing remark, realizing that the president is merely trying to break the tension that has already started building.

When everyone is seated, the president gets right to business. "Let's start by looking at the first scenario: what would we need to achieve a successful pre-emptive strike against Iran?"

General Sanford, the commandant of the Marine Corp, begins by saying, "Sir, number one on my list is intelligence. I can't stress strongly enough the importance of having the most accurate intelligence we can. Satellites can provide us with only so much. Most countries know when satellites are overhead and simply stop doing what they don't want us to see. My suggestion is we put a number of teams into Iran based on what we want to know."

"How many teams would you suggest," says the president.

"That depends, sir. What's it you want to identify, and what are you aiming to target?" replies Sanford.

"Good question," replies the president. "Okay, let's begin there. What do we need to achieve to bring Iran to its knees and eliminate the possibility of a counter attack?" asks the president.

"If I may speak, Mr. President," interrupts General Bradley. The president gives the commander of the Air Force the nod. "Are you looking to eliminate—or just cripple—their nuclear enrichment facilities?"

"Gentlemen, if we have a reason to attack Iran before they strike us, we better be prepared to take out any military installations that could cause us major concerns," the president answers unequivocally. "And we'll definitely need to destroy their nuclear enrichment facilities. And, if conditions in the world come to such an event, I would also want to take out the regime that has created this monster as well."

Admiral Smith raises a finger and takes the floor. "From a naval point of view, sir, we can use our submarines to fire cruise missiles at any and all positions you choose. My second concern would be having sufficient intelligence regarding the Iranian navy, so we can cripple it at the same time. I estimate it'd take two or more battle groups to do the job. My biggest concern is those four Kilos we know they have, plus the two more that are reportedly coming from Russia any day now."

"We put plenty of cruise missiles into Iraq. Were they effective?" President Egan asks rhetorically, then quickly answers his own question. "Yes, to some degree. Without going nuclear, do we have payloads to improve the punch?"

General Bradley answers, "Sir, the Pentagon has weapon loads available that we've never used militarily, more powerful weapons that can be delivered by cruise missiles, as well as laser-guided bombs that can be dropped from planes."

"Gentlemen," says the president, "If this becomes a reality—and I so hope it never does—my assumption is that we'll only have one chance to be successful. Israel took out Iraq's first reactor, but that only set the confrontation timetable to a later date. I want to stop World War III, and if we do take out Iran, I believe it will also take most of the wind out of the sails of the terrorist groups we've been combating on so many fronts for so long. After all, Iran is staking them most of their weapons. I also think it would serve to make Syria sit up and take notice."

"So, as I see it," General Sanford says, "you'd like us to take out the nuclear enrichment plants, the major military bases and the top echelon in Tehran. Would that be a correct assessment, sir?"

President Egan hesitates for a moment, and then forces himself to respond. "Yes," he says quietly and unequivocally.

General Sanford allows himself a thin smile. "Sir, you really had me worried for a while there. At first I thought I wouldn't have enough teams to go around. As I see it, satellites will tell us most of what we want to know about the facilities and the military bases. My teams can surveil the top dogs and any other sites you want, to identify how we can best hit them based on their routines."

The president smiles in response. "Victor, you don't have to worry." His smile quickly fades, however. "Now, for the rest of the morning, I'd like to hear and see what the three of you have prepared for an attack."

Three presentations are made to the president, then the four of them debate the strengths and weakness of each approach.

*

"It's now almost noon," the president observes. "I'm having Janet send sandwiches and drinks for lunch. Let's break now and go into our second scenario after we eat."

"Sir, if I may ask," says the admiral, "why is it that none of your staff nor any of the joint chiefs are with us?"

"Fair question," Egan acknowledges, "and I assume it's been on all of your minds. Politics, in short. The reality is that I have to make the final decision. There will be plenty of time for my staff to get their political comments in before I do. I also feel that when someone is promoted to the joint chiefs, they too get politically involved and may not give me the purely military answers I need to hear. Gentlemen, to put it bluntly, you're the ones with your asses on the line after I make that decision. I expect the best responses from the three of you. Which is why I said that nothing said here leaves this room."

There is a knock on the door. Secret Service allows an agent wheeling a lunch cart to enter the room. The agent can't help but notice that the president is meeting alone with top brass military. *What in the hell does this mean?* he wonders as he positions the cart, then quickly retreats back out to the hall.

Each of the men looks over the luncheon choices, takes one or more sandwiches and his choice of beverage. Janet has even been thoughtful enough to send down some fruit and cookies.

General Bradley remarks, "Your Janet doesn't miss a trick, Mr. President. She's ordered enough to feed us for a couple of days."

"You can stay a couple of days, Jim, if you want. Personally, I prefer a room with windows," laughs the president.

Over lunch the three military men start swapping war stories. Everyone is surprised when the president, who has seen active duty himself, jumps right in there with the rest of them.

As the stories finally wind down, the president reminds them all, "Remember, I said everything stays in this room—especially my old war stories." He waits out each of them until they've given him their word. Then, with a sigh, he changes tone. "Okay, let's move on to scenario number two: we're attacked by Iran. What's our plan of action if retaliation is called for?"

All three men recommend that a quick assessment of U.S. operational assets must be made. General Bradley takes it from there. "Sir, if we're attacked, I'm sure there will be thousands of civilian casualties. There could be hundreds of thousands—conceivably even millions. Do we retaliate in the same manner?"

The president bows his head for a moment, then looks up at Bradley. "Jim, I'm not going to attack civilians with revenge in mind. However, because of the reckless nature of Iran's government, civilians may die in our trying to counter-attack a government that wishes to see the United States destroyed."

In light of the president's answer, Bradley continues. "Sir, the Air Force could deploy from a number of locations throughout the Middle East and the European theater." He pauses, then continues. "Mr. President, I would suggest that targets be pre-assigned between the Navy and ourselves, in case we find ourselves faced with a scenario of this type. The fewer last-minute decisions, the better. It'd help cut down on the stress that'd come with such a scenario. Which, face it, would be enormous."

Admiral Smith speaks up. "I agree with Jim, Mr. President. If the Navy has pre-assigned targets, we could act on them almost immediately."

"All right, goddammit, Admiral, Generals," Egan explodes, "tell me how you plan to do that if Washington, D.C. no longer exists. If the government is no longer functioning? Who the hell is going to give you the go-ahead orders, Bob? Jim? Victor?"

General Sanford is the first to answer. "Mr. President, under the War Powers Act, you can make special provisions for immediate retaliatory action, now, as a safeguard to protect this country."

"Yeah, and what am I supposed to say to Congress, not to mention the people of these United States?" the president asks angrily.

"Now, just wait a fucking minute, sir," Admiral Smith fumes. "You just spelled out a scenario without a Congress or any form of working government. What do you want the people to do? Hold an election?"

General Sanford jumps in, equally frustrated. "Do you remember a few years back when we had a secretary of state telling everyone he was in charge, which was pure bullshit. With warfare in your front yard, we need to have the ability to make military decisions. I mean, give us a break."

Intentionally pushing their buttons, the president says, "So—you don't trust politicians like me to do that?"

"Sir, with all due respect," offers General Bradley, clearly trying to hold on to his temper, "we don't put you in that category. If you were, I doubt we'd be sitting here today. What we're concerned with is the fact that you only have two more years left to your term. If you should fail to get re-elected and we get some pussy in the office who can't make decisions—or some broad, for crissakes—well, this country could go down the tubes, very quickly." Bradley unconsciously snaps the pencil he's holding. The sound it makes stops all of them in their tracks.

The president stares down all three men, then finally says, "So, you're telling me that the military should have the only say to retaliate?"

General Sanford answers for all three, at the top of his voice. "Hell, no!" he yells, and he keeps yelling. "What we're all trying to tell you, sir, is that you need to have a damn good plan B in case we can't communicate with what's left of the government, or if we are under continued attack and the shit's literally hitting the fan."

President Egan raises his hands to them, a signal to just stop. "Okay. Okay. I appreciate your passion and your honesty, gentlemen. I need to investigate what you're proposing. Please don't misunderstand—I don't disagree with it. As a matter of fact, if anything, I do tend to agree with it. The thing that scares me though is, who replaces *you* should, God forbid, anything happen to you. And what kind of people are *they*? I could see special provisions to the War Powers Act becoming your proverbial double-edged sword." The president stands, leans his hands on the table in front of him and again looks all three in the eye.

"That's the question I want you to contemplate. I promise you we'll meet again, when I feel we have more facts in hand, when we have something substantive we can work with. I also want each of you to explore how best to insure that your replacement—and your replacement's replacement—can be trusted as well as I trust each of you."

Egan turns to Smith. "Admiral, how many boomers are currently floating around the Indian Ocean?"

"Two, sir."

"Based on their cruise missile carrying capacity, I want you to station two more in the Indian Ocean. They can be attached to the current flag officer, but I'd prefer that they run independently. Our fleet is under constant observation. I don't want any other government to be aware that we have four in the area."

"Yes, sir," Admiral Smith replies smartly.

"Good," the president says, then again addresses all three. "Gentlemen, I think we have accomplished what we wanted to do today. I suggest we leave the rest for another day."

As the president starts to leave, Admiral Smith says, "Sir, remember to put on your tie."

President Egan laughs and says, "Thanks, Bob."

The president exits the room first. The other three just sit and stare at each other.

Chapter Eighteen

Third Week of June

The phone rings in the office of Hidden Talents. Silberberg answers to find Schwartz on the other end. "Okay. We have an appointment at 1400 hours next Tuesday afternoon with Rabinowitz," he tells Silberberg. Jacob Rabinowitz is the current chief of staff of IDF. "Ariel said he'd be briefed," Schwartz continues, "but it couldn't have been much of a briefing. He appeared to be at a loss as to what's going on. That in itself is not surprising, but I feel his hesitancy when he realizes that two former IDF officers, now independent contractors, are going to be calling the shots."

"Natan, does that really surprise you?" Silberberg is glad Schwartz cannot see his facial expression over the phone, which clearly reads, *Natan, do you really think the chief of staff of the Israel Defense Forces—just the entire combined ground, air and naval forces of Israel—wants us to tell him what we plan to do?* Instead, he simply says, "An officer in any military expects to give the orders. When two civilians call in, tell you they have the prime minister's directive to get a project done, how do you expect him to respond?"

"Okay, okay," Schwartz allows. "You're right. I went into it assuming that as a military man, like any military man, he could take orders too. Clearly he has to hear it from the top. You know how 'assume' usually goes."

"Of course he wants to hear it from the top," Silberberg continues. "Only this time the top doesn't want to be associated with it, especially if it goes sour. I'm sure Mossad made it clear to him that this project will be strictly need-to-know, only for those involved."

"Anyway," Schwartz continues, "you and I need to create a brief presentation on the kind of mission we are deploying, one that doesn't give up much by way of details, just the broad strokes. We need to prepare a check list of items we'll need, by category: deployment, removal, emergency extraction. We need to be clear between ourselves what we want and who we want for each of these areas, before we go in to see him. Do you agree?"

"By all means," Silberberg says. "We need to be as prepared as possible. And we'll probably disagree on some options, if I know us. So we better get to work on it as soon as possible."

"Good. I can finish up the job for Feltman tonight. Let's plan to be in the office tomorrow and start hashing this out. Early."

"Got it. What time do you want me there? How about 0830?" Silberberg suggests.

"That works for me," replies Schwartz, "See you then."

*

"Natan, you look like you didn't get any sleep last night. I haven't seen bags under your eyes this bad since we went on that drunk after our last trek in the Negev. You need rollers for these bags."

"Very funny. I got some sleep," Schwartz protested, "but I couldn't get my mind to shut down on all the planning we need to do, the logistics of the operation. I just know that I will be a far happier man when we can get in there, get the job done and get out."

"You know, you could let me share some of that load," Silberberg offers with all sincerity.

"Mark, you have enough to do, making sure we have all of the equipment and supplies we need, making sure that everything is in operating order, making sure we haven't missed anything."

"Yeah, the pressure is on both of us," Silberberg agrees. "The last three desert treks we did, the IDF delivered all the equipment we needed. All we had to do was follow IDF orders. IDF did all the planning and supplying. But so can we. Now, though, I'm realizing how much we took for granted, what all goes into planning an operation on this scale. Holy shit, this can be a real mind trip when you're never done it before."

"Good. Face it and get it off your chest," Schwartz encourages his partner. "But we'll be okay, Mark. It's just new, having to rely on ourselves almost exclusively, except for Yosef and whoever ferries us in. This *is* our show."

"And speaking of Yosef," Silberberg interrupts, "let's give him a call and see how he's making out with his end of things."

Schwartz picks up the secure line on his desk, then dials the special number Bergman left with them. After the third ring, Bergman picks up. "Code words, please."

"A million dollars," says Schwartz.

"Okay, Natan. What can I do for you this morning."

"I just wanted to check and see how you're progressing on the equipment lists we gave you," Schwartz says calmly, his stomach rolling.

"Weapons, high-shock 9mm ammo, knives, light-weight Kevlar jackets, are all ordered from sources we know we can trust to maintain confidentiality," Bergman reels off. "Your laser burst communications equipment, long range listening devices and the 500-meter emission detection devices were ordered from the Belgian sources you gave us. Necessities for in-the-field have been ordered from the Brits, also as you suggested. Everything is being air-freighted in. We should have the whole lot by the end of this week."

Silberberg holds up a finger. "One moment, Yosef," Schwartz says. "Mark has a question."

"Ask him if he was able to reach the underwater equipment people I told him about," Silberberg asks quickly.

"Yosef, Mark wants to know if you got through to the underwater equipment supplier he gave you."

"Natan, tell Mark that I could not connect with the Amsterdam source, but I've been able to get everything he needs in that department from the Utrecht people he also mentioned, just as he thought I would. Our people consider them to be the very best."

"Okay, Yosef, let us know when everything arrives. In the meantime, we'll discuss how we can transport everything without people getting nosey."

"You're on, Natan," says Bergman. "By the way, just out of curiosity, why is Mark's password 'a half million?'"

Laughing, Schwartz says, "He's second in command. Just think of it as the military."

"Whatever," Bergman says, chuckling as he hangs up.

While Schwartz has been chatting with Bergman, Silberberg has been busily pinning up a series of satellite close-ups of their two target areas. He studies them carefully, using a ruler to compare distances to the scale provided with each image. When Schwartz hangs up, he comes over and joins him.

"Let's lay out a grid for ourselves," Silberberg suggests, "as to how we enter Iran, time to the first target area, time spent at the first site. What do you think?"

"What's the distance from the closest entry point to the first area?"

"Just under a hundred kilometers," replies Silberberg.

"Shit. I was afraid that's what you'd say."

"My thoughts are that they bring us in as close as they can by submarine, then have an underwater team with sleds take us as close to shore as possible. We pack the sled with everything we need."

"How close do you think a sled team could bring us to shore?" Silberberg asks, shaking his head dubiously.

"Satellite photos can only tell us so much. Up-to-date nautical charts of the area show it as navigable, but they don't factor in politics, of course," Schwartz grumbles. "I would like to hope they could get us to within thirty meters."

"Unless we get some kind of floatation devices to aid us in moving our gear the rest of the way, we'll sink like rocks," his partner points out.

"The Navy uses floatation devices to move heavy pieces of equipment. The problem is in making sure we can hide them quickly, so we won't be detected," replies Schwartz.

"I'm sure we can get our hands on something that's not outlandishly large. It can be buried with the gear we'll need on our return leg of the mission, extra supplies to last us and the spare equipment in case something turns out to be faulty."

"All right. We're on shore, then we head inland—about what you'd say—three, four kilometers off of a traveled roadway to bury our gear?" suggests Silberberg.

"Sounds right. We bury that batch, then we boogie about twenty k's a night to get to the target area. I see us getting dropped off on a Monday night, around 2200 hours. The first night will be used for concealing our stores. By traveling only at night, it should take us three, at most four nights to reach Bampur. I would want to be there Friday, which is the Muslim version of Shabbat. That should cut down on the number of people wandering around. They will be in prayer."

"Natan, I don't know about you, but I'm thinking that we could really be pushing our luck staying on site for five days. If we haven't been able to get emissions information and monitor some conversations in five days, we probably never will. We must take the amount of water we will require into consideration."

"Bampur has a small natural body of water nearby," Schwartz points out. "We can always re-supply our water." Then he thinks again. "The down side, however, is what else that body of water attracts. No, you're right, Mark—we carry the water we need for five days. Even five days on one site stretches the odds—but we have stretched odds before. Let's plan on four days of travel to the site, then a maximum of five on site. Now we have to consider travel back to the burial point and then onto site two."

"It looks like travel to the second site will be a bit further," Silberberg says, consulting the photos again. "We'll have to back-track south and then head west. I'm estimating that this leg will cover about one hundred twenty kilometers from where we bury the gear."

"What are your thoughts on how long we should allow for travel, then?" asks Schwartz.

"Well, after lying around for nearly a week, let's be realistic and say eight to nine nights. Nine tops."

"So, we set up near their base and listen in to what we can find out about their subs. Let's say five days maximum again. You know, it sounds easy enough to pull off, but Bandar Abbas is a city. It isn't going to be easy. I doubt the Iranians would ever consider somebody having the balls to do this," Schwartz concludes.

"Natan, my real concern is how we're going to be removed. I know, by submarine, but we are talking about another one hundred and twenty kilometer trek back to where we were dropped off in the first place."

"Let's discuss this with the Navy and see what they can come up with. Maybe they'd be willing to come in closer to Bandar Abbas." Silberberg nods, then goes contemplative.

"You know, Natan," he finally says, "this operation can never have an emergency extraction. If we get spotted inside of Iran, no one is going to do a fly-by to pull us out. It's our tit in the wringer."

"And why did you think they were willing to pay us the big bucks?" Schwartz says quietly, looking Silberberg straight in the eye. *Are you losing your nerve, partner? Where's the old Mark?*

Silberberg nods, slowly at first, and then with animation. "Forget I ever said that," he laughs, his confidence returning.

"Okay, let's plan what we want to say to the chief of staff and the Navy," Schwartz resumes, relieved. "And remember, if they can't back us up, if it doesn't look good, we always have the option to call it off."

"Natan, who are you bullshitting? You and I both know this has to be done. If it isn't, Israel could be in serious trouble. Even afterwards, Israel may still be in serious trouble. You and I both know that we took this job because of our sense of duty. For our country. It's not the money."

Schwartz is the one now nodding. "You're right. So let's make the best of it, and just hope we come out of this with our hides intact."

Chapter Nineteen

After Their Trip

Hussein and Dakham get a good night's sleep after their long journey. Following showers, they go down to breakfast in the hotel's dining room. Hussein decides to stop at the front desk on the way, to check for any messages.

"Yes, sir," the clerk tells him, "a wire just came in for you early this morning. I didn't want to wake you too early."

Hussein thanks him, takes the wire and nods to Dakham. At their table, he opens the wire and reads it. Then he passes the wire across the table.

Dakham reads: "Cousin, glad your trip was uneventful. My business partners will contact you tomorrow around noon your time. I'm sorry I couldn't send anyone else with you on this trip as we are short-handed right now. Signed, your fourth cousin, Ali."

Hussein speaks first. "What do you make of it?"

"Well," says Dakham, "it looks like we have a day and a half to prepare for our first meeting and maybe see some of the sights."

"That's not what I was referring to."

"I know that. My assumption is that our friend from the airport is not a friend of our cousin." Dakham shrugs. "We'll just have to see if we run across him again. My guess is, we will."

"Maybe, maybe not," says Hussein with a shrug of his own.

Scanning the breakfast menu both men are amazed at the number of selections it offers. Breakfast menus are nothing like this back home, nor in Pakistan. Hussein chooses a small juice and an order of French toast. Dakham decides to eat hardy. He orders a large juice, two eggs over easy, plus an order of pancakes.

Suddenly, as they are just starting to eat, just as both agree they could get to like living like this, the man from the newsstand walks into the dining room and takes a seat along the opposite wall facing them. They cannot miss noticing him; he's still wearing the same brown leather coat and bulky red sweater he wore on the plane yesterday.

"Shit," Dakham says quietly. "Can't we even have a comfortable breakfast?"

"Don't lose it!" Hussein jokes. "However, I don't believe in coincidences either, so I would venture to say we have a tail. Where he's from I have no clue, but he sure as hell wants us to know he's here. Any suggestions?"

Dakham replies, "Well, let's take our time with breakfast and see how much time he has to spare. If he's really a tail, he will wait until we move. If he's not, then we may be just overreacting."

"Maybe we are," Hussein concurs, "maybe a little, since let's face it, we *are* new at this. Yet my gut is telling me, other than how much it appreciates this French toast, that somehow this guy is here to play a part in whatever it is we are getting ourselves involved in."

"Me too," says Dakham. "I suggest we finish our breakfast and get out of the hotel for a while. See if he follows us, yes, but I will also lay you odds that our rooms are bugged. I would rather not say anything of importance within these walls."

"Very wise," Hussein compliments his partner.

*

The two Iranian operatives take over an hour, thoroughly enjoying their breakfast at a leisurely pace. The man opposite them sits there the entire time, drinking cup after cup of coffee.

"I hope he drinks enough coffee to bust his bladder," says Hussein.

"Well, let's go get our coats and walk off this breakfast," Dakham suggests. "Perhaps we could arrange to do a bus tour."

Walking out of the hotel, they are glad that they have had the foresight to bring jackets. The gusty winds and falling temperatures are chillier than they are used to.

As they walk, they rehearse their roles for the meeting tomorrow. First, they know they need to get a sense of who it is they are dealing with, to be sure they are not being set up by the Russian secret police. Second, they have to play the roles of businessmen sent in search of industrial replacement parts for their company, at least until they are certain who these people really are. It wouldn't do to jump into a conversation and say, "Hello. We are looking to purchase enriched uranium."

They realize the value of playing it cool and not getting over-anxious. Also, as Dakham points out, appearing too eager could affect price negotiations after they have had an opportunity to test some samples.

*

The next day, they choose to have their breakfast at a quaint, nearby restaurant they passed the previous afternoon. When they walk in, they are pleased with their selection. The interior is just as inviting as the exterior. There are many empty tables. They choose a booth near the bay window in front.

Sitting across from each other, even before they have had time to pick up their menus, they see the man who has been tailing them come through the door of the same establishment. "Oh, for crying out loud, this asshole is getting ridiculous," Dakham says angrily.

Only this time, the man in the brown leather coat approaches them and asks if he can sit at the same table for breakfast, since they clearly have room to spare—even though there are numerous empty tables close at hand.

Hussein looks across at Dakham. Dakham shrugs, gets up and moves out of the way so the stranger can maneuver his small frame into the back of the booth. Dakham sits back down, looks at Hussein, then at the stranger, who announces without preamble, "I waited for the two of you at the airport in Pakistan for three days. I'm sure glad to see you made it." He speaks to them in Farsi, but with an odd accent which gives no clue as to his true nationality.

"And why are you so anxious to see us?" asks Hussein evenly.

"To tell you the truth, the food down there was terrible. My stomach couldn't handle anymore of it."

All three of them smile at the obvious attempt to establish rapport.

"You're too damned obvious to be the secret police," Dakham confronts him.

"You're right, I'm not. I'm your ride to the noon-time meeting you have today. I will meet you in the hotel lobby at 1100."

"How can we be sure that you're telling us the truth?" Hussein asks, unconvinced.

"Your fourth cousin sent my boss the information that you were coming, and my boss wants me to spend some time with you, to see if you're what you say you are."

"But we haven't said what we are," Dakham says coolly.

"True enough," says the man. "And I don't know why he sent me, to tell the truth, but he will be able to judge after having a conversation with both of you. He's a much better judge of people than I am."

"I hope he's better at shadowing people, too," Hussein says, still unsmiling.

"What shall we call you?" Dakham asks. "Spook? Tail? Driver doesn't seem much of a fit."

Chapter Twenty

Authorized Mission

Three days following their presentation to Jacob Rabinowitz, Schwartz and Silberberg receive a phone call at their office from Israel's chief of staff.

"Natan, this is a secure line. Is your end secure?" Jacob asks warily.

"Yes, sir, it is," replies Schwartz.

"I would like you and your partner to meet with me this coming Friday afternoon at 1300 hours in my office. I've invited your sponsor for this meeting and the captain of the transportation you requested. I believe we can work out the details you need to start, and arrive at a satisfactory date for your departure.

"Mark and I will be there, sir." Schwartz, once again, is surprised that all this can move so quickly.

*

Fifteen minutes later, Schwartz receives a phone call from Bergman.

"I was just asked to attend a meeting this Friday at 1300 hours. Will you and Mark be attending?" Bergman asks guardedly. *Best to see what he knows.*

"Yes, of course." *Wasn't he told who else would be there?* Schwartz is surprised.

"Are you prepared to set up plans for a launch date for our project?" asks Bergman.

If he's still talking launch dates, I guess everything is still a go, Schwartz thinks with relief. "If Moshe—Captain Katz—is agreeable to our ideas and suggestions, Mark and I both agree that we can go ahead and plan a launch date, as you put it. Assuming that you have all of our necessary equipment and papers, Yosef."

"Everything is ready, Natan. We are prepared to deliver everything wherever you want it, whenever you want it."

"We'll work out a transfer of the materials after the meeting. It must happen in one shipment, during regular business hours, so as not to attract any undue attention. We can go into this further on Friday." Schwartz hangs up, still puzzled by that cat-and-mouse business at the beginning of the call.

*

Jacob Rabinowitz, the chief of staff himself, escorts Schwartz and Silberberg into the conference room. No sooner have they greeted Captain Moshe Katz, who is already seated at the table, than Wattenberg and Bergman join them. Everyone takes a seat, the chairs around the table upholstered in a plush velour. Glancing around, Bergman realizes that this conference room is as every bit as large as the one in the Knesset Building.

Jacob begins by introducing everyone, an unusual departure from Mossad protocol, as the director of the Mossad normally tries to keep his identity known only within Mossad itself. Captain Katz looks a bit perplexed after Wattenberg's introduction, understanding as he does the security risks involved. *What on earth is this mission about?* he has to wonder.

Jacob starts the meeting by informing all present that his office has authorized this mission. As requested by Silberberg and Schwartz, Captain Moshe Katz is to be the commanding officer of the submarine that will deploy them near their target. The same vessel will extract them from the area several weeks later, as will be discussed.

"Since Captain Katz only knows a few sketchy details about this mission at this point, I would like Natan and Mark to fill him in on their operational plans with all of us present."

Schwartz starts without hesitation. "We have chosen Captain Katz because we already have experience working with him on two IDF missions. He was the commanding officer of the submarines we rode in on. This mission, Captain Katz, will take anywhere from six to eight weeks for us to accomplish what the Mossad needs from us. Our greatest concern is how to be extracted if circumstances develop requiring us to either abort the mission for Israel's sake, or for our own safety."

Captain Katz smiles warmly. "Natan, I remember having you and Mark on the two missions you speak of, and I feel comfortable working with both of you on this one, even though I'm aware there is tremendous risk involved. But what are you really asking me? Will my submarine always be around in case of emergencies? Based on the information I've been given, we cannot wait offshore for you. Can we stay in the general area? Yes, if I'm given orders to do so. Is that what you want to hear?"

"Captain, we have the navigational charts for the drop point. It looks like you should be able to come within five kilometers of shore without the risk of bottoming out. We would require a team of underwater sleds and drivers to then take us and our gear as close in to the beach as possible. Would that be a problem?" Silberberg asks.

"No, I don't have a problem with that at all. How close do you wish this team to take you to shore?"

Schwartz picks up where Silberberg left off. "If we can get some floatation gear for our equipment, we could be dropped off within thirty meters. Mark and I can handle getting everything from there to shore."

"Yes, floatation equipment is available. I would recommend using the type that will float your equipment just near the surface. That part is fairly basic. My concern is how we handle an emergency extraction if needed," says the captain, "bearing in mind, in order of importance, first your safety, then Israel's anonymity being compromised, and then the possible loss of our submarine and its crew to our navy."

"When we took on this assignment we knew there was no way we could be airlifted out of the area in an emergency," Silberberg says. "An emergency extraction, from our point of view, would be that, first, we notify Yosef that we are up to our asses in alligators. Then we would then make for an extraction point. Once there, we would send you a signal from shore to be picked up. Depending where our assignment has us at the time, it could conceivably take us a couple of days or more to get there."

"Clearly, this mission will require me to stay in close enough proximity for us to be able to perform that kind of extraction. Needless to say, we too will have to deal with any unexpected situation that might come our way," Katz adds. "We have no way of knowing what the Iranian navy may be up to at the time."

"Captain, we certainly understand. All we want to know is, if the shit hits the fan, that we have at least a *chance* of getting out," replies Silberberg.

Schwartz speaks. "Captain, we have asked for your participation simply because we have working knowledge of your ability to get us there and get us back, even if the going gets a little rough. Neither Mark nor I were aware that you're now in command of a Dolphin-class sub. We thought you were still commanding one of the older gal designs."

Captain Katz smiles and sits back in his chair. "I'm there for you, boys," he says. What he would really like to say is far stronger. *I admire these two young men. I will do everything humanly possible to get them back home alive.*

"Well, that's settled," Jacob announces. "Captain Katz will have orders to remain within an area that will allow him to be at your pick-up point within twenty-four hours notice. Is that satisfactory, gentlemen?"

"Absolutely," says Silberberg. "That would be a fair response time. If we arrive earlier, it is up to us to conceal ourselves until you can get to us."

Jacob turns to the director of Mossad and asks, "Is there anything you wish to say or add your input to this operation, Ariel?"

"No, we have decided to rely on Natan and Mark's expertise to put this together which, as I don't have to tell any of you gentlemen, is a definite departure for us. My only question to you two," he says, turning to Schwartz and Silberberg, "is have you settled on a date to begin the operation?"

Silberberg looks over at Schwartz, who nods that Silberberg should take the question. Silberberg smiles.

"We'll be ready to set sail one week from Tuesday," Silberberg says with confidence. "This will give us sufficient time to check out all of the equipment, once it has arrived, have some time with the captain to go over things with him, and still allow for a drop day of two weeks from Monday, which is what we want to aim for. Unfortunately we do have to go the long way around the Cape, for security reasons."

"Getting dropped off on a Monday will give us sufficient time to arrive at our first target area by Friday, based on traveling only at night," Schwartz adds.

"Why Friday," Jacob asks.

Silberberg explains his theory of the Muslim equivalent of Shabbat. "We feel that we'll have the least intrusion into our activities, setting up on site, if we time our arrival then," Silberberg explains.

"Anything else before we complete this meeting?" asks Jacob.

"Only that Yosef and I still need to work out our transfer of goods to Hidden Talents, which we can take care of after this meeting," replies Schwartz.

Sitting there, sweat pouring down from his armpits, his hands icy cold, Bergman speaks up for the first time. "I will call you first thing in the morning, Natan."

"Captain, is there anything else?" Jacob asks.

"No, sir. We can handle this."

All of the men rise and shake hands as they leave the chief of staff's conference room. All are aware of Bergman's cold hands. Bergman leaves thinking, *Oh my God, this impossible idea of mine is really going to happen. God help us all.*

Chapter Twenty-One

July Departure

It is 0300 hours, the morning to sail. Yosef Bergman is not used to loading crates of equipment in the dead of night. Earlier in the day, he has rented a large van in Tel Aviv, which he then drove up to Hidden Talents' facility in Haifa. Now he, Schwartz and Silberberg are loading gear to take aboard the submarine.

"That's the last of it," Schwartz says. "Let's head out. I want to be dockside by first light. Captain Katz has promised us to have a work party ready to help us unload and store all this."

The three men are quiet on the short trip to the docks, each ruminating on his own thoughts . . . about the upcoming mission . . . and the question on all their minds: *will two of us be returning?*

*

At 0500 hours, the van pulls up to the entry gate of the navy base. "Identification, please," asks one of the sentries who matches IDs to the face, while another holds his weapon pointed at them. Once the first sentry is satisfied, they are flagged through. This group has been expected, by orders of Captain Katz.

As Bergman has never had the occasion to visit any of Israel's naval stations, this is a new experience for him. Looking about him, he can't help but think, *I'd much rather work with Mossad than be in the navy.* "So—where do they keep the subs?" he asks Schwartz.

"Go around to the third dock," says Schwartz. "You will see the submarine there."

Also seeing a sub up close for the first time, Bergman is struck by how menacing it looks, with its sleek black conning tower and long torpedo-shaped hull. Bergman could never conceive of how men could live for weeks at a time totally submerged in water.

As they pull up by the bow of the vessel, an armed petty officer walks out to the pier to again ask for their identification. When he assures himself that they match two of the men he's expecting, he calls out to the watch messenger on the deck, "Have the four-man work party in the mess decks come up to the pier." His order is acknowledged with a brisk salute.

As their gear is being unloaded and stored below decks, Schwartz, Silberberg and Bergman take a long look at each other. Nothing needs to be said. They all realize that this could very well be the last time they see each other.

"I expect to hear from both of you when you arrive on site," Bergman says, breaking the solemn moment. "Remember, if you're able to gather the information we need sooner than we have anticipated, move out. Do not remain any longer than you absolutely have to and put yourselves in unnecessary danger."

Both Schwartz and Silberberg give Bergman a warm hug, both realizing that Bergman is as committed to the mission and anxious for their safety as they are. The three shake hands and board the sub.

Bergman takes one last look at them going aboard and prays God to protect them, for Israel's sake, for their families' sakes, and for his sake. *Their loss on this mission, which for better or for worse was my idea, would be a burden I would bear for the rest of my life.*

Climbing back up into the rental truck, he backs around and heads south to Tel Aviv. His nerves grow tenser with each passing mile—and the knowledge that the mission is actually about to begin.

Aboard the submarine, the petty officer of the watch directs the messenger to escort both Schwartz and Silberberg to the wardroom where the captain is expecting them.

The messenger takes them below decks, through the forward hatch and down a narrow passageway to the wardroom. He knocks on the wardroom door, then opens it for them to enter.

Captain Katz rises from the table. "Welcome aboard the Renewal, my friends!"

Both respond, "Thank you, Captain," almost in perfect unison.

"It seems like old times, sir," Silberberg adds.

"Yes, it does, Mark, only this time my orders just tell me where to drop you off and how far I'm allowed to roam until I retrieve you. Whatever you're up to, this must be extremely top secret. I feel like I'm nothing but a ferry captain, not the skipper of a submarine."

"Sir, the less anyone knows, the better for all."

"Well, plan on enjoying breakfast. Our cook does wonders with navy provisions. After we are underway and clear the harbor, I want to introduce you to my XO. While you're aboard, you will be using his stateroom, which has two bunks. He will bunk in with the navigator. Later, you will be introduced to the sled team drivers, so the four of you can start to plan how you will disembark."

The wardroom steward appears at the door. Captain Katz turns and signals for him to come in. "Steward, please make sure these two gentlemen eat hearty meals while they are aboard," says the captain.

"Yes, sir," replies the wardroom steward, touching a couple fingers to the brim of his hat. "Gentlemen, we can do eggs any style and we have plenty of beef hash available, plus juice, toast, coffee, the usual. What's your pleasure?" he asks them.

"I think, I'll have some orange juice, two eggs over easy and rye toast, if you have it," Silberberg says, then adds, "and coffee."

Schwartz answers, "I'll ditto that."

"Rye toast for both of you?" Both nod. "I'll get you large orange juices," the steward says and makes good on his promise promptly.

As the men eat breakfast, the intercom announces, "Now all members of the special sea detail, man your stations for getting underway."

The wardroom door opens and the executive officer enters. "Gentlemen, I am Commander Micah Rubin, the ship's executive officer. The captain is getting us underway and wishes for both of you to remain here until we clear the harbor," the XO says stiffly. "I will return to formally greet you when we secure from special sea detail."

"Yes, sir," both Silberberg and Schwartz reply. The XO exits the wardroom, and Schwartz and Silberberg break into laughter. "That was informal?" Silberberg chuckles. "Nothing's changed since the last sub transfer they worked. Everything is by the book.

Suddenly, with a slight shudder, they feel the submarine pull away from dockside. Its engine makes slow revolutions to clear from alongside, then forward momentum pulls them out into the channel.

Twenty minutes later, Captain Katz and Commander Rubin enter the wardroom. Captain Katz speaks first. "Commander, this is Natan Schwartz and Mark Silberberg, private contractors for the government. I've known both of these gentlemen from IDF missions we did in my former command. All I can tell you about their current mission is what I know. We'll be dropping them off by sled and retrieving them some six to eight weeks later. Our drop-off point is near the coast of Iran, as is our retrieve point. We are assigned an area in the Indian Ocean for the duration which will allow us to reach our retrieve point within twenty-four hours."

"Commander, we can understand that you and the captain might find it awkward not being briefed on all the facts. That decision was made by the chief of staff. I just want you to know it was not our doing," says Silberberg.

"The only thing we can tell you, Commander, is that your vessel was selected because of our previous experience with Captain Katz," says Schwartz.

"Gentlemen, if the captain is fine with this arrangement, then I'm fine with this arrangement. So long as we have the coordinates to drop you off and retrieve you, we'll do our job."

"Let's have some coffee before we discuss anything else," suggests the captain.

"I'll pass on the coffee," says Schwartz. "I've had enough with breakfast, but I could use the head, if I remember the term correctly."

"Me, too," says Silberberg.

"Gentlemen, let me show you the closest head, and then we can continue our conversation," the XO tells them.

Back in the wardroom, the four of them discuss the route the sub will be taking. Captain Katz plans to exit the Mediterranean Sea by the Strait of Gibraltar during the night. He's counting on anyone observing them depart thinking the sub will be on patrol off Lebanon, or that it will be involved in exercises with the U.S. Sixth Fleet. Neither would be a reason for suspicion.

"After we leave the Mediterranean, we'll proceed in a southerly direction, around the southern tip of Africa, and then proceed north, keeping Madagascar to port. We should arrive on station in fourteen days." Captain Katz fills in Commander Rubin on the rest of the plan.

"Gentlemen, I'm sure you've had a long night getting your gear down to the dock. Why don't I show you to the stateroom that you'll be using while aboard and let you get some shut-eye? We can introduce you to the rest of the officers at dinner this evening, and you can meet the crew and your sled drivers tomorrow. Until then we have other assignments that need to be addressed," says the XO.

"Sounds good to us," Schwartz grins. "We'll see you at dinner time, Captain. Oh, by the way, what freedom limitations do we have while aboard?"

"I really admire both of you for past missions and for whatever reason you're making this trip. However because there is a real potential of your being captured, I can only authorize you to use the XO's stateroom, which has a head and shower, the wardroom, the crew's mess for the 2000 movie and the passageways to get to the disembarking chamber.

"Understood," Silberberg said, savoring the fact that he doesn't have to say sir.

*

Silberberg and Schwartz are escorted to the XO's stateroom. Their carry-on bags are already there. Both know that a submarine stateroom is not very large. However they also know they will appreciate it, compared to sharing a hole in the sand together for more days than they want to count. Schwartz says, "If you don't mind, I'll shower first—and flip you for the top bunk."

"Go ahead, million dollar man," Silberberg says with mock sarcasm. "Rank has its privileges."

Both men shower, then climb into the racks for some much needed sleep.

*

Knocking on the stateroom door, the messenger of the watch informs them that the captain requests their presence in the wardroom for dinner at 1800 hours.

"Please tell the captain that we'll be there," Schwartz calls out in response.

Both find the idea of having a dinner with a bunch of military officers, while they themselves are dressed in civilian clothes, amusing. "Big change from when we were in the IDF," Schwartz comments as they get ready.

Entering the wardroom, they are greeted by Captain Katz and Commander Rubin. The XO does the introductions around the table. Schwartz notices he sticks strictly to first names for everyone, including himself and Silberberg. Commander Rubin advises his officers, "Neither you or the crew are to question either of the men regarding their mission. The only members of the crew who are to have any idea will be the sled team that takes them close to shore. Otherwise, that topic is off limits." Everyone nods.

Dinner in the wardroom is great compared to what Silberberg and Schwartz were used to in the IDF. After dinner, they stay in the wardroom for a while to socialize with those officers who remain after dinner. The officers express surprise that Schwartz and Silberberg have two prior insertions from submarines.

The 2000 hours movie in the crew's mess brings with it a lot of stares. No one questions them, but they can just imagine the conjecture and rumors going around.

*

After breakfast the following morning, Schwartz asks Rubin, "Commander, is it convenient for us to meet with the sled team we'll be working with?"

"The team you're working with are both standing watch right now, Natan. I'll get word to them that they can meet with you in the wardroom at 1330. This will give the officers a chance to finish lunch without rushing, then you can use the wardroom as a meeting place with some privacy. I can't imagine trying to fit the four of you in my stateroom."

"I quite agree, Commander," Silberberg laughs. "That'd be a little tight."

At 1330 quartermaster first class Brian Greenberg and radioman second class Hal Michaelson knock on the wardroom door. Schwartz opens the door and invites them in, introduces himself and Silberberg, then the four shake hands and sit down at the dining table. Plans are discussed on how Hal and Brian can help them disembark from the submarine, going over every detail carefully. Silberberg also brings up plans for retrieve and the signaling process they will use to insure the team knows it is them.

"Are we correct in understanding that you want us to take you only to within thirty meters off shore?" Brian asks.

Silberberg replies, "Yes. We want to travel just below the surface until we reach that point. From there, we'll inflate the floatation devices, mount our air tanks onto your sleds and snorkel to shore."

"Will we be retrieving your gear when you return, as well as yourselves?" Hal asks. "We just need to know so we have the appropriate hookups on the sleds. I imagine you'll want us to just reverse the process, which means we'll also need to bring your tanks back."

Schwartz answers, "If all goes as planned, we'll be bringing back everything we haven't used while in the desert. We don't want to leave anything behind that could indicate we were ever there. And, yes, we'll need our tanks for the return to the sub."

Schwartz asks, "How many runs like this have you two made before?"

"I've made three others off of the coast of Lebanon," Brian responds. "And Hal has done a couple off the Gaza strip, right?" Hal nods in confirmation.

"Then for you two, this should be easy," Silberberg says. "We don't foresee anyone expecting us to do something of this nature, so we don't expect their navy to be on the lookout for anything special. Hopefully," he adds.

Hal says, "You're right, they shouldn't be, but I make a practice of playing it just as cautiously as any other military action. After all, if we get spotted, they will know a sub is in the vicinity and they'll go looking for us."

"Natan, when do you want us to get together before the drop?" asks Brian.

"If you have any questions, you can connect with us anytime. Just remember that we're restricted to certain areas, so you'll need to come to us. If you're comfortable with what we've discussed here, all we need to do is review everything twenty-four hours before we shove off."

With that said, the four shake hands, and Brian and Hal take their leave. Schwartz and Silberberg head back to the XO's stateroom.

"We have twelve days until we are on station," Schwartz says to Silberberg. "We should be using the time to check, double check and triple check everything we brought on board. We need to pack each of our bags so we can reach for our weapons quickly as soon as we hit the beach, and make sure that everything is absolutely watertight, so that it all works when we get ashore." Schwartz's stomach churns with tension as the operation builds. *I know it's nothing more than preplanning jitters, but I so dislike the feeling regardless,* he can't help thinking.

"Natan, you can relax on that, at least. The watertight bags we ordered are guaranteed to depths of sixty meters. This won't be a problem. However, we do need to make sure we don't leave any tracks from the water's edge."

"We'll use the same method we've used before. You're right—no trail from the beach and especially no trail from where we bury the first two loads of gear for replenishment," Schwartz says.

"We have plenty of time before dinner. Why don't we go over our maps. We can begin memorizing everything we need to know," suggests Silberberg. *Better to keep Natan's mind preoccupied,* his partner knows from experience. *But fourteen days of keeping him preoccupied? This is going to be one long voyage . . .*

Chapter Twenty-Two

Meeting the Mafiya

Vicktor, Hussein and Dakham's driver, stands in the lobby of the Best Eastern, waiting anxiously for the pair to come down from their rooms. Vicktor looks like he's come to audition for an old-style gangster movie. He even wears lifts in his shoes, to make up for his short stature. It also appears he's wearing a shoulder holster.

Precisely at 1100 hours, the elevator door opens, and Hussein and Dakham step out into the lobby. Both are dressed casually, as is typical of engineers.

"Hope we didn't keep you waiting very long. You did say 1100 hours, did you not?" Hussein asks.

"Let's go," says Vicktor briskly. "We have nearly an hour's ride to the meeting. My boss won't like it if we are late."

"Vicktor, we are potential clients, not soldiers in the military," Dakham reminds the driver. "What's the big deal if we get there a few minutes late?"

"You will see," Vicktor replies. "Dimitri is a very busy man. He likes things orderly. He gets very upset if things don't go according to his schedule."

Leaving the lobby of the Best Eastern, they cross the entranceway into a parking lot reserved for visitors. Hussein and Dakham follow Vicktor to a silver Mercedes 300S four-door sedan. "Now this is what I call comfort," Dakham says, impressed. "You can drive us around Russia anytime, Vicktor, on anybody's schedule."

"I'm glad that you like it. I can tell how much Dimitri wants to impress someone based on which car he sends me out in. I never said that."

"Of course you didn't," replies Hussein, elbowing Dakham in amusement.

Leaving the city in a north-easterly direction, the shocks on the Mercedes take a real beating as Vicktor and his passengers get bounced around the interior. *I wonder if these roads ever see any maintenance?* thinks Dakham, while Hussein is thinking, *You wouldn't have to remind your passengers to buckle their seat belts around here.*

*

Nearly an hour later, the Mercedes pulls up in front of a large old warehouse facing the Volga River. Two men stand on guard, on either side of the entrance. Vicktor parks the car across from the entrance, opens the car door for Dakham and Hussein and the three of them head towards the guards.

"You just made it on time, Vicktor," says the man on the left side. "Dimitri just called down to see if you were here."

The man standing on the right side, a large man, has the look of a longshoreman about him. He simply says, "This way," and hurriedly escorts Hussein and Dakham upstairs.

Vicktor brings up the rear as the four of them proceed through the doorway and up a long flight of stairs to a second level above the warehouse. The stairways of the old brick building seem to be made of ancient oak. As they make their way up the stairs, each step creaks under their weight, each sounding a bit different, depending on the step and the weight of the individual. The effect is, in an odd way, musical.

On the second level, the guard, who has only told them they can call him Igor, leads them down a long hallway to the very end. Facing the last door on his right he knocks and hears, "You can enter." Igor opens the door for them, holding it open as they pass, then silently closes it behind them.

They are in an office of sorts, with a window that overlooks the river and beyond to the opposite bank and woodlands. The office itself is sparse. Its furnishings consist of a desk and a few metal folding chairs. The walls are bare. The man they will only know as Dimitri sits at the desk. He rises to greet them.

Dimitri Kostovich, some five feet ten inches in height, Hussein estimates, has the looks and features of someone whose ancestors immigrated to Russia from the Slavic countries to the west. Dressed in a shirt, slacks and a bulky knit sweater, he looks to be about forty. Physically, he looks like he can handle any problem that might come his way himself, if necessary.

"Vicktor, you made it. I was worried about you for a minute there." Dimitri radiates anger rather than any concern for Vicktor's wellbeing.

"Traffic is a little slow getting out of the city," Vicktor offers in his own defense.

"I assume these are our guests who we have been expecting from Pakistan? Grab a seat, gentlemen. I don't have a great deal of time, so let's get to the point." He doesn't even bother with handshakes. His demeanor is grim.

"Yes," Hussein says, coming across brusquely himself. "We were told by our fourth cousin that you could assist us in finding replacement parts for our business back home."

"And what sort of business are you in?"

Dakham replies, "Our firm is a brokerage company that obtains used equipment for many types of industries. Primarily we work with utilities and processing plants."

"And what type of equipment are you looking for from me?"

"We have a list of various mechanical and electrical components that we are searching for, to fulfill the needs of several clients," replies Hussein.

"And what kinds of components would these be?" The comment is made in an aggravated, disparaging tone.

"The utilities we are working with are looking for large horsepower generators, impeller drives, gear reduction units, flow valves, steam turbines and switch gear panels, for their control rooms," Dakham tells him, unperturbed, then asks, "Is this something that you can assist us with, or perhaps you can recommend someone else for us to visit while we are here?"

"Do you have a list?" Dimitri asks, his words a command, not a question.

"Of course." Hussein produces a document and hands it over to Dimitri, who merely gives it a perfunctory, almost dismissive glance.

"Vicktor, bring Ivan up."

A couple of minutes later Vicktor returns with a small man who looks to be in his fifties, wearing grease-covered coveralls.

"Ivan, I want you to take this list and see if we have any of these things in inventory. If not, check our other sources."

"Yes, sir," Ivan says, taking the list, he promptly heads back downstairs.

"Gentlemen," returning his disdainful gaze to Hussein and Dakham, "give us a few days. We will get back to you if we can be of some assistance. If not, then I suppose we could recommend another source."

"Our fourth cousin was correct in sending us to you," says Hussein, forcing a smile as he and Dakham rise and extend their hands to shake that of Dimitri. Dimitri returns the gesture, though there is nothing cordial in his handshake.

Vicktor escorts them to the office door. Before leaving, Hussein looks back to see Dimitri watching them as they exit his office, clearly suspicious. Hussein raises a couple of fingers and offers what's meant to look like a confident little wave, then turns and follows Dakham and Vikctor down the stairs.

Vicktor drives them back to the Best Eastern without uttering a word, his passengers following suit. As he drops them off then he says, "See you in a couple of days."

Hussein and Dakham wave him off and head into the hotel.

"Well, what do you think?" Hussein finally asks Dakham once they are inside.

"I think he wants to take a good look at who we are. If he's who Atwan says he is, we'll get a call back in a couple of days to come back in and talk about what he's found for us and hopefully about what we really want. If we don't hear from him, either we spooked him or he's not what we've been told he is."

"Fair assessment, spoke Hussein. "We do need to stick with our roles until we're sure who we're really dealing with, however."

"Of course," says Dakham.

"I don't know about you, my friend, but this broker in used equipment for utilities and processing plants could really do with some lunch. Let's go somewhere outside of the hotel. Get some cold air in our lungs and stay clear of curious ears. I find dealing with the likes of Dimitri a bit unsettling."

"Me, too. Except I'd put it into stronger language than you."

Chapter Twenty-Three

Engineering Challenges

Muhammad Abdullah anxiously paces around the room as he waits for his engineering team to arrive for their weekly meeting. A white board and flip charts at the front of the room are covered with calculations regarding the Shahab-3 and his assignment of converting this missile into one that can be fired from ocean depths and successfully reach its target. The far wall of the room, with its bank of six windows overlooking the submarine docks, is the backdrop for Abdullah's presentation. He intentionally has positioned the white board and chairs so that, when seated, everyone can see both the calculations as well as the vessels outside of the windows.

Abdullah holds this meeting after noon prayers and lunch, so they will not be interrupted. Majid Nouri and Taher Abbas are the first two engineers on his team to arrive. They enter the room cautiously.

Nouri, the most outspoken member of the group, says, "This goes a long way from constantly meeting in the torpedo room and working on schematics in that dungeon we were using."

"I told you things would get better. You need to trust me," smiles Abdullah.

"Oh, we trust you, Muhammad. It's others we don't trust," Abbas replies candidly.

The door opens again and Rahim Givon and Kharam Farhani, the remainder of the team enter, Givon saying, "Hope we're not late."

"No, you're right on time," Abdullah assures them. "Let's everyone take a seat and get started. We've been at this project for six weeks now. You know we have a deadline of ten months. I want to hear from each of you about your ideas on what our next move should be."

The four engineers look back and forth at each other. No one seems to wants to speak first, to make any kind of commitment and possibly end up playing the fool.

"Look, we have measured those torpedo tubes down to the last millimeter," Abdullah exclaims with frustration. "We know what we are working with. Can we fire the missiles from submarines or not?"

Givon, normally the quiet one, speaks first. He may be quiet, but his thoughts on the subject are clear. "Not the way they are currently designed. In order to fire that missile from one of the Kilos, its physical structure must be altered. Torpedoes are not missiles, and missiles are not torpedoes. We must alter the fin design, so that they can fly effectively once they break the surface."

Farhani picks up on Givon's thought. "When we have the proper fin designs, we then have to create a special propulsion system, one that will allow the sub to fire the missiles electronically, to clear the tubes."

Nouri disagrees. "Kharam—you're always the optimist. That's only part of the propulsion problem. We need a discharge force great enough to allow a modified Shahab-3 to clear the submarine and get far enough away before its booster rocket fires and takes it to the surface."

Abbas, always the doubter, shakes his head. "Muhammad, everything built into that current missile is designed for dry land. This is a very different usage. Honestly, I have to wonder if ten months gives us enough time to solve all these problems."

"Gentlemen, I hear what you're saying," Abdullah says mildly. "We know that the Americans have overcome this issue. If they can, we can. If we cannot, then I guess we have no choice but to steal their secrets." Abbas looks up, wide-eyed. "Which at the moment is not an option on the table," Abdullah quickly assures them all.

"Rahim and Kharam, I want both of you to take a missile housing and begin working on the necessary alterations so it can clear the torpedo tubes and to make its flight efficient." Givon and Farhani look at each other and roll their eyes.

"Majid, Taher, I want you two to work on the initial firing system to get a missile underway and safely clear of the submarine before ignition." Nouri nods. Abbas shrugs.

"I myself will work on the calculations," Abdullah continues, "to compensate for any physical weight changes, whether internal or external, so we can attain accurate targeting. I want a working model to test fire out of a tube in twelve weeks. Does anyone have a problem with this? That still gives us five and a half months to come up with a working missile."

Nouri speaks up. "If we had some information from the original designers of the Shahab-3 missile, everything about its characteristics, maybe that might make our job a bit easier?"

"Majid, my thoughts exactly," responds Abdullah. "That's precisely what I plan to ask my boss when I report to him this evening.

The four engineers look at each other. Their eyes betray their doubts.

Chapter Twenty-Four

August Insertion

The Israeli submarine Renewal is maneuvering at a depth of five hundred meters just fifty kilometers off the Iranian shoreline. In the control room, Captain Katz is giving orders. "XO, have Mark, Schwartz and the sled drivers meet both you and me in the wardroom at 1400 hours."

"Yes, sir," replies Commander Rubin. He heads for his stateroom. Knocking on the door, he hears a response from inside, an invitation to come in.

Opening the doorway, the XO says formally, "Gentlemen, the captain requests your presence in the wardroom at 1400 hours, to go over last-minute details."

"We'll be there," says Schwartz. Schwartz and Silberberg have just been discussing the fact that both are beginning to feel what Silberberg likes to call 'pre-op nerves.' They just want to get going.

The XO heads back to the control room and orders the messenger of the watch to have Brian Greenberg and Hal Michaelson meet in the wardroom at the appointed hour.

*

At precisely 1400 hours, Silberberg and Schwartz enter the wardroom. Sitting at the dining table are Captain Katz, Commander Rubin, and their sled team.

"Have a seat, gentleman," says Captain Katz, who notices he's beginning to feel fatherly towards these two former IDF men. Silberberg and Schwartz select seats directly opposite Katz and Rubin.

"We will arrive on station for your departure at 2115," says Captain Katz. "I want to double check that each of us is fully aware of our individual and joint responsibilities. If there are any unanswered questions, I want them cleared up now, before we reach that point."

"Captain, Brian and Hal met with us yesterday to review everything that the four of us needed to go over," Schwartz reports. "Mark and I are comfortable with both their levels of experience and abilities. We're clear on the retrieve signal codes for pickup at the end of the mission. We believe everything is squared away on this end,"

"Are there any questions from either of you?"

"No, captain," says Brain. "We know what we need to do. We can get them close enough to shore," spoke Brian.

"I want the four of you ready to debark at 2145. I will bring the sub to the surface. The conning tower will be just above water line and the escape hatch right at the water's edge, which should make it easier to get the sleds and the gear out of the sub. I suggest that you travel the first stretch at a depth of ten meters." Four heads nod in unison.

"After you drop off Mark and Natan, I suggest you return in the same manner. Our listening devices will pick up the two sleds in plenty of time to resurface to reclaim the two of you."

"Captain, I want to remind you that our mission is open-ended, time-wise, because of its complexity," Silberberg says, catching Schwartz's eye as he speaks. *I know I keep going back to this*, Silberberg thinks defensively. *Hell, it's important to me.* "I just want to reconfirm that you'll be able to meet us there with twenty-four hours' notice."

"The Renewal will be cruising locally, staying within that twenty-four hour window," says the XO, coolly. Rubin knows this much, and little more. Maintaining his cool is becoming harder by the hour. *Dammit, I'm sick and tired of having been left out of the loop on this. That alone is highly unusual for naval operations. What on earth are these hot shot sled-jockeys up to?*

"On the return trip, we'll send out Brian and Hal when we have a location and time to pick you up. I don't want the sled team floating out there unprotected any longer than necessary," Captain Katz says.

"We'll notify you via satellite message that we have arrived near shore to be retrieved," says Schwartz. "By the time the sleds arrive within thirty meters, we'll already be just at the surface with our gear loaded. No one should be able to spot us at that time of night, unless they're already aware we're here."

"All right, then," says the captain. "Sounds good. Mark, Natan, I'm sure you have checked over your equipment a number of times to insure everything works." Both Silberberg and Schwartz nod emphatically. "So—I'll see both of you at dinner at 1800 hours, unless there are any more questions."

There aren't.

*

Dinner in the wardroom is tense. None of the officers want to ask anything that might infringe on secrecy. However, the navigator says, "Let's wish our departing guests a good trip. May they be successful, and may they have a safe return." All seated at the table nod in agreement.

At 2115 the navigator sends the messenger of the watch down to inform the captain that they are on station point alpha. The captain advises the messenger to inform the guests in the XO's stateroom, as well as Brian Greenberg and Hal Michaelson. He then proceeds to the control room.

The officer of the deck calls out, "Captain in the control room." Captain Katz gives a slight wave of his hand. "Captain has the conn," he announces as he takes over. "Bring her up slowly to periscope depth. Sonar, are you picking up anything?"

"No, Captain."

The junior officer of the deck reports, "Periscope depth, Captain."

Captain Katz has the night vision periscope raised so he can scan the surrounding water. Finding neither surface vessels nor aircraft in the vicinity, he orders the sub to the surface.

As soon as Renewal reaches the surface, the deck officer opens the forward hatch so Brian, Hal, Silberberg and Schwartz can climb up on deck. Two other enlisted men assist in lifting the two man-powered sleds to the top of the hatch.

Captain Katz, standing on the top rung of the escape ladder, tells Schwartz and Silberberg that all of Israel wishes them a safe return.

Schwartz and Silberberg, who are familiar with his caring send-offs, appreciate the captain's sincerity and concern nonetheless.

As soon as the sleds are in the water and moving, Captain Katz goes below and the deck officer closes the hatch.

"Dive to periscope depth," the captain orders.

"Sonar, control. Are you getting readings from the two sleds?"

"Control, sonar. We have readings from both sleds. Will advise when they reverse direction."

Thirty minutes later: "Control, sonar. We have readings indicating both sleds have reversed direction and should be nearing our location within twenty minutes."

*

Schwartz and Silberberg float near the shoreline of Iran, scanning the beach to be sure conditions are safe enough to come ashore.

As they get close in enough to stand, both men remove their fins. Just before they step out of the water, they load two packs each onto their backs. They will walk barefooted, dragging a rake-like tool to eliminate tracks behind them. They are headed inland to bury one half of their gear and flotation devices.

*

"Control, sonar. Both sleds are within three hundred meters of point alpha."

"Up periscope," says Captain Katz. Finding everything on the surface as clear as before, he orders the sub to surface and retrieves the sleds.

"Deck officer to control. Drivers and both sleds are on board."

"Dive to periscope depth. Take her on a course of 180 degrees. When we are twenty kilometers from shore, descend to three hundred meters," says the captain. "OOD, you may have the conn."

"OOD has the conn."

*

Schwartz and Silberberg trek about one thousand meters from the shoreline, each pulling one of the detracking devices, then dig a deep hole far enough off the beaten path for safety, and bury one half of their gear for the second phase of the operation. Schwartz takes a GPS reading so they can find the spot again without difficulty.

Before they head out, they put on socks and Iranian military boots, so that their tracks will conform with those of any Iranian who would have reason to be walking around this uninhabited area.

*

Aboard the Los Angeles-class nuclear submarine Trenton the sonar chief on watch is listening for unusual noises that might indicate movement from Iran.

"Control room, sonar. I have a sonar contact bearing 270 degrees, range ten thousand yards. It's making sounds like a Dolphin-class submarine, and it's rising to the surface."

"Sonar, control room. Are you positive of that, Chief?"

"Well, sir, if it's not, I'll buy you a bottle of Scotch."

"Messenger of the watch, ask the captain to come to the control room."

Captain James Blair arrives in the control room and asks the chief if he can tell them anything else.

"Captain, she's on the surface and it sounds like she's off-loaded two powered underwater sleds."

"Can you track those sleds, Chief?" asks the captain.

"Yes, sir. They're heading towards the shore."

Captain Blair checks with the OOD. "You're still on silent running as ordered, correct?"

"Yes, sir, we are."

"Chief, follow the tracks of those sleds. Keep us posted here in control."

"Aye aye, sir!"

"Captain, the sub is below the surface."

"Okay, Chief."

"Control, sonar. It appears that the sleds went in close to the shoreline and are now returning to open waters."

A minute later. "Control, sonar. The submarine's rising to the surface. They appear to be meeting the sleds."

A few moments after that: "Control, sonar. Sleds are off of our scope, so we can assume they were taken back aboard the sub and then she dived."

"OOD, wait thirty minutes so that sub can move out further, then take us near the surface so we can float a wire to send a message to sub fleet headquarters," says the captain.

"Sonar, control room. Nice work, Chief."

"Thank you, sir."

Chapter Twenty-Five

Same Night Off Iran

ENCRYTED MESSAGE TO: COMSUB ATLANTIC US SUB FLEET ATLANTIC HEADQUARTERS *BREAK* HIGH PRIORITY*BREAK* FROM USS TRENTON SSN*BREAK* ON STATION IN INDIAN OCEAN*BREAK*WE HAVE ON RECORD A DOLPHIN CLASS SUBMARINE OFF-LOADING TWO JET SLEDS*BREAK*SLEDS THEN PROCEED TO IRANIAN COASTLINE*BREAK*SLEDS RETURN WITHIN A THIRTY-MINUTE TIME FRAME*BREAK*SUBMARINE RETRIEVES SLEDS ABOARD THEN MOVES OFF IN A SOUTHERLY DIRECTION*END OF MESSAGE*

*

When senior intelligence officer Captain Peter Johnson receives his copy of the encrypted message, he's startled at first. To the best of his knowledge, only two countries have Dolphin-class subs, Germany, who builds them, and Israel, who has purchased a number of them. *Why do I get the feeling that this is not a German expedition?* muses the captain.

Quickly, he picks up the direct line to Admiral Robert Smith's office, and asks to speak to the admiral as soon as possible.

Five minutes later, Admiral Smith is on the secure line at Sub Fleet Atlantic Headquarters. "What's up, captain?" asks the admiral.

"Sir, one of the two additional boomers we have in the Indian Ocean is cruising silent running off of the coast of Iran. We've just received an encrypted message from the *Trenton* saying they have recordings of a Dolphin-class sub off-loading two sleds, then reacquiring those sleds after they'd gotten close to the shore of Iran. Said Dolphin then began moving in a southerly direction away from the coast."

"Captain, get me a copy of that message within the hour."

"Yes, sir. You'll have it by special courier."

Admiral Smith hangs up, then sits back in his chair and considers what he's just heard. Picking up the phone, he calls the Oval Office.

The switchboard answers and passes him onto Janet White.

"Admiral, how can I help you?" answers the president's secretary.

"Janet, I need to speak with the president on a secure line, as soon as possible."

"Admiral, he's in a meeting right now. I expect he'll be through in thirty minutes. I'm sure he will want to call you back as soon as he's finished."

"Thank you, Janet. I'll be waiting for his call."

*

Thirty-five minutes later, President Egan is on a secure line to Atlantic Sub Fleet Headquarters.

"Admiral, I know you're not calling to check on the weather. What's up?"

"Sir, I have an encrypted message from one of our boomers you ordered to the Indian Ocean to travel independently. I'd like to bring this to you as soon as you can fit me into your schedule. I believe we should have the directors of the NSA and the CIA in on this meeting."

"Sounds critical, Bob. I'll have Janet cancel my visitors' greeting at three this afternoon, and have her call the directors to meet with us."

*

By three o'clock, Admiral Smith, CIA director Allison McDonald and NSA director John Walker are sitting in front of the president's desk in the Oval Office. Admiral Smith hands the president the message, passes copies of it to both directors, then sits back and waits for their reactions.

"Reading this message, and the intelligence memo with it," says President Egan slowly, "I believe we can assume that our friends the Israelis are staging some kind of covert action."

"What in the Sam Hill are they tryin' to do now?" explodes John Walker.

"Sir, the CIA has no information of any Israeli action of this nature. Of course, I really wouldn't expect them to tell us. If you remember my suspicions at our previous meeting, Mr. President. I had a gut feeling they'd come up with something, the way things are headed."

"Can we confront the prime minister or Mossad about this, Allison?" asks the president.

"Well, we could always hint that we're aware of an operation on their part and see where it goes. Do I believe we'll get an honest answer? No, sir, I do not."

"John, how many additional satellites can we get focused on Iran?"

"I can have ya three additional birds watchin' 'em by mornin', sir."

"All right, people. This is what I want to do. Have the Navy give you co-ordinates on the drop-off and scope a radius inside Iran of a hundred miles. Have every satellite we can get taking pictures of everything. It sounds like they've dropped off a covert team. What their mission is, I haven't a clue yet. I want their body heat registered on our systems as soon as we can locate them. I want to know where they are, how many of them there are, and what they appear to be doing." The Admiral and the two directors are scribbling notes.

"I don't want this information out of this room," the president continues. "We don't want to jeopardize their team in any way. If they make it out safely, then we can put some pressure on Israel and get them to tell us what the hell they were up to there. If they don't make it out safely, Iran will most likely let the whole wide world know about it. Anyone have any better suggestions?"

"No sir," three voices answer.

"Then, let's get to it. John, I want daily top secret reports on this, and Allison, I want you to have your people do some more digging without revealing what we're looking for. Admiral, send the Trenton a good-heads-up reply."

The admiral and both directors rise and leave the Oval Office, shaking their heads, all agreeing that nothing surprises them anymore.

Chapter Twenty-Six

NSA Tracking Capabilities

In the basement at National Security Headquarters, Jim Stewart is studying satellite images of Iran. His desk and conference table are covered with them. As senior watch officer, he reviews photos that his staff feel deserve a second opinion.

Stewart picks up his phone then calls one of his analysts. "Jerry, what's it you want me to look at? You're acting like something's suspicious."

Taking a moment from one of the many consoles he monitors, Jerry Daniels says, "Jim, I've been getting heat registrations from two human forms moving northward in Iran, only during the hours of darkness, from say about 2100 to 0500 hours." *My gut says they're from the submarine.*

"Well, what's so odd about that? Maybe they're a night detail."

"Sure, Jerry, maybe they are. Or maybe they're what the director told us to look for. Those two forms stay hidden—covered—during daylight hours. If you're moving to a position and you don't want anyone to know you're coming, wouldn't you do it when you can't be seen?"

"All right, stay on top of your nighttime travelers. We'll see where this goes."

*

At his console the following night, Daniels continues to observe what he's come to believe are the two men he's been watching for. The signatures coming in from other movements leave no questions in his mind. And he finds them again on Thursday night of this week, still following their same routine.

Friday night he notices that the pair—the team, as he now thinks of them—continues moving until 0100 hours, then stops. *Either they're taking a break—or they've reached their destination.* He's sure of it. All night long he monitors them as they stay put. *Strange behavior for two individuals who've been moving freely for four nights during the dark to end their travels, unless they've gotten where they want to be.*

"Jim, I think we have something here. Our team's arrived at its destination. Bampur."

"Bampur? What the hell's there?" asks Stewart.

"Beats the shit out of me," Daniels replies. "Right now I need a cup of coffee and a cigarette break. Have someone relieve me, will you?"

"Cindy'll be through in about fifteen minutes. I'll have her relieve you."

Two hours later, Daniels finds that his pair are on the move again. *If I were one of these guys, what would I be doing this for? Maybe they're going for a better observation point, for whatever the hell it is they're planning to do. Yep. I'll bet they're repositioning themselves.*

"Jim, inform the director about this situation, first thing in the morning. He'll want to include it in his report to the president."

"Jerry, thanks for doing my job," Stewart says jokingly. He considers Daniels one of his best observers, and has no doubt that one day he'll make a good senior watch officer.

*

National Security Director John Walker arrives at the White House for his morning report to the president.

In the Oval Office, President Egan is already listening to Allison McDonald give him her latest update. Escorted into the Oval Office by the Secret Service, Walker takes a chair alongside McDonald. "Sorry I'm a couple minutes late today. Mr. Pres'dent," he says, ignoring the fact that he's interrupting McDonald. "We were stuck in traffic."

The president doesn't care for Walker's rudeness. Without acknowledging him, he says, "Allison, continue, please."

After she's finished her report, John Walker hands the president the original of his report, then passes McDonald a copy.

"Mr. Pres'dent, most of that report's pretty similar to what we discussed yesterday," Walker begins. "However, one of our satellite analysts has been watchin' two human forms for four days now. They travel only durin' the night."

John knows enough not to paint the whole picture all at once. The president falls for the bait. "And what's so special about that?" asks Egan.

"If we weren't lookin' for somethin' covert, possibly from Israel, I'd probably say nothin'. But here we have a team of two, movin' only under the cover of darkness. They seem to have arrived someplace and it looks like they've taken up residence. The place is called Bampur." He draws the second syllable out like he's imitating a cat.

"Bampur? What the hell do the Israeli's know about that we don't? Allison, does the CIA have any idea?"

"No, sir."

"John, what does NSA know about this place?"

"Sir, I have to plead ignorance, same as Allison. It just looks like a speck of a farmin' village with a little bit of water. We don't have a clue what's goin' on there."

"Well, I suggest we do a little spying of our own with our satellites and eavesdropping skills and see if we can't find out what the Israelis seem so anxious to learn."

"Sir, we've already programmed three of our satellites to give us continuous monit'rin' of that team. We'll probably have trouble listenin' to their satellite communications, though. It'll all be encrypted."

"John, get your best people on it, to try and figure out what those two are trying to accomplish. See if we can get a handle on whatever's they're there for."

"That's already in place, Mr. Pres'dent. Jim Stewart, one of my senior watch officers and Jerry Daniels, one of our analysts, have already been assigned, and other shifts'll be doin' likewise. Actually Jerry found this team. He's been trackin' like a hound dog on a rabbit."

"Tell him thanks for me, John."

"I will indeedy, sir."

"All right then, if there's nothing further to discuss, we'll meet again tomorrow morning."

Both McDonald and Walker get up and exit the Oval Office. In the waiting room outside, they trade baffled looks. *Bampur?*

Chapter Twenty-Seven

Second Guessing

It has been ten days after the meeting with Dimitri Kostovich, and so far, no word. Hussein and Dakham are beginning to wonder if Dimitri really is a viable source. Arriving back in their rooms after breakfast on the eleventh day, the message light on Hussein's phone is flashing. Calling down to the desk, he asks for his message.

"Just a minute, sir," the desk clerk says. "I'll check for you." After a pause, she returns to the phone. "Yes, sir, you do have a message. It reads: 'Vicktor will pick you up tomorrow morning in the lobby at nine.' That's it, sir."

"Thank you," replies Hussein. Smiling, he calls over to Dakham and tells him about the message.

"Well, then, we might as well do some more sightseeing again. I don't want to spend another whole day in this room," Dakham sighs.

"I'm tired of sightseeing, hanging around hotels, just lying around in general," agrees Hussein.

"Relax, Kamil. This project will get intense soon enough, if my suspicions are correct."

*

At 0855 the next morning, Hussein and Dakham are sitting in the front lobby waiting for Vicktor to show up. Just before 0900 hours, he comes through the door in his old-fashioned American gangster-style outfit, smoking a cigar. The overall effect seems just plain silly to the Iranian operatives. He blows a couple of smoke rings which, they suppose, are meant to impress them, then says, "You two ready to roll?"

"Vicktor, as observant Muslims we do not smoke nor do we drink alcohol," Dakham states disparagingly. "We are not accustomed to sitting in smoky environments and would appreciate it if you'd dispose of the cigar."

Wincing, Vicktor says, "Oh, yeah, sorry. I forgot my manners." He discards the cigar in a lobby receptacle. "Let's go. The car's right out front."

They all climb into the same Mercedes 300S sedan that they rode in to the first meeting. However, this time, Vicktor heads north instead of east. This road is in better condition, not as full of potholes as the road they'd taken on the previous trip.

"We aren't going to the warehouse where we met Dimitri before?" asks Dakham.

"No," says Vicktor. "Demitri is having us meet him at one of his source locations, so you can personally inspect some of the items you had on your list. It's too expensive to just move this stuff around. What you want is too big to handle any more than necessary."

Vicktor becomes their travel guide as he drives Hussein and Dakham through the countryside, pointing out what he believes are historical sites.

Although they appear interested, Hussein and Dakham's thoughts are only on the meeting, and if it will bring them any closer to the goal to their overall mission.

*

Two hours later, the Mercedes pulls up to an old secluded industrial building which appears is no longer doing any kind of manufacturing. The windows are boarded up.

Vicktor parks the car in front of the old, ivy-covered brick building, then instructs them to wait for him to return. He wants to be sure that Dimitri has already completed his previous appointment. Dimitri doesn't like visitors running into each other.

Ten minutes go by. Neither Hussein nor Dakham says a word. Both are thinking the same thing, however: *Is this a set up?*

Suddenly, Vicktor returns with Igor in tow. *The fellow who was at the door at our previous visit*, remembers Dakham. Vicktor and Igor escort the two of them into the warehouse. Inside it is very dark. *Just how are we supposed to see what Dimitri supposedly has for us?* Hussein wonders.

Inside, they hear and recognize Dimitri's voice from the rear of the space. "Wait just a minute," he says. "I will have Ivan put on the lights for us. Don't want to waste precious electricity, you know."

The lights go on. Startled, both Dakham and Hussein react in tandem. *What an enormous amount of goods he's got here, stored under plastic covers!*

"Ivan, you have their list," comes Dimitri's voice from afar. "Please, show our guests what they want to look at."

Ivan leads their tour from item to item. Hussein and Dakham look at each other in outright amazement. *This is not used equipment. It's brand new, possibly never been used before. Most probably, it's been stolen.*

"Ivan, we'd like to open up some of the housings to view the interiors," Hussein says calmly, as if he inspects hot goods every day for a living. "We have to make sure that none of the parts are damaged,".

Ivan looks to Dimitri, who gives him the nod to go ahead. He then begins taking off the inspection cover of the first parallel reducer, one with the specific ratios as detailed on their list.

"This unit is full of rust-preventative grease. It looks like it's never been run," Dakham says, acknowledging the obvious. Ivan opens several more for their inspection. They all look to be in similar condition.

"Dimitri, we are shopping for used equipment," Hussein grumbles. "Our budgets do not allow us to buy new. If we did, we could not afford all that we need to obtain."

"Look, when you're looking for specific equipment, you may not always have the option of finding used parts," Dimitri counters. "But do not worry. I can offer it to you at not much more than used pricing."

After an hour of looking around, Hussein walks back to where Dimitri has been sitting all this time. "Dimitri," he says, "give us a package price on the four reducers we opened and the four switchgear boxes you have on the third skid. And we have one more request."

"I'll have the pricing for you tomorrow. If we come to terms, you will have to pay in US dollars only. What's your other request?"

Hussein hesitates, then plunges into the real reason they are here. "The customer who needs this equipment is now requesting that we also look for some spent fuel rods."

"And where would I get spent fuel rods?" asks Dimitri.

"We don't know. We are only asking if you can. If not, we'll have to continue shopping for that part of the package," Dakham answers for Hussein. It is clear that these two are working as a team.

"You do know, I assume," Dimitri answers cautiously, "that if I could possibly supply them, the price would be . . . very expensive."

"You give us a price if you can deliver. Our firm would of course have to have a sample tested for quality. Then we'll make you an offer," responds Hussein firmly. "However, why don't we say that you wait on a quote for everything we need, to see if you can come up with a package deal we can live with." *You'd think I've been doing this all my life,* Hussein pats himself on the back, pleased with his performance.

"Ivan, put this stuff back together. Vicktor, take our guests back to the Best Eastern," Dimitri tells his men. Then he turns back to Dakham and Hussein. "Gentlemen, I will need some time to try and locate this last item you're looking for. Is there a specific amount you need? Or are you willing to take all I can find?" Dimitri's eyes, black as coal, stare them down unblinking.

"Let us know how much you can find and, if the quality is there, we'll give you an idea of what our client wants," answers Dakham ambiguously. Both he and Hussein are relieved when Vicktor ushers them out of the building and back into the light of day.

Inside, Dimitri Kostovich gets to his feet. "Igor, I want a tail on those two for the next two weeks. Make sure the tails rotate, so they don't get spotted. Either this is the kind of sale you wait half a lifetime for—or the government is trying new tricks to find missing nuclear materials lying around the country."

"What happens, sir, if we find out that they are government agents?"

"Well, Igor, it would not be the first automobile accident you ever rigged to happen."

"I'll take care of them so they can never be recognized again, if they are," Igor assures his boss.

"Now, I have some very important people to speak with," says Dimitri. "Get me back to the office. Ivan, close up here. Someone will pick you up in an hour."

"Yes, sir."

*

Hussein and Dakham arrive back at their hotel and head up to Hussein's room. As soon as they are inside, Hussein attaches the encryption device to the phone and dials the number in Pakistan. When he hears the three beeps, he knows it is safe to speak.

"This is Kamil. I want to leave a message for my fourth cousin. Tell him his request has been handled. We are now awaiting a confirmation. Expect to be sitting tight for a couple of weeks, at the least."

Chapter Twenty-Eight

Executive Power

President Egan calls his personal secretary on the intercom. "Janet, please come into the Oval Office. We have work to do and I need you now."

"Yes, sir," comes the quick reply.

Janet picks up her steno pad and the president's schedule log, walks over to the door and knocks. On hearing the president's okay, the Secret Service man standing in front of the door opens it for her. Janet takes her usual seat in front of the president's large desk.

"Before we start scheduling a meeting I'm planning, I'd like your opinion on something, Janet. Your security clearance allows me to ask you this. I'm looking for an opinion of an American citizen, not a politician."

Janet thinks about it for a moment, then nods. "I can do that. What are you asking, sir?"

"Picture this, if you would: a foreign government attacks the United States without warning and takes out top levels of our government. Our Constitution allows for a succession process that replaces those in authority. In fact, the process for successions goes eighteen levels deep, though if anyone on that list were not native-born, he or she would not be able to take office as president. Working through it would be long, tedious and difficult, particularly in the chaos of a such a situation. My question is: would you expect the remnants of the government to follow the Constitutional guidelines to a T? Or would you—just as a citizen, remember—be willing to consider having the nation's military commanders take charge of retaliation, to protect our country and our citizens?"

139

"Phew, sir," Janet says, clearly overwhelmed. "Let me digest this a moment." She pauses, half of her brain addressing the question, the other half wanting to cry out, *What are you telling me? Are we in imminent danger of attack?*

"Personally," she finally begins, "I believe the eighteen levels you say we have were never created for a time of national emergency on the scale we can imagine today. Secondly, if we were to be hit without warning, in a scenario such as you're suggesting, a good number of those sixteen individuals could be dead or dying. I'd think that, if the president and vice president are no longer alive, we should at least try to reach the next three positions listed in the Constitution. Given a good attempt to maintain the constitutional requirements, we probably should have some flexibility so our military commanders can make the necessary military calls to protect the nation and defeat our enemies. However, I do feel that when the dust settles and we can hold elections, they should then revert back to their regular responsibilities."

"Janet, are you sure you don't want to sit in this seat?"

"No thank you, sir!" *However, I'm certainly pleased that you confide in me and respect my opinion!*

"Thank you for your insight, Janet," the president says, nodding. "I knew I could count on you to tell me what you truly felt, not just what you think I want to hear. That's one of your many admirable traits. I think I can believe what you just said is probably representative of the majority of the American people."

Janet sits before her president more than a bit stunned. She manages a smile. "Thank you, sir. I'm your secretary because I believe you're the kind of president this country needs. You don't make your decisions by whichever way the political wind's blowing."

"Thank you, Janet," he says particularly sincerely, looking at her with new respect. *It's never occurred to me that she feels this way,* he reprimands himself. *I've been taking her loyalty for granted. No more of that.*

Clearing his throat a bit self-consciously, the president returns to the job at hand. "All right, then, now let's get down to business. I want a meeting two weeks from Friday in the Situation Room one p.m., and the following are required to attend—note I said *required*. The vice president, chief of staff, secretary of defense, the directors of the CIA and NSA, Admiral Smith and Generals Bradley and Sanford. I want you to speak to each of them personally, not just leave messages with their secretaries. Advise them to plan to spend the entire afternoon at this meeting." He thinks for a moment, then continues.

"Tell everyone this is an update from our previous meeting. And tell the military commanders that we'll be discussing broadening the war powers authority of the president, something I promised them when we last met. Oh yes, and have Marine guards stationed at the Situation Room door for the duration of the meeting."

"Is there anything else, sir?"

"Not right now. What time is my next appointment?"

"In half an hour you have the ambassador from Israel coming in at your request."

"Have the kitchen make up some strong coffee for us, to be ready when he arrives, please."

"Consider it done."

"I always do, Janet. And Janet, let me say, I've been remiss in telling you how much I appreciate your support and your competence. Truly."

Janet smiles. "It's my privilege," she says quietly.

Returning to her desk, Janet drops down into her chair harder than she meant to. *Ouch! But really, the emotional moment I've just been through—with the president of the United States!* she thinks in wonder. *I don't know if I've ever felt—what?—drained, scared and honored, all at the same time.*

It takes her a good five minutes to pull herself back together and get to work placing calls to each of the players the president wants at this meeting and letting them know everything he wants each of them to be aware of.

As she does, she realizes she's recognizing a pattern here. *Bill Egan can be so clever at times*, she thinks. *He likes to keep some people guessing and others on their toes. I guess you'd have to call it manipulation, but it's clearly how he gets original thinking, not rote answers. What a guy.*

Chapter Twenty-Nine

Second Week in August

After three days of staying under cover through daylight hours, and traveling during darkness, Schwartz and Silberberg arrive at their designated point around 0100 hours on the fourth night. No Iranians have appeared along the way to give them any trouble.

"Let's take a break here, Mark," Schwartz suggests, "and recon the area to find the most advantageous spot for us to set up. We need to keep within a range that'll allow us to obtain emissions readings and be able to record conversations."

"I'd like to suggest that when we leave here," Silberberg counters, "we take a dip in that body of water back where we filled our canteens. I don't know about you, but I feel filthy."

Schwartz is an easy sell. "Agreed. It'll be a long time before we see our next shower."

Viewing through night vision binoculars, they agree on a spot that will put them within the range they need, a natural rise in the desert that offers them some height, allowing them to observe what they believe is the front entrance of the facility.

Halfway up the rise, they dig out an area just large enough for them to maneuver around each other. During daylight, they'll record any readings they can obtain and attempt to record voice conversations as well. During the night, they'll move in closer to the facility to obtain more information.

Schwartz consults his watch. "It is almost 0415, Mark. Let's set up the camo cover and you catch some shut eye." Silberberg is entirely willing to sign on to this plan.

*

An hour later, Schwartz taps Silberberg on the shoulder; "Time to eat some more of that wonderful chow we're carrying."

Silberberg swallows his rations and smiles. "I guess it beats the fasting going on down there," he says, referring to the fact that the Islamic holy month of Ramadan has begun. "You remember how we said on the last trip that it would be the last one? Hah!"

"Sure, I remember," Schwartz grins. "Only this one seems to be more important than any promises we made ourselves." Silberberg nods. "How about I sleep for a while. You take the first watch and wake me up if you start seeing any activity."

Silberberg likes the particular camo cover they are using. With about six inches clearance for visibility, there is no need to be outside of the enclosure to keep watch.

The facility he's looking at is a complex of four buildings, each about the length of a soccer field. He sees no visible signs of security, but assumes there must be some.

While he keeps his eyes open for any activity, he cannot help but admire the beauty of the Iranian desert. Of course you have to love deserts to appreciate one. Silberberg grew up on a kibbutz in the Negev desert in Israel. His parents being immigrants from Russia, he enjoys the distinction of being native-born, a sabra. He remembers many happy years growing up in the desert, which is why he's so comfortable in one. His thoughts turn to Schwartz, remembering how the two of them met in the IDF, as company commanders taking part in various projects together, sometimes jointly on special operations, sometimes just the two of them alone. *It's uncanny,* Silberberg ruminates. *We both have the same way of approaching problems, doing things, and second guessing what the other will do. A useful sense to have—it's saved both of our lives more than once. I trust him explicitly, as he does me.*

*

Around 0720, Silberberg hears some heavy trucks coming towards their location. The trucks are on the opposite side of a large sand dune; he can follow their progress by the tell-tale dust clouds they're generating.

Giving him a nudge, Schwartz comes awake instantly. Both of them start following the dust clouds with their binoculars. When the trucks lumber into view, they count four heavy-duty vehicles that would normally be used to carry military equipment. Schwartz starts the log he will keep to support their findings.

As the vehicles approach the facility, an individual with an AK-47 semi-automatic steps out of the first building near the entrance and raises his free arm up to notify the driver to stop. When the vehicle stops, four other men with AK-47s emerge from the same building and begin searching each truck, checking each driver's paperwork, then looking into the cargo areas of each vehicle. When the four give the first guard the okay, he indicates to the driver the convoy can proceed. None of these people are wearing military uniforms.

Hmm . . . more security than we'd expected, thinks Silberberg.

The remainder of the daylight hours is quiet. Both attempt to identify some emissions readings without success. Whoever works here seems to be keeping inside during daylight hours, making the recording of communications more difficult. The equipment they are using needs to be directed at an exposed source. *It may be top-of-the-line and state-of-the-art, but everything has its limitations*, muses Silberberg.

They decide to rest through the twilight hours and then head in closer to see if they can get more recordings during total darkness. Resting means that one will keep watch for three hours while the other sleeps. Then they will switch roles, unless something gets their attention.

Around 2000 hours, they both decide it is time to make their way closer to the facility. As it is their first attempt, they crawl through the sand on their bellies.

Their first order of business is to make sure the outer perimeter is clear of mines. This process alone takes over three hours of painstaking, meticulous effort.

Now knowing they are safe to maneuver around, they head for the main entrance they saw the trucks enter. Much to their surprise the building that held the men with the AK-47s is empty. Is it possible that the plant really has no security after dark?

Not seeing the trucks leave today, their next instinct is to find where inside of the compound the trucks are parked. They come upon them parked alongside the last building in the complex. Inching their way over to within a hundred meters of the trucks, they take readings for radioactivity. Bingo! The readings indicate that whatever was or still is loaded on those trucks has a high percentage of radiation to it.

Hearing a sound, Silberberg spots a lone sentry walking the yards between the buildings and pulls Schwartz down closer to the ground before they can be seen. The sentry seems to be entirely relaxed. He lights up a cigarette, then pulls a walkie-talkie from his belt and, in Farsi, reports that everything is clear on this side of the plant.

Having seen enough for tonight, Schwartz and Silberberg head back up to their hideaway. The return trip is hardly as slow as the first leg, but it is nearly 0430 by the time that they get back, both soaked in perspiration. Between the physical and emotional exertion, they need some rest.

Immediately upon their return, Schwartz sets up the encrypted satellite blast transmitter they use for communications. He downloads the readings, accompanied by a short message to Bergman. It only takes seconds to locate the satellite and send the transmission. The signal is too brief for any land forces to identify the location of the transmission.

*

Inside Mossad headquarters, Yosef Bergman waits for a message that he's been expecting since the submarine inserted Schwartz and Silberberg. Actually, he'd expected a message saying they were on site the previous day. He's trying to maintain his patience, but it's becoming harder by the minute. *Have they been killed or captured? I'd at least like to know that they are alive.*

At 0600 hours Israeli time, his transmission equipment jumps to life. Bug-eyed with surprise, he gets up quickly, records the message and downloads the encrypted report. As soon as he's finished, he heads into Mossad's encryption center to get it translated into readable Hebrew.

His first reaction is satisfaction simply in knowing that Schwartz and Silberberg are alive and safe, at least for the time being. Schwartz provides a quick assessment of the facility, the grounds and security.

Bergman also downloads the readings report which will have to be deciphered and then interpreted by a nuclear scientist.

He will meet with Wattenberg as soon as he arrives this morning. *Ariel has been as anxious about the team as I. He just won't let it show.*

*

At 0800 Wattenberg arrives at Mossad headquarters. Bergman has already asked to see him before his day begins.

When Bergman steps into the director's office, Wattenberg locks eyes on him. He doesn't have to ask the obvious question that's written all over his face. *Do you have good news? They are still alive?* Bergman simply smiles and nods. Wattenberg, clearly relieved, welcomes him into his office and they both sit down.

"So, tell me what you have, Yosef."

"Our first report, Ariel."

"Really!"

"Yes. We now know that they are alive. They're situated near the facility at Bampur. From the report, the facility is receiving trucks which show radioactive readings. We will need one of our specialists to interpret the data. And they say that the site seems to be well guarded. That's all I know for certain so far."

"Good, Yosef. Your idea is beginning to pay off already. If this goes to completion it will be a blessing, one of course that unfortunately we can never talk about."

"Yeah, I know," Bergman accepts with a shrug," but that's our kind of life, isn't it?"

Chapter Thirty

Radioactive Readings

During daylight hours the next day, from the relative safety of their base, Schwartz finds that he's now able to pick up radioactivity from the building beside which the trucks are parked.

Silberberg can see some men congregating just outside of a third building who appear to be on some sort of work detail; they seem to be moving some heavy containers. One of the men calls out to the truck drivers parked nearby, telling them to bring a couple of the vehicles over to where the workmen are waiting.

Two of the trucks are driven over. The work detail loads a number of containers onto each truck, then the trucks leave the compound and head off the way they came.

Silberberg is recording all of these conversations. When the trucks leave, he's able to hear the man in charge of the detail tell the men under him that more material will be ready for the remainder of the trucks in three days.

Meanwhile Schwartz is able to zone in on the departing trucks with his radiation detector. His readings are much higher than those he took the night before when the trucks were supposedly empty. All this information he also enters into his log.

In the late afternoon, three men are seen exiting the last building on this side of the complex. Silberberg spots them with the voice recorder. He can hear their conversations as they are being recorded.

The first one says, "I'm leaving in two weeks. How many weeks do each of you have left?"

The shortest one says, "I have four more to go. This place is a hell hole, with nothing to do but work and pray."

The last one of the group remarks, "Be thankful that you're not in the processing group. They won't get to leave here for months. Have you seen the safety gear they have to wear?"

The shorter one responds, "They tell us we're safe doing what we're doing if we only stay here six weeks. I really don't believe any of it."

The first says again, "Two weeks and I'm out of here."

"Where will they send you next?" asks the short one. "This is my third plant."

"Only Allah knows," says the first.

*

After listening to the conversations, Silberberg shares them with Schwartz.

"Well, now we know why they insisted on us wearing rad badges on this site," says Schwartz.

"I hope we don't glow in the dark when we get out of here," Silberberg agrees.

That night they decide to go down near to the building from which the heavy containers were removed and loaded in the trucks.

Schwartz moves within fifty meters of the building while Silberberg hangs back as a rear guard. He removes his special emission detection equipment from its case and begins to take whatever readings he can obtain. Tonight his dials record much higher levels of emissions and radiation. *What in the hell do these guys think they are doing?* he wonders in disbelief. *This lack of containment could jeopardize their own country, as well as cause nuclear harm to others.*

Within fifteen minutes he's back with Silberberg and the two head back to their hideaway. At 0200 hours they send a burst back to Israel giving Bergman the recordings of radiation readings throughout that day and night, plus the conversations that were picked up.

*

At Mossad headquarters, Bergman receives the information almost instantaneously. He downloads everything, and has the encryptions deciphered. His eyes go wide as he reads what's before him. He quickly sends the data on emissions and radiation to the special science group monitoring this project.

Beads of sweat form on his forehead as the reality of what's going on in Iran, what they have feared all along, sinks in.

*

By 0730 the following day, Bergman has a report from the science group on the two days of data provided to them by his desert rats. It is not good.

The conversations the team has been able to record are mostly just typical gripe sessions between soldiers stuck in a lousy location. But some of the content suggests that these soldiers are aware of what they're being exposed to, leading the specialists to believe that the nuclear situation in this location is both highly suspect and critical.

They also believe that the levels of emissions and radioactivity suggest that this facility is not enriching uranium, but rather reprocessing plutonium. This conclusion is every bit as dangerous as if they were enriching uranium. Reprocessed plutonium can also be used in nuclear warheads.

At 0800 hours when Wattenberg walks through the door of the agency, Bergman nails him even before he takes off his hat. "We need to talk, and right now."

"What's so important that I cannot pour myself a cup of coffee, Yosef?"

"We have found what we were looking for, within only a couple of days at site one. I want to pull Natan and Mark off of there and send them on to site two."

"Well, let's see this report, my excitable aide."

After reviewing the report, Wattenberg agrees. "You're right, Yosef. We probably can't find out much more than what we already have here. We need to get them to Bandar Abbas."

"We need to get them off of a nuclear hot spot is more like it," says Bergman. "They have already done their job at Bampur. I don't want them exposed to any more radiation then they already have been."

"Your thinking is—admirable, Yosef," Wattenberg says, carefully choosing his words. "But my job is to make sure this project is completed thoroughly."

"I know what you're saying," Bergman says. "It is, I can assure you. I want to send a message to move to site two."

"If you're absolutely curtain, then do so. If not, have them stay a little longer."

Bergman shakes his head. "I will send them a burst tonight and have them move out."

"If that's your choice, then do it," says Wattenberg. Wattenberg smiles sadly as Bergman leaves his office. *I'm watching you go through the pain of being responsible for a team, something I've long been accustomed to. It never gets easy, my friend.*

*

Around 1800 hours Schwartz notices the receiving light on their communication gear is blinking. He turns the unit on and receives a transmission burst that reads out on the screen. "Move on to site two tonight," and nothing more.

He deletes the message, then tells Silberberg, "We're packing it up after dark and going to take that dip you talked about."

"Tonight? They're sure they have enough information in just four days? That's pretty damn quick," says Silberberg, skeptical.

"Whatever the reason, those are our orders," Schwartz reports. "We're moving out of here tonight. Let's start putting our gear together. We have a long haul back to where we buried the rest. We want to make sure this spot looks just like we found it. No one can know that we were ever here."

*

Later that evening, NSA's Jerry Daniels is watching his focus area at Bampur. Suddenly he sits up. The heat registrations from the two human forms are moving again. *Interesting,* he thinks. *Okay, my friends, let's see where you're headed now.*

As the night progresses he notices that the two seem to be doubling back along the same track they came in on. *Well, let's see how they leave Iran, if we can. Boy, Jim's gonna shit when he reads this.*

Chapter Thirty-One

Working a Deal

Hussein sees the message light blinking on his phone as they arrive back in their rooms after lunch and calls down to the desk to inquires about the message. The front desk finds a message that was left for him and Dakham. Someone named Vicktor will be picking them up tomorrow at ten a.m.

Hussein calls Dakham's room and asks if he received the same message. "Yes," Dakham replies. "Let's go for a walk."

"Agreed," says Hussein. "I'll meet you in the lobby in ten minutes."

As they walk along the avenue, Hussein says, "It has been exactly fourteen days since we have heard from Dimitri. He said a couple of weeks. I think his aim is make us sweat."

"Either that or now that we're starting to inquire about more than simply machine replacement parts, he's getting nervous," Dakham surmises.

"We need to keep our cover. I'm sure that we're being watched while we're here, and not just by Dimitri's people," says Hussein.

"Well, maybe our cover has made Dimitri more negotiable—or maybe he plans to run, as scared as a mouse," Dakham suggests dismissively. "The only thing we do know is that we can't know until we meet with him tomorrow. So how shall we spend today? Shall we visit the museum and see the Panorama for the fourth time, or shall we hike up and pay our respects to Mother Russia and the Heroes for the—what?—I can't remember, the fifth time?"

"Anything, just no more cruises on the Volga, okay?" Hussein begs.

*

Vicktor arrives five minutes before 1000 hours. He calls up to Hussein's and Dakham's rooms but gets no response. *Maybe they're on their way down,* he thinks.

Two minutes later, Hussein and Dakham step out of the elevator. Vicktor is so easy to spot, in his outlandish mobster mode of dress. "I tell you, that man has seen one too many gangster movies," Hussein whispers to Dakham before Vicktor spots them and waves them over to him.

"Gentlemen, gentlemen, it's so good to see you this morning," Vicktor says effusively. Hussein looks at Dakham and wonders what the cordial greeting is all about.

For some reason Vicktor continues in this warm and friendly manner this morning, not projecting his usual rough self. "The car's right out in front," he says affably. "No need to walk in the bitter cold."

The ride to the warehouse where they first met Dimitri is full of smiles, and warm compliments. *Something's going on,* thinks Dakham.

When they arrive at the front door, only one guard stands outside instead of the two previously. Igor holds the door open for them, and even tells them to go up to the office without an escort.

At the top of the stairs, Vicktor leads the way. When they stop at Dimitri's office, he knocks on the door. All three hear a response to come in. Vicktor holds the door so Hussein and Dakham can enter.

Dimitri jumps to his feet, though he does stay behind the desk. "My friends, my friends, it is so good to see you again," he greets them.

The shit is getting pretty deep in here and it doesn't even smell yet, thinks Dakham.

"Sit, sit," says Dimitri, pointing to some chairs and in front of his desk.

Hussein decides he might as well open the conversation. "Dimitri, have you found the special rods our client is looking for?"

"Yes—and no."

"By that you mean . . ."

"We have found a supply of spent rods that are still located in a reactor that's not functioning. To get them out would take many skilled people and would certainly draw attention—too much attention." He looks genuinely frustrated.

"However, we have located some projectiles that are, shall we say, unaccounted for," he quickly goes on. "They should be able to serve whatever purpose you need the rods for."

Dakham shakes his head. "We are not looking to ship projectiles. We are interested in purchasing those gear box housings to move nuclear materials we had hoped you'd been able to find. The projectiles would be useless to our client."

Dimitri looks at them both, then says evenly, "You'd have to reprocess the rods. The materials inside the projectiles should be usable without remanufacturing."

Hussein replies, "We can only advise our client of your dilemma. We will also tell them of your suggestion. However, I'd suggest that if you can find a way of removing the materials in question, we might have a better chance of reaching an agreement."

Dimitri lowers his eyelids to half mast, then says, "Have you found someone else who says he can supply what you want in Russia?"

Ah hah, so this is where this is going, thinks Dakham.

"There's not that much to do in Volgagrad," says Hussein with a shrug. "During the two weeks while we were sitting on our hands, we decided to see what other opportunities we might be able to find. So far everything is in the opening stages, of course, the getting-to-know-you part. But if you play your cards right, you won't have to worry about competition."

"However, we can't afford to continue to sit around forever. We must get back to Pakistan," adds Hussein.

"If you can come up with a sample of material for us to test, and are sure you can remove all of the materials from the projectiles, we'll consider doing business. Of course, only if the sample proves its worth," says Dakham.

"You know this is going to be expensive," says Dimitri.

"We cannot talk price until we see the quality of the product. But remember, the whole batch must match up to the quality of the sample, or you can expect problems," says Hussein.

"What . . . kind of problems?" asks Dimitri, cautiously.

"My fourth cousin doesn't like being taken advantage of," Hussein says, his tone well matched to the thinly veiled threat.

Hussein looks to Dakham, who nods. Both rise, signaling the meeting is over. Once again, Vicktor takes them back to the hotel. Unlike the ride over, this time he has returned to his usual silent self.

As they enter the lobby, they head for the front desk. "We will be checking out as soon as we can make arrangements for our trip back home," Hussein tells an attractive desk clerk. "Please have our bills ready for us when we call you to inform you of the time."

"Yes, sir," the young lady replies with only a professional smile.

Hussein and Dakham head for their rooms, and Dakham calls to book a flight for them back to Pakistan. They're pleased that the next flight is in six hours. This allows them enough time to pack, call Atwan, if they can reach him, and still get to the airport. They plan to eat dinner at the airport.

After packing, Hussein installs the encryption unit on his room phone and calls the designated number. As he expected, he cannot reach Atwan, but he does leave a message saying the trip is over and that they will look forward to seeing him when they return.

They check out and head for the airport.

Chapter Thirty-Two

End of the Second Week

During the morning CIA and NSA briefing with the president in the Oval Office, John Walker is finding it difficult to control his excitement. He listens impatiently while the director of the CIA goes first, presenting her agency's views on crucial happenings going on around the world.

"Seems like the same old, same old," says the president, wearily. "Does the CIA have any word on what we believe the Israelis are up to at Bampur?"

"Not yet, sir. We're trying to get one of our agents close enough to Bampur to eyeball the situation. He's posing as a nomad, complete with a couple of camels. I've spoken with the director of Mossad, to see if they're making any progress in identifying what might be going on in Iran, beyond what they've already told us. He just kept saying that they weren't aware of anything else."

"Well, keep at it, Allison. We know they're not sightseeing there. We need to find out what has them so fascinated." Turning to Walker, he says, "John, you're looking pretty perky this morning. What've you got up your sleeve?"

"Well, suh, my reg'lar report's just more of that same ol', same ol', like Allison's. Except," and he draws the word out for full dramatic effect, "our people have been monitorin' that covert team of Israelis. Report is, they spent three or four days at the Bampur site, but now they're on the move, reversin' themselves, headin' back towards their orig'nal deployment position."

155

"Sounds like they're gittin' out of Dodge," says the president. Walker's southern accent can be contagious. "You've gotta wonder what the hell they found out there. When you see they've been evacuated, I want to be notified. Then Allison and I are going to have a little four-way chat with their prime minister and the Mossad."

"Suh, I'll let y'all know the minute they get back in the watah," John Walker promises.

"Allison and John, thank you. It's not much, but for some reason I'm beginning to feel like we've got the cat by the tail—or at least by an inch of tail."

Chapter Thirty-Three

Fourth Week in August

Kamil Hussein and Hamid Dakham are sitting in the conference room of the Iranian Secret Police building, tired and haggard from the long journey home. All they want to do is drop off to sleep.

The phone in the room rings, jolting them out of their growing stupor. Dakham answers. "Jibril Atwan has asked me to inform you that he's on his way to the office. You're to continue to wait in the conference room," says a male voice "He said you're to make yourselves comfortable."

Hussein asks himself, *How could anyone to be comfortable sitting in any room in this building?*

*

Two hours later, Atwan walks through the door. His penetrating stare is enough to make people cringe. He takes the chair directly at the head of the table. Hussein and Dakham are sitting to either side of him. "Welcome back, gentlemen," says Atwan, his expression unreadable. "How was your little—vacation?"

"For the most part, it was truly boring, if you must know," says Hussein.

Atwan is not amused. "All right. I want to hear about every single thing you did and every single person you dealt with. Do not leave out any details. What may seem unimportant to the two of you may be very important to me." Atwan turns on a recorder.

For the next five hours, Hussein and Dakham give Atwan an exhaustive—and exhausting—description of everything they did, saw and heard on their trip. They tell him where they ate each meal and what they ordered. They tell him about people who rode elevators with them. They try to remember every fellow passenger on a two-hour trip on the Volga. They tell him about the lousy cab driver. Both get up at one time or another, to pace the room. Atwan sits quietly, the embodiment of patience, through the entire debriefing.

Finally both men run out of details. Looking across the table at each other, Dakham asks Hussein, "Is that all?" Hussein searches the farthest reaches of his excellent memory before finally nodding.

"Good," says Atwan, getting to his feet. "Wait here. I must speak with someone about some of the things you have just told me before we continue."

Hussein and Dakham's eyes lock on each other. *Continue?*

*

An hour later, Atwan returns to the room and sits back down in his chair, his face a grim mask. "This Dimitri fellow you met with is a low-level mob boss. We assume his job was to feel you out, to see what he can sell us, and what he must do to satisfy our demands."

"So, what would you like us to do?" asks Dakham.

"You will wait for three weeks. Then you will call him back, from this office. Depending on what he has to say for himself, we'll decide whether we continue to negotiate with him. Or come out and ask to speak with his boss. Of course that will be an uppercut to the ego for him. We will need to be very careful about how that's done, if we find we need to." Atwan stops talking, then starts shuffling through paperwork on his desk. Hussein and Dakham exchange surreptitious glances. *Is that it? Are we done here? What in the hell—*

Atwan suddenly looks up and interrupts their confused thoughts, as if there had been no break in the conversation. "Overall, you did well on your first assignment," he tells them. "I have one of our people checking into how much useable nuclear material we can expect to find in one of their projectiles."

"If our people think it is possible to use that material, do you think he's capable of dismantling the projectiles as we asked?" asks Dakham.

"He will do anything for the right price," Atwan says sarcastically.

"As I said, I told him I wanted samples to test the radioactive materials," says Hussein. "And warned him that my 'fourth cousin' would be most unhappy if everything were not of the same quality."

"How did he take that statement?"

"He doesn't like being threatened," says Hussein. "We assume he thinks he's invincible within Russia," adds Dakham.

"No one is invincible anywhere," Atwan states flatly. "Which is why we must see to it that he does not sell us out to a higher bidder. That would be a major mistake on his part." Atwan continues blandly. "So—go back to your homes and return here three weeks from today. You will be briefed for your conversation with Dimitri. Needless to say, I doubt I need to remind you not to discuss this assignment with anyone else. I would even prefer it if you do not discuss it with each other outside of these walls."

"Of course," says Hussein. Then, exhausted, he and Dakham rise slowly from the table and are escorted from the conference room to the front entrance. The door is held for them, and they step back out into the streets of Tehran.

Chapter Thirty-Four

Second Site

Natan Schwartz and Mark Silberberg are pleased to find that that their strength is up to par after phase one of their assignment; days of relatively inactivity can take their toll. They make it back to their buried supplies in roughly the same time as the trip north to Bampur had taken. Satisfied with their success at site one, they both feel cautiously optimistic about the remainder of the mission.

Their GPS coordinates are exact. It only takes fifteen minutes to dig down to the buried gear. The equipment they will need is well wrapped and free of sand—a supply of treated water, food and a change of clothes. They need to carry both sets of equipment at least as far as Jask, some 350 kilometers to the southwest, in the vicinity of their appointed pickup spot, where the submarine Renewal plans to meet them. Assuming all goes as intended, five or six nights of demanding terrain carrying heavy loads lays between them and this their next depot point.

The two are fastidious in leaving no trace of their presence behind them.

*

It takes three hard nights of travel to arrive near Jask. Again, they choose a remote area, dig in and bury their gear. They stow what they won't need for the next leg and refill the hole, disguising it well. "I suggest we move out a couple of hours, to distance ourselves from the site, just in case," proposes Schwartz.

"I agree. Let's head north until, say, 0430, then find ourselves a spot to sit out the daylight hours." The night is windy, which is annoying but also in their favor. As they travel, the wind saves them one chore, obliterating their tracks in the swirling sands. Wearing their night vision goggles and scarves over their noses and mouths, they head west until they come upon a well traveled road. They can move easily along this road, their tracks blending in with those already there.

Just before dawn, they pick a spot about one hundred meters north of the road, a small bowl amidst the dunes. Much to their liking, it is easily concealed. They dig out an area they can rest in while still maintaining vigilance under the camo cover they used at site one.

Staking the tarp in place, Silberberg flops down on the sand in its shadow. "Step one, cover. Step two, something to eat." As he opens yet another container of field rations, he groans. "Natan, how much I look forward to a nice home-cooked meal again. These preserved meals really suck, you know."

"Come on, enough bellyaching. It's only for about two to three more weeks, at the most," Schwartz chuckles, stretching before he wriggles into the confines of their new hole in the desert.

"I'll take the first three hours of watch," Silberberg offers. "It will give me time to savor my meal. Why don't you try to get some rest."

"Will do," Schwartz replies gratefully. "Just keep a sharp eye out for whatever might be traveling on that road to and from the direction of Bandar Abbas."

"I will," Silberberg says, "and from here on in, we need to get back to logging everything that moves. You never know what that could tell people back home."

Daylight brings some traffic on the roadway, in both directions. Most of it seems to be troop-transport military vehicles, but among them are a scattering of nomads, with their camels and their families. Both men are concerned about the possibility of nomads wandering off the road and discovering them. Their rules of engagement are to leave no witnesses.

*

After two more nights of travel they draw near the provincial capital of Bandar Abbas, a city with a population of roughly 350,000. Circling just to the north of the outlying village of Shaqu, they approach Bandar Abbas from the north till they are beyond the naval installation, then make their way due south, skirting cautiously around a scattering of tiny houses and make-shift truck depots until they reach the sea, just to the west of the navy base. A chain-link fence, most probably electrified, delineates the western perimeter. A good fifty meters of no-man's land lies empty between the fence and the compound within.

Laying on their bellies looking through their field glasses, Silberberg says, "Holy shit, Natan, how do they expect us to get close enough to find out about their Kilos? Everything looks tighter than a drum around the place."

"You're right," Schwartz whispers. "Let's not worry about it yet. Let's just get ourselves dug in. Tomorrow we can worry about how we pull this off."

"Bampur was a Boy Scout exercise compared to this."

"Right again," says Schwartz, always the voice of reason. "Just hang on to the fact that we've always been able to figure our way out of impossible situations before. Let's see what we need to do to work this one out. We definitely can't get inside this place or we may never get out. Let's try and find out a weak link in this fencing."

With some time left before dawn, the two men move parallel to the fencing heading in the direction of the water. The fence stops about six meters from the water's edge, then turns at a right angle toward what appears to be a docking area for Iranian naval vessels.

"I think we may have just found our weak link, Mark. They must be more concerned about entry into the base from land, I suspect. I'll lay you odds they think no one will get by their patrol boats, and therefore are less concerned with someone coming in from the sea. From the corner of this fencing, we should be able to pick up plenty of conversation, and maybe get lucky enough to hear something about the Kilos. And, if necessary, we could probably crawl along the fencing a ways to get in closer."

"You're right. Let's go dig our gopher hole," Silberberg says. "But before we start that, I need to take a piss, and am I ever tired of doing it lying on my side. It will be great to be able to stand up again in front of a urinal."

Schwartz just smiles. He knows the feeling.

*

Taking cover behind an earthworks that was most probably thrown up to reinforce the fencing, the two dig in about twenty meters off the corner of the fence. Once again, their desert camo tarp blends in well with the surroundings, providing them good cover. Silberberg takes the first watch.

Daylight brings a steady stream of naval vessels into the harbor area. Some pass close enough that whoever's standing watch is able, with the help of binoculars, to see the faces of those men topside.

They have carried the conversation-monitoring equipment with them from both sets of gear, the second set as backup, just in case anything in the first one malfunctions. Each daylight hour brings new vessels into the harbor; an almost equal number exit. Their data and what conversations they can pick up are recorded. *This site at least provides more activity than the previous one*, thinks Schwartz as he makes note of the departure of an oil supertanker flying the flag of Latvia, though the lettering on its hull is in Cyrillic.

*

When darkness falls on this moonless night, Natan Schwartz tosses a few stones at the perimeter fence, to see if it's rigged with an alarm system. All remains quiet.

Slowly the two approach the fence, moving quietly along the length of it to see what lies ahead. It ends about one kilometer away at a two-meter stone wall that runs perpendicular to the fence. Taking out a scope with fiber-optic cable and a night screen, and standing right alongside the wall to avoid slipping, they are able to drop cable over the top so they can see what lies on the other side.

From behind the wall, they now have a bird's-eye view of the docking area. Clearly visible are destroyers, high-speed patrol boats and two submarines at dockside. A number of guards are stationed outside one particular building near the submarines. "Interesting," Schwartz mumbles to Silberberg. "The base appears secure enough in itself not to require even more guards for any of its interior buildings."

They retract the fiber optic cable and retrace their steps to their base. Every step they take requires the elimination of the footprint it creates. Here they must take no chances.

Back at their the base, Schwartz puts together an encrypted message about what they've been able to see so far what little, badly garbled conversation they've been able to record. He also asks Bergman to see if a satellite can get any readings off that building being guarded inside the dock area. Within ten minutes he has created and sent the message via a satellite burst.

He expects that tomorrow will bring more of the same.

*

At Mossad headquarters, Bergman has been waiting eagerly to hear from the team as to whether or not they have reached Bandar Abbas. When his message light goes off, his nerves jump, worried at what he will find in the incoming message. He has expected this aspect of the mission to be the most difficult; he knows the base at Bandar Abbas will not be child's play.

But when he'd read and reread Schwartz's message, he still cannot believe his eyes. Not only have they arrived at Bandar Abbas intact, but they have already been able to transmit hard data as well. In the morning he will report to Wattenberg.

*

At the National Security Agency's headquarters at Fort Meade, Maryland, Jerry Daniels is still keeping an eye—or in this case, several satellite eyes—on his mystery pair, tracking them by heat measurement since they left Bampur. They travel by night, so he too has been working nights, for the most part. To his amazement, they return to their original set of coordinates near the coastline. The following night they turn westward.

Five nights later, he has them roaming around Bandar Abbas. Daniels knows what's at Bandar Abbas. *The balls!* he thinks. *This report's going right on Jim Stewart's desk.*

*

Wattenberg arrives at the office at his usual predictable hour. No surprise; the man prides himself on being punctual. Bergman allows him enough time to get his first cup of coffee before he nails him.

"Ariel, I need your time before anyone else does."

"How do you rate?" Wattenberg says gruffly.

"Because I do, that's why. We have word from the team from Bandar Abbas. They are there, Ariel. They have already sent an abundance of information about ship movements, classes of vessels, and the fact that two Kilos are docked. They've also requested that our satellite monitor a building being guarded inside of the base, right near dockside. There have seen no other building under heavy guard."

"Is our satellite as good as the Americans' for getting that kind of information?" asks Wattenberg.

"It better be," Bergman replies. "We bought it from them."

"Yosef, Yosef," Wattenberg chides him. "You know America is not going to sell us their best product—these they keep for themselves. But what we have will be more than adequate for the job. Make it happen and give me a report as soon as you have something."

*

Three days go by without any change in routine for Silberberg and Schwartz. The fourth day is like a gift from God. Just after noon, Silberberg gets a fix on five men walking down to the water's edge, just outside of the fence line. Silberberg directs the voice recorder and listens in as he records.

The men seem to be in discussion about something they are all working on. Silberberg assumes them to be engineers. The men change out of their clothes, which they leave on the rocks, and get into swim trunks. They spend about an hour in the water, swimming and taking part in some lighthearted grab-assing, as young men tend to do.

After they get out of the water, towel off and change back into their clothes, they start heading back up along the fence line. Silberberg hears a tall, bulky-bearded one say, "We deserved that swim. Our reward. Our work is done, praise Allah. Now it is up to the Revolutionary Council to arrange for testing. This new missile will work just as well as any American cruise missile, and won't they be surprised."

"Yes," says another, "and so will the Israelis."

Silberberg wakes Schwartz after the Iranians are well out of hearing, and plays the recording back for him. When the voices fade out, Schwartz and Silberberg sit staring at each other. Silberberg is speechless. "This is it," Schwartz whispers. "This is what we came for."

Both men decide not to circulate tonight and take any chance of being observed and caught. At 2400, they will send their message out, high priority.

*

"Okay, Jerry, so this team you're watching is now sitting somewhere around Bandar Abbas. What do you want me to do?" Jim Stewart asks.

"Look Jim, we were told to watch out for the unusual. I'm convinced that this team could be Israeli. And wouldn't you consider having two Israelis sitting outside of Iran's largest naval base a bit unusual?"

"Okay, put it into a report and I'll send it up the line. High priority."

*

Bergman hasn't heard much from the team for four nights. On the fifth night, he receives Silberberg's recordings. *My God*, he thinks, *this is it. We are in serious trouble.*

On his own authority, Bergman orders the team off the site and to give him twenty-four hours to co-ordinate their ride home.

That very night Silberberg and Schwartz pack up everything they have and refill the site they dug out for themselves. They leave nothing to indicate they were there, just as they did in Bampur. They start moving. Again fast, heading southeast towards Jask.

*

The next morning, Bergman is sitting in Wattenberg's office waiting for him to come in.

"So who gave you authority to be in my office without me?" asks Wattenberg, feigning aggravation.

"Ariel, no time for games," Bergman says hurriedly, jumping to his feet. "I've had very little sleep for the last three weeks, and this thing is suddenly starting to get serious. Here, listen to this." He had brought a tape recorder with him. Punching the play button, the voices of the two Iranians come through loud and clear.

As Wattenberg listens, his face goes pale. "If this is true," Wattenberg says, struggling to put unwelcome thoughts into words, "not only can Iran strike us with the new long-range missiles we know they have—now they can fire missiles from those damn Kilos off our coast." He turns to face Bergman directly. "Who else knows about this recording?"

"Only our team, you and I."

"Realistically, do you think they can find out any more information?" Wattenberg asks.

Bergman shakes his head conclusively. "No—I pulled them off site last night, so they wouldn't be found. This is so serious, I thought it best. They are headed to a rendezvous site to be withdrawn."

*

Jerry Daniels, holding a cup of coffee, leans on the doorjamb of his boss's office. "Just for your information, Jim, that team's on the move again. It looks like they're heading back where they came from. I'll bet a week's pay they're getting their tails outta there."

"I never bet where the Israelis are concerned," Stewart says seriously. "Keep your eyes open for what happens next, Jerry. I'll be talking to the director about this later today."

Chapter Thirty-Five

Leaving No Traces

Silberberg and Schwartz double-time it for one night, burrowing themselves into the sand during the daylight hours, eager to get off of Iranian sand and soil. Schwartz sends a message burst to Bergman that reads, "Requesting taxi 26x57.5 0200. Inform driver will confirm departure 15m before. Will be waiting with our luggage."

Bergman receives Schwartz's message and immediately forwards it as an encrypted message to the Renewal via satellite, adding "Confirm receipt of this message with me within twelve hours of transmission."

*

Aboard the Renewal, the radio shack records the encrypted message and notifies the captain he's needed; high priority messages must be signed for. Captain Katz makes his way down from the control room and enters the radio room.

Reading the message, he smiles. *They did it again,* he thinks, then advises the radioman to send out an encrypted confirmation and log the message.

Leaving the radio room he heads back to the control room. Entering, he advises his XO and the navigator to set course for the coordinates in the message he hands them. "I want us there at 0130, to pick up the team at 0200," he tells them. "XO, have Greenberg and Michaelson meet you and me in the wardroom at 1500. I want to go over the pickup with them personally."

*

At 2000, Schwartz and Silberberg pack up their gear, refill the depression they dug and head out to pick up the gear they had left on the shore line at Jask.

At 0115 they arrive at the GPS coordinates where they buried the rest of their gear. Silberberg starts digging while Schwartz sets up a satellite message to send Renewal. The message sent, both men place everything into the carry packs they brought with them. They cover the hole where the gear was stowed, then drag the packs down to the water's edge, again insuring that all traces of their tracks are erased.

At the water's edge, they attach the floatation devices they used coming ashore and slip into their scuba suits and fins. Moving slowly so as not to make any unnecessary noise, they slip into the water and walk their equipment out just to the point where they would have to swim.

*

Brian Greenberg and Hal Michaelson are moving swiftly under the surface to the rendezvous point on the GPS unit that Brian carries. Less than halfway to the rendezvous point, Brian gasps. The GPS unit has quit functioning. *Shit,* thinks Brian. Not now. Brian signals to Hal, miming the fact that the GPS unit has failed.

Hal points to the surface, suggesting they should go up. Brian nods in agreement and they both head upwards. On the surface, they are relieved to find the sea empty around them. Brian looks at his compass, points to the visible shoreline and signals Michaelson to follow him. As they proceed closer to shore, Brian consults his compass repeatedly.

Around 0200, Silberberg hears the first traces of motor sounds. "Natan, I think Brian and Hal are here," he whispers.

"Let's wait a few more seconds, Mark. I don't want to blow this now," Schwartz responds, straining to hear what Silberberg has heard. Finally he smiles in agreement. Five seconds later, they see the flicker of red lights, the go-ahead signal they have been waiting for. Schwartz responds with three flashes of his light, gets one in response, then he and Silberberg start swimming towards the sleds.

Both Brian and Hal are pleased to see the two men, but they are more concerned with attaching the equipment and getting down below. Brian explains that their GPS unit failed on them and asks if their unit will operate underwater. Silberberg says, "No problem. Ours could operate on the surface of the moon, if necessary."

Hal says, "We don't need to go that far to test it. Let's get out of here."

Schwartz and Silberberg slip into their oxygen tanks and each slides onto a sled behind one of the drivers sent to pick them up. Both sleds drop below the surface and head back to the Renewal.

As the sleds approach, Captain Katz orders her main deck to the surface. A group of sailors swarm out onto the deck to help all four men get aboard quickly. The sleds are dropped down the forward hatch for storage, and as soon as the hatches are secure, the Renewal drops below the surface, turns to course 180 degrees and maintains a depth of two hundred meters.

As soon as Schwartz and Silberberg remove their dive suits, the boat's medical officer is waiting to check the registrations on their dosimeters. Both meters read a satisfactory level of radiation, nothing more than what one would see on a nuclear submarine. Then, and only then, are they invited to the wardroom by the captain.

"It is nice to have you safely back aboard, my friends," he says warmly. "I trust your mission was successful. I hear we had GPS problems trying to retrieve you, though."

"Yes, captain," Schwartz states. "Everything went well for us, and we think we were able to record enough information for our people to better understand what's going on. Brian and Hal handled the GPS problem like pros."

"Good. We're heading home the same way we came. So now, besides a hot shower and a clean bunk, what would you gentlemen like?"

Silberberg doesn't have to think. "Something warm and home-cooked to eat," he tells the captain with a grin. "I can't choke down one more crappy field ration, no matter what delicious meal it claims to be on the label."

Laughing, the captain says, "Not a problem. Go get yourselves cleaned up. I'll have the wardroom cook get up and make whatever you want."

"A few fried eggs, some roasted potatoes, toast and a bottomless cup of coffee would be great," sighs Schwartz.

"Gentlemen, you've earned it. Just please remember that the restrictions of movement you had as we came are still in enforcement, since you're technically civilians."

"Yes, sir!" reply both men, snapping to attention and offering mock salutes as they do so. Schwartz salutes with his left hand; Silberberg's bisects his forehead. Captain Katz can't help but grin and shake his head. "The sooner we get you two goons off this ship, the better."

The captain then goes to the radio room and tells the radioman on duty to send an encrypted message. "Time: 0300 hours," he dictates. "Zulu, your birds have been picked up and are resting in the coop. End of message. SK."

*

Bergman receives the message and after reading the encryption, smiles. This good news calls for a good night's sleep. Tomorrow will come soon enough to have further discussions with Wattenberg. Debriefing will start as soon as the team arrives, and promises to be very interesting.

Chapter Thirty-Six

After Labor Day

President William Egan is sitting at his desk in the Oval Office. Sitting expectantly before him with their regular morning reports are Allison McDonald and John Walker. "I read both of your briefs over breakfast this morning," he begins, "and I must say, both of them are most interesting—to say the least. I'd like to hear your personal thoughts. Allison, ladies first."

"Well, sir," McDonald starts, "the most critical areas of my report relate to three issues: Bampur, Russian Kilos and the Russian mafiya. I'll start with Bampur." The president nods.

"You already know that we sent an operative we have inside Iran to get as close to Bampur as he could, to see if we could clarify the situation. Believing that the Israelis had a team on the ground and moving towards Bampur, we needed to be able to advise you on what's going on there. Our operative, a native, dressed himself as a nomad traveling across the desert. He had two camels with him, and only carried things that someone with his persona would." At this point, McDonald consults notes in her lap.

"As of 28 August, he was a week overdue returning home. Another operative was sent in to see if he could find him, which he did. Both our contact and the camels were shot to death. It appears that they were machine-gunned to death about five miles from Bampur. What that means exactly, we can't say. Most bandits do not carry machine guns for weapons. We suspect that he was murdered merely because he was close to Bampur. His personal belongings were strewn everywhere, we were told, leading us to believe that whoever murdered him and his animals were trying to find out if he was legit."

"Sounds like a logical conclusion," the president commented.

"Next, the Russian Kilos," McDonald goes on. "Earlier I mentioned the fact that the Russians had sold two more Kilos to the Iranians. At the time, we estimated that we could expect to see a delivery of anywhere from eighteen to twenty-four months from now. However, we now think that window has shrunk, to ten to twelve months. The Iranians have four now. We can't help but wonder what the rush is for the updated delivery."

"Good question," President Egan said quietly, then nodded for her to continue.

"Third, our contacts in Russia have observed two men masquerading as Pakistanis who have made a number of visits to one Dimitri Kostovich. Kostovich is a mid-level boss in the Russian mafiya. Now we hear he's searching for weapons-grade uranium for these two men, who we suspect are Iranians."

"Those all represent concerns," agrees the president. "What's of immediate urgency to me is why the Iranians are trying to purchase weapons-grade material when they are also trying to mass-produce it themselves? Something is starting to smell here, and there are no fish out of the pond yet. John, what do you have to add?"

"Well, suh," Walker drawls, "we're purty certain that a Dolphin-class sub from Israel dropped off a team of two onto Iranian shores. We been monitorin' them, from the time they landed. Their destination, it turns out, was Bampur. They spent three and a half days there, then headed back to their drop point. At first we figgered they were headin' out, then, for whatever reason, they turned around and went to Bandar Abbas."

"The Iranian naval base," says the President, rubbing his chin.

"Yes, suh, that's the one. Bear in mind we're trackin' them only by heat sourcin'—they were travelin' in total darkness. But our equipment's purty damned exceptional and we have confidence in our findin's. So, then they camped out around Bandar Abbas for five days. What they found out, who knows, but then they headed eastward for one night. Then, it appears, they were retrieved by submarine, somewhere around Jask, the middle of the second night."

"Jesus, those guys have balls. Excuse me, Allison," the president says, after the fact.

"I've heard worse, sir," McDonald grimaces. "Don't worry about it."

"Suh, NSA feels that Israel must have 'dentified what they went in for. The real issue heah is will they be sharin' whatever that is with us?"

"John, you say in your report that the sub picked them up about thirty-six hours ago. They surely won't return to Israel through the Suez Canal, which means they have to be going home the long way. Which means the powers that be in Israel won't have a real handle on it for at least ten days.

"Allison, I want you to call Ariel Wattenberg in two weeks. I want you to tell him we'd like to have him visit the U.S. to discuss the status of things going on in Iran. Tell him that you and John will be meeting with him. Don't tell him that we'll be holding the meeting here in the Oval Office."

"Yes, sir."

"Allison, I wish to commend you on keeping us on our toes with this Iranian situation. With Israel making such bold moves, I have to think that more's going on here than we realize. We can't afford to get behind the eight-ball on this one. These people play for keeps over there."

Turning his attention back to both of them, he continues, "Let's keep the information coming and, either of you, please call me with anything you feel might be urgent. No need to wait for the morning reports."

Walker and McDonald smile thinly in return. They know that if the president were to compute his paycheck by the hour—including all the lost hours of sleep—he probably makes a lot less than your average certified public accountant.

When they're both back out in the hallway, Walker turns to his counterpart from the CIA. "Hey, girl," he says condescendingly, "that was a great presentation,"

"What's this' hey, girl' stuff?" McDonald stops him cold. "Wake up, John. I've grown up. They tend to call that being a woman." She gives him a mirthless wink. "Though, I must say, you didn't do too badly in there yourself—boy."

"Touché!"

Chapter Thirty-Seven

Two Days Later

Atwan ushers Hussein and Dakham into the conference room of the Iranian Secret Police building, the same room in which they were debriefed weeks earlier, tells them to take a seat, and hands each one of them a set of papers. "You're going to call our friend Dimitri and ask him how he's coming with removal of the uranium materials from the warheads that he offered you," Atwan started. "Kamil, I want you to lead the conversation. You will both be on a speaker phone so, Hamid, you will be involved in the conversation with Dimitri as well."

Hussein asks, "What happens if he doesn't have an answer for us, or if he says he's just not interested?"

"Act as if it does not worry you. Tell him you're also talking to another source. If he doesn't have an answer within seven days, you won't be considering him any longer, regardless. He needs the pressure turned up on him."

"Suppose he tells us he's removed the materials and is ready to negotiate?" Dakham asks.

"Then you work from the documents I just gave you," Atwan answers him, "which basically cover what you say on the subject of setting up means and standards for testing the material. He will most probably want to set a price upfront. You're authorized to offer him up to a half a million American dollars to obtain a sample of the material to be tested. Based on test results we'll then consider further negotiations."

Dakham asks, "How are we to transport the sample for testing?"

"Needless to say, before you place the call to Dimitri, both of you will have read these documents." Atwan holds up his own set. "Everything is explained in detail. If you talk to Dimitri in this manner, using the terminology you will find in there, it'll sound like you handle matters similar to this all the time. Now, I want you to take a half an hour and read and discuss these between yourselves. Decide who'll handle what. I'll return to sit in on your conversation. You're to let him know that he's on speaker phone and able to converse with the two of you. He's not to know that I am in the room."

Scanning the pages before them, Hussein and Dakham are amazed that someone in the secret police compiled this presentation. *This guy must think he's the next Shakespeare. This reads more like a play than a phone conversation*, thinks Hussein. *And he's not much of a playwright, at that. They think we can just read this and sound real to Dimitri? They're out of their minds.*

Both Dakham and Hussein get to work, highlighting words and ideas they might want to use in the phone conversation.

*

True to his word, Atwan shows up a half hour later. "Well, gentlemen. Any questions?"

"No questions," says Hussein. "We understand what you want to us do, and what you want us to cover. However, we need to use our own words or this is going to come off all wrong."

"Why do you say that? You think our writer doesn't know what he's doing?"

Uh-oh, Hussein thinks. *Maybe it's Atwan who thinks he's the next Shakespeare* . . . "No, no, Jibril," he hurries to say, "it's just that Dimitri knows what we sound like in conversation. I need to start this the way I'd normally talk—not the way somebody else would. What's really important is that we get all your points across." Dakham is nodding his agreement as Hussein speaks.

"All right, expert," Atwan says to Hussein. "Dial the number, and make sure you're effective. Leave space for Hamid to say something so that he knows you two are still in this together."

Hussein lifts the receiver, then pushes the button for the Pakistani line. He recognizes the number as the same number he called from within Russia. After dialing, the call is routed through Pakistan for both incoming and outgoing calls. It rings four times before someone finally picks it up.

"Who's this?" says a voice that could be Dimitri's.

"Who am I speaking with?" says Hussein.

"Dimitri Kostovich. Who is this?"

"Dimitri, this is Kamil and I have Hamid with me on speaker phone, so that we can both hear you."

"You were supposed to call me in two weeks," Dimitri says. "It's now three weeks."

"Yes, I know, and I apologize." The expression on Hussein's face is not one of apology. "I did mention that we have other clients who also take up our time."

"Dimitri," Dakham cuts in. "Have you found a way to disassemble the goods we discussed in your office?"

"It can be done," Dimitri tells them, "but we have not started yet, since we have not heard from you. You need to know that if we do remove the materials that you want, the rest of the items become just worthless junk for us to dispose of. You will need to purchase the complete units, even if you only want part of them."

Hussein smiles. *This guy is full of shit, right up to his ears. But he has what we want.*

"When can you provide us with a sample of your merchandise, for us to test the quality of your goods?" Hussein asks. "Our people tell us that the part you'll be removing will weigh slightly less than two hundred twenty-seven grams."

"We will have to talk money first."

Dakham steps into the conversation. "Before we talk money, Dimitri, you need to know that we'll be providing you with a shipping container, and will handle all transportation arrangements. All you will need to do is remove the goods, place them in the container and seal the package."

Hussein now says, "We will forward you three-hundred thousand American dollars along with the container. After our testing we can arrive at a package price, providing all of the goods are of the same quality."

"You think I would cheat you?" Dimitri says, sounding infuriated.

Of course you wouldn't—unless you get the chance, Dakham thinks.

And I'm sure your expression no more mirrors your own words than mine does my words, Hussein assumes, grinning over at Dakham. "Really,

Dimitri, the thought of you cheating us has never entered our minds," Hussein assures him calmly.

"However," Dimitri continues to thunder, "three-hundred thousand is far too low!"

"Well, we don't think so," Dakham responds, sounding a bit irritated himself. "We have no idea how long the goods have been sitting around, how much they may have deteriorated. Look, we'll make this more than worth your while—once we know that everything is as you say."

"Call back in a week," Dimitri cuts him short. "I will tell you where to send the deposit and the container. Euros—no dollars. The global money market stinks right now. You understand."

Hussein looks towards Atwan who gives him the high sign. "Fine. So long as we are satisfied, Dimitri," Hussein says, then hangs up. Both he and Dakham immediately look to Atwan.

"I will tell my script writer to call you two in the next time he has ideas. You will call Dimitri back in ten days, not one week. He must not feel like he's in control."

Chapter Thirty-Eight

Second Week of September

Ten days after picking up Schwartz and Silberberg, the Renewal cruises into home port.

Captain Katz and executive officer Micah Rubin both watch them as they depart from the prow of the sub and onto the pier. The four of them have already said goodbye below decks, to call as little attention to their departure as possible. No need to offer unknown eyes anything unusual to witness. Four sailors carry the team's equipment and place it on the pier next to a blue van which sits idling there. Schwartz and Silberberg are happy to be on dry land. They are surprised to find they still feel drained and tired even after the restful trip back to Israel.

Standing just within the conning tower, Rubin muses. "Will we ever know what they learned, Captain?"

"Most likely not, Micah, which is probably for the best. So long as what they learned is well utilized by the powers-that-be. Those are two very brave young men. I'm glad to see they have returned safely."

As soon as Schwartz and Silberberg step off the gangway, Bergman jumps down from the back of the van and gives each of them a warm handshake. Without a word, he helps them quickly load their equipment, then the three get inside and head off the base. He waits to speak until they have passed through the gates and are several blocks away. When he finally feels the coast is clear, he offers them a hearty welcome home. "We are expected at headquarters. The first thing we want you to do, of course, is to call your families and let them know you're back safe. Then we'll sit you down for a debriefing—something we are sure you're quite familiar with from your IDF days." Silberberg groans at the memories.

In an hour, they pull up in front of Mossad headquarters. Wattenberg is there to greet them as soon as they walk through the door. He escorts them down the corridor, to an elevator that takes them down to the same secure room where Yosef Bergman, Shlomo Herzl and Avi Singer met to create this idea that has come so fully to fruition.

Bergman shows them how to get an outside line to reach their families. He and Wattenberg then leave the room to give them some time alone. "Just let us know when you're ready for us by pushing the yellow button on the phone system. It will ring in Ariel's office and we'll be right down," says Bergman.

*

"Gentlemen, you have accomplished what we once thought would be impossible. Yosef's faith in your abilities has paid off. You've supplied us with a great deal of valuable information. Let's start with each of you describing everything, from your departure from the Renewal to your return to the Renewal. Then we'll share with you what we have learned from your efforts."

Schwartz begins and describes his recollections of the mission. After a meal break, Silberberg takes his turn. A tape recorder runs, and Wattenberg and Bergman both take pages of notes as well. Eight hours after Schwartz began, Silberberg finishes.

"Now, we assume you'd want to know what we have been able to learn from the data you provided us," says Wattenberg.

"Yes, that would be interesting," says Schwartz.

"First, Bampur," Wattenberg says. "From Bampur, we have come to the conclusion that the facility there is a processing plant, that the facility is highly secured, and that the facility is somewhat radioactive. Our nuclear specialists tell us that Bampur is not an enrichment plant—but that it's just as dangerous. They believe the Iranians are reprocessing plutonium at Bampur." Silberberg's eyebrows rise. Schwartz purses his lips and nods.

"At Bandar Abbas, you found four piers in the area where the Kilo subs are moored, though only two subs were there. What concerns us is that the Iranians are purchasing two more Kilos from Russia." Wattenberg let that thought hang in the air before continuing.

"You were able to monitor daily surface-vessel traffic, both into and out of Bandar Abbas, for four days, which gives us some idea of their naval timetables, at least as far as Bandar Abbas is concerned. The conversations you recorded from these surface vessels, when you could, were routine as far as naval vessels go—mostly gibberish from their crews."

"Wish we could have gotten better," Schwartz says. "We could only work with what we had."

"Trust me, you did fine," Wattenberg assures them. "Now, the building you requested we monitor by satellite seems to be some type of technical assembly room for engineers. We have been watching it now for over two weeks. Only five men have been using it, which leads us to think that it must hold something of a highly secret nature. Especially as it appears to be guarded twenty-four hours a day."

"That was our impression," Silberberg confirms and Wattenberg nods.

"Last but not least, the conversations you picked up from the five men who went swimming outside of the fence area, is nothing short of alarming. It sounds as if Iran is redesigning their latest missile to be capable of being fired from a submerged submarine. Not the kind of news you want to hear as we prepare to celebrate Rosh Hashanah, I'm afraid."

Both Schwartz and Silberberg register a degree of alarm appropriate to Wattenberg's remarks.

"Is there anything else you'd like to add to this report?"

"No, Ariel, I think Mark and I would just like to go back to civilian life," Schwartz says for the both of them.

"One more thing, every piece of equipment you used is yours to keep."

Chapter Thirty-Nine

End of September

The president buzzes his secretary. "Janet, I need to speak with Yaakov Brumwell on a secure line."

"Yes, sir." Janet hangs up.

Five minutes later, Janet calls through to the president. "Sir, Prime Minister Brumwell is at a dinner meeting with members of the Knesset. I've left word for him to contact you after the dinner. Will that do?"

"Yes, that's fine, Janet. With seven hours' time difference, I'm not surprised you didn't find him in his office. Interrupt me when he calls, it is very important that I speak with him." Three in the afternoon, Washington time, is 2200 hours Israeli time.

*

Prime Minister Brumwell receives the message and heads for his office. When the president of the United States calls, you don't put him off until tomorrow. As requested, the prime minister selects a secure line and dials the White House. The call is forwarded to Janet White, who in turn advises the president that the prime minister is holding on a secure line.

President Egan picks up his phone. "Mr. Prime Minister, how was your dinner?"

"Well, Mr. President, dinner was the usual stuff, but I have to tell you, the Knesset discussion was more than enlightening for a change. However, you don't call me this late in the day without good reason,"

Yaakov says, quickly bringing the subject around to weightier matters. "What's going on?"

"Well, Yaakov, a certain situation has surfaced that we need to clear up immediately."

"A certain situation, Bill? Can you be more specific?"

"We identified one of your Dolphin subs off the coast of Iran a couple of weeks ago. We know the submarine placed a covert team inside of Iran."

Yaakov Brumwell says nothing.

"The Navy advised me regarding the drop and I ordered our National Security people to monitor the team," President Egan continues. "We tracked them to Bampur and then to Bandar Abbas. We do know that they've departed Iran, we assume also by submarine. I didn't want to contact you until the team was back on your soil."

"If what you say is true, sir," Yaakov says, choosing his words carefully, "I will have to check with our IDF to find out who authorized such a mission. It would be highly irregular for us to attempt to enter Iran."

"Well, we think so too, Yaakov. However, your people may have decided that it was necessary."

"Give me a couple of days, Bill, and I will get back to you."

"Fair enough." *You sly old fox,* Egan thinks. *Got yourself caught in the hen house, did you?*

*

The prime minister dials Ariel Wattenberg, who had just laid down to go to sleep when his bedside secure phone rings.

"Wattenberg," Wattenberg mumbles.

"What have you got scheduled tomorrow morning, first thing?" Wattenberg sits up, realizing the prime minister is on the other end of the line.

"I have a couple of meetings within the organization. Why?"

"Cancel them and be in my office at 0800. It seems that Uncle Sam has been observing our team and wants us to know it," Yaakov Brumwell says.

"How on earth did they do that?" Wattenberg responds, his mind just now fully waking up.

"I'll fill you in on the details in the morning, Ariel. Just be there." The prime minister hangs up the phone.

Wattenberg's night's sleep is ruined. His mind races, trying to think of all the ramifications of such knowledge on the Americans' part. Finally, some four hours later, he falls into a deep sleep.

*

At 0730, the prime minister advises his secretary that she's to cancel his first two morning appointments. "When Ariel Wattenberg arrives, have him come to my office immediately," he tells her.

Wattenberg arrives at 0745 and is shown directly to the prime minister's office. He wastes no time with formalities. "What the hell happened, Yaakov? Who told them what we did?"

"Nobody told them," the prime minister says calmly. "My best guess is that one of their nuclear subs was cruising off the coast of Iran and happened to notice our sub dispatch the team. Their report prompted closer satellite monitoring, which enabled someone with a quick eye to pick up the team before it got to Bampur. The Americans are aware of their entire route from that point on. What they don't know is what we learned, and this is what this conversation is really about."

"So, what do you plan on telling them?"

"I told the president that I'd return his call in a couple of days," Yaakov says. "The day after tomorrow, I plan to call him and tell him I'm sending you to Washington to meet with him."

Wattenberg blinks in surprise. "To tell him—what? That we put a covert team into Iran? To tell him everything we learned while they were there?"

"Ariel, I think it is time to address the fact that we may need help with this situation," Yaakov says pragmatically. "If Iranian submarines obtain the technology to fire cruise submarine-based missiles, we'd never be able to detect them before it was too late. It's hard enough to detect land-based missiles. I believe you told me that in one of those conversations they monitored, something was said about how the Americans were going to be surprised. I want you to play that up really big in Washington."

"If I do that, might they say that we already knew this, yet never let them know anything until they called us?"

"No, you will say that we are just getting the data now. They don't have to know when we first got it."

"When do I leave, Yaakov?"

"I will call President Egan the day after tomorrow and ask him when he can meet with you."

"Are we through, as least for now, Yaakov?"

"Yes," says Yaakov. "Just remember, Ariel, this is not the fault of anyone on the team. Maybe it will turn out to be a bit of divine providence for us."

Divine providence? Frustrated, Wattenberg leaves the prime minister's office and heads directly to his own.

*

Two days later, the prime minister calls President Egan.

"Mr. Prime Minister. I wondered if you'd forgotten about me," Egan complains.

"Now how could I forget a promise I made to you?" Yaakov says lightly.

"What did you find out?" *No point in beating around the bush*, the president thinks.

"You're correct, Mr. President. We made an insertion. I'm having Ariel Wattenberg, the director of Mossad, fly to Washington to meet with you, to brief you completely. We are just compiling the details from the team. It includes something of concern to your country. You will want to meet with him. When can that happen?"

"How serious is this, Yaakov?"

"Well, on a scale of one to ten, Bill, let's say it is a twenty."

"Can you get him here in the Oval Office within seventy-two hours?"

"He'll be there."

President Egan hangs up and calls Allison McDonald and John Walker on a conference line. "Allison, by any chance have you connected with the Mossad director yet?"

"No sir. I was planning on doing that tomorrow," replies McDonald.

"I confronted the prime minister on this insertion. He's sending Ariel Wattenberg here in seventy-two hours. It seems this team of theirs has learned something critical to the United States."

"You sure this isn't just some foot jockeyin' by the Israelis, suh?" remarks John Walker.

"I can't answer you, John, until I listen to what he has to say. I want both of you at that meeting."

"Yes, sir," they both respond, Walker's 'suh' overpowering Allison's.

"Janet will give you the particulars. If he's going to give us some detailed information, I want you to give him what you gave me the other morning. I have a feeling that, from that and what's happening with Mossad, we should be starting to look at some kind of reciprocal support here. Think about it. If you need to talk, contact me before he comes to town."

The president hangs up. *What the hell has Israel learned that could be vital to the United States? This visit from the director of Mossad could very well be the beginning of World War III.*

Chapter Forty

Seventy-Two Hours Later

Ariel Wattenberg's flight lands in Baltimore, and he is whisked away to the White House by limousine. He's not used to the nature of the American Secret Service personnel. As they roll up to the south gate, he's given an ID which allows him only to visit the Oval Office. When Secret Service escorts him directly to the president's secretary's desk, he finds himself standing in front of Janet White.

"Young lady, I have an appointment with the president," Wattenberg says a bit stiffly.

Smiling up at him, Janet says, "You are expected, Mr. Wattenberg. The president will be with you shortly. In the meantime, I do have to ask you for your papers. Just a formality, you understand."

"Of course," he says. As Wattenberg provides Janet with his ID, he's both relived and pleased to see Allison McDonald come around the corner.

"Janet, he's with me," she says. "When will the president be available?"

"In about fifteen minutes, Allison," Janet tells her. "You and Mr. Wattenberg may take a seat."

A few moments later, John Walker comes around the corner and sees McDonald and . . . he has a momentary memory lapse, forgetting the name of the director of Mossad. Sensing John's dilemma, McDonald comes to the rescue.

"John, Ariel Wattenberg," she says cheerfully.

"Of course, sir," Walker says smiling broadly as he shakes Wattenberg's hand. "Good to meet you."

"And you, Mr. Walker," Wattenberg says without hesitation or prompting.

Walker has to work to keep his smile in place as he catches McDonald's wink. "The president will see the three of us in about ten minutes, John," she adds.

Walker attempts small talk with Wattenberg, which keeps hitting dead ends. McDonald, on the other hand, seems to have no trouble engaging him. *They're peers*, he consoles himself. *Course they're gonna hit it off.*

After what seems an eternity, to Walker at least, Janet's intercom buzzes. She picks up the phone, then tells the three, "The President will see you now."

"Ariel, how good to meet you," says Egan as he stands, extending his offer of a handshake. Wattenberg grips the hand of the president and is pleased that Egan's shake shows strength of character. "Allison and John, I'm happy that you could meet with Ariel and myself. You've all met, I assume." They nod.

McDonald and Walker sit down across from the president and the Mossad director. Egan gets the discussion rolling. "Ariel, I suppose that the prime minister filled you in why I called him and what feedback he was able to give me. It wasn't much, to tell you the truth."

"Yes, sir, he did. At the time you called him, he was not aware of the nature of our insertion. We were still interpreting the materials our team brought back from inside of Iran."

What a bunch of bullshit, Egan thinks. *This operation had to be sanctioned by the prime minister. Mossad doesn't have that kind of authority.* "All right, Ariel, you've been sent here by the prime minister. Can you share with us why Israel took such a risk, sending a covert team into Iran?"

"Mr. President, you know the current president of Iran has been spitting out venom for a long time regarding the destruction of Israel. We received information that Bampur was another of a growing list of facilities capable of producing materials that could be used in nuclear weapons. We have also received information that they were in the midst of purchasing two more Kilo submarines from Russia."

President Egan replies, "We know of a number of facilities producing weapons grade materials. They already have four Kilos. What makes Bampur different, and what makes two more subs big news for you?"

"Their Shahab-3—outfitted with a nuclear warhead, capable of being fired from a submarine, represents very big news to us. In fact, it may be something America should be concerned about as well. It turns out, however, that Bampur is not enriching uranium. It is reprocessing plutonium." Wattenberg stuns the Americans into silence. All three stare at each other in alarm. *Damn*, thinks Egan, *this is new. No, this we weren't aware of.*

"John, why don't you share with Ariel how we found out about his insertion and how we monitored their movements until they departed," the president prompts his National Security advisor.

Walker goes into detailed explanation, from the time the Los Angeles-class submarine tracked their sub, to the National Security satellites tracking the team's return to the shoreline of Iran.

Wattenberg smiles thinly. "I have to say, I'm not surprised that this happened. I'm just terribly thankful it was not an Iranian submarine." The three Americans nod at the thought.

"Ariel," the president asks, "are you hearing anything about the Russian mafiya working with the Iranians?"

"No, sir, not to the best of my knowledge."

"Allison, tell Ariel what your contacts found around Bampur after his team left, what we know of the two remaining Kilos in Russia and the mafiya."

McDonald shares with Wattenberg the substance of her most recent report to the president. Again, Wattenberg is not surprised at what he's hearing.

"Thank you for sharing this information, Ms. McDonald. It is most helpful." Wattenberg stops momentarily, as if considering where to take the conversation from here. When he resumes, his tone has become trusting, confidential.

"The real reason I'm here, on the orders of our prime minister, is the following: our team recorded some conversations between five individuals who were swimming just off of the base at Bandar Abbas. They appear to be engineers, assigned, we believe, to the redesign of their Shahab-3 missile so that it can be fired from one of their Kilos. The comments which should be of particular interest to you were, 'Won't the United States be surprised.' You are not alone, however. Another one of them said, 'So will Israel.' If that does not put both of our countries in the same boat, I don't know what does."

No one says a word for at least a full thirty seconds.

Finally, the president turns to face Wattenberg. "Ariel, is there anything more you want to add to this conversation?"

"No, Mr. President," Ariel responds, "not at this time. We are continuing to review the information we learned from within Iran. If we come up with anything significant, we'll certainly contact you."

"Ariel," replies the president, "can you stay for dinner this evening or must you be returning immediately to Israel?"

"Thank you, Bill. I appreciate your kind invitation," Wattenberg says formally. "However, I plan on having dinner on the plane, and some much-needed sleep as well."

"All right then, let's call it a day," Egan says. "We thank you for coming. I will have the Secret Service escort you out. Allison, John, please stay behind. We have much to discuss."

Both of them acknowledge him with serious nods.

Chapter Forty-One

Pushing for a Sample

Ten days after speaking with Dimitri, Hussein and Dakham call him back, again on a speaker phone. As before, Atwan is in the room.

As soon as the phone is answered Hussein says, "Dimitri, do you have our sample ready for pickup?"

"What? Who is this?" Then realizing, he says, "You were supposed to call me back in one week. Can't you people count?"

"Of course we can count. We are three days late. Our schedule has been hectic."

"Yeah, yeah," Dimitri says dismissively. "I have your sample. You realize you can't leave this stuff sitting around like a loaf of bread."

"How much does it weigh and what size container do you need?" Dakham asks. "And do you want the container sent to your warehouse or to another location?"

"The sample weighs about twenty-four grams, nearly one ounce in mass. You can figure what size container from that. Send it to the warehouse where we first met. I assume you have the address."

"All right, Dimitri, this is what we will do. Hamid is going to send you a titanium container with a lead lining. We are going to ship you this container via United Parcel Service overnight. Your people will place the sample in this container and lead seal it so it cannot be tampered with. UPS will provide you with a return shipping label that will enable you to return the container to us at no charge. Mark the contents as x-ray materials for lab use. We are not intending to value the components at other than their normal insurance benefits, so as not to arouse any interest in it. The package will be returned to us the same way, via overnight delivery."

"And payment?"

"The day you send the package to UPS and we have a tracking number, we will electronically transfer the initial deposit."

"How will you know the tracking number from United Parcel Service?"

"Having an account with them, we will receive an e-mail saying the package has been picked up, plus time of delivery. Now it is up to you to give me your account number so we can wire you the money."

"Just a minute while I get it." Hussein, Dakham and Atwan trade silent, satisfied nods.

After obtaining the numbers, Hussein tells Dimitri, "The container will be shipped out to you tomorrow. You will receive it the following day. We expect you to turn it around for reshipment within twenty-four hours."

"My kind of twenty-four hours, or your kind of twenty-four hours," Dimitri says sarcastically.

Hussein deactivates the speaker button and hangs up. "So—what do we think?" Hussein asks, turning to the other two.

"I think Jibril's idea of waiting ten days has really made him anxious for his money," smiles Dakham.

"I believe you're right," agrees Hussein. "I don't believe both of us have to go to Pakistan to send the container and wait for the return shipment. Do you want to go or should I go?"

"I will go. You can keep Jibril company," replies Dakham, smiling as he says this.

*

United Parcel picks up the container from their store-front address in Karachi, Pakistan. The next day it is delivered to Volgograd. Two days later it is en route back to Karachi.

Dakham receives the package upon its return. So far everything has gone smoothly. In a couple of hours he will be back over the border to Iran and heading for Tehran. So far this has been the easiest part of the assignment. He has enjoyed two peaceful days in a hotel just lounging around. Besides, Pakistani food is good.

*

Atwan and Hussein greet Dakham when he arrives back at the Secret Police building. He hands the UPS package over to Atwan, who caresses it like it's a newborn child. *Well, I guess some guys get their rocks off in strange ways,* Dakham thinks, trying not to look amused.

"You two are free to go, for a few days at least," Atwan announces. "Check in with me in five days—five of Dimitri's kind of days."

Chapter Forty-Two

Succession Matters

The president has called a meeting. Present in the Situation Room are Patrick Devonshire, Maria Sterling, John Anderson, Allison McDonald, John Walker, Admiral Robert Smith, and Generals James Bradley and Victor Sanford.

"Ladies and gentlemen," the president opens the discussion, "This meeting has just one item on its agenda. There will be plenty of time for discussion. After the discussion, I'll make my statement."

He quickly moves into the meat of his presentation. "Having received a growing body of substantiated intelligence on a regular basis, it appears that the nation of Iran is threatening to attack both the United States and the State of Israel." This news creates a general stirring around the table.

"When that might happen, no one can say at this point. However, the information received to date indicates that sometime in the near future we are going to be involved in a confrontation with them. As president, it is my responsibility under the Constitution to protect our people and our nation to the best of my ability. Because of the serious nature of this intelligence, I've met privately with our admiral and generals sitting here this morning. We have discussed both preemptive confrontation and retaliatory confrontation.

"As the four of us see it, this country has a major problem if its shores are attacked on a larger scale than September 11th, 2001. If we are restricted to the Constitution's prescription for who takes over as acting president in the case of the death or inability of the president to function as commander-in-chief, we could become quickly crippled by our inability to make tactical military decisions to save our nation in a timely fashion.

"Therefore, I'm proposing the following: As president, I'm planning to exercise my authority to supplement the War Powers Act by executive order. In the event that this nation is attacked by foreign power which causes the death or disability of the president, and the first three replacements according to the Constitution as acting president, the military tactics required to save this nation will be placed in the hands of the Joint Chiefs of the Army, Navy, Marine Corp and Air Force. They are to confer and make joint majority decisions on how to respond in the best interest of our nation. This power is to remain in effect so long as this nation is in jeopardy and will revert back to the normal Constitutional constraints when the threat has been eliminated. The President or his replacements will have the authority to declare war based on factual intelligence that can be provided to the Armed Services Committee of Congress. We are now open for discussion."

"Mr. President, how many positions does the Constitution list for the succession of the president?" asks the vice president.

"Pat, the first one to replace the president would of course be you, if it happened during this administration. If something should happen to the vice president, thereafter it follows in this order: Speaker of the House, President Pro-Tempore of the Senate, the following Secretaries: State, Treasury, and Defense. The Attorney General is next in line. After the Attorney General we have: Secretaries of Interior, Agriculture, Commerce, Labor, Health and Human Services, Housing and Urban Development, Transportation, Energy, Education and Veterans Affairs. Seventeen individuals in total.

"However—if you look at this list, you realize what could happen in the midst of catastrophe. Total confusion, individuals required to make life and death decisions with little or no prior experience. This list was created in 1947, after we were victorious in World War II. At that time no one could begin to imagine what we are dealing with today. Just trying to find out who is alive on that list could be a major undertaking, under impossible circumstances."

By now most at the table appear to be profoundly moved by what they've been asked to consider, some from the realization of what a war with Iran would entail, others by the realization that this president is proposing taking unprecedented steps. The three military men appear to appreciate this president means what he says. All three are quietly nodding their heads, the only positive reaction to be seen.

"Mr. President, as Secretary of Defense, is there something that I need to be involved in that I'm not currently up to speed on?" asks Anderson.

"Yes, John. After this meeting, you, the vice president, the chief of staff and I will remain here. I'll give you highlights of what I know to date."

Turning to the rest of the group, the president asks, "Are there any further questions or discussions?"

No one indicates any further response.

"If there is no further discussion, we'll adjourn. I want each of you to be aware that I'm signing this executive order this afternoon. It will be on file in the event it must be utilized. Due to the gravity of the information you have just heard, I needn't remind you that you're not to discuss this meeting's subject matter with anyone. Doing so would put you in jeopardy of divulging top secret information."

The president rises, allowing those not remaining to depart.

Chapter Forty-Three

Early October

Jibril Atwan, advisor to the Supreme Leader, must now do some contacting of his own. Sitting in his office in the Ministry of Intelligence and Security, Atwan puts a call through to a phone number he has just looked up in his file. A phone rings in Russia.

"Hello. Who is this?"

"Your friend Jibril. Kolzak, how are things going for you?"

"Could always be better, Jibril. Are you calling on a secure line?"

"I wouldn't call you any other way."

"What did I do to deserve this pleasure, my friend?"

"The last time we spoke, you promised me two Kilos in ten to twelve months time. I'm merely calling to see if they are still on schedule."

"Jibril, you're fortunate that I like you," says Kolzak, his voice deep and gruff. "You know that I'm only the minister of defense, not somebody with power. But, yes, we are still on schedule for the ten to twelve months delivery date I gave you. However, Jibril, now that you have called, I think it is good that you consider paying us the moneys you're scheduled to pay since we have upgraded your delivery. I'm sure you know that it costs to get the needed parts as quickly as you want them. I also expect that you will have deposited the remainder when your crews arrive to receive delivery of the subs from our yards."

"I assume that when you require the balance," Atwan counters, "the subs will have undergone sea trials. I do not want any of my men finding what could be fatal leaks."

"Jibril, you can have your men here in four months, if you like. They can monitor and sign off on the sea trials and have any questions answered for them first-hand. That way we do not have to worry about any suspicious sub sinkings on the way home. I don't want you calling me back saying something is my fault."

Atwan just laughs. *Would I do something like that?*

"I wouldn't put it past you, Jibril."

"Your money will be wired tomorrow, my friend. I will take you up on sending my two crews up in four months." Atwan decides to push his luck. "Can they participate in the sea trials?"

"I can arrange that." *Of course. We have all been told—keep Iran happy, whatever the cost.*

"Kolzak, when my people leave for home, I would hope you can aid us in making sure they don't arouse suspicion when passing Norway, Sweden and Denmark on their way into the North Sea."

"So long as they don't go flying the Iranian flag, Jibril, they should have no problem. People are used to seeing our subs in the Baltic. Once they clear Denmark, they can run submerged for long periods."

"Good," Atwan replies. "I'm trying not to get too many people interested in our latest acquisition."

"Jibril," Kolzak laughs, "if you live in reality, most of the world probably already knows we are selling you the two Kilos. It is very difficult to keep things like this quiet. Just don't get us into any trouble because we sold them to you."

"With what we want them for, you will have nothing to worry about, my friend," Atwan promises. *Especially if everything goes off well.*

"Good. Call me when you have wired the money so I can get the finance secretary off my back."

"I will do that. Save me some of your good vodka for when I come up again."

"What? I thought you devout Muslims do not take liquor."

"Just for medical purposes, you know."

"Yeah, sure, Jibril, you're no different than me. Goodbye, now, my friend."

The line goes dead in Atwan's hand. *Don't be so sure, my friend. You are in for a big surprise as to how different my country and I can be.*

*

As he inserts yet another variation of encryption code into the translator, Dale Proctor checks the output. To his utter amazement, the output makes sense. "Wow! Wow, we did it, Jack! You hit the nail on the head—it was an elliptic curve-based cipher. You're a fuckin' genius, Ritter!" Proctor is so excited he can barely contain himself.

Deep in a subterranean room in the National Security Agency, Proctor and Ritter have been working diligently for months, attempting to break code used in communiqués between the Iranian military and the Supreme Command.

"Hold on, man," Ritter tries to calm his partner. "Let's run some other checks to be sure that what we've found is the real deal, not just a fluke. But we may have just gotten lucky on this one."

"Okay, Jack, let's do it. But I'd be willing to bet real money that we've hit the jackpot with this last code set."

For the next half hour they run these new codes against messages they've been storing from satellite-retrieved communications. Every one of the messages comes through making perfect sense. Both men gape at each other. *My God,* thinks Proctor, *this could be as important as when we broke the Japanese code in World War II.*

"Okay, step one, we record everything we did so we don't lose anything and have to start over," says Ritter. "Then we contact Carter."

After they record all of the work on their shift, Proctor picks up the phone and calls their supervisor. "David, we need to see you in the comm center. Can you come down? This is urgent."

"How urgent, Dale? I happen to be in the middle of something."

"Urgent enough, Dave, that I believe you might want to bring the director along with you."

"The director? You shitting me? Only an act of God brings him into the comm center."

"Well, tell the director that Jack and I just got a miracle from God that he might want to take a look at."

"I'll be down in five minutes, myself. If I agree with you crackpots, I'll call the director."

Seven minutes later David Carter, senior comm center leader, is staring at what Proctor and Ritter have to show him. After reading the first three translations, he grabs a chair near a phone and dials the director's office.

The director's secretary answers and puts Carter through to John Walker. "Sir, I feel you need to come to the comm center. This is important for you to see. I don't want to describe it over the phone."

"I'm just finishin' up a meetin' here, David," Walker says. "I should be through in fifteen minutes. I'll see y'all in twenty."

Carter hangs up and walks back over to Proctor and Ritter. Carter is still shaking his head in amazement. "This is a major breakthrough. You know you can't say a word about this outside this center to anyone. This goes right to the president and those with a need to know. You guys have any coffee on down here? I need some."

"I'll get you a cup," says Ritter. "How do you take it?"

"Black."

While the three wait impatiently for the director to arrive, they run more messages to see if they can trip up the codes. Every message they test comes through fine. The grammar might be a bit rough and some of the idioms give them trouble, but with the help of an Arabic translator, they know they can clean up any confusion. "There is no question about it, you've broken the code," says Carter, having just read the eighth message.

*

Thirty minutes later, John Walker walks into the comm center.

"So what's all this fuss about, David?" he asks.

"Dale, show him what we've been looking at for the last half hour. Sir, have a seat," Carter offers then puts a pile of decrypted messages on the table in front of him.

After reading the first half dozen messages in translation, John Walker turns around in his seat and addresses Proctor and Ritter. "You gen'lemen have just given the United States a majah advantage." Reaching for the phone next to him, he asks the operator to place him on a secure line to the president.

Janet White advises the president that John Walker is on a secure line and would like to speak with him immediately.

"John, this must be awfully urgent," President Egan remarks. "You rarely call me during the course of the day."

"Sir, y'all need to hear about somethin' I've just been made aware of. I'd rathah not do it over the phone, even if this is a secure line."

"How much time to do you need, John?"

"Fifteen minutes, tops, suh. That's all I need."

"All right, you get yourself over here right now and you can have your fifteen minutes."

"Y'all won't regret it," Walker assures him.

Walker has his secretary arrange to have his car and driver meet him at the side entrance. "And advise him he's to get me to the White House quickly. The driver complies, but finds himself wondering what the rush is all about. This is unusual behavior for the director.

*

"Janet, as soon as John Walker arrives, have the Secret Service escort him in and put my schedule off by a half hour. If anyone cannot accommodate me, cancel their appointment."

"Yes, sir!" *Something is going on,* figures Janet. *This isn't like the director or the president.*

John arrives in ten minutes and is escorted into the Oval Office.

"Have a seat and catch your breath, John," the president suggests. Walker is literally panting, having all but sprinted from the South Portico where his car just dropped him.

"I do thank y'all, suh."

"What's going on? Have the Chinese or the North Koreans gone to war?"

"No, suh. It's actually good news, Mr. Pres'dent."

"Good news that you couldn't tell me on the phone?"

"Suh, we've just broken the codes between Iran's military and their Supreme Command." For a moment, the president is speechless.

"You're sure of what you're telling me? You have no doubts about it?"

"We've been testing this for over an hour, suh. Every message we test it with gives us a good, workin' translation. This is for real, Mr. Pres'dent."

"Well, thank God for big favors! Not that I doubt what you just told me, John, but I'll want your people to continue testing this code against any messages they can pick up for a couple of days. When we're one hundred percent sure, I'll advise those with a need to know. We can only give this information to a trusted handful of people. Should there ever be a leak, we would totally lose our advantage, and probably never get a chance to crack their code again."

"I certainly agree, suh," says Walker. "What would you like to call this project?"

"Well, against the Japanese we called it Magic or something like that."

"That's right, suh," Walker says.

The president thinks for a moment. "I want this to be so quiet it'll just be a whisper. Let's call it Whispering."

"Project Whisperin' it is, suh. Now, I'll head back to the agency and brief each of my crews that'll be dealing directly with this."

"John, do you have any reservations about any of your teams in the center knowing what we just found?"

"No, suh. As a matter of fact, I believe it'll give them more incentive to scrutinize every last thin' that comes in from Iran now. There're only two other shifts that man the comm center beyond the two who broke the code, and I'll vouch for each an' ev'ry last one of them. And remembah, once we start utilizin' what we've found, I can't only have the two men on today's shift doing all the Iranian transmissions, for two reasons. One, it'd slow us down. Even if they took double shifts, they're only human. They'd still need to sleep. If somethin' critical came in while they were off duty, there'd be hell to pay. And two, the others might feel like we didn't trust them, and that could be bad for morale."

"Yes, I see both your points. I just want to be ever so careful with this."

"I un'erstand, suh. However, like I say, I vouch for my people. Now, my fifteen minutes has run way over. I'll get outta your hair and head back to the agency."

Chapter Forty-Four

Successful

Atwan sits at his desk nervously tapping his fingers. Two weeks have passed since he gave the lab the sample of uranium for testing. His anxiety level increases with every day, mainly because of the Euros equaling three hundred thousand American dollars that now sit in a mafiya account—and so far, nothing to show for it. Looking at the picture of the prophet Mohammad on his wall, he knows he must have faith. At least that's what he tells himself.

Finally, he cannot stand it any longer. He calls the lab. "This is Jibril Atwan. Where are the results from the sample I left with you? It's two weeks now."

The lab assistant, realizing the importance of the man who is calling, says, "I will get my director, sir."

The head of the lab comes to the phone. "Jibril, we are just putting our notes together as we speak. You will have a hard copy within the hour. We took our time so we could be absolutely positive of our findings."

"All right," Atwan says with a sigh. "I hope that you have good news for me."

"You will be satisfied, Jibril." The director hangs up his phone and shakes his head. *Bureaucrats,* he groans inwardly.

*

Joe Smiga

When the report arrives, it reads as follows:

> Material is considered to be a good grade of enriched uranium. Quantity appears consistent with the amount normally found in a warhead. There appears to have been no decay within the container in which it arrived that would indicate deterioration of this material, at least not in the foreseeable future.

Atwan's eyes light up as he reads the report. Quickly he picks up his phone and calls down to the Supreme Leader's office. He advises his superior of the report, and recommends they should complete negotiations to purchase the remainder of the materials.

Fadil Ahmajid tells Atwan, "I will bring this up with the council tomorrow. You will have an answer by the end of the day. "You have done well, Jibril. I am sure Allah is pleased with your efforts in this project—and what's to come."

Hanging up his phone, Atwan cannot foresee any reason why the council wouldn't purchase the remainder of the materials from Dimitri.

*

Meanwhile, the test firings of the newly designed missiles to be shot from Iran's Kilo submarines is not going as smoothly as the uranium purchase. The window of time allocated for testing is nearly a third over and, as the reports come in, there are still numerous problems. Muhammad Abdullah is not a happy engineer at this point. The council representatives are putting heavy pressures on him. He's taking all the heat for this problem, even though some of it more properly belongs with the submarine crew doing the testing.

*

The council okays the purchase of the enriched uranium from the Russians. Fadil Ahmajid calls Atwan and advises him to resume negotiations to purchase the balance.

Atwan is now soaring emotionally. He's visited with visions of an Iran as world conqueror. All that stands between today and that day is details.

This hurdle cleared, he has growing confidence that the problems the engineers are encountering will be solved in good time.

Picking up the phone, he calls Hussein and Dakham. "I want you to meet me in the conference room tomorrow at 1200 hours. We have an important phone call to make to our friend up north."

Both Hussein and Dakham assure him they will be there. *Things must have gone well in the testing*, each thinks to himself.

*

At noon the next day, Atwan, Hussein and Dakham spend an hour rehearsing how they will handle dealing with Dimitri. "All right," says Atwan, "I want you to call him the same way you did before when you arranged for the sample. I will be listening in and writing you notes if we have issues."

Hussein dials Dimitri's phone number, using the Pakistani phone line. Dakham again listens in on the speaker phone.

It takes four rings for Dimitri to answer. "This is Dimitri. What can we do for you?"

"Dimitri, this is Kamil, and I have Hamid in the room with me. You are on speaker phone."

"So, are you calling back for a refund or are you going to order the balance of the materials?"

Hussein laughs. *Who are you kidding. We both know that in this business there is no such thing as a refund.* "No, no refund, Dimitri. The sample has been tested and we now have our report."

"Well I'm sure that the report you have will confirm the one I have. You see, Kamil, I took the liberty of having a sample analysis done also, just so there's no argument about the value of the materials."

Hussein and Dakham look at Atwan. They hadn't anticipated Dimitri being thorough. Atwan writes a note and holds it up so both can see: *He's bluffing.*

"What grade did your testing report, Dimitri?" asks Dakham.

"Ours was evaluated as a very good grade of enriched uranium."

"Well, that's very interesting, Dimitri, because our report grades it only fair to good, possibly because it has been lying around for a long time. However, it is good enough to suit our customer's needs."

"Well, gentlemen, I guess we have a difference of opinion," says Dimitri. "Regardless, our asking price for the balance of eleven is eight million two hundred and fifty thousand euros. That is, seven hundred fifty thousand each."

"Dimitri, we agreed upon three hundred thousand American dollars beforehand," Hussein responds angrily. "Then you changed it to euros, and we agreed to that. But now you have raised your price more than fifty percent. We need to make a profit as well."

"Your profits are not my concern, my friend," Dimitri says. "I didn't realize the value of what I have until I had it tested."

"Dimitri, I'm sure you're a good businessman. We are not taking the projectiles themselves. Even though they are no longer nuclear, you should be able to get three hundred thousand euros each for them as is."

"Sorry, but I have another buyer who is interested and willing to pay more money."

Another bluff? "Dimitri," Dakham responds, "We can go up to five hundred thousand euros, but no higher. We offer you half today and the balance when the remainder leaves Russia."

Dimitri pauses for a few moments. There is nothing but silence on the phone. Finally he says, "How do you expect me to ship the materials to you if I agree to this?"

Atwan writes another note. *You got him. The deal is done.*

"When can you have the balance of the eleven removed from their housings?" Hussein asks.

"Two weeks."

"All right, we will wire you half of the money today. Hamid and I will arrive in Russia in fourteen days, and stay at the Best Eastern again. I'll expect you to call us there on the fifteenth day. Oh, and by the way, I expect that we will be getting the three reducer housings and our shipping requirements taken care of with this package."

"You push a hard bargain, Kamil."

"Dimitri, please," Dakham speaks up. "Surely your profit margin on this negotiation is much greater that ours will be."

Dimitri does not fall for the bait. "How will you arrange transportation out of Russia?" he asks quietly.

"Let Kamil and me handle that, Dimitri. We already have our plans in mind. However, only when we have departed safely from Russia, will you receive your balance."

"What do you mean, safely? Do you expect some kind of interference?"

"No, not really, but we know that you will make sure of that with that much money still owed to you. See you in fifteen days."

Hussein hangs up the phone. The three Iranians look at each other.

"He got a little more money, but not what he'd hoped for. He needs to show his bosses that he's doing his job," says Atwan. *Just as I do mine.*

Chapter Forty-Five

End of October

Deep inside of Teheran sits the parliamentary building used by the Iranian Ministry, the tallest building in the capital city. Its views assure the citizenry that they can always be observed. On the very top floor is the conference room, a square space of twenty by twenty meters. With the drapes fully open, the warm sunlight provides a pleasant atmosphere in the room. The conference table is large enough to accommodate twelve chairs. Lately, however, there have only been six chairs set up for the council.

Ayatollah Fadil Ahmajid enters and looks at the cluster of five council members standing together, waiting for him to appear. Only Jibril Atwan is absent. "Everyone take a seat. We have matters to attend to." They quickly do his bidding.

Looking at his notes, the Supreme Leader hesitates a moment to allow excitement to build within the room. Finally he announces, "Our current missile testing demonstrates that we now have the capability of delivering missiles to the entire European continent. In six months, we'll have sufficient enriched uranium to build twelve nuclear warheads. This will satisfy our needs to take over all of the Middle East and the European continent, as well.

"Jibril has just recently made a purchase from inside Russia which strengthens our position even more. We now have the nuclear materials to make the newly designed Shahab missiles more effective when fired from our Kilos. We will take the war to the Americans, when everything is finally tested and we are satisfied they work. In two more months, the Russians will have the last two Kilos we purchased ready to deliver. Each of our six Kilos will have two of these new missiles to bring to the Jews and the Great Satan."

Council member Ayatollah Mansour Hassan is the first to speak. "What's the proposed timetable to deliver all of this destruction?"

A second member, Ayatollah Ali Givon, appears quite nervous about the whole discussion. "Fadil, we have *tentatively* agreed to go ahead with this undertaking. But, before we commit to this, I would like to know who in our military is responsible for the whole operation."

"To answer Hassan's question first," Ahmajid replies calmly, "we have set a target date of ten months from now. All of our forces that will be involved should have sufficient training and coordination by that time. Ali, the council will have everything presented to it at least one month before the operation begins."

Ayatollah Sayed Abbas speaks. "Supreme Leader, we are undertaking a worldwide military campaign. What are the chances of having secrets leaked to the Europeans or to the West?"

"With the IAEA no longer allowed to monitor our nuclear enrichment sites, we have eliminated the biggest source of a leak to the outside world. Within our own borders, our secret police have been monitoring anyone and everyone connected with these affairs. If anyone—or a number of anyones—might be tempted to betray us, they will be handled with the fiercest repercussions."

Ayatollah Hossein Farook replies, "That's all well and good, Fadil. However, the more people involved in this, the more the project lends itself to becoming of some interest to the outside world. I would hope that each segment of this plan is being carried out without another segment being aware of its partnership to the project."

"Hossein, Jibril and I are the only ones who currently know the total scope of our plan. Others are performing their tasks without knowing their true nature or when, or if anything, will come of their efforts. It is easy to train people when they think that their contributions are for self-survival against the West."

"All well and good, Fadil. However, now you have exposed us to purchasing enriched uranium from outside of our borders. I hope that purchase doesn't come back to bite us." Farook's eyes betray his lack of confidence in what he's hearing.

Sternly Ahmajid replies, "Farook, Jibril is very good at what he does. I have complete confidence in how he's handling his end of this."

"I hope you're right. Only Allah knows, and time will tell us, if you are."

"Let us go then with Allah's blessing. Each of you know what your assignments are, am I correct?"

Each of the five nods his head in agreement.

"Till we meet again."

Each member of the council departs the room. The Supreme Leader is beginning to see inklings of reservations on their minds, now that the plan is beginning to unfold. *When we are successful, I will have these spineless, fat little men replaced on the council. A new Iran must have leaders, not merely dreamers.*

Chapter Forty-Six

Middle of November

As the president enters the Situation Room he smiles at the sight of three small clusters of individuals chatting. *Amazing how humans gather with 'their kind,' those similar to themselves, rather than branching out to mingle with others*, he muses.

Upon the president's entry, all conversation comes to a halt mid-sentence. Bound by protocol, everyone in the room waits for him to 'decide' where he will sit, in spite of the fact that they all know he will take the seat at the table nearest the door—the seat the Secret Service has chosen for him.

"Why doesn't everyone take a seat so we can get started," President Egan suggests as he sits down himself.

Patrick Devonshire, Maria Sterling, John Anderson, Allison McDonald, John Walker, Admiral Robert Smith, Air Force General James Bradley, and Marine Corp General Victor Sanford all select a seat. Today they are joined by the chairman of the joint chiefs, General Dean Hargrove.

The president looks around the table, then nods. *I am surrounded by some of the greatest talent in America. May they be equal to all that's before them.* Only then can he start.

"I know that all of you're aware of Project Whispering." He pauses a moment while this fact is uniformly acknowledged in the affirmative. "As of right now, with the exception of a couple of analysts in the NSA, you nine are the only members of the government who are aware of this project, and until necessary, it will remain that way." Again, he looks around the table for confirmation.

"Project Whispering," the president continues, "is beginning to yield some insight as to what might happen in the near future concerning the Middle East and the United States. This is why I've called for a meeting." The president pauses, looks down as if consulting with an inner advisor, then proceeds onto territory he never expected to have to face in his administration.

"Our top military people have suggested that, in the event of an attack on our shores, we designate pre-assigned targets to minimize reaction time—for retaliation." He pauses again, giving the group a moment to adjust to such a difficult reality. "It makes sense to me to do so, but I believe the responsibility for making those choices lies with all of us. Do I have any questions at this point?"

The vice president speaks. His tone is subdued, meek even. Formerly the governor of Vermont, Devonshire is a man passionate about ecology in general, and saving the earth in particular. The thought of retaliation—the thought of war—automatically goes against his grain, but his loyalty to his president is equally fierce. If William Egan says these choices are necessary, Pat Devonshire is prepared to trust him implicitly. "Sir, how much retaliation are we looking at? Will this be like Afghanistan after the World Trade Center, or are we looking at a major invasion like Iraq?"

"We cannot afford another Iraq," Maria Sterling volunteers, acknowledging the vice president's thoughts with a nod. "The people won't stand for it."

"Maybe I didn't make myself clear enough," the president interrupts. "We're not talking about how much retaliation we're looking at. What I want you to focus on today is strategic locations, tactical choices we would target."

The secretary of defense doesn't hesitate. "No question, we should target military installations. What else would you consider a worthwhile target?" he asks almost sheepishly.

"What about the core issue in this matter, the uranium enrichment facilities? Are we going to allow them to continue manufacturing?" demands Allison McDonald.

"No, no, Allison as far as I'm concerned they are military targets," responds Anderson, realizing his blunder.

"Well, we need to identify what's military and what's not," Maria Sterling says with exasperation. "I'd lump military bases and uranium enrichment facilities under the same heading."

"Would we consider the government itself a military target, since it would have made the decision to strike us in the first place?" asks President Egan. Now the room becomes very quiet. "Well, don't everyone just sit here. I'm looking for your opinions." *For more than five decades, since the end of World War II, governments worldwide have been following an unwritten policy: the use of force is okay, as long as it doesn't touch the top dogs. How shall we react?*

"Sir, if I may," says Dean Hargrove, "if we are attacked and only retaliate against military or whatever we consider military, then we are leaving the head of the snake attached to the body, so to speak. I've always been of the mind that, if you want to kill a snake, you better darned well make sure you take its head off."

"Dean, we aren't talking about killing snakes here," Sterling cuts in.

"No, Maria, we aren't," the president says, seemingly agreeing, but then he continues, "We're talking about people who will try, again and again, as long as they are alive."

Pat Devonshire replies, "Do you honestly think we can get in there and assassinate their entire government?"

"Hell, no, Pat," the president responds in frustration. "This isn't the old days of the CIA trying to undermine heads of state, like Sihanouk in Cambodia or Salvador Allende in Chile. I won't try to assassinate individuals. I plan to just bomb the hell out of all of them."

"My God, this is crazy," Sterling exclaims.

"John Walker," the president calls on his national security advisor, "I'm not hearing anything from you. Cat got your tongue on this issue?"

"No, suh," Walker answers, choosing his words carefully. "From the data we're collectin', I believe somethin' will happen within the next twelve months. With what we know, do y'all want to declare war and explain later to the world why we did what we did? Or do y'all think we should take the chance of bein' attacked first? Me, personally, I'd rather be the first to attack. As far as takin' out an entire foreign gov'ment, well, the gov'ment we're talkin' about is lyin' and connivin' all of us. They're a blood-thirsty bunch, and if we don't cut off the head of that there snake like Dean said, well, I believe history'll repeat itself somewhere down the road."

"John, you express my feelings precisely," says the president. He looks over at his top military people. "I'm recommending that you gentlemen of the military meet with Allison and John to pin point every military base and enrichment facility in the country of Iran. I want as many covert teams put into Iran as it takes to identify the routines of the current government and Guardian Council in Iran. I want to know how and when they eat, sleep and drink, if it can be done."

"Suh, my people can do just about all of that with the re-positionin' of spy satellites," says John Walker.

"Then do it, John, and do it starting today. I want to make sure we know about all of them. "As soon as the military is ready, and with whatever you've learned, John, and Allison as well, I want to meet with everyone involved to formulate a concrete list of targets. I will have the secretary of state arrange for the prime minister of Israel to visit us within the next month. I want them to share with us what they know, and see if we can sort this action out together."

"Sir, don't you think we'd be courting danger, involving Israel in this?" Sterling asks warily.

"Maria, Israel has already provided us with vital intelligence on this matter. It's vital, for both of our countries' sakes, to solve this problem."

Although he knows it will change no one's opinions, the president makes one more statement in closing the meeting. "One of my predecessors in this office once said something to the effect of, "if it's too hot for you in the kitchen, you can always leave." If any of you feel you cannot handle your responsibilities through what may be one of the most serious threats this country has ever faced, I will be sorry but willing to accept your resignation."

Everyone in the room looks shaken by his words. *Good*, the president thinks. *They know I mean business, both in what I'm saying and what I'm prepared to do.*

Chapter Forty-Seven

Same Time in November

"I don't know about you, Hamid," Hussein says, his voice reflecting his fatigue, "but my frustrations with setting this thing up are getting to me. I need to move around—get out of this room for a while. We have been at it for five days straight now, figuring out our route, learning how to handle and conceal the uranium in the reducer housings."

"I'm with you," Dakham agrees, tossing a yellow pad, filled with page after page of technical data, down on the table. "Let's take an hour or two, walk around, maybe grab a bite to eat. When we get back, we can review everything with clear heads. And we need to work out a schedule for what still needs doing."

"All I know is, it was a good thing that Dimitri said he needed two weeks. Who knew we'd need every day of it ourselves," Hussein said, shaking his head in amazement. "It will still take us another day or two to firm everything up. I want to go over what the scientists told us about the concealment issues once more, too." Hussein stands up and stretches. *My nerves are getting taut. Not good. Definitely time for a break.*

"Look Kamil, everything will work out," Dakham says. He's seen his partner like this many times before. "Once we get the uranium concealed and incorporate the false bottoms, no one will suspect a thing. Our departure will take longer than our first visit did, but you'll see, everything will go well."

"I wish I could be as confident as you are, Hamid. I don't trust Dimitri. Who knows what can happen to us before we get back to Iran."

"Come," Dakham says and pushes Hussein towards the door. "No more negativity. Let's get out of here."

Leaving the building, they head around the corner and over several blocks to an area of numerous cafes. They do not notice the tail Atwan has placed on them.

Today, it's Hussein's turn to pick a place to eat. This is the arrangement they have always had between the two of them whenever they eat out together. "Let's go down to the Café Niavaran. They've got tables outside. It is too nice a day to be eating inside. We've been inside enough, and will be back inside soon enough."

"Good choice," says Dakham, "and good reason. Besides, they make great falafel sandwiches and tabouli."

Arriving at the café, they find they have just missed the lunch crowd and a number of outside tables are available. Hussein picks one with an umbrella to give them some protection from the sun.

Coming to the table, a middle-aged waiter with a thin moustache and goatee asks, "Are you two having lunch or just something to drink?"

"We'll both have the falafel sandwich, with a side order of tabouli," Dakham tells him. "Oh, and would you please add hummus to those sandwiches? Thanks."

"Do you wish to have anything to drink, or just water?"

"Just water for me," "Hussein replies. "Hamid, what do you want?"

"I'll have your iced sweet tea, the large size."

After the waiter goes, Dakham says, "Don't turn around, but I see a black jeep parked a short distance up the street. I could swear I've seen the same car parked in the police parking lot. Do you think we are being tailed?"

"I wouldn't put it past Jibril," Hussein says with a shrug. "Why don't we take our time having lunch and let whoever's in the car roast in the sun for a while."

*

Two days later, Atwan meets with Hussein and Dakham in the conference room. This is a very different Atwan from the one they've done business with up until now. This Atwan is in executive mode.

"Give me your proposed routes and transportation requirements and I'll handle everything here," Atwan says in an almost patronizing tone. "I expected you have everything complete by now."

"Jibril, we do not want to use the same means of transportation we did for the last trip to Russia," says Dakham, pulling a map out and laying it on the table. "We shouldn't attract anymore attention to ourselves than we have to. We plan a different border crossing into Pakistan, here, at Turbat," he says, pointing, "in the southern end of the country, not going in again from Zahedan. And here is the name of a service we can use to get us from the border to the Karachi airport. As we told you yesterday, we'll need a minimum of five days at Dimitri's place to conceal the uranium in the housings, and we'll need a flat-bed truck to carry the three reducers down to the port at the mouth of the Volga. And not just any flat-bed truck. This transport must have adequate shock absorbers to protect the units from being bounced around." Dakham's delivery is terse; his annoyance is beginning to show.

Hussein jumps in, taking over from here. "At the seaport," he says, "we'll need the services of a stevedore who knows what he's doing, so the units are handled properly and are well secured inside of the ship's hold. Everything needs to be labeled with a final destination of Pakistan, traveling through Iran. We have everything laid out. All you have to do is approve it. We have already taken the time to investigate every option."

"All right, all right," Atwan says, somewhat mollified. "Clearly the two of you have put a lot of research into these plans. You seem to have everything covered, just as you said you would. However, I might want to use other carriers than those you have in mind." Hussein shrugs. *We get it, Jibril: this is your show.*

"Go take a couple of days off and get yourselves some rest." This offer comes as a pleasant surprise to both Dakham and Hussein, and goes a long way to dissipate the tension in the room. "I will send you up to Russia by the route you have selected. While you're there, you can advise me of your progress and when you know you will need the truck. Tell me how long it will be before you can reach the mouth of the river. Then leave the rest to me."

Stymied, Hussein and Dakham just nod at each other, then pack up their copies of their reports and leave. Hussein walks down the hall, silent, perplexed at having been given an assignment, following it through—and then not being allowed to execute it. *All this work and then he tells us he will be making all the arrangements?*

Once they are clear of the building and far enough away, he finally speaks his mind. "What the hell was that all about?"

"Beats the shit out of me," Dakham fumes. "Did he just give us work to keep us busy? Perhaps he'll use some of what we came up with to make his job easier."

"More likely, he'll pass off our work as his own," Hussein suggests. "The man is a control freak. Be careful, Hamid. This is a man you don't push. I was watching his eyes the entire time. They are not the eyes of a friend."

"Well, let's go enjoy the time off, and screw him," Dakham vents. "I will use the time to be with my family, in Hamadan."

"And I think I shall go up to Rasht. I can stay with my uncle, and do some hiking in the hills."

Each of them go their own way, as do the tails that have been assigned to follow them.

*

They arrive in Russia on the fifteenth day, exactly as they told Dimitri they would. By now seasoned "Pakistani businessmen," their roles come easier for them. No longer do they experience the feelings of the first trip. They are seated in business class on Aeroflot, flying in and out of Pakistan. It seems that customs is more lenient with business travelers; passing through at the airport this time is a breeze, nothing but a few quick questions and they are sent on their way.

After claiming their luggage, however, they find the chore of getting a taxi to take them to the Best Eastern to be just like the first trip all over again. They try waving to get a driver's attention without success.

"Taxi, taxi," Dakham hollers. "That's the third asshole that refused to stop, even though they are empty."

Suddenly Vicktor pulls up in the Mercedes. "Well, I see you made it all right," he calls out the window as he pulls alongside the pair. "Dimitri sent me to give you a lift to your hotel. He wants to have dinner together tonight before the meeting in the morning. Is there any problem with that arrangement?"

Hussein and Dakham look at each other and both shake their heads. "No problem at all," Hussein says, wondering *I sure hope it's no problem at all. Dinner with the mafiya. What next.*

Vicktor opens the trunk, they throw in their luggage and settle into the back seat. Vicktor reminds them that they should wear their seat belts, which amuses Dakham to such a degree that he spends most of the ride trying to control the urge to laugh.

The traffic is no lighter than on the previous trip from the airport to their hotel. It takes Vicktor less than half the time to get to the Best Eastern as it did the first time they made the journey, confirming their earlier hunch that their former cab driver had in fact ripped them off.

Before they have a chance to get out of the car, Vicktor turns back to speak to them. "We will pick you up for dinner at 1800 hours. Dimitri would like the two of you waiting outside of the hotel."

"Will you be using this car, so we know what to look for when you arrive?" asks Hussein.

"Most likely, but I cannot say for sure."

"Where is Dimitri planning to take us for dinner, might I ask?" Dakham says.

"Don't know," Vicktor replies with a shrug. "He never tells me until he's ready to go. Don't worry, it will be somewhere exquisite."

Exquisite? Dakham thinks. *This I've got to see.*

Vicktor pulls the trunk release and the trunk opens with a quiet pop, which sounds like a form of audible punctuation. Realizing they are not going to get any further information from him, Hussein and Dakham exit the Mercedes and pull their luggage out of the trunk. The moment Hussein shuts the trunk, Vicktor leaves with tires squealing. "Well, Hamid, look on the bright side—at least we didn't have to tip anyone."

"Let's get inside and check in," says Dakham. "Why do I get the feeling that we have stepped out on a stage, the curtain's just gone up and suddenly a whole lot of eyes are trained on us, like we're some kinds of celebrities, like they are there to watch our performance—or in this case, our movements?"

Dakham pauses and thinks about what he's just said. *Or am I just getting paranoid? This is not good. But*—"And, come to think of it, do you not find it awfully odd that not one of the empty cabs we saw stopped for us?" he adds.

"I agree. Let's go," Hussein replies, equally nervous. "Dinner should be very interesting tonight."

Chapter Forty-Eight

Arranging a Return

David Carter, NSA communications center supervisor, stares at the reports on his desk intently. He has assigned three teams the job of monitoring all Iranian communications, in support of Project Whispering. With thirty years in NSA, he cannot shake the feeling that he's dealing with something potentially more perilous than he ever has before. Project Whispering is keeping him up at night. *What in the hell are they thinking—and what the hell are they planning on doing? It's time to put some heads together to see if we can sort this out.*

Carter calls down to Jack Ritter and Dale Proctor, the two analysts who created the codes to intercept and decipher these messages. Ritter answers the phone. "Jack, when you and Dale are off your regular watch, I need both of you to meet with me in my office," Carter tells him.

"Another all-nighter, Dave?" asks Ritter.

"Maybe. Did you have anything planned for tonight?"

Ritter stops to think, scratching his head. *Damn, I swear this job's making that bald spot bigger by the day.* "No, I can be there. Mary's planning to go out with the girls tonight. Let me call her and have her get a sitter for the kids."

"What about Dale? Do you know if he's got plans?"

"Dale? Of course Dale has plans. Dale's single. But, you know, it's downright amazing how flexible his schedule can be when he needs to change plans for whatever reason. You don't need to worry about him. Even if it means breaking someone's heart, he'll make it."

"Good. I'll have three dinners sent up to my office so we can eat before we begin. Any preferences?" his boss asks him.

"Just don't order any of that crap they called beef stroganoff on the lunch menu today," Ritter says with a mock dramatic groan. "I don't know who the hell cooked that shit up."

Ritter hangs up, then shares the news with Proctor, who slams down his pen. "No, not again!" Proctor cries. "What the hell is this? I've already logged in over sixty hours this week."

"That's why we're rolling in it, Dale."

"Yeah, right. If you look at it by the hour, this job sucks."

*

At the end of their watch, Ritter and Proctor go up to Dave's office.

"I hope you've ordered a fine wine to go along with dinner, Dave," Proctor says as he comes through the door. "That's the least you can do."

Laughing, Dave replies, "Bitch, bitch, bitch. That's all I ever hear around here. "I got the kitchen crew to do up three medium-rare New York sirloins for us. Is that good enough?"

"All depends on what the rest of the plate looks like," says Proctor.

"Two came with rice and vegetables, and one with a baked potato and vegetables. Who wants to be the odd man out?"

"Give the potato to Jack," Proctor says. "He's definitely odd."

The three have dinner, enjoying a good bout of friendly verbal jousting and some very strong coffee afterwards.

"Okay, Dave, what's all this expense money going for?" Proctor asks, finishing his coffee.

Dave Carter is best known for being able to go from casual camaraderie to serious business faster than anyone else at NSA, and he doesn't bother with preambles. "As senior watch men, both of you are fully aware of our group's Iranian message reports. I'm beginning to see something of a trend developing. I want to review my thoughts with you two before I pass my report upstairs."

"What do you think you're seeing?" asks Ritter, fishing out a pack of cigarettes from his jacket pocket. Carter's clearly negative reaction inspires Ritter to drop them back in.

"I'm getting the sense of an increasing intensity in making deadlines by the military," Dave informs them. "It's almost like they've got some kind of major deadline they're shooting for. I'm seeing traffic that suggests the two Kilos they're buying from Russia are undergoing sea trials, with two Iranian crews already in Russia. In the past the Russians always delivered their Kilos, and sea trials were conducted in Iranian waters."

"I don't know if that really means anything in and of itself," Proctor says, pushing his chair back from the table.

"Maybe you're right. Maybe it doesn't," Dave concedes. "It's a gut thing. Have either of you gotten any sense of a red flag? I need your views besides my own."

Ritter gets up and paces the floor, thinking. Then it hits him. "There's been a pick-up in messages between the Council and the navy, about missile firings that aren't going as satisfactorily as they'd like. I can't put a finger on what kind of missiles they are talking about, but there does seem to be a lot of internal pressure going into the problem, whatever it is."

"Internal pressure. What do you mean by internal pressure, Jack?" asks Proctor as he puts his feet up on the conference room table.

"Its hard to put into words. It's—it's as if some project of theirs isn't measuring up to somebody's expectations." Ritter tries to put the pieces of a hunch together. "But whatever this is, I get the sense that the navy's trying to pass the buck. Have either of you seen anything that might suggest they're having missile malfunctions?"

"No," says Dave. "If anything, they've been putting out more propaganda than usual, bragging endlessly about their surface-to-surface and surface-to-air missiles that work so well, like they're warning the world to back off. They're even bragging about new torpedoes."

"Shit, don't start believing that crap as gospel," Proctor says with a snort, "but if it's not surface-to-surface and surface-to-air, might it be possible they're working on missiles that can be fired from a Kilo?"

"You mean like our cruise missiles?" says Ritter stunned.

Dave goes wide-eyed too. "I'm not aware that they have the technology to do that."

"Well, hell, they could have stolen it from somewhere," Proctor says.

"And you're thinking they don't have the bugs worked out yet . . ." suggests Dave.

"More than that. Maybe Dale's bugs are creating problems with this deadline you think they're working toward, Dave," Ritter murmurs, thinking out loud.

"I'll certainly make note of these possible scenarios in my report," says Dave. "Okay. Next, their nuclear missile program. Where do you see that going?"

Ritter answers first. "The army has charge of their nuclear missile program. I'm not hearing much about it. I do know that their new long-range Shahab was tested successfully three times. However, we don't have a handle on how quickly they can produce enough enriched uranium to make a significant number of nukes," says Ritter, tapping his fingers on the surface of Dave's desk unconsciously.

"More than zero would be a significant number in my book," Proctor comments. "Any word from the CIA on that?"

"If they have anything, the director isn't passing it down, at least not yet," says Dave. "Walker told me they'd been told to share everything—but he didn't sound like he put much store in that actually happening. Okay, you've helped me come up with several key issues to go in my report—and it only took us a couple of hours and three steak dinners to do it," he joked, then quickly grew serious. "From here on in, I want you to keep your ears and eyes open for even the slightest hint of anything that might be going on over there, anything at all. I can't say why, but I have a very bad feeling about this one."

Ritter rises to leave, then hesitates, "Dave, you been around twice as long as I have. What are you suspecting?"

"This doesn't leave this room, you hear? If they even end up with only two workable nukes that they can deliver from a sub, I can't help thinking number one would be fired into Israel. And they'd come after us with number two."

Proctor drops his feet to the floor and sits bolt upright. "You're shitting me, right, Dave?"

"No," Dave says quietly, shaking his head. "I'm not."

Ritter sits back down and stares at Proctor. The thought of a nuke being delivered to a coastal city in the United States has clearly never entered either of their minds.

Chapter Forty-Nine

End of November

"Today, we'll be making decisions critical to the safety of our country and its citizens. These decisions will entail military action which will lead to the destruction of facilities and human lives. I don't have to say, none of these decisions can be taken lightly. Each one, in and of itself, will be a very heavy burden, a burden we must all carry for the rest of our days," President Egan says gravely. "Yet it is vital that, as leaders of the United States, we make these decisions,"

Looking around the Situation Room at those seated before him—the chairman of the joint chiefs, an admiral, two generals, the directors of the CIA and the NSA, his secretary of defense—the president assesses the realities of this moment. *Though I'm commander in chief, I feel inadequate to the task before me. Only these four military men have any strategic planning and military experience at the command level. I am humbled in their presence.*

"Dean, you said that you wanted to start with the list of military sites we need to consider. Let's have it," Egan says with a sigh.

Dean Hargrove rises and walks to the podium. After adjusting a sheaf of papers in front of him, he turns on a computer. The Great Seal of the United States of America appears on the screen at the front of the room; all eyes are drawn to the thirteen arrows in the grip of the eagle's talon.

A no-nonsense presenter, Hargrove turns to the group before launching into his presentation. "Let me just say, folks, that I tell it like

I see it. I also welcome questions. Now, I just want you to know that Ms. McDonald, Mr. Walker, Mr. Anderson, the admiral, and both of the generals have met with me a number of times since our last meeting. This is what we see needs to be addressed for a successful preemptive strike on Iran."

Hargrove puts up the first screen showing the locations of Iran's air force commands. "As you can see, the Iranian air force command is broken up into three sections, the largest being the western command, then the southern command and third, the eastern command. From our intelligence they comprise a total of twelve airfields." The image on the screen changes to a more detailed topographic map of the country.

Picking up a pen-style laser pointer from the podium, Hargrove circles each position of interest. "The western command, as you see, has seven airfields. The southern command has three and the eastern command, two airfields."

Now he brings up a montage of aircraft. "Their military jets are a combination of French, Russian and Chinese. Some of these planes they have had since Saddam Hussein landed his air force in Iran to avoid losing them in the first Gulf War—Iran simply never gave them back."

A closer view of each airfield comes up one at a time. "We know of two Shahab-3 missile sites at each of the airfields," Hargrove goes on, pointing to the telltale signs in each image.

"If we intend to pre-empt a strike, these would be our first targets. We would need to take out each set of Shahab-3 sites before they could be launched at any other country. It is an adjunct possibility that we could take out the majority of their air force at the same time."

An image labeled 'Bandar Abbas" now fills the screen. "Bandar Abbas is our biggest concern. The city, with a population of close to 400,000, is a major port of entry for Iran. It also serves as a monumental navy base. Chinese missiles systems are located in areas of strategic protection. This base has the capability of closing the Strait of Hormuz within a short time frame, thereby locking up the Persian Gulf's flow of oil. The Strait, at its narrowest point, is a mere fifty-five kilometers or thirty-four miles in width.

A new image appears. "The Iranian navy has at least twenty frigates and destroyers moored there as well as a number of high speed torpedo boats, but our biggest concern is their Kilo subs. We've determined that they currently have four Kilos and are awaiting delivery of two more from Russia. This base must be a primary target as well."

The chairman of the joint chiefs flips to the another screen. "Before we go on, Dean," asks the president, "what, if anything, can we do to diminish their army?"

"Sir, Iran's revolutionary guard is a sizeable force. However, if we can immobilize the air force, the missile sites and the navy without major disruption in the Persian Gulf, the army is temporarily neutered as a fighting force."

"Continue then," says the president.

"Thank you, sir. This next image you see is of the tanker traffic coming in and out of the Persian Gulf. If we launch this strike, it is vital that we have complete control of the sea lanes inside of the Strait of Hormuz, that critical thirty-four miles. If we don't, Iran could make a last-ditch effort to disrupt the sea lanes. They could sink enough tankers in the Strait that it would take decades to clear."

"I assume, Admiral Smith, that you and your staff have considered this matter and have a plan to see that we are successful?" says President Egan, turning to address the admiral.

Smith stands up at his seat, "Mr. President, the Navy's plan is to coordinate time tables with the Air Force so we're hitting them on all fronts at the same time. We see the Strait as our biggest challenge. We recommend attacking at a time when the Strait has the least amount of tanker traffic. There's a window, between 2100 and 0500 hours, that most tanker captains avoid the Strait, which isn't the easiest thing to navigate, as you can imagine. Once in a while you get a die-hard who'll attempt it. We would want to be able to plan against that eventuality," Admiral Smith says, then pauses. *Killing defenseless merchant mariners*, he thinks. *I just couldn't let that happen.*

"The Navy will have two squadrons of fighters over the Strait at any one time to deal with Iranian aircraft or missile launches from those Chinese missile sites. However, we need to understand one thing. Once a battle starts, all of the greatest plans go to pieces. Then it's up to the men and women fighting them to make them successful. Can we do this? We believe so. Is this going to be a cake walk? Hell no! This isn't fiction, no military thriller."

"How do we develop this simultaneous assault without Iran's radar seeing an air and sea build-up?" asks the president.

General Bradley joins the discussion. "Sir, again using the window of opportunity the admiral just mentioned, beginning at 2400 hours, electronic jamming from our three AWACS segmenting Iran will begin taking out their communication and detection equipment. Within minutes, our attack will follow. Before 2400 hours, our forces will go into holding patterns just far enough away not to be detected. For safety's sake, to cover the western end, we'll be announcing joint NATO exercises with the Turkish fleet and air forces. For cover to the east and the south, we are also going to publicize that we are doing joint naval exercises with the Indian navy."

The president nods, thoughtfully. Admiral Smith sits back down.

"And you all expect the Iranians to buy this?" the president asks everyone present.

"Sir," says General Sanford, "We have a plan that should totally disorient them for a number of hours, giving us the opportunity to complete our mission successfully. My understanding was, however, that this meeting was called to pick out the targets, not brief you on how it will come about. Far more work's needed before I'm going to be satisfied with preparations."

"You're one hundred percent correct, Victor," the president smiles. "Okay, just tell me what other targets we'll hit besides military ones."

Dean Hargrove puts his papers back in order then says, "I believe John Walker was planning to speak next?"

Walker stands up from his chair and walks around the podium, inserts a DVD into the computer and opens his first window. "What y'all see heah is the city of Tehran. For a numbah of weeks now, we've been monitorin' their gov'ment buildin's and the members of the Supreme Council. We know where they meet, when they get together and where they live. We know how big their families are, and just about how many cups of coffee they drink each day. The Council's comprised of six members, but we're also aware of a seventh member, who seems to be some kind of advisor. We think he's associated with the secret police. The NSA's selected target for the purposes of this meetin' is that group of individuals. If we're to target the real gov'ment, the pres'dent plus six individuals need to be on that list."

"You're suggesting we get them to call a meeting at 2400 hours to get them together?" the president asks. "Otherwise, what we're talking about is taking out their families with them, if we attack them in their homes."

Shuffling his papers, John is clearly uneasy with this question. "Suh, we don't have a concrete answer on that as yet."

President Egan places his hands together as if praying, then says, "Are you leaving that decision to the president?"

"No, suh, we just haven't figgered it out yet. We'll come up with somethin'. It's just the tip of the iceberg, suh. We've got a lot more to work out to minimize civilian casualties."

"What else do you recommend, John?" asks the president.

"NSA will propose any and all targets necessary to address these individuals. We feel that's our portion of the responsibility for target acquisition."

Walker leaves the podium and Allison McDonald walks to the head of the room.

"Sir, CIA recommends that we hit every known nuclear enrichment site and every site that may be involved in the process of nuclear enrichment. We know for a fact that a number of these sites are buried deep under ground. It's imperative that we demolish them completely and we use weapons strong enough to do so."

"Are you saying go nuclear, Allison?"

"No, sir, that I'm not. If I remember correctly, our military leaders told us in a previous meeting that we've got warheads with a stronger punch, warheads that we've never used before. If they're as powerful as they were represented to be, we won't need to go nuclear."

"Good memory, Allison," says General Bradley.

"What does it take for the Pentagon to use these warheads, gentlemen?"

"Just your say-so, sir," answers General Sanford.

"And the Pentagon is sure that these warheads will work without creating tremendous havoc on a civilian population?"

"Sir, after the Iraq war ended, we learned how many of our cruise missiles hit their targets but were not as effective as we would have liked them to be. The Pentagon has upgraded their punch power. If they hit their targets, they shouldn't be any more hazardous to the civilian population than our standard missiles," says Admiral Smith.

"General Bradley, does the same stand for your pin-point laser bombs?"

"Yes, sir."

The president begins to wrap the meeting up. "Okay, this is where we'll go with all this. I want you all to put your minds to all of the concerns that have surfaced this morning. I want plans to attack each of these concerns. I want to know how each plan will operate and how the coordination will work to make it happen. Nothing—I repeat, nothing happens until I give the go-ahead. Or, God help us, unless we are attacked first. Am I clear on this?"

Everyone responds in unison with a "Yes, sir!"

"Meeting adjourned, everyone. Let's turn this into a real plan."

The president rises and exits the room. Everyone else gets up from the table with the exception of McDonald, who is still standing at the podium where she was when the president gave his directive. She feels rooted to the spot. *Beginning a war of this magnitude can end one of two ways: either simply, or as a world-wide catastrophe. Which way will it go?*

Her thoughts pretty much match those of the rest who are starting to leave, each lost in his or her own world of worry.

Chapter Fifty

After Thanksgiving

Headline on the front page of The Washington Post:

Israeli PM to meet with President Egan

Israel's Prime Minister Yaakov Brumwell is flying in today to meet with President William Egan. White House press releases indicate the prime minister and the president will be discussing Israel's latest proposal for a Middle East peace settlement with the Palestinians . . .

The president scans the article. *Well, the press release should give us room to work in, the excuse we need to hold our meeting without a lot of second-guessing as to our agenda,* he thinks after finishing the front page article while eating his breakfast.

With the meticulousness of an hourly wage-earner punching a time clock, the president finishes his breakfast at 6:00 a.m. every morning, then he and his Secret Service detail head for the Oval Office. He has the next hour to himself to read and digest the various reports that await him in a neat pile on his desk. He finds this quiet time refreshing. He takes notes on the various subjects if he needs to seek clarification from the appropriate parties. One thing he has always said: "If you're going to read something, make damn sure you understand what you're reading. Otherwise you can get into serious trouble."

The lead agent of the Secret Service detail opens the Oval Office door and announces that Janet White, the president's secretary, is at her desk.

"Jack, ask Janet to please come in. Thank you."

"Yes, sir."

As Janet walks into the office, the president takes in her yellow business suit matched with an equally stunning blue blouse. *Those are good colors for her*, he ruminates as the Secret Service agent closes the door behind her. *I wonder if she's one of those women who picks out her clothes by that whole skin tone thing.*

Amused at himself, he gets down to business. "Have a seat, Janet," he says. "I need you to manage something for me. When the Israeli prime minister arrives, have the Secret Service escort him directly into the Oval Office and away from the news vultures. And I'd like you to bring Dean Hargrove into the office through the side door from the cabinet offices."

"As soon as the prime minister arrives, or would you like some time alone with him?"

"Give us ten minutes for the social pleasantries and protocol routines. I just don't want anyone seeing Dean here."

"Not a problem sir. The prime minister's El Al flight is due into Ronald Reagan at 11:00. I doubt if he will get here before 11:45. Actually, I could arrange to have a private lunch for you and the prime minister as soon as he arrives, then Dean could be sitting in here for when you two return. I'll tell Dean he needs to grab a quick lunch on his own."

"You keep reminding me of why I consider you my right-hand, uh, person." He smiles ruefully. "I swear, so many of the best expressions just don't translate into unisex-speak."

"That's okay," Janet laughs. "We women are pretty much used to it."

"Anyway," the president continues. "I like your plan. Nobody would expect that somebody'd be sitting here waiting for me to arrive."

"No one will have the foggiest, promise."

*

The limousine carrying Prime Minister Yaakov Brumwell arrives at the West Wing of the White House at 11:40. After the Marine guards on duty provide the proper protocols for the arrival of a head of state, two Secret Service agents escort the prime minister into the Oval Office to meet President Egan.

"Yaakov, it's great to see you. How was the flight?" The president comes around his desk and joyfully shakes hands with the prime minister.

"Too long as usual," Yaakov complains. "I'm getting too old for this stuff anymore."

"Don't hand me that. Your mind is as sharp as a tack, my boy. I've known you too long for you to start playing the Denny-the-Dunce routine."

"Well, sometimes I get away with it," he admits, smiling. "It works wonders in negotiations. You'd be amazed. You should try it sometimes."

"Well, this is not going to be negotiations. This meeting is to be strictly informative, to see if and how we can work together to solve a joint dilemma. Look, Janet has lunch all set for us. It's vegetarian, and guaranteed kosher. Let's go into the dining room. You must be starved by now."

"Tell her I appreciate her thoughtfulness, and her sensitivity to an old man's wishes."

"I will, but enough of this 'old man' talk. Let's go before someone else eats our food."

After lunch the president and the prime minister take some time to walk outside into the brilliant sunlight of a warm late November day. *It is good for both of us to feel the warm rays of the sun, especially when we'll be dealing with such dark issues,* Egan thinks as they approach a small mob of photo-op hungry reporters waiting to get some pictures and maybe a hint of what the two men are discussing today. The two take a few questions, then the president turns to the prime minister. "Yaakov, it is time to get to work. Let's head back to the Oval Office."

As they enter the office, Yaakov is appropriately surprised to find Dean Hargrove awaiting them. He knows that it is not customary for anyone to be alone in the Oval Office without the president being there. Hargrove jumps to his feet.

Dean Hargrove, chairman of the joint chiefs, is technically a civilian, serving in a post that had once only gone to top-rank military men. Hargrove is a retired Marine one-star general, who took early retirement rather than follow what he believed to be orders not in the best interest of his men and women, nor what he believed to be morally right for the United States. His six-foot, six-inch stature coupled with close-cropped hair and a trim navy blue suit, makes for a perfect specimen to represent American strength and integrity.

"Dean, it's good to see you, though I must say I am surprised," says Yaakov. "You must have an enormous amount of respect from the president to be left sitting in his office alone. Now I know this meeting will be serious."

Hargrove reaches out and shakes Yaakov's hand. "Thank you for the compliment, sir. Of course, he didn't tell you that he had me use the butler's entrance." The comment breaks the ice and the three have a good laugh as the president indicates a semi-circle of three chairs off to one side of the office, the area of the office most conducive to small meetings. Everyone settles in for what they all know will be a most significant discussion.

"Mr. President, we both know that you didn't call me over here to discuss the Palestinian issues in the Middle East. What's so urgent that it could not wait for my scheduled trip here in January?"

"Let me be direct, Yaakov," the president opens. "Is Israel planning any direct action on Iran's uranium enrichment sites?"

"You know that I could not tell you that, even if I knew it was so. Why do you ask?" Yaakov, a small man, looks up at the president over the rims of his glasses which he wears perched halfway down his nose.

"Because I can foresee, if both of our countries were to become involved in an all-out war with Iran, we could get our signals crossed and end up killing each other's people," the president says rather casually, considering the seriousness of his words.

Yaakov blinks several times before he answers. "What do you mean 'both of our countries'? You only asked me if Israel is planning any action."

"That's right. That's what I asked"

"So, what—is this a game, or do I go into my 'Denny-the-Dunce routine,' as you call it?"

President Egan and Hargrove both laugh out loud, not expecting this kind of response from an Israeli leader best known for his lack of a sense of humor.

"Dean, you tell him," President Egan says.

"Mr. Prime Minister, the president asked me to sit in on this meeting because he felt you'd believe what I am about to tell you as the truth, to the best of our knowledge."

"Okay," Yaakov says. "Go ahead. What's this truth, as you know it."

"Our intelligence is giving us information that Iran will have at least a dozen nuclear warheads within the next nine to twelve months," the chairman of the joint chiefs says. "We also believe Iran is actively attempting to purchase nuclear materials on the black market. We have good reason to suspect that they will have double the original amount, at the very least, that we thought they had to put into warheads."

"So what's the American concern? You aren't telling me their missiles can cross the oceans, are you?"

"No, of course not," Hargrove continues. "However, Kilo submarines can and we suspect they are working to modify their missiles so they can be launched from their subs. They also have another two new Kilos coming down from Russia at any time, once their sea trials are over. With this addition, their fleet will number six Kilos."

Yaakov is thunderstruck. "You think they are fools enough to fire on the United States!"

"We suspect they will attempt to hit both of us at the same time," President Egan says. "We are getting indications that Israel will come under conventional attack on two fronts as a diversion. One front will be from Gaza, the second from southern Lebanon. Once you're engaged on the ground, they will attack with missiles from Iran."

"I have no information from the Mossad on this," Yaakov sputters. "What makes you think this is so?"

"Yaakov, I can't answer that for you," Egan says. "What I'm asking you to do is go back to Israel and speak to those who you can trust with the utmost secrets. Tell them what we suspect. Ask them if we can work jointly somehow. I know this cannot be decided now, just between us. My primary concert, Yaakov, is that we don't want Israeli blood on our hands if we have to retaliate with Iran."

"Mr. President and you, Dean, both of you feel very certain about this?"

"Yes, we both do," says President Egan somberly. Hargrove nods in the affirmative as well.

"Shit," Yaakov says softly, looking off into space momentarily. "This makes the Palestinian issue look like a bad barbeque! I will do as you ask. I know for fact that some of my military leaders may feel they should deal with Iran themselves. I'm not so sure they trust the security of Israel to anyone but themselves."

"Yaakov, I fully understand their feelings and commitment," Egan says. "However, this time I think both of us are going to have our hands full and, as I said, we don't need to be stepping over each other as we try to deal with whatever comes our way."

"Taking my dunce cap off for a moment, if I may," Yaakov says wryly, "I get the idea you're talking more than retaliation. Is it possible that I'm correct?"

Hargrove looks to the president who gives him the go-ahead nod. "Mr. Prime Minister, we are looking at all options. One, a very likely plan, involves a pre-emptive strike on Iran, when and if we feel the situation gives us no other choice. Our intelligence is telling us that Hamas and Hezbollah, specifically, will attempt to strike at Israel as a distraction before Iran attacks. The United States would like to see Israel develop a plan to eliminate both Hamas and Hezbollah without killing too many civilians. This will allow us to deal with Iran without Israeli casualties."

"You know and I know, Dean, that what you're proposing is not the easiest thing to do. Both Hamas and Hezbollah hide within civilian populations."

"We never said it would be easy, Yaakov," says the president. "We just ask that you do the best you can. There are thousands of Palestinians and Lebanese who have no responsibility for what's going on."

"I know," agrees Yaakov wearily. "It's just that I see my own people having no responsibility for this as well, other than being Jewish—being blown apart by rockets and mortars or suicide bombers."

"Yaakov, it's true that it is very lonely at the top." The two heads of state lock eyes.

"Yes, my friends, it is," Yaakov finally says. "It would be so much easier to make these decisions if we had no hearts."

"Then, can we agree that you will talk with your people in complete secrecy? I cannot stress this enough, Yaakov."

"I will talk with the key leaders of the military, the Mossad and a few key Knesset members. Can I have two weeks to call you back on this?"

"Of course you can."

The president rises and goes to his desk, picks up some papers and returns to the others. "Now that we have cleared our agenda, Yaakov, I took the liberty of having Janet prepare two press releases for us. It's up to you to decide which one you'd prefer we give to the media regarding our Middle East peace plan."

"Are you shitting me, Bill?"

"No, I'm not, Yaakov. I'm giving you the choice of which one to offer the media dogs out there. Take a few minutes to read each and let me know which one you choose." Five minutes later, Yaakov hands the president his selection.

"Oh, so you're going to make me the bad guy," says the president, grinning wryly.

"What do you Americans say? 'It comes with the territory'? Anyway, you can always blame Janet. She put them together."

"Sounds like this might be one of her get-even days," says the president, laughing.

The three men get up from their chairs, shake hands and promise to speak again. Hargrove leaves through the same door he came in.

President Egan calls Janet and asks her to come into the office. When she enters, he hands her Yaakov's selection for the media. He also asks, "It's almost four o'clock. What time is dinner scheduled?"

"Dinner is scheduled for six, and the prime minister has a room upstairs if he would like to freshen up beforehand."

"How kind of you, my dear," smiles the little man.

Chapter Fifty-One

Early December

It is 1810; Hussein and Dakham have been standing outside of the Best Eastern since 1750.

Anxious, Hussein says, "Vicktor did say 1800, correct?"

"Yes, he did, my guess it's Dimitri. It's okay if he's late, just not us. They're either late because they left late, or they're stuck in traffic."

Hardly relieved, Hussein goes on, "I don't know, Hamid. I still get the feeling all of these antics are part of a game. The man has control issues."

"Maybe you're right, but I don't see it that way. What I do know is that he's dying to get his hands on the balance of the money, and I doubt he'll screw this up, at least until he gets paid."

"Which is why he doesn't get the balance until we are safely away from Russian soil," Hussein finishes Dakham's sentence for him. "Or as you are so fond of saying, it's our insurance policy so he will not screw up."

Pointing off in the distance, Dakham says, "Over there, Kamil. The Mercedes, turning the corner. With two people inside. Be nice now. We do not want to piss him off more than we have to."

Vicktor pulls up in front of the Best Eastern, and Hussein and Dakham get into the back seat. Hussein begins to settle down. "Sorry we are late," Vicktor says. "Traffic is terrible. I cannot imagine how countries with large automobile populations handle it."

Meanwhile Dimitri, who is sitting in the passenger seat, is talking on his cell phone as if he's alone in a phone booth. After a few minutes, he

237

ends the conversation, closes his phone and pockets it. "Sorry, but this is important business that I need to conclude today. It's good to see the two of you again. I'm taking you out to one of Russia's finest American style restaurants Do you like American food?"

Hussein answers for both of them. "We don't eat American food. What's it like?"

"You'll see for yourself. One thing you'll learn, the Americans, like the French, know how to eat!"

Vicktor pulls the Mercedes up to the front of a building that doesn't seem to fit with its neighborhood. The front of the building is aglow with lighting; a doorman stands outside. A pair of uniformed parking valets offer to take the Mercedes and park it for them. Both Hussein and Dakham, who have never seen the likes of this, gape as Vicktor hands the keys to the first fellow who offers to park it for them. In return, he hands Vicktor a small chit of paper, jumps in the driver's seat and takes off with the Mercedes' tires screeching. *What an odd bargain this is,* thinks Dakham.

Dimitri leads the way inside while the doorman holds the door open for each of them to enter. Inside, they walk down a flight of stairs where a pretty, young coat check girl gives Dimitri a quick peek on the cheek as he hands her his coat. Just like the car, he has traded his coat for a small, round disk, which he pockets.

An elegant hostess stands at the doorway of the dining room. She has pulled out four menus and a wine list the moment she saw Dimitri come through the door. "Dimitri, so good to see you again," she says cordially. "Your table is all set for you. Maria will be your waitress this evening."

She escorts them to a table at the far end of the dining room, a section that seems darker than rest of the room. The table seats four. Dimitri sits down first, positioning himself so his back is to the wall, giving him a clear view of the doorway. Vicktor sits to his left, Hussein to his right and Dakham sits across from him.

"Gentlemen, gentlemen. Let's start our dinner off with some refreshments. What kinds of wine would you enjoy?"

"Dimitri, we are sorry and certainly don't mean to offend you," Hussein says. "However, being observant Muslims, we do not partake of alcoholic beverages."

"Are you serious?" Dimitri reacts, seemingly in genuine amazement. "Even when you are out of the country and can do as you wish?"

"The practices of our faith are not limited to the boundaries of our country," replies Dakham.

"Okay, okay, you drink what you wish. I'm going to order a bottle of Merlot. Vicktor is driving and so he can't drink. It appears that I'm the only one who will partake of the gifts of the gods." He's still shaking his head. "Well, then, as to food," he continues, "I recommend that you try the western beef from the United States. I like mine medium-rare. It is very tender and I can assure you, you will never get a better meal anywhere else in the world."

A uniformed wine steward arrives at the table, and Dimitri orders a French Merlot. Hussein and Dakham order herbal tea. Vicktor is content with just a glass of water.

The waitress, Maria, appears and guides Hussein and Dakham in making their dinner selections. Both of them choose the marinated steak tips, along with a potato and vegetable. Dimitri gives her an order for a one-pound New York sirloin. Vicktor orders a twelve ounce steak. She asks Hussein and Dakham if she should deliver the tea with their meals. They reply in the affirmative.

Dimitri settles back into his chair. "So, then, welcome back to Russia. I believe we will satisfy your requirements and possibly do more business in the years to come."

"Is everything all set for us to start degreasing the reducers and placing the lead containers inside?" asks Hussein.

"Yes—and no." Dimitri says, his face a mask.

"What do you mean 'yes and no'?" Hussein asks, shocked.

"So far we have removed nine of the material portions you are purchasing. I will need another week to remove the other two."

"Why do you need another week, if you have already removed nine in two weeks?"

"Our regular man who does this became ill. We are looking for a substitute for him to finish the job. That person will arrive in three days."

Just as he finishes his explanation, the wine steward returns to the table and all conversation ceases. "Would you like me to pour a sample for you to try, Dimitri?" he asks.

"Yes, I would."

The steward pours a small portion in Dimitri's wine glass, then stands back waiting for him to check its flavor. Dimitri knows how to sample wine. He goes through the whole process of holding it in various spots in his mouth and then swallows what he sipped, which Dakham finds amusing. He dares not make eye contact with Hussein or he knows he will laugh out loud.

The hovering wine steward seems to be taking all this using-wine-for-mouthwash business seriously, however, Dakham observes. When Dimitri finally swallows, the steward asks anxiously, "Is it satisfactory, sir?"

"Yes, my friend," Dimitri responds warmly. "You can fill the glass and leave the bottle." He does as asked, then withdraws. Dimitri picks up the conversation where it had been dropped.

"So, as I was saying, our man got ill. Sometimes such things happen in life. Another week is the latest we expect."

"All right," says Hussein. "We will start working on cleaning up the three reducers. We will be placing four containers into two of them. The final three will go in the third. You do have the materials we requested, I trust, for us to build buffers between the lead boxes and construct the false bottoms over the units?"

"Yes, yes," Dimitry responds. "Everything is all set for you to work at the warehouse where you first saw the reducers. Vicktor will pick you up tomorrow at whatever time you wish him to. He'll take you there and bring you back at the end of each day. When you are finished loading the reducers, how are you going to transport them?"

"Our fourth cousin is working on arranging transportation for us to move the reducers. He will also provide us with the proper papers to export them out of the country."

"And when do I get the balance of the money I am owed for this project?"

Just then dinner arrives. Dakham looks down at his plate, then across at Vicktor's and Dimitri's. *There is enough food on my plate to feed three. Dimitri's would feed four or five.*

"Try the steak sauce on your meat," Dimitri suggests. "You may find it very appetizing." As soon as the waitress leaves, the conversation continues precisely where it left off.

"Dimitri, you will receive the balance of the purchase price," Hussein states firmly, "when we are clear of Russian territory. And I trust there will be no game of switch played on us,"

"What you think, I would cheat you?" *Insulting amateurs*, Dimitri thinks. He has just put his first bite of meat into his mouth, and realizes he's grinding his teeth as he chews.

"We just suggest that no one considers it."

"Hamid, is that a threat?"

"No, Dimitri, that's a promise."

At that, all conversation comes to a halt as the four forget negotiations and set to work devouring their meals. Hussein and Dakham find this exotic American beef very tasty, and proceed to finish everything on their plates, as do Dimitri and Vicktor.

When the plates are being cleared, Dimitri asks, "Anyone for dessert?"

Hussein and Dakham just look at each other. *This guy either has a bottomless pit for a stomach or is just one hungry son-of-a-bitch,* Dakham thinks, then has to suppress the laughter he feels welling up once again.

Since no one other than himself wants dessert, Dimitri passes as well. He signs the check, retrieves his coat, then everyone heads out. Dakham elbows Hussein as Vicktor hands the small piece of paper to the parking valet. As they wait, Dimitri takes some money from his wallet, then hands it over to Vicktor. *He will pay a bribe to get his car back?* is all Dakham can make of all this. When the Mercedes pulls up to the curb, the valet jumps back out, and Vicktor presses the bribe into his hand. *Paying a bribe after he returns the car. Now I've seen it all.*

Vicktor drives back to the Best Eastern and they agree he will pick them up at 0830 the next morning. The Mercedes pulls up in front of the Best Eastern, Hussein and Dakham exit the vehicle and head up to their rooms.

Hussein dials the number they use in Pakistan and receives a voice mail prompt to leave a message. He leaves the following update: "Your nephew here. Met with Dimitri this evening for dinner. He has not completed the removal of all the materials. We are short two pieces and need to wait one week for the completion of the job. Will work on restoring what was been removed and will complete packing for shipment."

Chapter Fifty-Two

Packing the Goods

The ride to the warehouse the next morning is subdued. Vicktor is not his talkative self and Hussein is contemplating what they will encounter. Dakham on the other hand is taking in the view while they ride. They pull up to the warehouse and drive around to the back before Vicktor parks the car.

"I've been told we need to go in the back door this time. Dimitri doesn't want anyone nosing around to see what you're doing here."

"Not a problem for us, Vicktor," replies Hussein. "Will you be staying with us throughout the day or leaving us to ourselves? Is there anyone else in the building in case we need something we can't find?"

"I'll be staying with you all of the time you are here. If you don't have something you need then I will attempt to get it for you." At that, Vicktor gets out of the car, opens the back door and takes them inside and directly to where the reducers are located.

Hussein gives them a quick check. "Good," he says, once he's convinced that the reducers are in exactly the same shape as they were when saw them on their first visit.

"Vicktor, we can handle this from here," says Dakham. "Just tell us where the materials are that we ordered, and where the goods are stored."

Vicktor points out the nine storage boxes containing the nuclear materials, staying as far from the boxes as he can. Then he takes them into another room, where they find the materials they'd ordered, plus an assortment of tools that they can use. Vicktor says, "I'll be in the back office. Holler if you need me."

"Good, Hamid, now we can work in peace," Hussein says once Vicktor's out of hearing. "First, check and see if any radiation's leaked from the boxes?"

Dakham gets the hand-held Geiger counter from his briefcase and turns it on. State-of-the-art, it can detect the standard beta and gamma rays, and alpha radiation as well.

Scanning the storage box containing the nine small leaded boxes results in no radioactive readings. *Either these leaded boxes are very good or we are getting a hose job on what's inside. However, we have no choice but to take their word for it without the protective clothing to open one to make sure,* Dakham thinks. *Great planning. That I'd have to classify as a major oversight.*

Hussein is thinking, *I wonder if the guy Dimitri used to remove these materials had the proper gear, or is he dying of radioactive poisoning right now?*

"So far so good, Kamil," Hamid reports. "Based on the readings I'm getting, we can safely work with the leaded boxes."

The reducers are very large and very heavy. Reducers are mechanical components of a power transmission system. The greater the torque inserted into the reducer, the larger the unit. That factor also has a lot to do with the ratio of the unit. The larger the ratio, the higher the output torque. These particular units are designed for 100-150 horsepower input, with large ratios.

"Damn, these things have so much paint on them it'll take both of us and a much larger wrench to get these bolts loose," Dakham says as he starts working with the first one. "I know one thing for sure: whoever ran these units never took the covers off for inspections."

They spent a full two hours removing the cover of the first reducer, then taking out the shafting, gears and bearings. Then they set to work degreasing the lower portion of the housing so they can epoxy four of the lead units onto the base. It takes four hours for the epoxy to take permanent form, and then they add the wooden shims they had made to insure that nothing moves while being shipped.

Things have been quiet all day. All of a sudden they hear Vicktor holler, "Don't you guys ever take a break and eat?" He's coming back to check up on them. "Let's go and get something."

"We took a break for our noon time prayers and had a snack while the epoxy was drying, Vicktor," says Hussein. "We'll pass on going out for a meal. We have too much to do. Why don't you go out and get yourself something,"

"I can't. I'm supposed to stay with you."

"Your choice, Vicktor. At the rate we're going, we should be done in another hour. We'll do the second reducer tomorrow."

By the time they're finished for the day, they have been able to insert the special false bottom on top of the leaded containers. Everything fits perfectly. They apply a skim coat of adhesive they brought with them to indicate if the bottom has been tampered with before the goods arrive in Iran.

They are pleased with their progress. It has only taken a total of seven hours to install the units and replace the reducer's components to look as if they were never touched. *Tomorrow we'll do the second reducer, but before we go I'm going to mark the units, so if there's a switch we'll know it before we leave,* Hussein plans.

"Let's go Vicktor. It's time for us to get cleaned up and then go for an early dinner. Are you buying?"

*

As Hussein and Dakham enter the Best Eastern after dinner, they stop by the front desk to check for messages.

As expected, they have received the following from Jibril Atwan. STAY THE EXTRA WEEK AND ENJOY THE SIGHTS. HAVE ARRANGED FOR TRANSPORTATION FROM YOUR STORAGE AREA TO THE COAST. NEED TWO DAYS NOTICE TO HAVE A FLAT BED AT YOUR LOCATION. NO NEED TO REPLY TO THIS MESSAGE. YOUR FOURTH COUSIN.

*

The next day is a duplicate of the previous day for Hussein and Dakham. The only thing that differs is that Vicktor is smart enough to bring lunch for himself.

At the end of the day, Hussein says, "Vicktor, is Dimitri's new man in town yet to deal with the other two units? We can't do any more until we have them, and we need to notify our office when we'll be ready to leave."

"Dimitri told me he arrives in two days with your two boxes."

"Well, let's head back to the hotel for dinner. Since you paid last night, we'll spring for dinner tonight," states Dakham, smiling.

*

Sitting in Dakham's room, the two of them review their progress and what they believe they can expect next.

"Okay, so this new man arrives in two days with the boxes," Dakham says. "If he arrives as expected and we finish loading the last reducer without any difficulty, then we can give our fourth cousin the two days' notice he's looking for and be out of here at the end of one full week."

"Right. Then three days travel time to the port at the mouth of the Volga. I hope our cousin doesn't plan on us sitting around the docks waiting for some freighter to arrive."

"Kamil, if this screws up, it's his ass on the line with his bosses, even more than ours are. I think he's smart enough to make sure the timing of our arrival results in a minimum delay at the docks before we're on board."

"But, Hamid, we also need to have our transportation papers and shipping documents in order before we leave here. Do you think he'll have them ready in time, or will we end up stuck sitting around here with three hot reducers waiting for a KGB raid?"

"Kamil, relax. You can't be happy if you don't have something to worry about," Dakham groans. "They'll make it happen."

Chapter Fifty-Three

Reporting to the Guardian Council

"So, Jibril," says Ayatollah Fadil Ahmajid, the intimidating Supreme Leader, "what can you report to us regarding the Russian Kilo delivery and your surprise package from Russia?"

Jibril Atwan looks into the eyes of the five members of the Guardian Council, the real decision makers in Iran. Since Ahmajid hired him as a military advisor to the council, Ahmajid is someone he believes he can trust. The other five Imams look desperate for information to satisfy some sort of dreams they have. What these dreams are, he cannot know. Trusting them would be only for the foolhardy, which Atwan is not.

"Ayatollah, members of the Council, I have just received word that the two Kilos we recently purchased from the Russians have completed their sea trials. At my insistence," Jibril says, then takes a split-second to think, *I might as well take credit for the idea*, "We provided the Russians with Iranian crews to bring the Kilos back to Iran without any other foreign assistance. They will be leaving Russia four days from now, after they have been re-supplied."

"How long will it take the two subs to reach Iranian waters from where they are located?" says Rahim Givon nervously.

"We have given them six weeks to arrive; they will be conducting sea trials of their own on the way back—things we want them to be qualified for that we didn't want the Russians to be aware of." Atwan stares at each of the council members except Ahmajid.

"How long will it take these two crews to be up to par with the crews that we currently have on the four Kilos we have in port?" Hossein Farook wants to know. "I understand that the four crews we have now are not sufficiently experienced in firing our Shahab missiles. Can we still meet our supposed target date of nine months from now?" Farook's tone is decidedly negative.

Ahmajid interrupts angrily, "The navy has assured me that the four current crews and the two new crews will be ready in six months. They say that the difficulties they are having are minor in nature."

Sayed Abbas gets up from the table and walks to a window and looks out. Then he turns back. "Supreme Leader, Jibril, my concern is that, if we aren't fully operational in eight months, we may need to re-think our launch date." Having had his say, Abbas rejoins the table quietly.

"I agree with Sayed," says Mansour Hassan, "We know that our Shahab missile will fire effectively and inserting the nuclear materials is not a major issue. However, if we don't cripple the United States at first strike, we set ourselves up for major retaliation. Those missiles must work and those subs must be able to deliver them."

"So far we are right on schedule, gentlemen," Atwan says, trying to come across as the picture of confidence. "Our own plants will be providing us with enough enriched uranium for twelve warheads within eight months. It will only take a couple of weeks for us to install those materials into existing warheads and bring them on board."

"So what is this surprise package that the Supreme Leader says you picked up in Russia?" asks Givon, suspiciously.

"As we speak, two agents are moving overland with enough nuclear materials for us to create twelve more nuclear warheads for our missiles. They should arrive within forty-five days."

"Are you not taking chances, moving this material overland?" asks Farook.

"Sparing you all of the details, yes, we are moving it overland. Our means of transportation is good and we have concealed the materials in a manner that no one would ever suspect what they carry."

Hassan turns to Ahmajid. "Our military must be well coordinated to make this strike successful."

The Supreme Leader looks hurt by Hassan's question. "You know me better than that, Mansour. My plans have been underway for months now, preparing the military to be ready to launch into our mission without hesitation. I am beginning to feel insulted with all of your negative questions. Of course, we can cancel the whole thing if the Council wishes, and then tell the world that we—lick the boots of the foreigners and kiss their asses as well." His voice rises with each word he spits out.

"Calm down, Fadil. No one questions your abilities,' says Givon. "But the fact is, your plan can turn Iran into a major player worldwide—or it can destroy us as a nation. We need total assurance that everything is being done that needs to be done."

"Well, it is—if you just listen to Atwan and me instead of to your petty fears, you will help Iran become the leader of the Islamic world."

Chapter Fifty-Four

In the Prime Minister's Office

"Prime Minister," Chief of Staff Jacob Rabinowitz says in a loud and agitated voice, "I'm hearing what President Egan told you, but I have serious doubts about letting any country be responsible for the welfare of our people."

Before answering Jacob, Yaakov Brumwell faces those sitting around the table, Ariel Wattenberg and Yaakov Bergman, who he has requested to be here. With them are Yonatan Levy and Adam Rosenberg, two trusted members of the Knesset.

"Your response to the president's suggestion, Jacob, is something I told him would arise. Personally, I agree with you. Realistically, I think we need to consider the pros and cons of his suggestions. The president has asked for an answer in two weeks. It may not be the answer he wants to hear but, we'll give him an answer. Before we go into further discussion on this matter, Ariel, are you picking up any new intel on what the president seems to think is going on?"

"As you already know, Yaakov, we have information that leads us to believe that Iran is planning a strike at Israel, and we also believe that they are planning on targeting the United States as well. It does sound as if the president has more information than we have to date. I do have to wonder if it's accurate enough to make these kinds of decisions, but I suppose going ahead under those assumptions is better than doing nothing at all."

"Yosef, what do you think about the president's considerations?"

"Well, I do agree that if we are both to attack Iran independently, there will certainly be casualties on both sides due to lack of communication and human error. I look at this in a couple of ways. If we go with the U.S. retaliating against Iran scenario, and assuming we are attacked simultaneously, our air force will most probably have been severely compromised and we will be desperate for their help. If it ends up as a pre-emptive strike, I agree with the president, to really nip this terrorism bullshit once and for all. If this does come about, we will have to tell Syria, Egypt and Iraq to stay the hell out of the air and keep their ground forces immobilized."

Yonatan Levy speaks, "We have two weeks to come to a conclusion. Let's each take a look at what we individually believe are the pros and cons and meet next week at this time to build a consensus. Obviously, I assume we are not to discuss this matter outside of this small group, Prime Minister?"

"Obviously," Yaakov Brumwell says grimly.

Chapter Fifty-Five

Transporting Purchases

With the final three lead boxes in hand, Hussein goes about the task of installing them and sealing up the third reducer, the final step in completing this portion of the shipment. As soon as that is done, they will notify Atwan they are ready for pickup.

*

Two days later, Dimitri and Vicktor pick up Hussein and Dakham from the Best Eastern. "Nice of you to give us a good send off, Dimitri," says Dakham, his words only tinged with disdain.

"I just want to make sure you get off without any hitches," Dimitri responds. His words are tinged with power. "Don't forget, you owe me a lot of money."

"We know. You keep reminding us," says Hussein, his voice cautiously mocking. "Presuming all goes as planned, I expect you'l have the balance of your money within five to six days from today."

As the Mercedes pulls up to the warehouse, they see a large, black flat-bed rental truck out in front.

"Well, it looks like our fourth cousin employs someone who's prompt at least," remarks Hussein. "A good sign."

Vicktor, Dimitri and Hussein head for the warehouse while Dakham walks to the truck to speak with the driver, who has the windows closed against a cold November wind. He rolls down his window as Dakham approaches him. "Can I see the paperwork you're supposed to have for us?" Dakham asks him. The driver hands over a large sealed pouch.

Dakham breaks the seal, opens the pouch, then opens the single envelope it contains. The bills of lading are in order, indicating the driver is to pick up three used reducers. The units are to be transported to the mouth of the Volga River, along with two passengers. There they will be loaded aboard a Pakistani freighter. All of the paperwork indicates a purchase made in Russia with a final destination in Pakistan.

"Good. All is in order," Dakham says. "You'll need to back up to the loading dock so we can have a fork lift load the goods." Dakham could swear that he's seen this driver before but can't seem to place him.

On his way back to the warehouse, it hits him. *This is the same guy who took us on an early-morning tour of Tehran that day they started their training. Jibril sure has his connections.*

Inside the warehouse Dakham says, "Dimitri, I'm having the driver back up to the loading dock. Who's going to run the fork lift to load the truck?"

"What, you don't know how to run a fork lift, Hamid?" Dimitri laughs. "I'll show you how it works. Driving a fork lift is how I got started in this business, working on docks on the Black Sea."

As Dimitri goes for a fork lift from the back of the warehouse, Dakham has a chance to ask Hussein, "Each reducer is now on a skid. Did you check the marks you made so we know there's been no switch?"

"No switch," Hussein says quietly.

"You're sure?" Dakham asks. Hussein answers his question with a quick shake of the head. Dimitri is returning.

"Everything's fine, Hamid," he whispers. "If someone tried to make a switch, we'd know. No one would recognize my marks as identification."

"Nice work, my friend. Now for some other news. I think our driver is the same guy that gave us a tour of Tehran the morning we started our training."

"You've got to be kidding!" Hussein says, surprised.

"I could be wrong, but I don't think so. Don't let on if you think I'm right."

Dimitri loads the first reducer on the flatbed of the truck. It is obvious that he does know how to operate a fork lift. Rather than wasting time trying to teach one of the young men how to handle it, he thinks again, and goes ahead loading the second and third himself.

"See how easy that is!" Dimitri says as he steps off the fork lift. He and Vicktor wish the pair a safe journey.

Of course Dimitri wants us to have a safe journey, chuckles Dakham to himself. *He wants his money.*

*

The driver says, "The cab is designed for four. You can sit in the back of the cab, or one of you can ride in front if you wish. Put your luggage in the locker on the flat bed. You will be more comfortable that way. My instructions are to get to the port as quickly as possible. I plan on driving straight through without stopping except for fuel and for meals."

"Really? A three day trip without stopping?" says Hussein.

"I have done four days before. This is not a problem. Your fourth cousin has approved this."

"Okay," Hussein says, throwing his hands up in surrender. "Who are we to argue with the powers that be."

Hussein climbs up to the front of the cab alongside the driver and Dakham stretches out in the back of the cab. The two of them decided they will ride this way and rotate whenever they stop for fuel or meals.

Hussein turns to the driver and asks, "Do you have a name we can call you?"

"Oh, yes. Please excuse me. My name is Azim."

"Well, Azim, let's get this rig moving. We have a ship to meet."

"We'll be there in plenty of time," Azim assures him.

*

After two and a half days and numerous hair-raising driving incidents, the flatbed arrives at the mouth of the Volga River. Azim seems to know exactly which pier the Pakistan freighter Emir is docked. He maneuvers his flatbed through the traffic around the docks and pulls up to a gate.

Hussein cannot believe how lax customs security is at the gate. The agent inquires what's on the truck. Azim tells him used equipment bound for Pakistan. There is no discussion of anyone going aboard the vessel along with the equipment. An envelope changes hand, papers are stamped and the truck rolls through the gate down to a large blue and white freighter moored between two other freighters on the same side of the dock.

Azim tells Hussein and Dakham that one of them will have to go aboard the ship and advise the cargo officer they have materials to be loaded. Whoever goes should also advise the watch officer that two cabins have been reserved for them.

Azim stays with them until the reducers are removed from the flatbed and placed on the dock. Hussein stays with the goods until he sees the cargo officer direct a loading crane to take the reducers on board. All three units are placed in the forward cargo hold and secured so they will not move around during the trip should they hit rough seas.

Azim then bids Hussein and Dakham goodbye. As he starts to head back to the freighter, Dakham turns around to Azim and asks, "Will we see you in Tehran again?"

"I wondered if you remembered," Azim says with a smile. "Yes, brother, we will see each other again."

Once their cargo is aboard there is nothing else for them to do. They board the vessel and find their cabins. The Best Eastern has it all over a freighter cabin.

Only one more item needs to be taken care of: a five day trip on the Caspian Sea before they reach the Iranian port of Khurramabad. On the third day, Hussein will wire Atwan to release the balance of the funds to Dimitri.

The following morning, the Emir leaves the pier with the assistance of tugs, standard practice for all large vessels as they cannot maneuver very easily alongside a pier.

Out in the main channel, the tugs leave the freighter, and at the end of the channel the freighter enters open waters.

Five days to digest all that we have accomplished, thinks Hussein, standing at the rail, looking across the Caspian Sea to the horizon. *Five days to think about what our endeavor will deliver to the West.*

Chapter Fifty-Six

Do We or Don't We?

One week later, the prime minister's conference room is filled with what he calls the unholy six. Sitting around the table are Jacob Rabinowitz, Ariel Wattenberg, Yosef Bergman, Yonatan Levy and Adam Rosenberg of the Knesset; and himself.

"Don't everyone look so damn happy," Yaakov Brumwell opens the meeting. "If I didn't know what was going on in this room, I would think we were sitting shiva. Cheer up. Nobody's dead yet anyway."

"You know, Yaakov, this is not an easy task," says Rosenberg.

"No shit, Adam," Yaakov says. "If it were easy, I wouldn't need your opinions. You left this room last week with the suggestion that all of us put our pros and cons down on paper, so that we might be able to build consensus. So who wants to start? Pro means agreeing with the US terms. Con means against the president's suggestion. We can place the options on the flip chart."

For two hours the conversation goes back and forth. Some pros and cons are obvious. Others require discussion to decide whether they qualify as a pro or a con.

"All right, all right, enough already. I'm hearing the same damn things being said all sorts of ways. Let's put the common ideas on the board. Yosef, please be kind enough to be our flip chart master."

"I knew you wanted me in on this meeting for something," laughs Bergman.

"Don't be so smart, Yosef. It's just because you're the youngest in the room."

Bergman walks to the far end of the room and moves the flip chart and the easel on which it sits to a position where everyone can see what he will be writing. He decides to use a red pen for the pros, a blue pen for the cons. "Can everyone see the board comfortably?" he asks. The bunch of nods he receives that indicate that he got it right the on the first try.

"Before we start why don't we take a five minute stretch break," Yaakov suggests.

Everyone gets up from their chairs and tries to free up the tensions in their bodies, each in their own way, then cluster around as Yonatan Levy entertains them with stories of fishing recently off an ancient rock jetty in Tel Aviv. It helps keep their minds off the serious discussion ahead.

Ten minutes later Yaakov says, "Let's get back to it." They all head for their seats.

Jacob Rabinowitz opens. "I would like to list the cons first as I personally feel that they will form the structure for making our decision."

"Fair enough," says Yaakov.

The commonalities of the opinions are listed as following:

CON:

- The security of Israel should never be left to a foreign nation.
- This joint venture would not give Israel the full scope of military authority, which could affect battlefield decisions.
- Would Israel be running its own military actions, or would our troops be under the direction of the United States?

PRO:

- Israel has never fought an enemy as far away logistically as Iran. Our supply lines and engagement capabilities are limited.
- Dealing with the Gaza Strip, the West Bank and southern Lebanon as battlefronts is more practical in terms of our capabilities.
- Allowing the US to handle the Iranians would allow Israel to prepare for possible counter attacks.
- We must be vigilant for other Arab countries who might take advantage of our dealing with an attack by trying to engage against us as well.

"It appears that we have some very strong arguments and feelings on both sides of this issue," says Yaakov.

"Now I ask each and every one of you, if you were in the shoes of the prime minister, what conclusion would you come to?"

Jacob again responds first. "It is my nature to say only we can preserve our security. However, as we have talked and as a military man who has spent much of his career dealing with logistics, I know that we cannot sustain a long military action in Iran on our own."

Wattenberg speaks next. "If we have the assurances of the president that our military actions are under our own direction, I could feel comfortable about this choice."

Bergman says, "My concern is timing. I would want to have our attacks well coordinated with the American timetable so that we don't go on the attack, inadvertently causing something terrible to happen on their end. The Bay of Pigs situation in Cuba comes to mind."

"Damn good point, Yosef. I believe we must have clear assurances if we get into this agreement," says Yaakov. "Yonatan, Adam, do you have any input?"

Yonatan speaks up. "I can envision major counter attacks in this situation, as I'm sure Hezbollah and the Palestinians will see this as an opportunity to jump in. I think we need our troops close to our borders."

Rosenberg adds his thoughts. "Our air force will have its hands full within our own borders and quite possibly dealing with one or more Arab states that try to, as Yonatan says, take advantage of the situation."

"So what I think I'm hearing," Yaakov says slowly, carefully, "is that if we have these assurances from the president, we'll agree to work with the Americans as he has suggested."

Equally slowly, everyone finally nods in agreement.

"I will call him tomorrow. I've ordered lunch so, please, relax, use the facilities. Lunch will be delivered in ten minutes."

Chapter Fifty-Seven

Middle of December

Jibril Atwan and the Ayatollah Fadil Ahmajid sit across the desk from Iran's president, Mahmoud Khasanjani, in Mahmoud's office. This is the first time that Atwan has ever set foot in the president's office. They sit patiently while President Mahmoud speaks on the phone.

As he waits for the president to end his phone conversation Atwan thinks to himself, *if I didn't know any better I would think this office was designed by someone from the western world. Maybe it's because of the public image he wants to project. Whatever his reasons, I really feel uncomfortable sitting here.*

President Mahmoud ends his phone conversation, hangs up and turns to Atwan first. "Jibril, good to see you again."

"And you, sir," answers Atwan.

"It is important for us to lay out some definite plans, now that our efforts are beginning to bear fruit, reaching the point that we can move into phase two as it were," says the president.

"Mahmoud, we are nine months away from our target date," says Atwan. "In seven more months we'll have enough materials to load twelve of our Shahab-3s with nuclear warheads. In two more weeks we expect the twelve containers we purchased to be arriving in Tehran. We will then be able to say that we have nuclear cruise missile capability."

"Excellent, excellent," Khasanjani exclaims, clearly pleased. "Now we must think ahead so we can achieve the end of phase two on time. Phase two must get us to the point of initiating our strikes. Our strikes are phase three—the final agenda," he adds, the final three words as quiet as any he has spoken so far in this meeting. Both Atwan and Ahmajid are struck by the meaning of these words.

"Fadil," Khasanjani says after several moments' silence, "what are you planning to happen in phase two?"

"Mahmoud and Jibril, this is what I see which needs to be accomplished in phase two. With the Council's approval, we must get started on taking steps to be ready to strike when the iron is hot. For one, we must be certain that Hamas and Hezbollah are fully prepared to be our diversion before we strike Israel."

"Our agents have already told us that they have promised loyalty and would welcome the chance to become part of the takeover of Israel," replies Atwan.

"All well and good, Jibril," says Ahmajid. "However, we need a representative that the council and I trust meeting with both of these groups, coordinating their plans of action so that we know they will be effective. All of this must be done with the utmost secrecy, without stipulating any launch date for Israel's spies to uncover."

Atwan looks at Ahmajid and sees in his eyes why he was brought to this meeting. "Both of you know that I've never operated outside of Iran. I don't even have formal training to do this."

"You're right on both counts," says Mahmoud. "However, you have the natural skills we need for this assignment, and we cannot afford to have anyone outside of this circle knowledgeable of what we are planning to do."

"I would have to live in Gaza and Lebanon for a period of time?"

"Fadil and I feel that you should be able to accomplish your mission by spending no more than two months with each of the groups," says the president. "You agree, Fadil, do you not?"

"Yes, yes. Two months maximum in each of the camps should allow you sufficient time to earn their trust, work out strategies with them and build up their passions, to make their plans a reality once we reveal an actual timetable."

Somehow, I'm not as sure of my ability to take this on as these two appear to be, Atwan thinks. "So—when am I supposed to leave on this mission?"

"Mahmoud will have all of the necessary paperwork for you to travel as an Iranian diplomat. You should be able to leave within two days," says the Supreme Leader.

Atwan looks at Ahmajid. *Who do you think you are? Where do you get off, not even giving me a clue that this would be coming down? After all the years I have been your faithful advisor, I'm now to be treated like some common field agent?*

Ahmajid sees anger bordering on rage in Atwan eyes. *Not now,* Ahmajid thinks, *please Allah. It will be a enough of a job to handle your emotions as you work to accomplish this mission for me.*

Ahmajid quickly rises, wanting to get Atwan out of the room before he explodes. Mahmoud gets to his feet and kisses the hand of the Ayatollah. Atwan takes his time, an insult to both of the others. Shaking the hand of the president on his part is stiff, formal and obviously insincere. Atwan and Ahmajid leave the president's office.

The moment they are outside of the president's office, Atwan turns on the Supreme Leader. "Why, Fadil? You know that I've never been out in the field. Why now?"

"You heard Mahmoud. We simply cannot afford to have anyone else aware of our plans."

"We have plenty of agents who would love to have the opportunity to fire up Hamas and Hezbollah for attacks on Israel."

Ahmajid stops and turns on his advisor. "Jibril, I am getting the feeling that you do not trust our judgment. Can you do this mission—or not?"

"Oh, I will go," Atwan immediately caves. "However, I thought I was part of the management team on this project. I have dedicated my life to making sure everything goes as perfectly as humanly possible. Who will handle my responsibilities while I'm away?"

"I will personally take over your position until you return. At most, you will be gone four months. After that you will be back here planning the intimidation processes and the strike dates. Does that not satisfy you?"

"Yes, I guess it does," Atwan says, toning down. "It might have been easier to swallow, however, if you had given me some warning."

"You're right, it might have. However, Mahmoud asked that you not be advised beforehand. I wanted to appease him in this instance. It's complicated."

Both men then walked down the hallway and out into the sunlight at the front entrance of the president's headquarters. The Ayatollah turns to Atwan before getting in the car waiting for him. "Allah will be with you, Jibril. You will accomplish great things for Iran and Islam on this mission."

"You owe me one for this, Fadil," Atwan insists on protesting. "Four months sleeping with the peasants is not going to be entertaining."

"This project is not meant to be entertaining," the Supreme Leader says, looking placid as he speaks but working to keep his own anger in check. "It is a major undertaking for which we all must make sacrifices—and which we must win."

"I guess that's the only thing on which you and I can agree," says Atwan, taking Ahmajid's proffered hand and kissing it. "Get me my papers and I will be on my way. How do you want to communicate with me?"

"You will have a brief along with your papers, giving you all of the necessary information."

Chapter Fifty-Eight

Before the Holidays

President Egan and Dean Hargrove are sitting on sofas in the Oval Office trying to second guess what Israel might be deciding relative to the President's suggestion of a coordinated joint military venture. "The prime minister did say he would have an answer in two weeks," says the chairman of the joint chiefs, "Which is tomorrow."

"You know, Dean, if I were Yaakov, it would be very difficult for me to make the decision to place my country's security in another country's hands."

"I tend to agree with you, sir," says Hargrove. "However, we are not just another country. We have been, and will continue to be, the largest friend and benefactor that Israel has."

"Yes, I know the logic of it all. However the gut feeling that creates, the potential insecurity of it all could work against the part we want them to play."

Just then, the phone on the president's desk rings and he rises to answer it.

Seeing it's Janet's line to him, he picks up the receiver. "Yes, Janet."

"Sir, the prime minister of Israel is on a secure line and would like to speak with you."

"Thank you, Janet. Put him through. It's Yaakov," he says to Hargrove before he picks up the secure line, his concern as to what the conversation may amount to showing clearly.

He picks up the phone. "Yaakov, thank you for calling. I didn't expect to hear from you until tomorrow."

"Well, Mr. President, Israelis can move quicker when they want to."

"We all can move quicker, like you say, when we want to," the president says coolly. "So—may I ask, how did our proposal go over with your people?"

"I have to tell you, there's a great deal of concern on our part that if we give up the right to deal with Iran directly, then we are placing Israel's safety in the decision-making process of others."

Hargrove, watching the look of concern on the president's face, feels his powerlessness, like a phantom observer who can do nothing but watch what's going on.

"You know, Yaakov, if I were making this decision, I know I'd be having the same reservations. However, you have my word that, if necessary, the United States will do everything in its power to eliminate the threat against Israel."

"I believe you, Bill." Egan fights the temptation to hope that this indicates a yes. Yaakov Brumwell takes his time before he finally continues. "As you know, we have never participated in a military campaign so far from our borders before. Therefore, we believe your proposal has a good deal of merit and could enable us to solve our border problems with Hamas and Hezbollah at the same time."

"So, if I'm correct, Yaakov, Israel is agreeing to work with us on this joint venture, should it prove necessary?"

"Yes, Israel is agreeing."

Hargrove watches a smile break across the president's face and takes a deep breath of relief.

"What we would need from you, Mr. President," the prime minister continues, "is some preplanning with your military people before we begin this venture."

"No question about it, Yaakov. I want that to happen. We will come up with some reason that would bring your people here, learning new tank tactics or whatever."

"Good, Bill, I want you to understand that Israel's safety is now in your hands."

"A responsibility we do not take lightly, Mr. Prime Minister," the president says formally, and with great relief. "Yaakov, we will do everything in our power to make sure that both your people and your nation are safe."

"That's all I want to say for now. And, of course, I will not be making any statements about this publicly because of the security of this issue."

"Thank you, Yaakov." Quietly, the president hangs up his phone.

President Egan sits back down with Hargrove, but remains lost in thought for a moment. *I now have the security of two countries to be concerned about. What a Christmas present.*

Chapter Fifty-Nine

January 2011

Janet White is busy working on assembling the attendees for the 9:00 a.m. meeting the president wants held in the Situation Room this coming Friday morning. As she reaches the office of each party, she puts a circle next to the name on her list; once confirmed she fills in the circle, as if she were casting a ballot or taking a machine-graded test. Her list reads: Pat Devonshire, Maria Sterling, John Anderson, Allison McDonald, John Walker, Dean Hargrove, Robert Smith, James Bradley and Victor Sanford.

Two hours later she calls into the Oval Office. "Sir, everyone has been notified of your meeting on Friday, is aware that it's a must-attend situation and I have confirmations from all but two. Is there anything else you'd like me to do at this time?"

"Not right now, Janet. Thank you."

Based on a growing pile of Whispering data, satellite and human intelligence data, and input from sources within Israel, President Egan is preparing his staff to plan for war with Iran. He has the commitment of Israel to stay out of Iranian air space and to coordinate attacks on Hamas and Hezbollah when the time comes. He wants everyone at the meeting to know of his decision and to prepare themselves and their forces for when concept become reality. He has decided not to advise the Senate and House Armed Services Committee at this time. No actual date has been set yet, and he's determined to reduce the chance of a leak.

*

Everyone, including the president, is seated inside of the Situation Room with the exception of Maria Sterling. Anxiety has the upper hand on several of the faces around the table. The president doesn't normally call for "must-attend" meetings.

A Secret Service agent escorts Sterling in five minutes after the hour. "I'm sorry I'm late, sir," she says to the president. "My apologies to you all. An important phone call." *Maria looks like she didn't get a moment's sleep last night,* the president notes.

"Well now, with everyone here, let's begin," says President Egan, steeling himself for what he will say next. "In front of each one of you are reports detailing an accumulation of factual information which has caused me to reach the decision I've made. I suggest you take ten to fifteen minutes to read your file and then we'll discuss what I am about to do. When this meeting adjourns you'll leave the material right where you found it. The reports will be shredded by the Secret Service."

The president, deep in thought at first, finds himself scrutinizing each face around the table, taking mental notes on what he suspects each person is thinking. And watching the clock.

At the end of the fifteen minutes, he states, "As president of the United States of America, I am going to prepare this country for a war which appears imminent with Iran." He pauses, then adds, "I'd like your comments."

Maria Sterling is the first with a question. "With all due respect, sir, aren't we rushing to judgment? If I read these papers correctly, they say that some of this information is based on Israeli intelligence. Can we really trust their intelligence?"

John Walker nods to the president. The president points to him to speak.

"Suh, if I may respond to Maria before you reply?" He gets a nod from the president. "Maria, everythin' in the Israeli intelligence report has been verified by our own intelligence. NSA stands behind our intelligence."

Sterling shrinks back into her seat like a child who had just been scolded.

Allison McDonald speaks. "Sir, we are continuously receiving satellite data and intelligence from other sources that we recognize as the seed of something big, something planned to happen within the next twelve months. Our sources inside of Russia just advised us yesterday that a shipment of large-scale, heavy-duty industrial equipment left Russia several weeks ago. It is believed that nuclear materials was hidden inside of those units, which were purchased from the Russia mafiya. The destination of those units was listed as Pakistan. However, to the best of our knowledge, they never reached the Pakistani border."

"Where do you think they went?" asks the president.

"Sir, our sources say they traveled by freighter from the Volga River across the Caspian Sea to Iran. The papers say they were to be delivered to a warehouse in Pakistan. Two passengers on that freighter traveled with the shipment, posing as two Pakistani engineers who went to Russia looking for "used parts.' However, we were able to confirm that they're nothing of the sort. They are really Iranians schooled by the Iranian secret police."

"Interesting. Very interesting," replies the president.

"Allison, what's the status of the two Kilos that Iran's purchasing from Russia?" Admiral Smith inquires.

"Admiral, the two new Kilos left Russian waters two weeks ago and are heading for their Iranian berths. We have them under surveillance by satellite, and occasionally spot them on the surface. Those two will give the Iranians six Kilos that we know of."

The vice president speaks. "If Iran has to purchase nuclear materials from the Russian mafiya, that doesn't speak well for their nuclear enrichment program. Is it possible that the enrichment program is all a charade?"

"No, the enrichment program is no charade," President Egan responds. "Nuclear enrichment takes time. I believe, as do others, that they purchased additional nuclear materials to give themselves greater capacity than they can currently produce." The president rises to his feet and stands before the assembled group.

"Starting today, I want our country to begin preparations for war. Our military will draw up concrete plans to strike a first blow when and if we feel it is necessary. This is to be considered both of the highest priority and top secret. No leaks, is that clear?" Everyone present nods.

"If and when it becomes necessary to implement our plans, I will meet with the House and Senate Armed Services Committees."

John Anderson asks, "Sir, as secretary of defense, how am I to go to the United Nations and explain what by then will be a fait accompli?"

"After our mission is completed, I plan to broadcast to the Iranian people why we attacked their nation. I'm also going to offer them our protection from any other nation while they can rebuild their country and their government. Secondly," he says as he bends down and plants both hands on the table in front of him and looks each of his carefully chosen appointees in the eye, "I will speak before the United Nations myself and present the documentation as to why we did what we did. Let the world know what the Iranians had been planning to do before we stopped them."

Again he surveys his team. "Are there any other questions? If not, we all have work to do."

Chapter Sixty

Council Pressure

Ayatollah Fadil Ahmajid is just finishing reading his weekly report from Atwan who has been meeting with Hamas over the past two weeks. Atwan's report indicates that Hamas is willing to play a role in the joint incident designed to tie up Israeli forces along the Gaza strip. Jibril plans to spend six more weeks with the leaders of Hamas to get them accustomed to acting like a military force instead of "a bunch of hit-and-run bandits," as he calls them in his report. They will need to attack the border with a coordinated effort, not the way they've been accustomed to. Afterwards, Atwan plans to head to Lebanon to repeat the same process with Hezbollah. Ahmajid smiles. *How easy it is to raise armies just by providing money and motivation.* He chuckles quietly.

Just as Ahmajid closes Atwan's report, the five other Imams of the Guardian Council enter the conference room for their meeting. Hossein Farook, Mansour Hassan, Sayed Abbas, Karim Farhani and Rahim Givon each take a seat. The air is heavy with tension.

"How are things progressing, Fadil?" asks Farook.

"We are right on schedule. Our purchase from Russia has arrived safely. It is being held in storage within the containers it was shipped in. Our own enrichment process is still on schedule. We will have sufficient materials for twelve warheads within seven months. Our plan is to insert the nuclear materials in the missiles one week before our target date."

Abbas says, "I hear that Jibril is in Gaza."

"Where did you hear that?" Ahmajid snaps.

"You may think only you and the president know of this, Fadil, but there are more eyes and ears out than you realize paying attention to what we do."

"That doesn't answer my question, Abbas!" The supreme leader is angry now.

"I heard it from Jibril himself, if you must know. He told me he was going. What's his assignment there? I have never known Jibril to have worked outside of Iran before."

Ahmajid calms down. "The president wants someone to meet with Hamas and Hezbollah directly in order for them to fully understand their part in our plans. I agreed with him that Jibril would be the best person to fulfill that responsibility. He's sending us weekly reports. I was just reading this week's. So far he's pleased with what he's finding in Gaza."

"How is it that the president and you are making all these decisions without any of the five of us being involved?" Givon questions.

Ahmajid's answer to Givon comes out in an outburst of fury. "What are you saying, Givon? The five of you are usually involved in your mosques and whatever works you do in the community. The five of you are not always available to make decisions. Do you expect us to wait around to hold meetings to get things done?"

"No, no, Fadil," Hassan jumps in, trying to placate the man. His tone is soothing, almost fawning. "That's why you are the Council leader. Yet, the five of us sense that you and the president are beginning to run away with this plan. I speak for all of us in telling you that we are growing concerned. Can you assure us the two of you aren't becoming power-driven instead of making this the jihad we originally planned."

"The five of you are beginning to make me laugh," Ahmajid snorts. Pointing to each of them in turn, he goes on. "You spout hate and anger in your sermons, Farook. But when it comes to action and plans, you want someone else to make those plans work, don't you, Abbas. Then when things don't seems quite religious enough, Givon, you want to take back control of the reins. Go ahead run your jihad, Hassan. I will gladly step down and let any one of you, along with the president, make everything happen."

"That's not what we are saying Fadil," says Farook quickly.

"Then what are you saying, Farook?"

"As a council, things are happening but we are not being kept informed. You want to make the necessary decisions, fine. We understand that need. If Jibril hadn't told Abbas that he, Jibril, would be going to Gaza, when did you plan to tell us?"

Recovering his normal solemn demeanor, Ahmajid, speaking as the voice of wisdom, says, "I would have told you at this meeting. Are you satisfied?" The five nodded. "Now, if we can get on with the business at hand. The five of you need to come up with ideas about how we are going to address the United Nations Assembly to lift the sanctions placed on us, making it clear that if they are not, we'll definitely take action they will be sorry for. This is important."

The mood in the room changes and Ahmajid realizes he's once again in control. *Let these petty mullahs bicker. They don't know what true leadership really is.*

They close their deliberations with a proposal for the president to address the UN.

Chapter Sixty-One

Bringing the Navy Aboard

Ayatollah Fadil Ahmajid and Admiral Aziz Kerubi, head of the Iranian navy, sit in the conference room awaiting the arrival of President Mahmoud Khasanjani.

"Thank you for coming, Admiral," Ahmajid says to Aziz. "It is most important that we begin to discuss how your Kilos will take part in our future plans."

The admiral replies with zest, "Yes, sir. It is, of course, my pleasure to be here and be of service to my country."

"Would you like some tea while we wait for the president to arrive?"

"Why, yes, I would enjoy that very much, if you will join me as well," Aziz smiles.

Ahmajid picks up his receiver, dials, and orders herbal tea for three to be sent up to the conference room.

Waiting for the tea, Ahmajid and the admiral engage in small talk about the admiral's naval career. He really doesn't need to do this as he has read the file on the admiral closely.

Ten minutes later the tea is brought into the room by a security person. "Come, let us have our tea while we wait for Mahmoud to arrive."

Admiral Aziz and Ahmajid sit across from each other, sipping their hot tea, each trying to sense what the other is thinking and each planning his own strategy for what he may encounter.

Within a few minutes after the tea arrives, President Mahmoud walks through the door and expresses his apologies for being late. "Admiral, it is so good to see you again. It has been a while since our last meeting."

"Yes, Mr. President. I must say I'm pleased that you remember, considering all that you have to deal with." The president looks at the admiral and says to himself, *this guy is a real ass kisser. I wonder what we can get him to commit to.* His thoughts are not far different from those of the ayatollah.

Once the three of them are seated, the president begins. "Admiral, we have plans to use your Kilos that will make Iran the leader of the Islamic world." He lets that thought hang for a few moments. Then he proceeds to say, "Our plan will make you the most heroic naval Muslim in the history of the entire Middle East."

"Am I to destroy Israel with the Kilos?" Aziz wonders aloud. Ahmajid sits back and watches the president play this egotistical officer like plucking the strings of a harp.

"Actually, more than just Israel, Aziz. You will be attacking the United States as well."

Aziz sits blinking, dumbfounded for a few moments. He shakes his head as if trying to get this information to fall into its proper slot, regains his composure, starts to lose it again, pulls himself together and finally is able to ask, "With only six Kilos you expect our navy to attack the United States?"

"Yes, admiral. The United States. You, I know, are well aware of the missiles we are converting to cruise-missile capability. Very soon we will have nuclear material to place in their warheads." Aziz jumps at the word 'nuclear.' "Your navy will bring the Great Satan to its knees. When their major cities have been hit, on both of their coasts, you watch, their determination to continue to fight us will evaporate. We are taking the war to them. The oceans will no longer protect them as they have in the past. We will conquer them."

Aziz again goes silent at the enormity of what he's being told. Ahmajid and Mahmoud watch his reactions closely. He asks another question. "Mr. President, Fadil, our cruise missiles are only in the testing stage. How much time do we need before we enact your plan of attack?"

Ahmajid smiles. "Jibril has told me that the engineering group working on the missiles reported to him that they completed their design modifications and are satisfied with their testing."

"They may be satisfied, but we are still finding some inaccuracies which are causing field problems. I'm looking at three more months at the very least before I'd want to undertake a plan of this magnitude."

"Then three months you have, Aziz. However," says Ahmajid, raising a finger, "no more than that."

"Gentlemen, if I may, what's your launch date for this project?" the admiral asks his third question.

"It is not exactly firmed up yet," the president replies. "But we can guarantee that we will give you at least a full month's notice before we want the Kilos to depart on their mission."

"Will the captains know what their missions are when they depart?"

"Your job is to motivate your captains. They must realize that their part of this plan is vital to the success of Iran's becoming the ruler of the Muslim world," Mahmoud tells him. "Their orders will be delivered sealed to the captains. They will be instructed to open them only after they have departed. Only the three of us will know where each vessel is headed. Security is of the utmost importance. Do I make myself clear?"

"Yes, Mr. President." Aziz is now quivering inside, though he's determined not to let it show. *I cannot comprehend the boldness of this plan—or are these men insane?*

"Admiral, we will want weekly reports on your progress with the missile systems," remarks Mahmoud.

"You will have them," he replies calmly.

"You may leave now, Admiral. We look forward to hearing your reports. We trust you will be successful."

Aziz gets up and starts for the door, then hesitates. "May I ask one more question before I leave?"

"What's it?" Ahmajid asks.

"How many other aspects of your plan are there?"

"Admiral, you only need to be concerned about what involves the navy." Aziz nods, then leaves, closing the door behind him. As he departs the building, again he finds himself wondering where the government is taking him and his country.

"Well, Fadil, what do you think of Aziz's reaction?" asks Mahmoud.

"It is as I expected—the scale of it scares him like he has never been scared before."

Chapter Sixty-Two

Creating Fear

Standing before a crowd of thousands in the Iranian capital of Tehran, President Mahmoud Khasajani announces to the world, "Iran is coming closer to its destined position in the world. We will unite the Muslim world. We will fight the Zionist. We will conquer the land of Israel. Then the United States will taste what it is like to be alone."

The throng gathered in front of him, there by invitation in the form of bribery, erupts into wild cheering to such an extent that Mahmoud cannot continue his speech for a full five minutes.

When he's finally able to resume, he tells them, "Allah be praised, as I stand before you this day, you will see all of this come about."

Every word Mahmoud speaks is being transmitted over Al-Jazeera, BBC and CNN.

Analysts the world over wonder, and start writing about, what this saber-rattling and rhetoric might signify. Is it just clichés, something to whip up enthusiasm for a populace who has suffered long and hard under sanctions imposed by the West? Or is something deeper being revealed to the Iranian people?

Is the president preparing his nation for war, or is he still just a politician full of hot air?

*

Joe Smiga

Two days later, London experiences another subway bombing, again at rush hour. The 2005 bombings had resulted in fifty-two deaths; this bombing kills hundreds. No one claims responsibility for it. Scotland Yard receives only a one-sentence call, made from a phone booth by a man with an Arabic accent. All the man says is, "This is just the beginning—if you continue to side with the Great Satan."

*

At almost the same moment, Paris suffers a similar bombing in its Metro. Two hundred eighty dead. In Madrid, a major transportation hub is also hit. The death toll there numbers in the thousands. Both the Paris Préfecture de Police and the Policia Municipal de Madrid receive exactly the same message as did Scotland Yard.

*

The House of Saud, the ruling family of Saudi Arabia, receives a message that warns of its destruction if it continues to side with the United States militarily.

Chapter Sixty-Three

Assassination

Almost as soon as he arrives in Gaza, Jibril Atwan's presence is noted by Mossad agents operating in the region. Their instructions are to tail him, and attempt to find out why Atwan, of all people, is visiting with the leaders of Hamas.

Passing what information they can find back to headquarters, Mossad assumes that Atwan's visit is to establish some kind of coordinated plan, in which Hamas has most probably been given a role to play in an attack against the state of Israel. What that plan is, the agents have not been able to discern.

Following their instructions, they continue to monitor Atwan's every move. Surprisingly, he remains in Gaza for close to eight weeks. Whatever he's transmitting to the leadership of Hamas is taking much time for them to digest.

In the middle of the eighth week, the agents watch as Hamas places Atwan on a high-speed water craft. Word the agents receive via the pipeline is that their visitor is on his way to spend time with Hezbollah.

*

Ariel Wattenberg is studying his agents' reports from Gaza. The fact that Iran has sent Jibril Atwan to visit with Hamas has major implications. Wattenberg's face shows signs of the stress of not knowing what's going on. Wattenberg picks up his phone and puts a call into the prime minister, asking that the prime minister return his call on a secure line.

Within the hour, Yaakov Brumwell returns his call.

"Ariel, what are we dealing with that you want a secure line?"

"Do you know the name Jibril Atwan?" Wattenberg asks.

Surprised, Yaakov responds, "Yes, I do. He's some sort of special advisor to the Supreme Leader of the Iranian Council."

"We have been watching him for close to eight weeks now. It seems he's getting much further in bed with Hamas than has been the case heretofore. However we haven't learned very much."

"We've always known Iran supports Hamas. However, this does sound a little bit unusual. I'm not aware that Atwan is the messenger type."

"You're right, Yaakov—he's not. What this is telling me is that whatever he's sharing with Hamas has to be of major importance. They would trust no one else."

"Has he headed back to Iran yet?"

"No, we've just learned that he's traveling by high-speed boat to the shores of Lebanon."

"So, a meeting with Hezbollah as well?"

"It would seem so, Yaakov. Something is brewing. The first thing that comes to mind, of course, is a major confrontation for us."

"See if our people on the ground in Lebanon can find out anything more than what our people in Gaza did, Ariel. We obviously need more information than what we have."

"We'll do our best, Yaakov."

Wattenberg hangs up with a bad feeling. *Not another war,* he sighs.

*

It takes three days for Israeli Mossad agents working in Lebanon to locate Atwan. No one back at headquarters is surprised to be told he's spending time with known leaders of Hezbollah.

The fifth week that Atwan is in Lebanon, one of the agents learns from one of his informants that Atwan is talking about a joint attack of Hezbollah and Hamas on Israel. His plan is simple: have Hezbollah strike along the whole northern border of Israel and Hamas strike along the whole Gaza strip simultaneously. According to his source, no date had yet been set as to when this is to take place.

Wattenberg doesn't even hang up the phone after receiving this information. Cradling the receiver on his shoulder, he breaks the connection and immediately puts a call through to the prime minister. When he gets him on the phone, he quickly tells him what his agent has just reported.

"Do you believe this information to be true, Ariel?"

"Yes, Yaakov, I do. This information plus the amount of time that Atwan is spending with each group lends credence to what we've found out."

"What do you plan to do, Ariel?"

"Well, our choices are that we can do nothing and just continue to monitor both groups to see if we can learn more without their realizing we know anything."

"That's just one choice," Yaakov says. "What's another choice?"

Wattenberg thinks out his response as he talks. "You know, I believe that Iran may have sent Atwan for more than one reason. Maybe they don't trust anyone else to deliver this particular message. However, with Atwan spending so much time with each group, I think Iran wants to know how effective each group will be for whatever it is they have planned."

"Okay . . . that makes sense to me."

"I also doubt that Atwan would have put much information regarding these groups in writing, in his reports."

"So, what are you saying then?"

"I'm saying that if the fountain of information never gets back to Iran in one piece, that could create problems for Iran, or at least create a delay long enough for us to learn more about what's going on."

"I see where you're going with this. You want to take out Atwan."

"That's correct, sir. He certainly is not the top dog in Iran, but he's a heavy hitter in his own right. We may never get another chance at him again."

"How would you do this?" the prime minister asks.

"That I do not know as yet. But—do I have your okay?"

"You certainly do," Yaakov says grimly.

"Thank you, sir. I believe you've just made a very positive tactical decision."

*

For three weeks in a row, around 2100 hours, Atwan takes a stroll along the beach where Hezbollah has him quartered. He usually walks for half

Joe Smiga

an hour heading north and then retraces his steps back to his lodging. He appears to like his solitude, enjoying a cigarette or two along the way.

Tonight, around 2000 hours, three figures dressed in commando suits and swim gear come ashore nearly one hundred meters north of the path where Atwan habitually begins his walk. Each of them finds cover and removes his swim fins and snorkels.

There is no moon tonight; the night vision scopes they use looking for their quarry are very helpful. Everything is quiet along the shoreline. No one has noticed their arrival.

Around 2100, just as they expect, they see a lone figure walking along the shoreline. And just as they expect, he lights a cigarette. He's walking so slowly that they begin to wonder if they are positioned too far north of his path.

The team leader whispers into a voice-activated mike. "Two, when he gets past you, let him get about five yards away. Then move in behind him." The leader hears a click on his mike and knows he's acknowledged.

"Three, I will move in on him with two behind him. I need you to watch our backs." Again, he hears the confirming click.

Atwan continues to stroll, a man who looks as if he doesn't have a care in the world. Passing number two, he continues on. A little further up the shoreline he thinks he hears something and instinctively spins around.

Number two freezes in the sand. With his jet black suit and darkened face Atwan doesn't make him out in the shadows. Assuming it's merely his imagination, Atwan turns around and walks a little further. Before he realizes it, he's grabbed from behind. Another commando steps in front of him and whispers, "You are Jibril Atwan, I hope."

"Yes. Yes, I am. What's this, some kind of game?"

"No, we just wanted to be sure."

Those are the last words Atwan will ever hear. He's quickly dragged into the ocean and drowned by the team of Israeli seals. When the men are sure their quarry is dead, they pull his body about fifty meters further out into the sea.

Number three brings up their gear and the team moves out to be retrieved by submarine.

The next morning members of Hezbollah find Atwan's body floating in the ocean. It is obvious he was not out for an evening swim with his clothes on. Iran will not be happy about this.

Chapter Sixty-Four

Early February

Dean Hargrove, chairman of the joint chiefs, sits along side Admiral Robert Smith. Generals James Bradley and Victor Sanford are situated on the opposite table. The tables today are set up to form a U-shape. The president will sit at the connecting table, the bottom of the U, when he arrives in the Situation Room. Each pair exchanges small talk, keeping clear of the reality that's before them. Five minutes later the president arrives. As he's escorted into the room, he asks the Secret Service to remain outside of the doors.

"Gentlemen, I'm sorry to have kept you waiting," he apologizes, "but things needed to be addressed before I could come down for this meeting." All four of the men nod; they understand that he has a country to run, on top of preparing to fight a possible war. "I have some ideas of my own. However, first I'd like to hear from each of you as to what you feel our best strategy would be with Iran."

Hargrove suggests that Admiral Smith should start off, which he does with no hesitation.

"Mr. President, the Navy proposes the following for a first-strike approach. In the initial stage, we would use two Ohio-class submarines, with a payload of forty-eight Trident II D-5 missiles, to be fired from a distance of 1,500 miles from the shores of Iran. From that distance, it's doubtful that their launches will be monitored by anyone other than ourselves. Those missiles will enter the upper atmosphere long before their flight patterns can be detected. When they re-enter the atmosphere they will almost be on top of their targets, leaving very little time to counter their approaches.

"The payloads in these missiles are the heaviest we have in our arsenal," the admiral continues, "Without going nuclear. We would expect very efficient results from this first assault. To insure keeping the Persian Gulf open, we'd target Bandar Abbas with two of these Tridents." Everyone is taking rapid notes as he speaks.

"The Iranian navy deploys their night patrols, usually six vessels of different sizes, around 2000 hours. They stay out until 0800 hours the following morning. After the night patrols leave, we propose having one of our Seawolf subs lay at the least a hundred mines in the harbor of Bandar Abbas. We would begin mine-laying at 2100 hours, which should insure that the complete night patrol has set sail. We would also recommend having three Los Angeles-class subs cruising offshore of Iran. They would be there to take out any of the surface craft on night patrol when and if we deem it necessary."

"How are you sure they can do that, Admiral?"

"Mr. President, we would monitor what classes of surface vessels depart on night patrol. Those we feel should be eliminated would be followed, and taken out when we give them the word."

"Yes, but you said they usually send out six vessels?"

"Correct, sir," Smith answers. "Normally three of them appear to be high speed boats, rather like our old PTs. We don't consider them much of a threat."

"Admiral, my concern is to make sure those Kilos are docked when we make our attack. I don't want any Kilos showing up by surprise, not with their new cruise missile capability."

"I understand, sir. You, of course, will have the say as to what day and what time we launch our attack."

Oh, right. God forbid I should forget—the buck stops here, thinks the president. He nods for the admiral to continue.

"After the missiles, if we haven't needed to use any of the Tomahawks from the LA-class subs, our naval air fleet will launch attacks on whatever is left of their military installations." He stops, and within moments so does the note-taking. "Dean, I believe General Bradley should go next," he suggests.

"Thank you Admiral," Hargrove says. "General?"

"Certainly," Bradley says, then launches into his presentation. "Mr. President, when we're good and sure that the air's clear of our missiles, our B-2A stealth bombers, taking off from Diego Garcia, will make a run on the designated targets you choose to eliminate the Iranian hierarchy. We'll use pin-point laser-guided bombs, designed to penetrate concrete before they explode."

"General, how will you know whether or not you'll be dealing with anti-aircraft missile sites still remaining?" the president asks.

"Sir, after talking with both the directors of the CIA and the NSA, we've been assured that we'll have second-to-second coverage of Tehran, and most all of Iran, for a full twelve hours when we need it. With our B-2As, we plan to eradicate the government of Iran. Remember, sir, the B-2A is the most advanced aircraft in the world. They don't call them stealth bombers for nothing."

"I hear you, James, but you and I aren't the pilots sitting in those cockpits." The president then looks to General Sanford to continue. "Victor, what do you want to add to this proposal?"

"Mr. President, I can insert teams into Iran whenever and wherever you want, to assure that we're doing everything possible to be totally successful."

"I hear you, Victor, but what can your people do that our satellites can't do?"

"Sir, only teams on the ground can inform us of any last minute changes they see that we need to be aware of. They could also assist on guiding in the laser bombs, should it be necessary. Their participation could prove critical."

"With the enormous proportions of what we are considering, I'll have to think that one through, Victor."

The president sits, hands folded in front of him, eyes down, seemingly lost in though for a moment, then looks up at his top military men. "I thank you, gentlemen. I like what you've proposed and if we need to, we'll go this way. Victor, we'll wait on putting people on the ground. I'd not want that done unless it was absolutely necessary. If only one were captured, it could compromise the entire undertaking. No, if this is to work to our advantage, we must have the utmost in secrecy, and our timing must be planned to the split second."

Joe Smiga

President Egan rises and thanks everyone for their input. He heads for the door. His Secret Service bodyguard moves to his side the moment he opens the door.

Each of the senior military people looks at each other, each thinking his own variation of what the chairman of the joint chiefs is thinking. *This is going to happen.* No one speaks as they leave. They all understand the terrible tragic loss of human lives this plan will incur—even if the United States of America wins.

Chapter Sixty-Five

The Same Week

Chief of Staff Maria Sterling is just getting up for work. She's two hours late and didn't sleep at all the previous night. As a matter of fact, she hasn't slept well for the past few weeks, ever since the president made it clear he was preparing to go to war with Iran.

The same words echo through her mind whenever her brain isn't otherwise engaged. *What, is he nuts? We just got out of Iraq a couple of years ago. And where did that get us? The world's no safer today.*

She quickly showers and tries to make herself look presentable for her staff. She'd made the decision upon awakening that she will talk to the vice president this morning. She's tired of carrying this burden alone.

*

Entering her office, she asks her secretary to call the vice president's office to see if he has time in his schedule to see her this morning, preferably, or this afternoon, if not. She goes into her office, sits down behind her desk and sighs wearily. Within a few minutes, her secretary rings through. "Maria, the vice president has time for you at 11:30 this morning. Shall I confirm that," she asks.

"Yes, Jenny, that will be fine."

Now Sterling wonders how she's going to keep her mind on her work for another two hours.

*

At 11:25, Sterling leaves her office and heads down the hall to Pat Devonshire's office. Entering, his secretary greets her warmly and suggests the chief of staff take a seat while she can check to see if the vice president is ready for her. She picks up her phone. "Sir, Maria Sterling's waiting for you in the outer office. Shall I send her in?"

"Yes, by all means—and, Joan, please hold my calls."

As Sterling enters Devonshire's office, he gets to his feet and welcomes her with a broad smile. "And to what do I owe the pleasure of this visit, Maria?" A short, dapper man in a city of tall politicians, Devonshire was a state governor before coming to Washington. His main preoccupation since taking office has been the ecology and conservation. This man's chief concern, she knows, is to save the planet.

Nothing about war is compatible with conservation, Sterling thinks as she shakes his proffered hand. "This isn't going to be fun, Pat. I need to talk with you about something—several things, actually, which are quite serious."

"Serious calls for physical comfort," says the vice president, ushering her to a pair of armchairs at the other end of his office. "Where do you want to start, Maria?"

"Pat, this whole thing, a pre-emptive strike on Iran, is wrong. I haven't gotten a full night's sleep since the president shared his plans with us and told us to keep a lid on it."

"Maria, he hasn't said he's definitely going to war," the vice president reminds her. "The way I see it, he's making plans in case we have no choice but to go to war."

"I hear you," Sterling says, "speaking like a true-blue vice president. Remember, it's me you're talking to, not the media."

"Maria, we have good intelligence coming from Whispering. This is something we can't ignore. Besides, the Israelis are providing us with additional intelligence that certainly seems to confirm everything we have."

"Why shouldn't they, Pat? They're no fools. They'll get the full might and muscle of the United States to fight a war that's really their war."

"Maria, are you being objective? Or do I sense a touch of anti-Semitism in your thinking?"

Sterling stops and does some soul-searching. "Maybe," she admits. "I've never trusted Jews. However, this isn't just about Israel. We've just gotten out of Iraq, and that was a debacle. This could be a hell of a lot worse. I don't want to sound paranoid, but it isn't much of a stretch of the imagination to see this battle being brought to our shores this time. Not to mention that the political fallout from this could be the end of our party."

Pat Devonshire hesitates a few moments before he responds. "Are you suggesting that we let it get out?"

"If I ran the Iranian government and got word of what Egan's planning, I sure wouldn't want to see the United States coming. I think the intimidation factor would be enormous for them."

"Do you have a plan in mind?" Pat asks warily. "You know we have a directive from the president—you know this is classified top secret."

"I don't really know yet. Yet, I—I just feel I have a moral responsibility that something should be done. I wanted to ask you if you share any of my feelings about this. If you do, perhaps we could work together?"

The vice president takes a deep breath. "Maria, I don't know if you know it, but I've been a pacifist all my life. I don't want to see us going to war if we can avoid it. Somewhere deep down, this doesn't seem right to me, either. Regardless, you and I are bound to obey the president's orders. We could get thrown in jail, for Christ's sake."

"Or," Maria answers him, "we could be the ones who save this country by doing our moral duty, Pat."

"Look, why don't we take a couple of days to think intelligently about this? My wife and kids are away for two weeks with her family. We could meet somewhere for dinner where we can have some privacy?" Sterling starts nodding halfway through his thought.

"Yes. That's a good idea. I'll call you Friday. We can meet somewhere good and clear of the beltway."

Sterling rises up from the couch and shakes Devonshire's hand. "If nothing else, thank you for listening to me, Pat. At least I don't feel so alone now."

As she walks slowly back to her office, her mind is working full-time. *This can't be that hard. All I have to do is play to his hopes of being elected president in the next election to get him to go along with me.*

*

Roberto's Restaurant in Arlington, Virginia, has a great reputation for fine Italian food. Not only is the food superb but the setting is intentionally dark as well, offering a good deal of privacy to its clientele, many of whom come here for just that reason.

Pat Devonshire and Maria Sterling are having dinner in the quiet area reserved for VIPs in the rear of the restaurant; there's ample room for their Secret Service details to observe their safety but removed far enough from curious ears.

"Maria, we need to make this look like just a friendly night out, so let's order a bottle of wine and take some time studying the menu before we order."

"Sounds fine with me," Sterling says. "I do need time with the menu. I've never been here before."

After their meals are ordered and the wine arrives, the two of them look at each other. Neither knows how to start this conversation. Sterling finally takes the plunge.

"Well, Pat, do you think it's possible to bypass the president's directive and maybe go to one of the members of the armed services committee in Congress?"

Just then their waiter arrives with their salads. Conversation stops.

After he departs, Pat replies, "Yes. I thought about that, but I don't think it's a good idea. It'd get back to the president so quick our heads would spin—before getting chopped off. Congress doesn't even know about his executive order for the war powers presidential succession business. They'd be up in arms, on principle alone."

They both go quiet as they eat their salads. Their entrées arrive, along with home-made Italian bread. Just like the wine, everything is excellent.

"This place is wonderful!" says Sterling.

"You should come back here again," Pat suggests quietly. "With somebody else—just in case anyone's wondering why we're here together. Make it look like it's one of your favorites. Get my point?"

"Point well taken, Pat," Sterling says. "I'll be sure to come back here again with someone else."

"Well then, Maria, how would you approach this idea of yours?"

Sterling stiffens. *Oh, that smarts,* she thinks. *He's making damned sure I understand this is my responsibility, not his. So he thinks he can just play the part of the advisor and observer, eh.*

"I know someone on the Post who might be able to get things printed the way we'd want, and keep his mouth shut," Sterling says, putting heavy emphasis on the 'we,' just to test where it might lead.

"Then may I suggest that we develop some press releases together and feed them out in small increments, so we don't panic the administration or the public."

Good boy—he fell for it, Sterling congratulates herself. "I agree, completely, Pat," she says, then adds, "And I think we'll need to be extra careful that we aren't seen together at the White House. Normally we don't interact without the president's being present."

"Shit," the vice president groans. "This has to be a huge success or we're going to go down like Tokyo Rose."

"Pat, just keep in mind that you're doing this to save the nation, not to mention the planet. God, if this thing went nuclear . . ." She pauses for effect, then adds quietly. "And the nation would have the opportunity to see you as playing a courageous, positive role. You know and I know, it's never too early to think about 2012 . . ."

"I hope you're right, Maria."

"Now, let's just enjoy the rest of this dinner. This is really a fine place, Pat. Do you bring your wife here very often?"

"Actually, no. She doesn't appreciate Italian food like I do. She's more of a health food type, wants to be sure any meat she eats had a nice upbringing."

After dinner they enjoy dessert and some espresso. Signing the dinner check, the vice president tells the waiter to put the bill on his personal account.

As they rise from the table, Sterling says, "Thank you for dinner, Pat. I wasn't expecting you to do that. If anything, I should be treating you."

"You can get the next one if we need to meet like this again," he assures her. The two of them head for the door as the vice president's Secret Service detail takes up positions in front and behind him. "Thanks for joining me for dinner while my wife's away, Maria," he says, deliberately speaking loud enough for them to hear.

Sterling smiles as she steps into a taxi. *The vice president has taken the bait. He's motivated enough that he'll do everything in his power to make this happen. The important thing is to be sure that neither he nor I gets credited with any of this. President Egan would be furious if he had an inkling of what we're up to.*

Joe Smiga

Not once has she allowed herself to think about the fact that what she's brought to the vice president qualifies as treason against the United States of America.

*

Two weeks later, a piece appears in the Washington Post suggesting that the United States might consider going to war with Iran if that country doesn't abide by the sanctions they are under. Two short paragraphs in length, it appears on page two in a column that recaps news of the week, which runs without a by-line.

Two weeks after that, another similar piece implies that the United States might be planning a war strategy.

*

All that can be heard from the president's breakfast parlor when seeing the first press release is a roaring "God damn it!"

When he reads the second release, he first goes white as if the wind has been knocked out of him, then beet red as the blood comes rushing back. He knows he's dealing with a deliberate leak. *There isn't a way in hell anyone can tell me this is a coincidence*, he screams to himself, suppressing the urge to scream it out the window of the Oval Office.

Chapter Sixty-Six

Middle of February

The president is livid. In all the years she has worked for him, his secretary has never heard him use the tone of voice she's hearing.

"Janet, I want the chairman of the joint chiefs, the national security director and the director of the CIA in the Oval Office at 1:00 this afternoon. No excuses."

Whoa, something's going on. She can't put a finger on it right now, but she does know she wouldn't want to have to answer for it.

Fifteen minutes later she has replies from the three, who will all be there. Even though she doesn't understand the reason behind his tone of voice, she gives each of them a heads-up to be prepared for an unpleasant meeting.

*

At exactly 1:00 p.m., all three individuals are escorted into the Oval Office.

"Let's sit on the couches so we can be more comfortable," the president suggests, but his tone is far from convivial. Once they are seated, he gets right to the point. "I'm going to ask one question and I want each one of you to answer it honestly. Is there any chance that someone in your department could have given the Washington Post information as to what we're planning?"

Dean Hargrove looks totally stunned. "Sir, I'll stake my career on the fact that no one in the military would have. Right now only those with the need to know have even the slightest idea of what we are doing, and I can assure you that no one has the complete picture—and that's deliberate, sir, for all the reasons you told us not to let any information out."

John Walker says, "Mr. President, the NSA has only a handful of folks workin' on this, and I'd trust each an' ev'ry one of them with my life."

"You may have to," says the president. He couldn't sound more pissed off. "Allison, what about the CIA?"

"Sir, we are not in the position to be planning any of the strategy. Therefore, only my deputy director and I have any idea of what you're doing. I can truthfully say it's neither of us."

"The Post printed two brief releases over the last two weeks. The first I took as gossip, but this second one can't be a coincidence." He passes both around. "I'll find out how this happened, and God help the person who leaked this information, if that's the case. I want all of you to remind your people of the need for absolute security on this planning. We aren't dealing with sane people over there. They're power-hungry individuals using religion as a front for their own conquests."

Dean Hargrove nods. John Walker and Allison McDonald both reply, "Yes, sir."

"I know that I'm reacting very strongly to some very negative thinking on my part right now. However, I can't emphasize enough that we are not playing toy soldiers here. This is real life." He stops and looks each of them in the eye again. No one ducks his gaze. He feels they are being frank with him.

"Allison, I have some other issues I need to discuss with you," he says, slipping back into a more normal version of himself. "I'd like you to remain for a few minutes. As far as this meeting is concerned, it's over—and I hope we never have to repeat it."

"I don't have any schedule conflicts, sir," McDonald responds. "I can stay as long as you wish."

Dean and Walker rise and leave the Oval Office, each of them realizing the seriousness of these leaks and the furor they could cause if the wrong people happened to notice them.

"What would you like to discuss, Mr. President?"

"Allison, I know by definition that the CIA is supposed to work outside of the country and the FBI is supposed to handle internal affairs, while abiding by the checks and balances accorded by the Constitution."

"Yes, sir. What are you getting at?"

"Allison, I want your black ops people to do some investigation into this possible leak. If the FBI does it, they'll go straight by the book and it'll become public knowledge even before either you or I know it."

"You know that your request could turn into a political nightmare, sir?"

"You're not telling me anything I don't know, Allison," Egan says with a grimace. "However, I'm entrusting you to try and find out if there's a leak or not, and if there is, how we can best deal with it."

"I'll handle this personally, sir, directly with the team leader. I won't even involve my deputy director," she assures the president. She considers for a moment, then adds, "On anything relevant to this, I'll only call you on your secure line, sir. And—there'll be no paper trail."

McDonald rises and leaves the Oval Office aware of the confidence that has just been given her.

Once she's out the door, President Egan sits back down and stares out the window. Without noticing that he's doing it, he massages his temples. Only then does he realize he has a throbbing headache.

Chapter Sixty-Seven

End of February

Mary Johnsen, the first woman secretary general of the United Nations, anxiously waits for the assembly to get seated and come to order. She looks out over the auditorium and senses that the next presenter is going to cause conflict, if not chaos. She shudders to think what may be awaiting the world some day, hopefully in the not too near future.

Summoning her resolve, Mary stands and opens the session. "Members of the General Assembly, we have a request from the nation of Iran to discuss hardships that are being imposed upon that nation by U.N. sanctions that have been in place for several years now. Please give President Mahmoud Khasanjani your undivided attention."

Mary takes her seat as President Khasanjani walks to the podium and members don earphones to be able to hear his speech in their native tongues.

"Madam Secretary, members of the General Assembly," he begins, speaking in Farsi. "As president of Iran, I feel it is imperative for me to explain the hardships that are being imposed on my country merely because we seek to develop nuclear power for internal use."

He pauses, allowing the translators time to catch up with him, then launches into his complaints, his speech weighty with pathos. "Our children are starving. Our economy is being crippled. Opportunities for our people are being suppressed. We wish to enter the world marketplace, which in turn would allow us to become self-sufficient. Many other countries have nuclear capabilities. No one questions them. No one sanctions them."

Again, he pauses. "Our government has decided that, if you as a governing body, choose not to recognize that we are merely trying to establish ourselves as a first world nation, then we'll have to resort to other methods." Again, he allows time for his words to be translated—and this time, to let them sink in. Suddenly, the large chamber goes silent as the members realize what they have just heard.

"We as a nation are not seeking to dominate the world as the United States does, colonizing, forcing its ideas down the throats of nations with their own ideas. We are a peace loving nation that follows the will of Allah. We request that you rescind the current sanctions and allow us to rebuild our economy. We expect that this body would be willing to help us so that we do not become a greater burden on its resources, as other countries have become. The decision is yours to make. If you choose to continue the sanctions, then I must take that decision back to my government, and we'll see where that leads us as a nation."

President Khasanjani then leaves the podium and takes his seat.

Conversation erupts on all sides among the various members of the General Assembly. It would appear that Khasanjani's message has made a very clear point: either you give us what we want, or somehow, someone will pay the consequences. Some members would do anything to avoid conflict. Others are tired of being pushed around by leaders like Khasanjani.

Mary Johnsen gets up from her seat. She turns and thanks the president of Iran for his presentation. Then she stands before the great assembly. "You are the representatives of our world body. We need to hear from you regarding Iran's request to eliminate the current sanctions. We will reconvene in three hours. I hope that will give you sufficient time to make your decisions."

Members jump to their feet and leave quickly, off to contact their governments as to how they should vote on this unexpected state of affairs.

Mary watches them clear the hall. *I knew I sensed trouble, but dear heavens, not this. I wonder what the final outcome will be.*

*

Three hours later, the assembly reconvenes. The secretary general opens the matter for discussion. Syria's ambassador makes the first statement. "As the representative of the Syrian government, we agree with our Iranian brothers that sanctions should be lifted."

The Saudi ambassador states, "It is the opinion of my government that the sanctions should remain in place. The president of Iran has only given us his word that his people are suffering. There is no transparency here—Iran's borders are closed to us. We would want more detailed information before we could consider changing our vote."

Both Pakistan and India concur with the Saudi ambassador.

Great Britain's ambassador speaks next. "It is my government's suggestion that until Iran allows the IAEA to monitor their nuclear enrichment program, we have no choice but to vote to continue the sanctions."

Egypt speaks next. "As a fellow Arab nation, our country has difficultly believing that Iran doesn't have another agenda. Therefore we, too, will vote to continue the sanctions."

On and on, messages of support or lack thereof are tossed into the ring. Finally, the secretary general ends the period of discussion, stating firmly, "It is now time to place a vote. If you vote yes, you're voting to maintain the sanctions on Iran. If you vote no, then you're willing to see the sanctions lifted."

Of the 192 members of the General Assembly, the vote reads as follows: 126 vote "yes" and 66 vote "no." The sanctions will be maintained. Saudi Arabia and Egypt are the only Arab countries voting in favor of maintaining the sanctions.

Both President Khasanjani and the ambassador from Iran rise and storm out of the General Assembly. Little does anyone realize it, but these theatrics are being played out exactly as planned. Iran knows it could count on the member nations to vote against the sanctions being lifted, providing them with a clear rationale for revenge.

At the end of the day, the U.S. ambassador, David Gates, calls the White House and advises the president of what has transpired.

"Well, Dave, how do you feel this affects the future?"

"Mr. President, I have a gut feeling that Pandora's box has just been opened. My honest opinion? The president of Iran stood there today and threatened the world."

"You might be right, Dave," the president says somberly. "I can't help but think that the recent round of terrorism on the European continent is meant as a wake-up call for what we can expect next from Iran. Keep your eyes and ears open. We need any information we can get our hand on to contain these fanatics."

"Yes, sir, I certainly will," Gates tells him.

Ambassador Gates closes his office at the United Nations. On the way out, he's stopped by the ambassadors from Great Britain and France. Both of them express great concern that today's vote will lead to serious consequences.

Chapter Sixty-Eight

Early March

Four individuals handle administrative details In the office of the Iranian ambassador, located on the thirtieth floor of the Secretariat Building of the U.N. complex. Two of these are legitimate office staff and two, Soheil Asim and Aboudi Feroz, are plants from the Iran's Ministry of Intelligence and Security.

While reading the current issue of the Washington Post, Feroz comes across a short article hinting that the United States is preparing for war with Iran. "Asim, look at this. The Post must have a source within the government that's feeding it military information."

"Why do you say that, Feroz?"

"You know as well as I that the *Post* will print any leaks it can get its hands on. Two weeks ago, I read a small blurb just like this one," he remarks, pointing to a paragraph in a column of political tidbits and trivia, "saying that it's possible that the United States and Iran could to go to war over the nuclear enrichment issue."

Asim shakes his head. "Sounds like a lot of conjecture to me, Feroz. I don't think it's any big deal."

"I thought so too, when I read the first piece. But now I read this. They are saying war is 'highly probable' between the two countries."

"You think it's a leak from the administration? We haven't picked up anything like that from any of our contacts in Congress or from anyone here in the U.N."

"I know, it's just that I feel the Post has something it's trying to get out, and that this is the safest way they can do it."

"Feroz, put your supposition into a report and let headquarters have someone contact the Post to see if they can learn who the source is. That's the safest way for us to handle it. Personally, I don't think their president has the balls." Asim laughs.

Feroz gets up from his desk and walks across the room to get some tea from an electric samovar. "You know, Asim, if this is true, our people need to get ready. We can't afford to lose ground with our nuclear capabilities. There's a great deal at stake."

Asim nods but repeats, "Let headquarters sweat over it. You've done your job. I need you to help me with the new assignment we now have. Don't waste any more time on that."

*

"Why should I meet you for dinner?" asks Scott Brubaker of the Washington Post.

"Because I'm in town and, if you recall, the last time we met, we had a wonderful time together. Or do you have so many girls hanging around your neck you can't remember them all?"

Brubaker laughs. "No, Melanie, I remember just fine. It's just that you're hard to keep track of. I thought we had something special—and then off you go, like a wisp of air."

"Look, we've talked about this. My career's global—it keeps me on the go. I can't get tied down, definitely not for the next five years, if I'm going to meet my personal goals. Can't you see that a woman needs to have her own life every bit a much as a man does? Or are you so macho you can't handle a mature woman?"

"Melanie, get off it," Brubaker says, sounding a bit irritated.

Melanie Jacobs smiles. *I'm getting under his skin,* she thinks. She likes the feel of it.

"Okay, I'll meet you for dinner," he says. "How about seven o'clock. We can meet at the Wild Rooster."

"Oh, you dog, you. You do have a memory."

*

Sitting in the third booth at the Wild Rooster in downtown D.C., Brubaker sees Melanie Jacobs walk in the door; the waiter points her in his direction. Both he and Jacobs have dined here numerous times. Not only is the food excellent, but the atmosphere is cozy and low lighting does wonders for the ambiance.

"So, what have you been planning since I called you?" Jacobs asks with a wicked glint in her eye.

"Where are you staying this trip?"

"I haven't made any hotel reservations—not yet, anyway. I thought that maybe we could do your place." She winks at him.

"Pretty sure of yourself, aren't you, lady," Brubaker laughs. He loves this in a woman.

"Kind of, but the way I see it, I'm worth changing schedules for, don't you think?"

"Hey, no fair. No matter how I answer that, I'm going to be in deep trouble."

"Right," Jacobs agrees, "so let's order a drink, look at the menu and see where things go from there."

Three drinks later, Brubaker orders the sirloin steak special and Jacobs orders a baked stuffed lobster. A fourth round of drinks is ordered while waiting for their salads. Fascinated by her beautiful eyes in particular and the whole package in general, Brubaker asks, "So what brings you to town this time, Melanie?" Their salads are set before them.

"My firm is investigating a client we might want to do business with."

"And who might that be?"

"Scott, you know I can't tell you, just like you can't tell me who your sources are." After this minor parry, conversation retreats to safer small talk.

The salad plates are removed and dinner arrives.

Melanie Jacobs takes her first bite and closes her eyes as she savors it. "Oh, this is so good," she says. "I haven't been anywhere lately where I could get a good lobster."

Dinner closes with another round of drinks. Finally Jacobs says outright, "So, are you taking me home or not?"

"I'm still thinking about it."

"You brat," she giggled, more than a bit tipsy. "After our last time you're supposed to be drooling."

"Oh, I'm drooling, all right. But, I keep wondering what's it you're really after. Maybe something for your client?"

"Scott, how dare you! I thought that we cared enough about each other to be able to just have some fun together." Jacobs does a good impersonation of a four-year-old going into a pout.

"I guess we do, but then I never hear from you for ages, and there never seems to be any way I can get in touch with you. And then all of a sudden, you drop back into my life."

"What a skeptic you are, Scott Brubaker!"

With that, Brubaker and Melanie Jacobs exit the Wild Rooster. Brubaker decides to leave his car in overnight parking, having wits sufficient about him to know he's consumed more alcohol than he should. Surprisingly, Jacobs seems to be able to hold her liquor. He hails a cab and gives the driver the cross streets for his condo.

*

"Well, you haven't changed a thing since I was here last time. I need to wash up. Can you pour me a brandy?"

"Okay. I'll make it a double."

Melanie Jacobs returns from the bathroom with nothing but a towel around her. Her silky brunette hair hangs halfway down her back, and her long, slender legs add to her air of casual elegance.

Brubaker throws off his jacket, tie and shoes and gets comfortable on the couch. "Your drink's on the counter," he says.

"Aren't you going to have one with me?"

"No, I think I've had enough. Hell, I have to work tomorrow. We're short in the office and I know they're going to be busting my balls for stories."

"Not before I bust your balls tonight."

Jacobs downs her liqueur, takes Brubaker's hand and leads him up the stairs to his bedroom. "Admit it. Isn't this what you really wanted, not that sirloin steak?"

*

Seven o'clock the morning after comes awful early, Brubaker berates himself as the alarm goes off, *after you've been screwed, blued and tattooed. Boy, she's good. Matter of fact she may just be the best I've ever had.* His eyes pop open at this thought. And he discovers that he's the only one in bed.

Brubaker jumps into the shower, then heads down to grab a quick breakfast, where he finds Melanie Jacobs down already, having toast and coffee, sitting in one of his bathrobes. "I couldn't sleep very well. Guess it's all the time changes for me," she explains.

"Will you be here this evening?" he asks. *Bet she says no.*

"Sorry, but I have to leave for the west coast. Maybe I can come back on my return trip, though."

"I'd love you if you did." *Damn, I think I really mean that. Phew...*

"Scott, I always read your column on the internet. That thing about the country going to war with Iran—do you really think that's possible?"

"I don't know," Brubaker answers with a shrug. "It might just be disinformation. You know, a ploy to get someone's attention or I suppose, God forbid, it could be the real thing. Why do you ask?"

"Because it scares me."

"It scares me too, which is why I think the source that gave it to me wanted it leaked to the public."

"Good God, are you saying that this administration could actually be considering that, after what happened to us in Iraq?"

"Hey, you never know," Brubaker answers as he throws down some cereal and juice. He decides to grab a latte at Starbucks on the way to the office.

Melanie Jacobs tells him she'll let herself out.

*

Encrypted message sent to Iranian Headquarter from 'the Lobster':

> PRESS RELEASES WERE A LEAK. DOESN'T KNOW WHETHER THIS IS DISINFORMATION OR FOR REAL. RECOMMEND YOU TAKE PRECAUTIONS IN ALL AVENUES.

*

Melanie Jacobs takes a flight out of Ronald Regan International Airport, just to protect her cover. Just as she told Brubaker, her flight is heading for the west coast. There's no knowing who's watching whom these days.

*

Jim Stewart, part of McDonald's special team, has been following Scott Brubaker for three days now. He doesn't know who the broad is, but he'll find out. Brubaker seems like he looks forward to her arrival. Stewart's partner will follow her on her flight.

It's time to meet Brubaker head on.

*

Brubaker has a number of voice-mail messages awaiting him this morning. One in particular piques his curiosity. "Mr. Brubaker, my name is Don Wilson. I work with congressional committees. Can I have some of your time? We're interested in your recent press releases regarding our country going to war. I'm sure that you can understand our concern, after the Iraq catastrophe. When is it convenient to meet with you, and where would you like to meet? Would the Wild Rooster be a good choice? You can reach me at 202-555-5555."

Chapter Sixty-Nine

Last Week of April

The five members of the Guardian Council sit down for their meeting. In the silence, one could hear a pin drop. Each one looking solemn, no one wants to be the first to speak about what's on all their minds: what might have happened to Atwan.

Finally, Farook speaks. "Well what does our esteemed president have to say about losing Jibril, Fadil?"

Evading the question, Ahmajid replies, "Hezbollah has no answer for us as to how he drowned. There were no signs of foul play when they found him."

"Fadil, I may be an Imam but I am not totally ignorant to the ways of the world," Farook bristles. "Jibril wasn't in the habit of going swimming with his clothes on. As a matter of fact, I happen to know that Jibril hated swimming. Either we have a traitor within Hezbollah or a major assassination by the Israelis."

"Unfortunately, we can never know what really happened," Ahmajid replies with a fatalistic shrug. "We do have some reports from Jibril, but he was extremely cautious making contact. What we'll never have is the major debriefing I was hoping to get from him when he returned. I need time to put his notes together."

"Will this set us back?" Farook asks. "I don't think we should change our time table, except if we have equipment problems, which are coming along with only minor glitches."

"About equipment," Hassan interrupts loudly, "it's my understanding that Admiral Aziz agreed to have cruise missile capability within three months. We are now two months into that period and I haven't heard a word as to where we stand on that."

"Admiral Aziz is still saying that at the end of the next thirty days, he's confident he will have the missiles operational and ready to be converted with nuclear warheads."

Givon brings up another point. "The admiral is telling us the missiles will be operational, but will his Kilo crews be capable of working with them?"

"The submarine crews will be ready to handle their assignments," Ahmajid says with a confidence he doesn't necessarily feel.

"You know, Fadil, you told us that our own enrichment processes would enable us to load twelve missiles in six months. That was two months ago," Givon complains. "We can't attempt a strategy such as we plan without those missiles being armed and ready, with crews fully trained to handle them. They are key."

"Our processing people tell me we'll have sufficient materials four months from now. That still enables us to keep our target date of eight months from now. Abbas, what are you staring at?" asks Ahmajid.

"You, my friend. You seem so sure that all of this is falling into place as we have planned. But I'm braced for something to happen to change our timetable. You know, hope for the best but plan for the worst."

"Well, actually, we have just learned about something that we do need to discuss," Ahmajid acknowledges. *It had to come up. Oh, well.*

"What has happened?" Farook asks, immediately smelling trouble. *Ahmajid likes to paint a rosy picture, but that's just the background,* Farook thinks. *He hates when he has to paint in the details, especially when they spoil the effect.*

"What has happened is that our intelligence people have come across two small press releases in the Washington Post suggesting that the United States might be planning to go to war. With us." Surprise registers on all the others' faces.

"Do they think there's a leak in their government?" Abbas questions Ahmajid.

"They could not tell. In their report, they advised that we should check into it."

"And I assume that we've taken their advice?" says Givon.

"Of course," Ahmajid responds, letting more than a bit of aggravation show. "One of our agents made contact with the reporter who wrote the article. Her report says that the reporter implied a leak in the government, though he has no idea if this is deliberately planted disinformation or if in fact it might be a reality."

"Are we hearing anything from our other sources within the United States?" asks Hassan.

"No," Ahmajid replies, "we aren't. However, in order to protect ourselves, I would like to suggest that when we get word from the admiral that his crews and the missiles are ready, we should put the Kilos to sea immediately. They can always use the extra time to reach their destinations, traveling at a much slower, quieter and less detectable pace."

Everyone at the table considers this idea, then one by one, nods in agreement.

"All right, for now this is all we have to discuss. I will call you together when we get closer to our launch dates."

Chapter Seventy

End of May

The Ayatollah Fadil Ahmajid is sitting before the President of Iran, in the president's office.

"Well, Mahmoud, what do you expect Aziz to report today? Ahmajid asks the president. "He's predictably punctual, a man of his word. It is exactly three months."

"Yes, Aziz is always a keeper of his word. You must remember, Fadil, that's how he survives in his position. I have no way of knowing what he's going to report. However, I expect that most of what he has to say will be favorable."

Just then, the president's phone rings and his secretary advises him that Admiral Aziz has arrived. "Please, do send the admiral in," he tells her, nodding as he looks over at Ahmajid.

As the Admiral enters the president's office, both Ahmajid and Mahmoud stand to greet him. "Admiral, we were just talking about what you might have to report today. We hope that you have good news for us," says Mahmoud.

Taking a chair in front of the president's desk next to the one in which Ahmajid is sitting, Aziz settles down, pulls a binder from his briefcase and sets it on the president's desk.

"The navy wishes to advise you, sir, that all six of our Kilos are ready to depart on whatever mission you ask of us. The only thing that may delay that mission is the problems we encountered trying to improve the firing and telemetry of the new missiles you supplied us."

"What problems?" asks Ahmajid, his eyes flashing angrily. "Jibril's reports said we were making good headway with those missiles."

"Fadil, it is not a problem on our end. Your engineers did a good job of modifying those missiles and making sure we could fire them. However, Russian tolerances in their submarines and the precision characteristics we require sometimes can be a world apart." The look on Ahmajid's face at this news doesn't daunt the admiral. He has faced far angrier men in his lifetime.

"After a number of tests, we found that if we sleeve a torpedo tube with a stainless liner, we have a smoother cargo area for the missiles to be fired from. Second, there is a difference between our firing sequences for regular torpedoes and those required for firing missiles. The fact that missiles need to be distanced from the submarine, then lifted towards the surface for the booster rockets to ignite, has caused us a great deal of trouble, but I can report that we have finally gotten that problem solved. What we do have now, however, is a shortage of missiles."

"What do you mean, a shortage of missiles?" Mahmoud jumps in. "I thought you were retrieving those you were expending?"

"Mr. President, when you're firing missiles of that type, it is very difficult to retrieve usable missiles for a second shot. As I understood my orders, I am to have our six Kilos ready for a mission and to be certain that the missiles we designed would function properly. I've delivered on that promise. Resupplying missiles for our submarines is not a function of the navy. It is a function of those responsible for equipping us with the materials needed to accomplish the task."

"Fadil, I'm afraid that Admiral Aziz is correct," Mahmoud says. Turning back to the admiral, he asks, "How long will it take us to have twelve functional missiles that we can then install the new warheads in?"

Ahmajid answers for Aziz. "Mahmoud, in the past, we have been able to supply our experimental team with one missile a week, assuming we work our people around the clock."

"Then make it happen. That means that both the submarine and land missiles will be ready within the same time frame."

The president turns back to Aziz. "Admiral, you have given us what we need. Now I want you to make sure your crews stay in top form. Three months from now, we are planning to deploy them on six very secret missions. Each one of them will have tremendous responsibility, but you, Admiral, have the greatest responsibility of all. You need to make sure that your people are up to the task."

"Yes, sir!"

"Admiral, you can leave now. Fadil and I have a great deal to do."

Mahmoud waits until the admiral has left the room before commenting, "Shrewd little bastard, isn't he, taking us on that little rollercoaster ride. Providing bad news, which he then tells us is good news, before giving us the actual bad news."

"Regardless, we will still be ready, Mahmoud," Ahmajid assures him with utter confidence. "And then, my friend, Iran will take its rightful place as the leader of the Muslim world."

Chapter Seventy-One

Middle of June

Three floors below the ground level, a special ops team consisting of Jim Stewart, Tony Romano and Jane St. John are sitting at a table discussing their current assignment.

"Before we get started, how about some coffee?" Stewart suggests.

"Okay, with a little milk for me," says St. John. Romano passes. Stewart brings two cups to the table.

Sitting down, he begins, "As you know, I met with Scott Brubaker last week. I suggested the Wild Rooster to him, since that was where he met his lady friend while I was observing him. The fact that I proposed the Wild Rooster seemed to have no effect on him, so I can't be sure whether or not she plays a role in what we're looking for.

"During our dinner meeting he told me that he could not divulge his sources, that he only passes on information he feels is of interest to the public. He allowed that some of what he reports may only be disinformation. Or as we call it, bullshit to blind-side the enemy.

"He remained cordial even after I made him aware that the congressional committee seeking this information could call him before an inquiry panel and that, if he chose to plead the fifth, they could put pressure on his employer. After dinner I said we might have to meet again if the committee felt it necessary. He didn't seem to have a problem with that."

"Cool character," Romano comments. "But the media thinks they're above the law anyway." Stewart shakes his head at this comment.

"Mr. Cool may not be so cool after all," he goes on. "A team bugged his home phone while we had dinner. It appears he called the White House late last night and left an unusual voice message for someone there. I don't know who yet, but I'll lay you odds it's either his source or close to it. I need to check who has that extension."

"What did the message say?" St. John asks. "Did it make any sense?"

"Word for word: Congress is making inquiries. I need protection."

"Protection from what?"

"Don't know yet," says Stewart.

"What I know" Romano says, "is that our friend Melanie got off the plane in Frisco and took a cab over to Oakland, to . . ." He consults his notes. "4315 Blueberry Drive, where she lives. With her parents. Who just happen to be Iranian. Who became American citizens twenty years ago."

"Now, isn't that interesting," says Stewart and St. John in unison, then laugh.

"What does our Ms. Melanie do for work, Tony, or are you just waiting for us to ask?" says St. John.

Romano gives her the finger. "It appears that 'our' Melanie, as you put it, works for something in Sacramento called Global Connections. She has a track record of traveling a great deal, mostly to the Middle East. Up front, the company seems to be legit, but it's too early to tell."

"So you're suggesting that Brubaker's involved with a possible Iranian agent? Or is he just a dumb reporter who prints anything to make a buck?" wonders Stewart.

"The real key here isn't Brubaker so much, but who his source is," St. John points out.

"Right, Jane," Stewart agrees. "However, at least we've limited the possible avenues that the leaks could be coming from for now. It seems like they're coming from within the administration." He stops for a moment, then ends the meeting, "Oh God, the president is going to split a gut when Allison tells him what we think."

*

At 7:30 the next morning, Allison McDonald places the call she really wishes she didn't have to make, to President Egan on his secure line in the Oval Office.

"Are you sitting down, sir?"

"Do I have to be?"

"You might want to." McDonald presents her team's findings to the president.

"My God! Betrayed by my own staff? I—who do you—why would anyone do something like this?" The president, normally an articulate man, finds him at a loss for words.

"We don't know yet, sir. However, I'm asking you for your permission to continue this ops order. There's a lot to it, more so I'm afraid than what meets the eye."

"By all means, Allison. You have to get to the bottom of this, and fast. What a ghastly feeling, suddenly thinking you can't trust your own staff. Never in my career . . ." He lets the thought trail away.

*

The next call McDonald makes is to her team leader, Jim Stewart. "Jim, just as you expected, the president's having a hard time swallowing this pill."

"I know I would if I were him," Stewart says.

"I want you to put some pressure on Brubaker, by degrees. With the right amount, he might just make a mistake and take us right to his source or sources. Since Tony tailed Melanie, I'd like you to switch Jane onto her. Have Tony make inquires of the Post's management, saying he's checking on the validity of their reports that we might be going to war. Between your pressure on Brubaker and hopefully some matching pressure from the top, we might be able to spring a trap."

"I may need more manpower to do some of this. Do I have your permission to use another team of, say, three?"

"Jim, you use whatever you feel you need to get the job done. Nice work so far. Your team's making steady progress. The key now is to give Humpty Dumpty a few little shoves, so he'll fall and crack. Get back to me with whatever you feel I need to tell the president. This is top priority, and right now he's afraid to make a decision without Iran finding out. Until we figure out who's involved, he's basically paralyzed."

*

"What do you mean the White House wants to know who my source is for those little blurbs? You know I can't divulge my sources. No one will ever trust me again."

"I know the routine, Scott," says his boss, "At the same time, you know the White House hates our guts and when we start getting calls about an IRS audit of our organization, which could tie us up for years and, man, the costs alone could murder us, well . . ."

"They can't do that and you know it," Brubaker fumes.

"Legally you're right, but shit happens. The word from the top is for you to comply."

Chapter Seventy-Two

End of July

Ahmed Rassi, chief engineer at the missile manufacturing facility, receives a call from his president.

"Ahmed, what's the delay? We were expecting twelve cruise missiles to be completed in three months. It is now three-and-a-half months and you have only supplied eight."

"President Mahmoud," says a decidedly nervous Ahmed, "you ordered us to have twelve Shahab missiles ready for you by the end of this month. And then you ordered twelve new cruise missiles with the modifications the navy requests and you want them two weeks ago. I'm not playing with a product that you just throw together. Not only are the components sometimes difficult to obtain, the manufacturing process of the units themselves takes time, even without all the necessary changes the navy ordered. We have tried our best to meet your orders. You now have ten of the Shahab missiles ready, plus eight of the cruise missiles. We have done our very best to satisfy you, but we cannot pull missiles out of thin air."

"When will you have the six remaining missiles ready?"

"I can promise you that they will be ready in four weeks, sir."

"How long will it take your technicians to install the nuclear materials in each warhead after you have all the missiles I require?"

"Sir, we are currently installing the nuclear materials in each warhead of the missiles we've already built, and will continue to do so as each of the remainder is finished. All twenty-four will be ready at the end of four weeks."

"Ahmed, let me be clear," says Mahmoud quietly. "You have no longer than four weeks. Do you understand?"

"Yes, sir, I understand," Ahmed replies mournfully. *I am a dead man if my people cannot pull off the impossible. The ignorance of these people! What do they know about manufacturing times and material deliveries? They seem to think that just because they say it is so, then things will appear as if by magic.*

Ahmed makes a decision; he will move his family out of Iran after this is all over. Whatever the government has planned is not going to be good for Iran. He knows his talents will be appreciated elsewhere—without the threats.

*

President Mahmoud dials the Supreme Leader. "Fadil, we must talk. We have fallen slightly behind schedule. I have another thought about the date."

"I will be in your office in two hours. Let's not discuss this on the phone."

Two hours later Fadil Ahmajid walks into the president's office. "So why the great panic I hear in your voice?"

"By the time all the missiles are completed and loaded with nuclear materials, it now appears that we will only have two and a half months left before our target date."

"So? What's the problem? As a matter of fact, that works out well since we have already decided to ship the Kilos out early."

Mahmoud is confused. "You told me we had no longer than four months preparation time."

"Mahmoud," Ahmajid says, almost casually, "what do you think I've been doing with my time? I am laying out all of the plans for the Kilos and for the land-based missiles as well. We will be ready to begin with our threats right on schedule, just as we've planned."

"And you're absolutely sure that every one of those countries will bow to our demands?"

"They will when we give them a demonstration of what happens to those who don't," Ahmajid smiles.

"You foresee no major retaliation from anyone? Not even from the United States?"

"I don't believe the American public is ready to accept a nuclear attack from us. What they did to Japan still lingers in their minds. They don't have the stomach to confront us."

"I only hope that you're right. If this doesn't go as you plan, the repercussions will be enormous. Our country will be set back decades, if not generations."

"You worry too much, Mahmoud," Ahmajid says soothingly. "You need to relax. You need to trust and be confident in our strengths and abilities."

"May Allah be with us, Fadil."

Chapter Seventy-Three

Tuesday After Labor Day

Supreme Leader Fadil Ahmajid, President Mahmoud and Admiral Aziz are meeting in the president's office. Aziz is uncomfortable, looking into the eyes of the others. He has no idea why, yet he's filled with a deep feeling of uncertainty.

"Aziz," says Ahmajid, "your missiles are finally complete. They will be loaded aboard your vessels in the next two days. Do you see any problems with your crews departing on the third day?"

"Number 106 has developed a bearing problem in her prop, which will need to be repaired before she can get underway. Otherwise it could seize up, and the noise alone will let everyone know where she is. The other five are being loaded with supplies as we speak. How long do you expect them to be out to sea on this operation? I need to know how much to load them with, in terms of supplies."

Mahmoud replies, "Provision them with supplies for ninety days. That should carry them through comfortably."

"You know, Mr. President, our submarines have never been out that long before," Aziz points out. "That long a time can create a major strain on the crews."

"They are Iranians and submariners both. I am confident that they will be able to handle their assignments," says Ahmajid. "They will depart as soon as they are properly loaded."

This guy, thinks Aziz, *may be the Supreme Leader, but he doesn't understand shit about what I'm talking about. I know the stresses these men will go through.*

"You have told me that they will be attacking the United States. Who, may I ask, is assigning the targets?" *As if I didn't already know.*

"Our president and I will be assigning the targets, Aziz. Only we three will know, you being the third. The Kilo captains will open their sealed orders after they move out of the harbor. Then each captain is entirely responsible for the actions and success of their mission. At the moment, until we make our final decisions, you should know that four kilos will attack the U.S. mainland. Two will attack Israel. Number 101 will definitely be selected for Israel, along with 106, due to time required for repairs and the travel distances involved."

"I'm sorry if I appear uninformed," Aziz says meekly, "but no one has given me a date to commence any action. Or do you expect each captain to make that decision himself?"

"Admiral, you're asking more questions than you should. Let us just says that your submarines will have instructions to communicate when they are within five hundred kilometers of their assigned targets. We'll then give them a launch time and date."

"You will be giving them the date, not naval headquarters?"

"Yes, admiral," Ahmajid says with growing irritation. "Once those subs leave the harbor, your responsibility is complete." Mahmoud looks off into the distance as if he doesn't have a care in the world.

Aziz has heard enough. *These fucking men are insane and purely power-hungry. They know shit about what they are doing—and could bring the world to the brink of disaster.* He, of course, knows better than to put these thoughts into words. "I will do my job as you have instructed. I pray that Allah will give you the insight to make the military decisions you need to make."

"Is that a compliment, Aziz, or a shrewd way of zinging us?"

"Gentlemen, I've served my country for many years and history has always proven that when politicians run the military, things tend to go astray. I have nothing else to say. I request that I leave this meeting as I feel there is no further need for me to be here."

"Granted," says Ahmajid. "Just make sure that you do your job."

Aziz bites his tongue. *Oh, rest assured, 'gentlemen.' I will do my job. At the very least, perhaps I can save one sub crew by having its repairs delayed beyond your time frames. Where did you get the idea you need two submarines to destroy Israel, anyway?* What he actually says is, "Yes, sir." *By the will of Allah, what's my country coming to?*

*

The six captains of the Kilos are invited to a dinner with the President and the Supreme Leader. Admiral Aziz is also there, though he seems to have taken a back seat to his superiors.

At the dining table, President Mahmoud stands and announces, "Gentlemen, in one day you will be leaving the harbor of Bandar Abbas and voyaging out into new waters. Our great nation is about to make its mark on the world and you're the vanguard of our message. Each of you will be given sealed orders just before your departure. They are to be opened only after you are underway, and followed through to the letter, to ensure all of our mutual success."

"Will we be acting as a pack on this mission, sir, or will we be acting independently?" asks one of the commanders, addressing the question to the admiral. However, the Supreme Leader rises to answer the question.

"Each of you will be acting independently," addressing all of the captains. "We have great faith in your abilities and, Allah be praised, for his will to prevail."

Mahmoud goes on, "It is vital that you keep tonight's conversations a total secret. No one is to know of this until after you leave the harbor, and only then are you free to discuss the matter with your officers. Your instructions will advise you at what point you are to share the nature of your missions with your whole crew."

Puzzled, each of the officers begins to look around at the rest. Never has the admiral treated them in this manner. As military men, they are excited to be involved in some kind of obviously significant operation. However, each of them senses that something unusual is brewing here. The fact that this announcement comes, not from their admiral but from the top two political leaders of Iran, makes them uncomfortable.

When dinner is over, the commanders leave quietly, one at a time, and head for their vessels. All of them have work to do in preparation for departure.

Joe Smiga

*

In the very early dawn, some thirty hours after the dinner ended, Iranian submarines 101, 102, 103, 104 and 105 each depart from their berth and head for open waters. As they clear the coastal waters, they dive and head out into the Arabian Sea and then onto the Indian Ocean.

Once they reach the Indian Ocean, each commanding officer opens and reads his orders. The meaning behind the strange dinner two nights earlier becomes crystal clear. Every one of them is awed by the boldness of their mission. Each realizes the perils that they and their crews will face in attempting to carry out their orders. Each plans to succeed.

Chapter Seventy-Four

That Same Day

"Son-of-a-bitch! Where the fuck did they go?" cries Jerry Daniels in dismay, his voice carrying to the farthest reaches of the NSA operations room.

Hurriedly, Daniels checks the log books of the previous watch, which ran from 0800 this morning to 1400 hours this afternoon, when Daniels came on. He can find no mention of the Kilos being absent from their docks. *How could they have missed them?* he wonders angrily.

Working backwards, he then checks the log books from 0200 to 0800. Again, no mention of the Kilos being absent from their mooring sites. Grabbing the phone, he calls down to Jim Stewart. He fidgets nervously until his senior watch officer answers.

"Jim, I just got on watch, and the first thing that catches my eye is that five of the six Kilos aren't in their berths. Why the sixth one's there, I have no idea, but what really worries me is that I've never seen more than two of the damned things ever leave at any one time."

"You're sure about that?" says Stewart.

"Oh yes, I'm good and goddamn sure. Why the hell do you think I'm calling you? Something's up. I can smell it."

"Okay, calm down, Jerry. I'll call the previous watches at home and find out if maybe they noticed something and just forgot to log it."

Jim Stewart calls both watch officers at home, getting both of them out of bed, which they do not appreciate. However, when he makes known what he's looking for, they both realize they did see something, and no, did not log it.

Stewart calls Daniels back. "Got what you're looking for. Around 0430 Iranian time the Kilos began to depart from their berths. They moved out one at a time, submerging when they got into the Arabian Sea. Nothing was noted as this was taken to be another exercise for the Iranians."

"Exercise, my ass," says Jerry Daniels. "Whose brilliant conclusion was that?"

"Calm down, Jerry. I'll handle the whos, hows and whys. More to the point, I have a call into the director."

"Jim, knowing what we do about Whispering, I'm surprised we haven't seen any communications about the subs departing. My gut tells me these bastards are really being tight-lipped about this. As in total blackout."

"Do you think they realize we've broken their codes?" asks Stewart.

"Doubt it," Daniels says, "not yet, anyway. We're still intercepting messages on a regular basis. My guess: leadership's playing it tight to the chest on this, not letting the left hand have any idea what the right hand's up to. Probably to make sure nothing gets out."

"That could be good news. Or—that could spell disaster, for them and for us," Stewart says quietly.

"You sure as shit are right, for people who think logically."

Just then Stewart's phone rings. "Hang on a sec, Jerry. It's the director." Putting Daniels on hold, he takes the incoming call. "Watch officer Jim Stewart."

"John Walker here. Y'all called?"

"Yes, Director, I did call. We've just learned that five of the six Iranian Kilos in Bandar Abbas left their berths early this morning. We doubt it's an exercise. Our gut feeling is that something's getting underway."

"I'll advise the pres'dent. Thanks, Jim. Y'all are doin' a good job."

*

President Egan takes the call from John Walker.

"Mr. Pres'dent, I need to inform you," John says, his tone stiff and formal, "that we have satellite ev'dence that five Kilos have gone missin' from their berths in Bandar Abbas, since just before dawn this mornin', suh."

"Shit, this is just what I was afraid was going to happen," the president replies, throwing formality to the winds. "Why do you think the sixth one's still there?"

"We don't really know yet, suh."
"Thank you for calling, John. I'll take it from here."

*

"Admiral Smith, the president is on the line," says the admiral's staff secretary.

"Bob, we just got word that five of the six Kilos in Iran have left their berths. I want you to work up how quickly they could make it to our shores."

"Yes, sir!"

Chapter Seventy-Five

Thursday That Week

Usually the last to arrive, President Egan is currently the only one sitting in the Situation Room, going over his thoughts once more before his military leaders arrive. This is no time to be indecisive, yet he must also be absolutely certain that he isn't jumping the gun and unintentionally starting a world war.

He picks up the secure phone in front of him and dials NSA Director John Walker on a speed dial already set up for him. "John, President Egan. I'm glad you're up at this hour. What's the latest you're getting on our Whispering reports?"

"With the Kilos departed, I haven't been to bed yet, suh. There's nothin' unusual in this mornin's reports, just what we'd expect—except we did intercept ordahs to have the main propellah bearin' replaced in that one Kilo remainin' behind, so now we know why it's still there. A reply message said that the parts'll have to be ordahed from the Russians. Seems they have no inventory on that item."

"Are you getting any messages indicating military movement, John?"

"No, suh, we are not. However, their missile people are tellin' the military that it'll take four weeks for them to redo the warheads in the last dozen they manufactured."

"Redo the warheads? What do you make of that, John? Those are land based missiles, correct?"

"To answer your first question, suh, we're not sure what they mean by 'redoin' the warheads.' However, our gut feelin's that they're plannin' some type of military confrontation usin' both land-based missiles, as well as their five operating Kilos." John just let the rest of the statement hang in mid-air.

"Do you have a launch date, or anything we can hang our hats on, to make a strategic decision, John?"

"No, suh, I do not. Right now that's the best I can give you, Mr. Pres'dent."

"Enough for now, John. Call me if anything changes."

"Yes, suh!"

The president hangs up the phone. No sooner does he place the receiver in its cradle than the door to the Situation Room opens and Admiral Smith and Generals Bradley and Sanford come in. As they enter, Admiral Smith looks into the face of a tired man. "Mr. President, it's five o'clock in the morning. How long have you been here?"

"To tell you the truth, Bob, I've been here since three. I really never went to bed last night after receiving word that the Kilos departed. "Let's get some coffee and whatever else you want before we sit down and start."

"Good idea. I don't imagine any of us had breakfast this morning," says General Bradley.

"Uh-oh," laughs the president. "You guys are starting to sound soft."

"Right," Victor says, "We just get wake-up calls with messages saying 'Situation Room in one hour.' All of us live at least forty-five minutes away."

"Victor, that's forty-five minutes in traffic, not at this time of the morning. I did take that into account," the president responds, smiling.

The four of them take some selections from the trays, then fill their coffee cups. They sit around a much smaller table for this meeting, which gives them more eye-to-eye contact. The president is looking for every signal he can get from his people as they talk.

"Bob, let's start with you. I'm sure you have the information that I asked you for late yesterday."

"Yes, sir, I do. The president has requested that I compile data on how long it would take for Kilo-class subs to get close enough to our shores, as well as Israel's, to make a first strike. Bear in mind that we have no idea of what speeds they will be traveling at, nor what courses they are taking, if they are in fact headed here. I decided to compute these figures using speeds we would use if our main concern was to remain undetected." He stops and pulls a notepad from his briefcase.

"I'm going to give you two speeds and two times based on those speeds," he continues. "To our east coast, we are talking round figures of 6,500 miles of travel. Based on 8 knots, we'd be looking at about 34 days, assuming they'd be attacking from somewhere between 200 to 300 miles off shore. Based on 5 knots, we're talking roughly 54 days." He waits till everyone has finished jotting his figures down.

"To our West coast, we are talking round figures of 8,000 miles. Based on 8 knots, now we're talking around 42 days, assuming the same firing range. Based on 5 knots, it's more like 67 days. To Israel's shoreline, we're into round figures of 5500 miles of travel. Based on 8 knots, about 28 days. Based on 5 knots, 46 days."

"Thank you, Bob," the president says soberly. "So what I'm hearing is that, worst case scenario, they could be off our coast in as few as thirty days, in round figures."

"Sir, that's of course depending on where the Kilos are headed and who their targets might be," the admiral emphasizes.

"Duly noted. Bob, what's the current status of our carrier group in the Indian Ocean?"

"Sir, the carrier itself is carrying its full complement of planes and bomb loads. Each of the support vessels with her are fully loaded for any action as well. The two subs regularly assigned to her are there with her as well. The other two boomers you requested are in the area but operating independently."

"Our naval strategy talked about Ohio-class and Seawolves. Can you give me their status?"

"Sir, both of our Ohio-class subs and the one Seawolf we plan to use are ten days away from the area. Our Ohios will stay outside of the fifteen-hundred-mile range to Iran until we need them. The Seawolf will be operating about fifty miles from shore."

"Do we have another carrier group close enough if we need them?"

"We have a second carrier group that's currently moving to within three hundred miles off the southern tip of India. This group can operate as back-up support, if necessary."

"So you're telling me the Navy's ready to go anytime we might need to."

"Yes, sir. We're ready. Just give the word."

"Jim, what's the status of the B-2s you're bringing into Diego Garcia?" the president asks General Bradley.

"Sir, we are planning on having three of our four squadrons on Diego Garcia whenever you need them. Each B2 will be carrying two one-thousand pound laser-guided bombs."

"When do the bombers arrive there, Jim?"

"They've got two there right now, and we're adding two a week, so as not to arouse suspicion."

"So you're saying that you will be at full compliment in five weeks." The general nods. "Jim, I want to you have three arrive each week so we can reach full compliment in a month."

"I can do that, sir, barring any unforeseen circumstances."

"Gentlemen, right now I do not want to hear about any 'unforeseen circumstances,' clear?"

All three men respond, "Clear."

"Victor, right now I have no desire to put anyone on Iranian soil, as much as you and your people would like to. We need those Tridents to take out everything they're supposed to. We'll have CIA and NSA's satellites straining to get everything we can possibly get, to check damage assessments.

"Bob, we need to be prepared to use our Tomahawks before we send any aircraft over Iran. I don't want to give any of their SAM batteries the opportunity to take out any of our pilots. Now we need to find those five Kilos and track them to see if they really are heading our way, or if they're just out playing sailor. Bob, Jim, the Air Force and the Navy have one hell of a job to prepare for." The admiral and the general both nod gravely.

"NSA is listening to all Whispering data, to try and get us an early-warning signal somehow. The sixth Kilo is waiting for a bearing for its prop, which seems to be the only reason it's still dockside—they have to go to the Russians for a replacement part. It will probably be a while, if I know them." All three respond with grim chuckles.

"Gentlemen, I don't have to tell you that this doesn't look good," President Egan says candidly. "However, we're not totally caught with our pants down. I'm sure you understand how bad this could be. Well, at the moment there's nothing we can do. Let's go upstairs and get ourselves a real breakfast."

Chapter Seventy-Six

Jibril Atwan's Death

"Prime Minister, the president of the United States is calling on a secure line. You can take it on line three," says his secretary.

"Thank you."

Smiling, Yaakov says, "Mr. President, to what do I owe this occasion—and why the secure line, may I ask?"

"Yaakov, I wish I could say it's nothing, that I was just calling to pass along some good news. However, it's not good, or at least we have reason to believe it's not good."

"What's not so good?" Yaakov begins to frown.

"Within the last twenty-four hours, five of the six Iranian Kilos have departed Bandar Abbas. We have never seen more than two ever leave at any one time. Based on what you and I've been observing, we are concerned they are putting battle plans into action."

"Why five and not all six?"

"Our intelligence tells us that the sixth has a prop bearing problem. They have to wait for spare parts from Russia." President Egan hesitates to say anything about Whispering.

"You found out about the repair problem in twenty-four hours? That's damn good intelligence. What else are you hearing you might want to share?"

Yaakov Brumwell misses nothing. "We are getting word that they are going to replace twelve currently built Shahab missiles with different warheads."

"Shit, I knew it," Yaakov says. "They've developed enough enriched uranium to make twelve nuclear warheads. Now the real game begins. This fits with information we have learned recently. Do you know of a Jibril Atwan?"

"I believe I've seen his name in reports, but no, not really."

"Atwan is—was—an advisor to their supreme leader. It seems that he has been spending time in both the Gaza Strip and Lebanon. This is highly unusual—to the best of our knowledge, he has never left Iran before."

"Why is he so special all of a sudden?"

"Our intelligence has learned that Atwan was involved in some sort of plan with Hamas and Hezbollah. Apparently, he was working with both groups, organizing them to carry out a joint diversionary action against us. We suspect this was meant to keep our minds off of the real issue, which is, of course, Iran."

"How positive are you of this, Yaakov?"

"It's only supposition right now. However, it seems that this Atwan drowned while he was visiting Hezbollah, so we are not hearing any more about what plans he was working on."

"Drowned? Accidentally or on purpose?"

"We honestly don't know. Quite possibly he had enemies within Hezbollah."

Sure or maybe some Israeli seal team took him out, President Egan surmises.

"Mr. President, what do you really feel is going on with these Kilos?"

"Right now, we're searching to locate them and estimate their courses. This might give us an idea of what they are planning. Until then, we have nothing concrete. I just wanted to pass on to you what we do have, so that you know as much as we do."

"Thank you, sir. I will return the courtesy when I have information as well."

Yaakov hangs up and has his secretary place, first, a call to Jacob Rabinowitz, the IDF chief of staff, and then a call to Ariel Wattenberg, the director of Mossad.

As each of the men call him back, Yaakov gives them the same message. "It's beginning. We need to prepare. Be in my office tomorrow at 0900."

Yaakov sits back in his chair and stares out of his window. His mind is flirting with the old story of Paul Revere, the American, when he rode to warn the colonists. *We need to learn whether they are going to hit us by land or by sea. Or both. Damn!*

Chapter Seventy-Seven

Same Week

At nearly nine o'clock at night, the vice president receives a call from the administration's chief of staff.

"Pat, we have a problem," Maria Sterling says tersely. "Are you free to talk?"

"Yes, my wife and the kids are upstairs. What kind of problem, Maria?"

"The kind of problem that we could lose our jobs over, maybe even go to jail."

"Are you shitting me?"

"Hell, no," she responds angrily. "Why do you think I'm calling you right now."

"What happened?"

"Scott Brubaker just called me at home. He says he had dinner with a congressional investigator—who wanted to verify that we are going to war."

"Jesus H. Christ!"

"That alone didn't bother him. What's really troubling him is that the Post is getting threatened by someone in the administration, saying that if he doesn't reveal his source, the Post could get an IRS audit."

"That's bullshit and you know it, Maria."

"You and I know it, but as his boss told him, shit happens, and the word from the top is that he should reveal his source if he continues to be questioned."

"Maria, you told me nothing like this could ever happen. Goddammit, woman, we could be in a world of shit."

"Look, Pat, I told Scott that I'd do some checking around to see how true that rumor is and let him know. In the meantime, I asked him to keep our identities confidential. He agreed that for now he would." Sterling knows what she's dealing with. *Pat's going to lose it, if this gets hot.*

"Okay, Maria," says the vice president, trying to pull himself together. "Call my secretary the minute you find out anything and get in to see me. I'll be traveling on a fund-raiser for the next three days. If it's urgent, call me on my private number and leave a message. I check it daily."

*

Jane St. John is following up on Global Connections. It appears that Global is a consulting firm which utilizes the expertise of proven problem-solvers. Their 'managers,' as they refer to these expert problem-solvers, operate worldwide for clients who are willing to pay Global's fees.

This could be an ideal cover for someone who wishes to do a little off-the-books consulting. thinks St. John. *Now, how do we go about checking out Ms. Body Beautiful?*

St. John calls Jim Stewart and gives him the low-down on Melanie Jacobs, including the fact that her last name is different from her parent's name.

"It could be a cover, or it could just be some personal whim," Stewart observes. He directs St. John to continue her search and then passes what she has told him onto McDonald.

*

Jim Stewart dials the White House operator. When an operator answers, he says, "Can you please help me? Someone from the White House called my number from extension 4788. I don't know who to return the call to."

After a brief pause, the operator says, "Sir, that's the extension for the chief of staff. Would you like me to connect you to her voice mail? I know that she's in a meeting right now."

"No, thank you. I hate voice mail," Stewart says with a laugh. The operator agrees with him. "No, I'll just call later. I appreciate your help."

Chief of staff! Oh, boy, is Allison going to love this one! Stewart dials the director of the CIA for the second time today. When she answers, he simply says, "I believe what I'm about to tell you isn't going to surprise you."

"And what are you going to tell me, Jim?"

"Just that Scott Brubaker's late-night call to the White House went to the chief of staff's direct line."

McDonald is struck dumb. When she recovered from the immediate shock, she went right into executive mode. "Jim, I want a tail on Maria, and I want some legwork done. Find out about her travels over the past month or two. Get me a listing of her home and office phone records, and see if she has anything wireless that we might need to check out as well."

"Allison, I need some kind of court order for that information," Stewart objected.

"You'll have it before noon tomorrow. Call me back with anything you come up with."

*

President Egan is signing papers in the Oval Office when his private line rings. He answers, "President Egan."

"Sir, its Allison. I need a court order to investigate phone records for our ongoing investigation."

"I can have one later this evening from the attorney general's office. What rationale do you want me to use? And I'll need the numbers for the order."

"Um, this is going to get touchy, sir. They are the office and home numbers of your chief of staff. And we need to look into whether or not she has a cell phone."

"Oh, my God!" the president reels at the thought. "Do you think she's doing this by herself, or is she working with others as well?"

"I don't have an answer for you yet, Mr. President. Honestly I don't know what we could use for a reason at the moment."

"We can place the order on the pretext that we're checking her lines for nuisance calls, in order to stop the caller."

"That won't get back to her?" asks McDonald.

"Maybe. We'll just have to hope it's not," the president says pragmatically, "until we've found out if she's the key to Scott Brubaker and the articles."

"I'll wait to hear that you have the court order, sir, before I have my team continue their investigation."

*

Tony Romano, one of Stewart's team, is very close with the Secret Service details located at the White House. Over a few beers at one of their favorite pit stops, Romano hears one of the agents say, "Guess who was having dinner in Arlington together the other night?" He shot a few feeble guesses down, then conspiratorially moved in close. "Just the vice president and the chief of staff."

His private scoop is met with derision. "Ya mean, Pat Perfect and Maria the Ball Buster are gettin' it on?" Romano laughs along with the rest.

"Okay, so they did go their own way afterwards, but I don't know—it just felt odd. I mean, they can meet in their offices to conduct business."

It could just be scuttlebutt, Romano thinks, *but you never know where scuttlebutt can lead.*

The next day when Romano reports to Stewart, he mentions the Secret Service agent's remarks.

"The old loose lips routine. That's how rumors get set in motion, Tony. Last I heard, it wasn't against the law in this country to have dinner with someone not your spouse."

"Yeah, that's what I thought too," Romano agrees. "But, I don't know. It still feels funny. Why, I'm not sure. Its like something wants to pop up at me about it."

"Well, when you get your pop-up, you just let me know."

Stewart hangs up from talking with Romano. *Well, I know who's getting the next tail,* he decides on the spot. *Only it can be tough tailing a VP, what with his Secret Service detail all over him. The chief of staff will be a piece of cake compared to him.*

*

Stewart has an electronics team bug the condo of the chief of staff. They are thorough—bugs are installed in numerous places, to pick up conversations from any room. He also locates a second team across the street from her home with video cameras and additional eavesdropping equipment. He will have a tail on Sterling as well.

He locates a third team in a house across the street from Devonshire's Georgetown four-story townhouse.

*

Allison McDonald is speaking with the president on his direct line. "Sir, we have confirmed Maria's calls to Scott Brubaker before the articles were printed, as well as incoming and outgoing calls to Brubaker after the articles were printed. As you know, we have a tail on Maria and we have video of her meeting Brubaker two days ago."

"So you think Maria is the source of our leak." The president is stating a fact, not asking a question.

"Sir, we also have evidence that the vice president had dinner with Maria in Arlington while his wife was away. That in itself wouldn't trouble us. However, Maria called Pat a couple of nights ago, and the two spoke for over a half hour. I have strong suspicions that both of them are in this together."

"Oh God, what will the country think of us?"

"Sir, I hate to say this, but my job isn't what the country thinks. We have a serious breach of security here and it needs to be addressed."

"I hear you, Allison," President Egan says reluctantly. "No, you're right. Thank you for bringing me to my senses." He pauses to think, staring out the window, then looks back at her. "I want you to continue your investigation, Allison. I want us to have enough rope to hang these two if it turns out this is true. I can send Pat off on a number of trips, to keep him out of the decision making process. His staff doesn't have a need-to-know. Therefore he can be put totally in the dark." Again he stops and considers.

"It might be a little more difficult with Maria," he continues. "She'll catch on that she's being excluded. Although, no, that may not be as difficult as I just thought. I can send her out on party fact-finding missions, have her meet with the heads of our party to work on pre-election tactics. That's right up her alley, anyway."

"Sir, when we put everything together, how are you going to handle this, if I may ask?"

"You may ask," Egan smiles, "but, in all truth, I don't have an answer for you at this point. This is leaking information, of course, but that doesn't make her an enemy spy. Honestly, I don't want to deal with this until after I've dealt with the possibility of going to war. Those leaks could have a bearing on what's happening. I intend to plug the leaks for now, until such a time that we have sufficient evidence to do something. Then, I'll be able to decide exactly what to do."

"I understand, sir," McDonald says, her tone empathetic. "I know this isn't easy."

"No, its not," the president replies. "For now, I can only do what I believe is in the best interests of our country."

McDonald nods at this man she so admires. "My team will continue its search, Mr. President, and we'll present you with whatever evidence we find. I know you'll make the best decision—the right decision—when you have a clearer picture."

"Thank you, Allison. Right now it is nice to hear someone say that."

The president hangs up and sits at his desk, again staring out at the Rose Garden beyond. The roses are still in full bloom. *I wonder how the hell all of this will wash out in the future . . .*

Chapter Seventy-Eight

Tracking Melanie Jacobs

McDonald, who sits staring out her office window at the Potomac River, has a thought. The president has ordered that their two agencies collaborate. She puts a call into John Walker at NSA.

"Allison," he greets her warmly. "and what can I do for y'all?"

"John, are you seeing any reports on Whispering that might relate to the Post articles the president spoke to us about?"

"None that I'm aware of, but let me check. Give me some time, Allison, and I'll get back to y'all."

Four hours later, John Walker calls Allison McDonald back. "What I have needs for y'all to be on a secure line. Call me back."

"Will do, John," McDonald says. Within seconds she has him on her secure line, "What have you found, John?"

"I'm not sure if this is what y'all are looking for, but I found out the Iranian ambassador's office at the U.N. has referred to the two articles in the Post. We have tape of them concerned that they should be checked out furthah."

"Did they say how they might be checked out?"

"No, but we've also picked up an encrypted message to the Iranians saying: 'Articles'—I think we can assume means the two Post articles—'a leak. Not sure if information or disinformation. Take precautions on all avenues.' That's it, verbatim."

'Roughly when did this message come in, John?"

"About ten days after the ambassador's message went out. And the funny thing is, it originated from D.C."

"Really?" McDonald couldn't keep the shock—and anger—out of her voice. "And no one made a connection?"

"Sorry to say, Allison, we didn't. What are y'all dealin' with?"

"I really can't say right now, John, but—thank you." The last two words were ripe with righteous indignation.

*

McDonald calls her team leader. "Jim, I really want to find out if our Melanie might be an Iranian agent. Things are falling into place. Our possible leak may have opened up the flood gates."

"I still have Jane working on it," Stewart says, "but I can give her another person or two to dig a little quicker."

"Jim, this is vital. I cannot express how crucial I feel this connection is. I may be wrong, but my intuition tells me I'm not."

"I'll take care of it and confirm what you're looking for, one way or the other, as soon as I can, Allison."

"Jim, thanks." Then she adds, "Please be very sure of your facts before you call me."

*

Jane St. John watches Melanie Jacobs show up at her workplace, Global Connections, every morning promptly at nine, and depart like clockwork at five. St. John has a perfect view of the front entrance from a stool in the window of a Sacramento Starbucks located conveniently across the street. St. John thanks her lucky stars it isn't a biker bar.

After observing her movements for several days, filing reports back to headquarters daily, she sits in her usual spot and watches passively as Jacobs departs from the entrance way and heads for the parking garage a block away she always uses.

Over one shoulder, Jacobs carries her purse; over the other shoulder, she carries her laptop case, just as always. She always walks alone. Suddenly men come from behind, then move to pass around each side of her. As they do so, they both grab the items from her shoulders and push her to the ground.

"What the hell are you doing?" she screams, hitting the pavement hard. "That's my purse! My laptop!"

The men run from the scene and are long gone before anyone has a chance to identify them.

"Can I help you, lady?" asks a passerby. "You're bleeding." Several more are drawn to the commotion.

"Somebody, please call the police for me," Jacobs cries. "I've just been robbed."

A second passerby helps her to her feet and helps her to a bench, then calls the police on his cell phone while Jacobs tries to staunch the flow of blood from her knees.

When the police arrive, the first officer on the scene records everything Melanie Jacobs has to say, then questions the two witnesses who have stayed to do their patriotic duty, as one has been repeating over and over since the phone call had been placed. A particularly attentive fellow, the fantastic amount of detail he's able to recall finally strains the credulity of the police. By the time he's finally finished, they've written him off as a fraud. What they don't discover is the fact that he was part of the team of three sent to perpetrate this day-light robbery.

As they are leaving, the officer who took Jacob's statement gives her a card and tells her, "Call the station next week and ask if they've found your computer and your purse. Probably won't, though," he says, offhand. "These things happen twenty times a day around here."

The laptop arrives in Washington and is put in the hands of forensic computer experts within five hours.

Chapter Seventy-Nine

Top Secret Orders

All five of the Kilos head on a southern course as directed by their captains. Each captain then heads to his cabin to open the sealed orders he was given. This manner of receiving their orders is a new experience for each of them. In the past Admiral Azis gave them their orders personally, followed by his wishing them a safe voyage. The admiral was no where in sight at the piers today, even as they departed.

As each captain reads his orders he has no way of knowing that, except for their specific targets, they are all receiving the same information.

YOU ARE TO MAINTAIN MINIMUM SPEEDS AND SUFFICENT DEPTHS TO AVOID ANY CHANCE OF YOUR BEING DETECTED. YOU ARE TO BE WITHIN 500 KILOMETERS OF YOUR TARGET IN FORTY-FIVE DAYS. THEN YOU ARE TO RAISE YOUR SIGNAL MASTS AND COMMUNICATE WITH US FOR A LAUNCH DATE AND TIME.

REMEMBER THAT YOUR BOW MUST HAVE THE PROPER INCLINE IN ORDER TO ACCURATELY LAUNCH YOUR MISSILES. UNLESS YOU HAVE A FIRING FAILURE, YOU ARE ONLY TO LAUNCH ONE MISSILE, SAVING THE SECOND FOR ANOTHER TARGET AFTER RECEIVING FURTHER INSTRUCTIONS.

YOU MAY DISCUSS YOUR ORDERS WITH YOUR OFFICERS AFTER YOU HAVE READ THEM. HOWEVER, DO *NOT* DISCUSS YOUR OPERATION WITH YOUR CREW UNTIL AFTER YOU HAVE YOUR LAUNCH DATE AND TIME.

Each of the captains begins to wonder where the other submarines are heading. Kilo 101, commanded by Captain Farzeen Ali, is heading for Israel. Kilo 102, commanded by Captain Habib Mukhtar, is heading for San Francisco. Kilo 103, commanded by Captain Asghar Hafiz, is heading for Los Angeles. Kilo 104, commanded by Captain Reza Kadir, is heading for New York. Kilo 105, commanded by Captain Mehrang Emir, is heading for Washington, D.C.

They also wonder whether they will ever return to their families after a mission such as this. Those heading for American targets realize that the United States will most certainly be watching for them as they approach their shores.

Chapter Eighty

Second Week of September

Admiral Robert Smith is holding a staff meeting at headquarters that will put into place two carrier battle groups and maintain Mediterranean coverage with the U.S. Sixth Fleet. His chief of staff, Captain Bruce McKay is leading the presentation for everyone on staff who has a need to know.

"Gentlemen, what we discuss here remains in this room or will be encrypted before being sent to the appropriate vessels. We are positioning our forces in case of a need for armed confrontation with Iran. By order of the President of the United States, we are going to assign the following:

"The Sixth Fleet, operating in the Mediterranean, will begin cruising eastbound to position itself within four hundred miles off the coast of Israel in the next thirty days.

"The Carrier Strike Group in the Indian Ocean will position itself six hundred miles due south of Karachi, Pakistan. This force will be the commanding presence over two Ohio-class submarines and one Seawolf. The Ohios will remain fifteen hundred miles off the coast of Karachi. The Seawolf will position itself within fifty miles of the coast when ordered to do so." He pauses. "Are there any questions so far?"

Commander Jack Nadeau speaks first. "May I ask how we plan to refuel these vessels so close to the Middle East, never mind resupply them."

"Good question, Jack," replies the captain. "We will have all vessels topped off before they arrive too close to their stations. A detailed schedule of refueling will be arranged so that all vessels will have sufficient fuel. Resupply will happen concurrently. Of course we don't have to worry about the subs."

That statement brings a chuckle to those sitting around the table.

"I don't wish to throw cold water on any of this," Nadeau speaks up again. "But with our vessels so close to other Arab nations, aren't we inviting air attacks while we are vulnerable?"

Admiral Smith steps in. "Jack, your question is one that I'd expect someone to ask. I'm glad that you did. We're planning for a second Carrier Strike Group, based out of Japan, sitting six hundred miles due west of Bangalore, India, which would put them about ten miles behind the first group. This will definitely give us sufficient coverage to protect the first group and discourage anyone from trying to play hero at our expense."

"Thank you, sir," replies Commander Nadeau.

The admiral goes on. "Gentlemen, this in no way should be construed as our have been given the go-ahead to commence any action. We are just preparing ourselves in case we need to. Five Kilo subs left Iran two days ago. So far they're running deep and we don't know where the hell they are. May I tell you that makes us very uncomfortable."

Those assembled can only return his thoughts with an equal sense of unease.

"Action orders will be sent to the designated groups as soon as this meeting ends," says the admiral. "That'll be all for now."

*

General Jim Bradley has called his operations officer to his office. "I want three B2As landing at Diego Garcia each week until we have twelve on the ground, no later than four weeks from now.'

"Sir, I'm not a fuckin' wizard, you know. How do you expect me to do this?'

"Well, Merlin, that's why the Uncle Sam pays you the big bucks. Find a way, goddammit, or both you and my ass is grass. And the president's the lawn mower."

"Yes, sir! General Bradley, sir, your wish is my command. I just became a wizard."

"I know you can do it, Tom. Some jobs are just harder than others. However this is one of those times that we don't have a choice. I want you to report back to me when all twelve are on the ground, fully-loaded, in Diego Garcia."

"Will do, sir. If I may observe, sir, you're really busting my balls on this one."

"Tom, when this is all over, you and I will have a drink together," General Bradley promises his ops officer, "and you'll probably be thanking me for being such a hard-ass."

Chapter Eighty-One

NSA's Nightmare

NSA director John Walker calls his two most senior officers into his office and asks them to close the door behind them. Jim Stewart and Dave Carter take the seats Walker gestures to in front of his desk. They've never seen the director look so serious.

"Gen'lmen, right now we're lookin' in every cranny, nook and corner of the waters of the world to find those five Kilo subs that departed Iran last week," the director says, his frustration showing. "The first priority of every American vessel, above the surface or below, is to report any sightin's, direction of travel, et cetera. The Air Force has been flyin' special missions from the moment we discovered them gone, to see if we can locate any or all of them before they get too far away. We gotta keep track of them." Walker pauses. "Y'all both know that we've reconfigured ev'ry satellite we have to keep a sharp eye over the whole area. However, the biggest part of the problem is that, by their very nature, subs aren't the easiest vessels to detect."

"John, those subs are probably only surfacing late at night to replenish their batteries," says Jim Stewart. "Hell, they don't even have to surface—they can just snorkel. And Kilos are damn quiet. We're going to need some lucky breaks on this one."

"The president realizes that, Jim," offers Carter. "That's what's got him so worried."

"Well, what do we expect five subs to do? Destroy shipping or cause port problems?" asks Stewart.

"No, it's a bit bigger than that," Walker says quietly. "We suspect the Iranians are carryin' cruise missiles on those submarines."

Both Stewart and Carter make long whistling sounds as the thought sinks in.

"What might happen would make 9/11 look like nothin' compared to what those missiles could do," the director continues. "Especially if they have nuclear warheads mounted on them things—which we think they do. I want every available person on duty till this thing's over. Cancel leaves. Make sure our weekend and night crews are full, not just skeleton crews. We cannot afford to miss these guys. Dave, it's imperative that we check and double check everythin' out of Whisperin'. We need to analyze the whole picture—and then analyze the analysis. We simply can't miss anything'."

"Sir, it sounds as if you and the president are working with a timeframe in mind," observes Carter.

"You're right," the director says. "We think that if anythin's gonna go down, we'll know about it within the next sixty days."

"How on earth will we be able to respond quickly enough?" Stewart asks, agitated.

"The pres'dent's already taken action to see that we're not caught sittin' behind the eight ball. We need to give him that heads-up. He wants the option of bein' proactive, not reactive."

"Is the CIA picking up anything that could reinforce our findings one way or another?" Carter asks pragmatically.

"More than just the CIA," the director tells him. "The CIA and the president are working with Israel. They've provided us with intelligence suggestin' that both the U.S. and Israel are designated targets. However, they don't have any sense of a timetable as yet. The president informed them about the Kilos leavin' and now they're concerned that they'll be attacked from three fronts—they'd already gotten intel that this is gonna begin with both Hamas and Hezbollah creatin' separate coordinated diversions on their borders."

"So now all we can do is sit and wait?" Stewart says, bewildered. *And watch for invisible subs anywhere around the world?*

John Walker rises from his desk. "Not entirely, Jim. We're makin' some moves on our own, along with Israel. Right now all I can tell you is what we've just discussed. Our job is to find those subs so the Navy and the Air Force can do their jobs, if and when we've decided the Kilos pose genuine threats."

Joe Smiga

Stewart and Carter also rise. Carter says, "I guess we should have expected this. They've been sending subliminal messages for years. We just never wanted to face it before."

"Enough talk. Let's get to work, Dave," says Stewart, already heading for the door. "We've got a big assignment on our plates."

Chapter Eighty-Two

Feeling Blind

Admiral Robert Smith and General James Bradley sit, side-by-side and ramrod straight, before the president's desk in the Oval Office.

"Are you getting anywhere in locating any of the five Kilos?" the president asks, taking off his glasses and rubbing the bridge of his nose. His fatigue shows. *Don't worry*, he thinks. *I'd probably faint from the shock if you told me you have.*

"Mr. President, finding a diesel submarine that runs as quiet as these Kilos and doesn't even need to fully surface to charge their batteries—it's like trying to find five needles in a haystack twice the size of China," says Admiral Smith.

"Anything from the Air Force yet, Jim?"

"We've got the same problem the Navy has. The only positive thing I can tell you, sir, is that the Air Force would have found them at some point if they were just out on standard maneuvers."

"So you're telling me that the Air Force thinks they're in attack mode."

"I'd put my career on the line for it, sir."

"You just did, Jim. Bob, do you concur with Jim?"

"Yes, sir, I do."

"Then what would your recommendations be now?"

Admiral Smith answers first. "Sir, I'd set up a line of listening posts, beginning two thousand miles from our shores. I'd recommend a cordon of surface vessels at two thousand miles, then a corridor of planes between two thousand and fifteen hundred. Finally, I'd want to see a line of our own subs at one thousand miles. We'd want to get as many vessels into those lines as we can, to minimize the distances between them, to optimize their search capabilities. Then, once everything's in place, I'd suggest we begin moving those lines closer to our shores. Daily. When those subs try to cross over SOSUS, we'll be able to get their locations. By having that many vessels and planes operating we should be able to corner them, maybe even be able to track them. Once we know where to start."

"Jim, what do you think of this?"

"Sir, I like it. The Air Force could cover these corridors with our anti-sub aircraft operating from our shores. As we get closer we can even use our anti-sub helos. What I do want to bring up, though, is the possibility that these birds might try to hit us on two shores simultaneously. I hate to state the obvious but we've got a lot of vulnerable coastline. We'd need to set this up on the east coast, the west coast, and the Gulf as well."

"If I remember correctly, we have SOSUS on both coasts, correct?" asks the president, referring to the Navy's Sound Surveillance System.

Both officers respond, "Yes, sir, we do."

"Do we have enough vessels and planes operating within our shores to actually do this?"

"Sir, it's not going to be difficult to rearrange our subs. I can pull vessels from enough surface groups by changing fleet orders and redirecting ships that are moving across the oceans or from the Caribbean."

"Then let's get it going," President Egan says. "I want both of you to work together on this and coordinate your thinking on how far you should pull back each day. It's been a week now and, dammit, no one has seen or heard from them."

Just then the president's line rings. He holds up a finger and apologizes for taking the call. "Yes, Janet," he says into the phone.

"John Walker wishes to speak with you on a secure line."

"Put him through on line two," he tells her, then turns to the two men sitting before him. "I'm going to have to take this, but I don't want you to leave yet." The admiral and the general nod their understanding as the phone rings again.

"John, have you found anything?" asks the president.

"Well suh, we've located one of the Kilos. It surfaced outside of the Strait of Gibraltar last night. It was only completely above the surface for half an hour. Then it dropped until only its mast showed and traveled like that for another hour. It appeared to be moving easterly, as if it planned to be go through the Strait and into the Mediterranean."

"You're people are sure it is one of the Kilos, John?"

"I can bring our images over to for you to see, suh. They're clear as can be. We had a full moon out last night."

"Yes," President Egan responds. "I do want to see them immediately. Thank you."

The president hangs up his phone. Turning back to the two military men in front of him, he says, "Gentlemen, don't plan on going anywhere yet. John Walker's coming over with images. From what he just told me, I want you to be around to look at them too."

President Egan picks up his phone again and buzzes his secretary. "Janet, John Walker is coming over very shortly. Tell him I'd rather have him meet me in the Situation Room."

"Yes, sir. Is there anything you want me to have set up down there for you?"

"That won't be necessary, Janet. If I find we need something, I'll call you." Again he hangs up, and turns back to the admiral and the general. "Gentlemen, let's head down to the Situation Room."

*

Twenty minutes later John Walker is escorted to the Situation Room, and smiles as he enters, glad to see the military presence here. *This is good. Somethin's happenin' and the pres'dent's just not waitin' around.*

"Mr. Pres'dent, Admiral, General, it is good to see you."

"Now, let us see what you have, John," says the president.

"Suh, fortunately we've had two birds watchin' the entrance to the Mediterranean through all of this. With the moon bein' full last night, we were able to pick up the sub when she surfaced. We were also able to keep her in sight the whole time she was surfaced, since both birds were concentrating on that particular area."

"John, how sure are you that it was an Iranian Kilo?" asks the admiral.

"If you look at this particular photo," Walker responds, "you'll see Arabic writing on her mast head. Translated, it reads one hundred one.

Joe Smiga

I checked other photos. That sub's been in Bandar Abbas for at least two years now."

"Great work, John. We'll notify the Sixth Fleet to keep an eye out for her and advise Israel of what we know." The president grimaces. "Now we just need to find four more."

Chapter Eighty-Three

Second Week of October

ENCRYPTED MESSAGE TO: COMPAC FLEET HEADQUARTERS * BREAK * TOP SECRET PRIORITY * BREAK* FROM NAVAL HEADQUARTERS HAWAII * BREAK * TWO SUBS LOCATED ONE HUNDRED MILES NORTHEAST OF HAWAIIAN ISLANDS * BREAK * VESSELS ARE RUNNING APPROXIAMATELY ONE MILE APART * BREAK * HEADED NORTHEAST * BREAK * VESSELS WERE SEEN BELOW THE SURFACE BY SQUADRON OF OUR HARRIERS * BREAK * DEAD RECKONING NAVIGATION PLACES THEM HEADING FOR OUR WEST COAST * BREAK * WE DO NOT HAVE ANY TWO OF OUR SUBMARINES CURRENTLY WORKING IN CLOSE PROXIMITY OF EACH OTHER * BREAK * SPECULATE THAT THESE MIGHT BE PART OF WHAT YOU ARE LOOKING FOR * BREAK * WILL AWAIT YOUR RESPONSE BEFORE PROCEEDING* END OF MESSAGE *

The watch officer quickly deciphers the message, then calls the commander's office on a secure line. A hard copy is sent by special naval courier for the commander to sign.

Vice-Admiral Kevin O'Rourke reads the hard copy of the message and calls Fleet Admiral Robert Smith on a secure line. "Sir, I think we've located two of the Kilos. I'll send you a copy of Hawaii's message. I've ordered a box search to try and regain their positions."

"Kevin, that'll work if they don't go deep. I want you to continue putting the screen that we discussed into place and keep everyone sharp."

"We'll have your screen up and running by midday tomorrow, sir. Those two should still be outside of the perimeter we're planning."

"I hope so. Let's see how good we are at locating them. Pretty soon they'll be entering the SOSUS zones. That'll help us. I'll advise the president of your peoples' find. Nice work!"

Fleet Admiral Robert Smith sits back in his chair before calling the president, trying to think. *Are we overlooking something?*

Unaware they have been spotted, Kilos 102 and 103 are heading according to their orders to positions off of the west coast of the United States.

*

Meanwhile, southeast of Bermuda in the North American Basin, Kilos 104 and 105 are cruising to their designated positions off of the east coast of the United States.

Commander Atlantic Fleet Vice-Admiral Daniel Peterson is laying out the screen orders given him by Fleet Admiral Smith. His vessels will cover a distance of two thousand miles from New Brunswick, Canada, to the north and the Bahamas to the south. He's set his vessels to run zigzag searches through the areas they are assigned. Their courses are to be set to allow minimal open areas between vessels and planes in their respective search areas.

As he looks at his directives to his fleet, he prays that the Iranians aren't as good as American submariners. *They need to make mistakes if we are to find them.*

*

When they arrive near Bermuda, Kilos 104 and 105 break away from each other and set different courses to achieve their objectives.

*

Very shortly all four of the Kilos will be entering the undersea surveillance lines known as SOSUS. Created after World War II and continuously upgraded over the years, with this threat, SOSUS faces its first test. Lives of millions of Americans will depend on it, though all but a few have any idea of the danger the country faces. The administration is trying desperately to resolve this situation, to avoid outright panic in the nation's streets.

Chapter Eighty-Four

Halfway Through the Mediterranean

At 2100 hours Captain Ali orders his crew to raise Kilo 101 to periscope depth. Viewing the surface and the nighttime sky for intruders he sees nothing to prevent him from surfacing and recharging his batteries. He also knows that his crew will benefit from the circulation of fresh air inside of the vessel.

"Prepare to surface," he tells his first officer. "When we are on the surface, open the forward and aft hatches as well as the mast hatch. Post a man at each hatch in case we need to dive quickly."

"Yes, sir," says the first officer, who in turn gives the command to bring 101 to surface level. Men swing into action, quickly and quietly opening the hatches and posting the necessary surface watches.

"Captain," the first officer asks, "how long do you plan to run on the surface?"

"How much time do we need to completely charge our batteries, number one?"

"If we could get six hours on the surface, we'd be in good shape, sir."

"Then let's do that. Bearing in mind, of course, that we might have to alter that plan based on what we come in contact with."

*

Flying at twenty thousand feet, an American P3 Orion has just left its base at Palermo, Sicily. Half an hour into the flight, one of the communications people says, "I just got a blip on my screen five miles off our starboard wing."

"What do you make of it?" asks his watch officer.

"It's too big to be a fishing vessel from around here. It's traveling at fifteen knots. Can anyone make out any nav lights out there for me?"

The co-pilot and the watch officer each look out into the distance. Even on a night like this, they should be able to see some type of illumination from navigational lights, but neither man can.

"Well, the funny thing about this contact is that the surface was clear for a half hour into the flight, then all of a sudden—he's just there."

"Do you think you have a sub contact?" the watch officer asks.

"Well, based on the briefing before we took off, I'd say it's a good possibility."

"Who do you think it might belong to? Can you ID it?"

"If we try to ID it, we'll probably scare him off. My suggestion, sir, since we have no rules of engagement yet, why don't we try making him think we're different commercial planes in flight? Fly patterns around him, this way and that, at different altitudes. It might let us dog him, as long as he stays on the surface, of course."

"Good idea," the watch officer nods. "Let me go talk with the pilot and co-pilot and work out a plan. Meanwhile, I'll have our radioman contact the base and let them know what we're doing. I'll also have them contact the commander of Sixth Fleet and advise him of our contact."

*

Standing up in the mast as Kilo 101 cruises on the surface, the captain is pleased that they have no surface contacts.

His first officer hears the roar of the turbo props on the P3. "Captain, shouldn't we be concerned about that aircraft?" he asks.

"No, number one. It's probably commercial, making a run somewhere here in the Mediterranean."

*

Joe Smiga

Meanwhile aboard the P3, a message comes in: EXECUTE YOUR IDEA AND GIVE US REGULAR HALF-HOURLY REPORTS ON YOUR CONTACT. NOTIFY OF ANY IMMEDIATE CHANGES. RECORD ALL COURSE CHANGES. GOOD HUNTING. BASE COMMANDER.

Chapter Eighty-Five

The Same Week in October

Sitting around the conference table on the top floor of the Guardian Council building are Mahmoud Khasanjani, Fadil Ahmajid and the five Imams on the council, Hossein Farook, Mansour Hassan, Sayed Abbas, Karim Farhani and Rahim Givon.

Khasanjani speaks. "In one week we expect our Kilos to be on their assigned stations. After we communicate with them we'll give them their instructions to launch their attacks."

"When will Hezbollah and Hamas begin their diversions?" Farook inquires.

"That commencement date will be coordinated with the Kilos arriving at their final firing positions. We will give the Kilos three days to arrive after we communicate, and then the diversions will begin. On the fourth day of the diversions, the Kilos will strike. And we will fire on Israel from within our borders," says Ahmajid. Beards are stroked and heads nod around the table.

"We now have twelve nuclear armed Shahab-3 land based missiles ready for positioning," Khasanjani continues. "Two will be used against Israel. The remaining ten will be in position to fire against countries that we feel might try to counter our moves. No one will know that, at that point, we'll only have ten more."

"Do you really expect that to happen after they see what happens to Israel and the United States?" asks Givon.

"One cannot assume anything in battle," replies Khasanjani. "One must be prepared for all contingencies."

"So, say the attack comes off as planned. Afterwards, what kind of retaliation would you expect from the United States," asks Abbas.

"We will advise them that our submarine fleet is still off their shores and, if any retaliation is attempted, we'll continue to fire nuclear warheads into their country," Ahmajid answers.

"And you think that will stop them?" asks Hassan.

"Yes, both the president and I feel that their media will put so much pressure on the administration that they will not dare retaliate, at least not then. What we must do is keep demonstrating our might, so that no one is brave enough to try to confront us."

"Mr. President, after all of the missiles fall, what are your plans?" asks Farook.

"We will make it known through the media that Iran is now the true leader of the Muslim world, that all countries need to honor our status."

"Fadil, all of your talk about power is great. However, even if we pull this off, what's to say that our actions won't unify the rest of the world against us. We could be creating a world-wide movement, nations forgetting their grievances and combining their strengths to stop us," says Givon.

"Givon, if you took the time to notice the Muslim populations that are already planted in every European nation, and in North and South America, you will see that what follows will be internal conflict beyond anyone's expectations."

"So you look at them as a fifth column inside each and every country, one that we can rely on?" says Farook.

"With Allah's blessing, yes, I do." Ahmajid is unshakable in his convictions.

"Now, back to my question, Mr. President," Farook speaks again. "What are your plans for our regional and worldwide conquests?"

"Farook, we are laying out plans to take over one country at a time, with the help of our fundamentalist brothers who live there."

"And you really expect no resistance?"

"No, no major resistance, anyway."

"Gentlemen, like all of you, I believe Allah wishes us to bring the true faith to the infidels," says Hassan. "However if history repeats itself, the crusades will come back to haunt us, and this time not on horseback."

"You Imans are acting like frightened children as we approach launch date," the Supreme Leader says.

"Fadil, we aren't afraid to die for our country," says Abbas firmly. "However, to not have a plan beyond what you have already told us is sheer insanity."

"Our future is in Allah's hands," Hassan reminds them all. "We just have to listen to Him."

Chapter Eighty-Six

Third Week in October

While a good idea, Admiral Smith's screen has not produced any significant results as yet on either coast. Submarines are simply damned hard to find. Then suddenly from the SOSUS listening posts comes a message to Commander Pacific Fleet aboard his flag ship by comm phone. The admiral comes to the phone.

DEFINITE KILO-CLASS SIGNATURE HEADED EASTBOUND ON A COURSE OF ZERO-NINE-ZERO DISTANCE FROM COASTLINE IS APPROXIMATELY FIFTEEN HUNDRED MILES DESIGNATE THIS KILO AS KILO ONE. IF THEY CONTINUE ON COURSE THEY ARE HEADED FOR LOS ANGELES OVER.

SOSUS CENTER IS THERE ANY WORD OF A SECOND SUB OVER.

NEGATIVE WE WILL CONTINUE TO MONITOR. HOW OFTEN DO YOU REQUIRE OUR READINGS OVER.

GIVE US AN UPDATE EVERY HOUR UNLESS KILO CHANGES COURSE WE NEED A FIX FROM LOS ANGELES SO WE CAN TRIANGULATE OUR SHIPS' COURSES TO INTERSECT OVER.

SOSUS CENTER AYE YOU'LL HAVE LONGITUDE AND LATITUDE IN ONE MINUTE OVER.

"Okay, people," the admiral says to those gathered around him. "We know that one sub is some fifteen hundred miles west of L.A. Once we get an approximate fix, we can move part of our screen to surround that one. Then we wait for word from the White House."

Admiral O'Rouke notifies a squadron of his destroyers and frigates to intersect Kilo one. *May God be with them,* he will remember thinking for the rest of his days.

*

TIGER ONE THIS IS MAINSTAY TIGER ONE THIS IS MAINSTAY OVER.

THIS IS TIGER ONE GO AHEAD.

YOUR SQUADRON FOUR DESTROYERS AND TWO FRIGATES IS TO HEAD TO INTERSECT KILO CONTACT CURRENT POSTION IS 31 DEGREES NORTH 140 DEGREES WEST SURROUND AND KEEP UNDER SURVEILLANCE AWAIT FURTHER INSTRUCTIONS KILO COURSE IS CURRENTLY ZERO-NINE-ZERO SPEED FIVE KNOTS OVER.

MAINSTAY THIS IS TIGER ONE WHAT RANGE DO YOU WANT US TO USE TO BOX THIS GUY IN OVER.

TIGER ONE FOUR THOUSAND YARDS WE HAVE A P3-ORION LEAVING SAN DIEGO SHOULD ARRIVE ON SITE BEFORE YOU DO OVER.

The four destroyers and two frigates crank their speed up to forty knots and haul ass to make the intersect. Everyone on board the ships is aware of the urgency of the situation. Bows of the smaller crafts lift out of the water as the six ships race towards the contact.

*

PAC FLEET THIS IS SOSUS CENTER OVER.

GO AHEAD SOSUS CENTER.

DESIGNATE KILO TWO APPROXIMATELY SIXTEEN HUNDRED MILES OFF THE WEST COAST IF CURRENT COURSE IS MAINTAINED HEADED FOR SAN FRANCISCO SPEED FIVE KNOTS OVER.

GIVE US A FIX FROM SAN FRANCISCO SO WE CAN INTERCEPT OVER.

Vice-Admiral O'Rourke picks up the comm phone and handles the call himself.

BLACK ANGUS BLACK ANGUS THIS IS MAINSTAY OVER.

THIS IS BLACK ANGUS GO AHEAD.

BLACK ANGUS TAKE YOUR SQUADRON TO INTERCEPT WHAT WE CONSIDER TO BE KILO TWO THEIR POSITION APPROXIMATELY 38 DEGREES NORTH 143 DEGREES WEST SPEED FIVE KNOTS HEADING COURSE ZERO NINE ZERO OVER.

MAINSTAY THIS IS BLACK ANGUS DO RULES OF ENGAGEMENT REMAIN THE SAME OVER.

BLACK ANGUS, THIS IS MAINSTAY FOR THE MOMENT RULES ARE THE SAME USE FOUR THOUSAND YARDS AS A RANGE TO QUARRY OVER.

BLACK ANGUS AYE OVER.

At least they have some idea of where they are, thinks Vice-Admiral O'Rourke. *Now to tell Admiral Smith so he can report it to the president.*
Vice-Admiral O'Rourke reaches Admiral Smith promptly. "May I suggest, sir, that the screen be reconfigured so they form lines above and below these targets?"
"Go ahead, Kevin. That sounds good. I hope we hear something soon on the east coast."

*

The president's phone rings as he's trying to close out what he considered to be a ridiculous meeting, strictly for public relations. "Gentlemen, duty calls," he says, feigning reluctance. "I'm afraid I must answer my phone, and I believe we are through."

Three members of the board of the Green Peace movement leave the Oval Office realizing they have just been given the boot.

The president reaches for the phone. "Yes, Janet, roughly what's it?"

"Sir, Admiral Smith is on a secure phone. I have him on line two for you."

"Thank you, Janet. I'm sorry if I came off a bit rude there. It's been a long morning."

"No problem, sir," Janet responds. "I have thick skin." The president smiles at her remark as he switches lines. "Bob, what have we got?"

"SOSUS picked up two subs on the west coast. Admiral O'Rourke has his squadrons of ships and a P3 Orion out of San Diego intercepting them. Do you wish to change the rules of engagement yet, sir?"

"How far out are they, Bob?"

"One was sixteen hundred miles, the other fifteen hundred miles when we picked them up."

"We won't change engagement just yet. Where do they seem to be headed?"

"One appears to be headed for Los Angeles. The second one is making for San Francisco."

"Good God!" The president closes his eyes for a moment. "Bob, do you think others will show up on the west coast or will they head for the east coast?"

"Sir, if we don't see anything off the east coast in twelve more hours, I wouldn't be able to tell you where the hell they're sending them. My guess, though, is that they'll be off your front lawn soon."

"I hear you," the president responds.

Both men hang up. Each finds himself looking off into space.

The president pulls himself out of his brief meditation, picks up his phone and asks Janet to have Dean Hargrove come to his office.

Five minutes later, the chairman of the joint chiefs arrives at the Oval Office door and is sent in by the Secret Service.

"You rang, sir?" Hargrove says, trying to inject a little humor into the tense environment. The president chuckles.

"You know, I'm glad I appointed you chairman of the joint chiefs. You can be funny at times, Dean, and right now I could use a small laugh. Yes, I called. Here's what's happening right now. We've located three of the subs and are still searching for the two others. Admiral Smith will be calling you in fifteen minutes. I want you to set up the Situation Room to monitor and display every move that Admiral Smith gives you on screens."

"Do I do this by myself, or can I use staff?"

"Do you have staff that will keep their mouths shut?"

"You're right. I'll do this myself. Can you send a car out to my place to pick up my emergency travel bag? I expect I'll need it."

"Done."

*

Four hours later.

TIGER ONE THIS IS YELLOWBIRD OVER.

THIS IS TIGER ONE GO AHEAD OVER.

YOUR CONTACT IS STILL ON COURSE ZERO NINE ZERO EVIDENTLY THEY DON'T REALIZE WE ARE ABOVE THEM. BUT WE BELIEVE WHEN HE HEARD YOUR PROPS TURNING HE DIVED TO A POINT I CAN BARELY SEE HIM OVER.

YELLOWBIRD THIS IS TIGER ONE COPY YOUR LAST TRANSMISSION OVER.

YELLOWBIRD TIGER ONE ALIGNING VESSELS TO CREATE LINE FIVE NAUTICAL MILES WIDE WILL REDUCE OUR SPEED TO TEN KNOTS OVER.

TIGER ONE YELLOWBIRD BE AWARE THAT KILOS ARE DEAD QUIET AT VERY LOW SPEEDS RESULTING IN SUBSTANTIAL REDUCTION IN ACOUSTIC SIGNATURE OVER.

YELLOWBIRD TIGER ONE ARE YOU STAYING WITH US OR DO YOU HAVE OTHER ORDERS OVER?

TIGER ONE YELLOWBIRD WE HAVE ORDERS THAT ONCE YOU ARRIVE WE ARE TO HEAD TO KILO TWO THEY WANT US TO JOCKEY BACK AND FORTH SINCE THEY ARE IN CLOSE PROXIMITY OVER.

YELLOWBIRD TIGER ONE LET US KNOW WHEN YOU ARE CUTTING OUT AND WHEN YOU ARE CLOSE BY AGAIN OVER.

TIGER ONE YELLOWBIRD WILL DO OVER.

Two hundred meters below the surface Captain Hafiz, commanding officer of Kilo 103 orders his ship to dive a further two hundred meters and reduce speed to three knots. Sonar picked up high speed surface vessels approaching; he wants to remain quiet so as not to be detected. *Are they looking for us or are they just out on exercises?* he wonders.

TIGER ONE YELLOWBIRD OVER.

TIGER ONE GO AHEAD OVER.

WE HAVE JUST CROSSED OVER WHERE WE ESTIMATE YOUR CONTACT SHOULD BE LOCATED HAS DIVED DEEP ENOUGH WE CANNOT GET A VISUAL ANY LONGER WILL LEAVE IT UP TO YOUR TEAM TO REMAIN IN CONTACT OVER.

YELLOWBIRD TIGER ONE AFFIRMATIVE ON YOUR LAST LET US KNOW WHEN YOU HEAD BACK THIS WAY OVER.

*

The six American vessels start a search pattern to locate the submarine. After finding it they must insure that they maintain its position. This will not be easy, even given the first-class equipment and training they have.

At a depth of six hundred meters, Captain Hafiz realizes the surface vessels are looking for 103. He orders all unnecessary machinery and

Joe Smiga

ventilation equipment shut down and reduces speed to one knot just to remain stable. Now they can only wait and see what happens next. At this rate, they should be able to reach their station, at which point they can communicate with their government.

His men have never seen battle, nor have they ever experienced being hunted by a hostile navy. The tension of hearing propellers overhead and the fear of being identified are building inside each sailor aboard 103. Though the sub is actually growing chillier, sweat begins to pour from their pores. Their eyes reveal glimmers of the terror that's making inroads into their usual composure.

Chapter Eighty-Seven

Same Day

Admiral Smith is on the phone to Vice-Admiral Dave Peterson, commander of the Atlantic Fleet.

"Dave is there any word from SOSUS or your screen identifying a Kilo?"

"No, sir, not as yet."

"SOSUS picked up two Kilos headed to the west coast," the admiral says. "I cannot believe they are going to leave the east coast clear, Dave."

"I can't either, sir. Not with such a tempting target as Washington."

"Okay, Dave, keep me posted. We're running a display screen in the Situation Room on every move we see."

*

Acoustical sound signals are adversely affected in cooler waters than in warmer waters. SOSUS does not pick up the other two Kilos until they get closer to the mainland.

*

Admiral Smith's phone rings. He grabs it fiercely without even realizing he does. If it were a sub sandwich, he'd have broken it in two. "Admiral, Dave Peterson here. SOSUS has two Kilos approximately a thousand miles off of our east coast. One is on a heading for Washington. The other is on a heading for New York."

"I knew it, dammit, I knew it," Peterson hears Admiral Smith say. "Dave, get me the particulars. I want everything you know sent down to the Situation Room. I plan to be there in twenty minutes."

"Yes, sir. I'll have it all for you."

Within the next twenty minutes, Vice-Admiral Peterson directs his fleet to intercept and place borders. Those Kilos won't escape if he can help it.

*

In the Situation Room, Dean Hargrove is plotting each submarine as information on it comes in. To his frustration, much of the time, the subs' locations are unknown. He feels like he's flying blind. He's not used to this type of analysis and feels utter frustration between sightings.

Just as he has received the latest information from the Sixth Fleet in the Mediterranean on the sub headed for Israel, he sees General James Bradley walk through the door.

"Dean, it's good to see you have everything under control," the general tells him.

"Yeah, Jim, sure I do," Hargrove scowls. "Hope it looks convincing, anyway."

"Dean, we're doing the best we can. We've got the best fighting force in the world. We'll take care of this, I promise you."

"Thanks, Jim, because right now, I don't mind admitting I don't feel very comfortable with what's going on."

"We didn't start it, Dean, but we damn well will finish it."

Just then Admiral Smith arrives. "Jim, I'm glad you're here," Hargrove welcomes him. "We need to set up some parameters between our vessels and our planes. The latest will be coming in from SOSUS on the east coast in about five minutes. Then we can move on into a new plan."

"Damn right, we will," the admiral replies with much the same degree of certainty as Hargrove had just heard from General Bradley. "I'm tired of these rag-heads screwing up the world," the admiral added.

Five minutes later, Vice-Admiral Peterson calls into the Situation Room and updates Admiral Smith. Both Smith and General Bradley put their heads together and quickly come up with a plan to protect the shores of the United States, insuring at the same time that those enemy submarines will never return to their shores.

MESSAGE TO: COMMANDERS ATLANTIC AND PACIFIC FLEETS * BREAK * POSITION SUBS TO STRETCH ACROSS A TWELVE MILE LINE AT THE CITIES OF: WASHINGTON DC, NEW YORK, LOS ANGELES AND SAN FRANCISCO. THESE SUBS ARE TO CRUISE AT A DISTANCE FROM SHORE OF TWO HUNDRED FIFTY TO THREE HUNDRED MILES * BREAK * AIR FORCE WILL COVER THE CORRIDOR OF THREE HUNDRED TO THREE HUNDRED FIFTY MILES * BREAK * SURFACE SHIPS ARE TO BE STATIONED AT THREE HUNDRED FIFTY TO FOUR HUNDRED MILES * BREAK * ALL ADDITIONAL SURFACE VESSELS AVAILABLE ARE TO BE SENT NORTH AND SOUTH OF THESE LOCATIONS TO CREATE A COMPLETE BOX. * BREAK *

The message is confirmed by Admiral Smith and sent by both fleet admirals. General Bradley sends the same message to his Air Force commands, leaving it up to each individual command to use its best judgment as to what planes they will use.

Just as the general's message is given, the President walks into the Situation Room.

"Well, gentlemen, what have we got so far?" he asks quietly.

Admiral Smith and General Bradley use Hargrove's screens to show the president what's known up to this point. They then explain their new plan, reminding the president that, of course, the most critical decision must come from him. "Even though these boats are running in international waters, we have no doubt as to their true intent," the admiral says.

"Bob, Jim, in my gut I know both of you're right. I just have to be sure that I'm not ordering the opening salvos of World War Three."

General Bradley speaks up. "Sir, the closer you allow them come to our coasts, the worse things may turn out."

"Right now I wish we had a two-hundred-mile rule of sovereignty like other countries. How many miles does the U.S. enforce? Three bloody miles." His frustration is obvious. Turning to the rest, he says, "I suspect that the four of us will be spending a great deal of time in this room together over the next few days. What do each of you need to be more comfortable?"

Admiral Smith says, "I've already told my wife not to expect me for a couple of days."

General Bradley says, "Not having a wife at a time like this makes it easier, I do have to say."

"My wife and kids are in Ohio visiting her folks," Hargrove says. "Boy, am I grateful that they're in the midwest."

"I'll have rooms set up for all three of you upstairs. This way we can all be readily available, and maybe even grab a little shuteye if possible."

Chapter Eighty-Eight

Changing Tactics

Admiral Smith picks up his satellite phone to the fleet and calls out to Vice-Admiral Kevin O'Rourke. "Kevin, what kind of success are your two squadrons having finding the Kilos they're trailing?"

"They're reporting only intermittent success so far, sir, I regret to say," he says.

"No, that's okay. I want you to pull both squadrons back to the lines in the previous message I just sent you. Concentrating the greater number of vessels and planes we can there will give us a better chance of finding them."

"You're saying you just want us to break off as if we quit looking for them?" O'Rourke questions.

"That's exactly what I want you to do," the admiral replies. "If they believe we've quit, we may find it easier for us to corner them closer to our shores."

"That's a real gamble, sir," the vice-admiral says without considering the impact such words might have.

In frustration, the admiral replies, "No shit, Kevin, but do it my way, will you?"

"Yes, sir. Will do." Kevin O'Rourke knows the admiral will remember those four careless words for some time to come.

*

Joe Smiga

BLACK ANGUS BLACK ANGUS THIS IS MAINTSTAY OVER.

THIS IS BLACK ANGUS GO AHEAD.

YOU ARE TO PROCEED FULL SPEED TO 38 DEGREES NORTH 125 DEGREES WEST TO MEET WITH PICKET LINE UNDER DESFLOT 4. YOU WILL BE GIVEN YOUR PICKET STATION UPON ARRIVAL OVER.

MAINSTAY BLACK ANGUS YOU WANT US TO LEAVE THIS GUY OVER?

THAT'S AFFIRMATIVE OVER.

*

TIGER ONE TIGER ONE THIS IS MAINSTAY OVER.

THIS IS TIGER ONE GO AHEAD.

YOU ARE TO PROCEED FULL SPEED TO 33 DEGREES NORTH 125 DEGREES WEST TO MEET WITH PICKET LINE UNDER DESFLOT 4. YOU WILL BE GIVEN YOUR PICKET STATION UPON ARRIVAL OVER.

MAINSTAY TIGER ONE PLEASE REPEAT YOU ARE ORDERING US OFF OF THIS CONTACT.

THAT IS AFFIRMATIVE TIGER I REPEAT YOU ARE DIRECTED TO 33 DEGREES NORTH 125 DEGREES WEST OVER.

TIGER ONE OUT.

*

Both squadrons of ships proceed as directed, twelve ships' bridge officers and captains all wondering what the hell is going on, all thinking variations on: *Somebody or somebodies sure damn well better have their shit together.*

*

Meanwhile in the Situation Room, SOSUS is giving Admiral Smith a sufficient reading on positions of the Kilos to make it possible to get an overall sense of direction. Dean Hargrove is plotting everything on the status boards so that everyone has a clear a picture of what's happening at a glance. The admiral finds this amusing. *Hargrove should have been working in operations in the Navy,* he smirks.

*

Kilos 102 and 103 are both relieved that the U.S. vessels have departed. At least for the time being, they feel comfortable proceeding on schedule to reach their stations and report in. However, both captains are not naïve enough to be fooled into thinking that this is the end of the episode.

*

As they get closer to the U.S. coastlines, both captains of Kilos 102 and 103 see and hear for themselves what they are confronting. This is going to be a challenge just to get off a message, never mind fire a missile.

Kilos 104 and 105, on the other hand, are unaware that they are being tracked by SOSUS. Up to this point, they would characterize their voyage as a walk in the park. They are beginning to get a little complacent in their thinking.

Over confidence can be as threatening as lack of confidence, if not more so.

*

President Egan steps into the Situation Room and everyone stands.

"Please, everyone relax. We've enough pressure without having protocol to deal with too. Dean, give me a run-down of what you have on the screens."

"Sir, we've set up screens of surface vessels and subs with corridors of ASW—anti-sub aircraft—flying between them on both coasts. We've been able to identify and locate positions on two Kilos on the west coast, beginning at approximately fifteen hundred to sixteen hundred miles off of our shore. And on the east coast, we picked up the remaining two at approximately one thousand miles distance."

"Why's that, Admiral?" asks the president, bewildered.

"Sir, because of colder water temperatures and different thermal layers, we were unable to pick them us sooner. If you're thinking it might be the fault of equipment, it isn't. It's merely a case of what the oceans will allow us to read, based on their own characteristics."

"Admiral, if they're going to fire at us instead of merely threatening us, at what range would you expect that to happen?"

"Sir, their Shahab-3 has a land range of approximately one thousand miles. On the east coast they are within that range right now. However, I'd say they'd probably want to come in to within two to four hundred miles to ensure a higher degree of accuracy. Bear in mind, this cruise missile business is new for them. I have no idea what their test results are like for these things. However, firing under actual combat conditions does a lot of things to people and equipment."

"Let's just hope their stress levels are higher than ours, and that they screw up royally," says President Egan.

Chapter Eighty-Nine

The First of the Four Days

Each Kilo reaches its station, at points three hundred miles off their targets. The four Kilos off the U.S. coastline have spent a great deal of their recent time at six hundred meters depth, running at one knot. This enables them to evade the surface vessels they know are looking for them. Now all they can do is sit on station and wait for the clock to run out until they can receive their final communication.

At 2400 hours Atlantic Time, 2100 hours Pacific Time and 0700 hours when the sun has risen over Israel, each Kilo raises its periscope to check the surface and then raises their radio masts to receive their orders. The orders come in exactly on time.

TO KILOS 101 THROUGH 105—PROCEED TO A DISTANCE OF 300 KMS FROM YOUR TARGETS—TAKE 3 DAYS TO ARRIVE THERE—ON THE 4TH DAY AT 2400 HOURS GMT YOU ARE TO EXECUTE YOUR ORDERS—ACKNOWLEDGE RECEIVING THIS BY SENDING ONE WORD ONLY (UNDERSTOOD)—DO NOT TRANSMIT ANY FURTHER COMMUNICATION UNLESS YOU ARE AT LEAST 3000 KMS FROM YOUR TARGETS—

All five Kilos transmit their UNDERSTOODs.

Ahmajid receives the replies from each Kilo by radio messenger. He calls the president. "We are on target and every Kilo has acknowledged. We haven't lost any advantage.

"Now it is time for Hamas and Hezbollah to play their part in the diversion. Allah is Great."

*

In the Situation Room, Admiral Smith receives Whispering data from NSA regarding the transmissions from Iran to the Kilos. Along with the information coming in from SOSUS, he knows that the subs have by-passed his surface vessels. Nothing about this is surprising; he knows how quiet Kilos can be. He doubts that any of the Kilo's are aware, however, of the sub screen he has put into place.

Chapter Ninety

Convincing Evidence

President Egan enters the Situation Room to review the data being entered onto the screens displaying the positions of each of the five Kilo submarines and the direction each appears to be traveling.

"Dean, Admiral, General, I know you have your hands full. However, I'm calling an emergency meeting here so we can all hear what Whispering has been able to discover, to keep everyone who needs to know on top of everything. Janet's in the process of reaching everyone I want to be here, asap."

John Anderson, Secretary of Defense, is the first to arrive. He appears astonished to see Dean Hargrove maintaining status screens in the room as ably as if he now were a tactical plotter.

General Sanford arrives next and smiles as he enters what he is now thinking of as the War Room, not the Situation Room. He doesn't need to be told what's going down. He knows what he expects to hear.

John Walker and Allison McDonald walk in together, having met in the hallway and taken the elevator down in each other's company, comparing notes all the way.

"Let's everyone take a seat," President Egan says. "We have a great deal to cover. John Walker, I'd like you to give everyone a report regarding what NSA has learned recently from Whispering."

Chairs get shuffled around as the attendees pick a spot in which they suppose they'll be comfortable; they all expect this meeting to be a hard one. As they look around the table at each other, taking mental inventory of the players today, they can't help but notice the absence of both the vice president and the chief of staff. Their expressions range from puzzled to dubious.

John Walker begins. "Okay, folks, 'round 2400 hours Atlantic time last night, Project Whisperin' picked up a communication intended for the five Kilo subs. Basically it told them they were to proceed to a position two hun'red miles from their targets and that they were to be there in three days. The message went on to say that at 2400 hours Greenwich Mean Time on the fourth day from today, they were to execute their ordahs. We're 'sumin' that each sub received its ordahs when they set sail and already know what their ordahs are. The communication said they should acknowledge receipt of this ordah by merely sending a one-word reply, presumably so's not to reveal their positions. Which I gotta admit worked—we weren't able to locate any of 'em by their responses. They were then told not to communicate with Iran 'til they were at least two thousand miles—I repeat, two thousand miles from their targets."

Admiral Smith speaks, "That tells me they expect to pull off this attack, and want their vessels somewhere safe enough from retaliation for use another day."

President Egan's eyes roam the room, watching for signs that someone has something to say. Seeing none, he says, "John, go on. I know you have more."

"Yes, suh, I do. The hierarchy of Hamas and Hezbollah received coded e-mails just after the Kilo communication was sent. Based on previous intelligence, we 'spect that both Hamas and Hezbollah are part of Iran's plan, that they've signed up to provide inland diversions for what's to happen when Israel's attacked by sea."

"You mean to keep our attention over there instead of over here?" says John Anderson, clearly frustrated.

"Partly. But we think it's really meant to preoccupy Israel, that dealin' with confrontations by two of their most powerful enemies at the same time, they may never see what's comin' at them from Kilos right off their shores."

"You mean they won't be attacking Israel with land based missiles?"

"If I can go on, this might become more understandable," says John Walker, clearing his throat. "To answer Allison's question first, we feel Israel's gonna get hit from both land *and* sea. Why do we think this? Our satellites have picked up a dozen Shahab-3 missiles being moved around Iran since midnight last night. It looks like each missile's being positioned for launchin'."

"They don't need a dozen missiles to take out Israel, John. What are you really saying?" asks General Sanford.

"What we think is that, after the attacks on the U.S. and Israel, Iran wants any other nation who might think 'bout leadin' a retaliatory action against 'em to be taken out by one or more of these othah missiles. A couple of those would let the air out of any more plans for interference."

General Sanford sits back in his seat and lets out an entire lungful of air through pursed lips.

"Now, I think y'all should listen to Allison before I continue or answer anymore questions. Allison."

"Thank you, John."

"Mr. President, gentlemen, as per previous intelligence reports you've heard from the CIA, this all seems to be coming to a head. We reported that the Russian mafiya supposedly sold materials for the production of nuclear warheads to the Iranians. Based on the number of centrifuges in operation in Iran, we don't believe they could have created large quantities of enriched uranium by now. From the Israelis, we've learned that Iran is also reprocessing plutonium into nuclear enriched materials.

"We suspect that the Iranians may have a small number of nuclear cruise missiles with which to attack us and we believe, based on recent Whispering intel, that a dozen warheads have been converted into nuclear warheads. The CIA believes that, having such a small nuclear capability, that Iran is out to frighten the world by sheer audacity. They know no one truly knows what they have. Based on the Europeans' lack of will over the last decade, it might even work. John, the floor is yours again." Walker picks up where she's left off.

"What the NSA sees is that we have seventy-two to ninety-six hours before four Kilos will attack the U.S. mainland with nuclear warheads. A fifth will strike the state of Israel about the same time. This will seriously damage us and probably wipe out most of Israel. It appears that there won't be any further contact between Iran and those Kilos. Even if we attack Iran, the Kilos are out of communication now. They could even be on some sort of suicide mission, for all we know."

The president says, "John, could Iran be thinking that we might find out about these Kilos and try to negotiate before they hit us?"

"Maybe, suh. I really don't know. Howevah, if we do that, I think Iran then gets to call itself the supah powah of the Middle East, maybe even the world. Either way, if we negotiate or we are attacked, the entire Muslim world will see them as their leader. That's where we believe this is all headed. They want to first rule the Muslim world, and then go for global conquest."

John Walker sits back in his chair feeling emotionally exhausted. McDonald tries to give him a heads-up smile hoping he'll realize he has done everything possible that he can.

No one says a word for at least two minutes.

Chapter Ninety-One

Plans Set in Motion

Finally, the president breaks the silence. "Based on the information presented, I think that Iran is trying to put us in a compromising situation. Realizing how much we value life, it's entirely possible that they may think we'd rather negotiate rather than have our homeland attacked." The president stops, considers, then continues, almost painfully. "As president, I am bound by the Constitution to protect its shores and its people. However, not at the mercy of people who have no or very little regard for human life."

The president gets to his feet and faces the group squarely. His voice grows more strident with every word he utters. "Let me make one thing clear. This nation will never go down in defeat. If we must endure being attacked, our casualties will harden us to continue the fight and take it where it belongs. If Iran thinks it can attack this nation, Iran is going to learn a lesson it most probably does not expect. We are going to war as of right now. Admiral Smith and General Bradley, are you able to have your forces deployed where and as we have previously discussed?"

"We are already in position, sir," Admiral Smith replies. "I've ordered all units into position when we first received confirmed SOSUS reports."

General Bradley's answer follows on the admiral's heels. "Sir, my forces have been at maximum levels in Diego Garcia for a week now."

The president can smile, if only slightly. Even in the midst of this terrible challenge, he can only admire the men this country has put in leadership roles. Then he grows serious again. "This meeting is now over. I'm going back to the Oval Office to speak to the prime minister of Israel. After that I do need to attend to a few things, after which I'll be calling a meeting of the House Armed Services Committee. That meeting will coincide will our launch against Iran. I won't address the American public until *after* we get those Kilos. The last thing I want is national panic."

Turning to the director of the CIA, he adds, "Allison, I need to speak with you in . . . say, give me half an hour."

"No problem, sir. I'll head upstairs and get a bite to eat. I haven't had lunch yet."

"Lunch? What's lunch?" Dean Hargrove asks nobody in particular.

*

Heading to the Oval Office, the president passes through Janet's office. As he does so, he asks her to get the prime minister of Israel on a secure line. "Don't take any excuses from anyone that we need to wait," he says emphatically. "I must speak with him now."

"Yes, sir," Janet says. Her radar tells her something very serious is happening. Janet's radar is never wrong.

Five minutes later Yaakov Brumwell is on the phone. "Couldn't you at least wait until I finished dinner, Mr. President?" he complains.

"No. This way you'll have less to throw up."

"That bad?"

"Yes, Yaakov, that bad and maybe worse. Prime Minister, we told you about the Kilos leaving Iran, and that one had entered the Mediterranean."

"Yes," Brumwell answers. "So now you're going to tell me you can't find him?"

"No, we know exactly where he is, and he doesn't even know it. What you need to know is that our intelligence says you're going to have border problems, tonight, tomorrow, any minute now. Hamas and Hezbollah are cooperating with Iran in planning border skirmishes which we think are merely meant as a diversion. We believe that the Iranians plan to launch a newly designed cruise missile into Israel—a missile with a nuclear warhead. It's also possible that they'll attack your country from inside of Iran as well."

"When do you think this launch will happen?"

"In four days, Yaakov—four days."

"Bill, aren't there four other Kilos out there?"

"Yes, there are. And they are heading for us, with the same mission and the same time table."

There is a silence before Yaakov Brumwell asks his next question. "Then what are you planning to do, may I ask?"

The president takes a deep breath. "I am calling you, Mr. Prime Minister, to tell you that the Sixth Fleet will be under orders, as soon as we hang up, to take out your underwater threat. What I can't do is protect your backside from Iran."

"Mr. President, the state of Israel thanks you from the bottom of our hearts. We will do our best to take care of our backside. Thank you again. You are in our prayers, Bill."

"And you in ours, Yaakov." President Egan hangs up with Brumwell, then asks Janet to put him through to Admiral Smith on a secure line.

Within a few minutes Janet rings to tell him that Admiral Smith is on line two.

"Mr. President, I didn't expect to hear from you again so soon."

"Well, Bob, I guess you better get used to me living with you until this thing's over."

"No problem on my end, sir. As a matter of fact, I'm enjoying working with you."

"Thank you," the president says, surprised at the bracing effect those few words have on him. "Now, onto why I called. I want the Sixth Fleet to take out that Kilo in the Med, and I want you to get word to every vessel you have on our coasts to take out the other four. As of right now, am I understood?"

"Yes, sir, and I totally agree."

Both men hang up, knowing their decisions will cause men to die.

*

Janet White calls into the Oval Office., "Sir, Allison McDonald is here and says you want to see her."

"Yes, I do. Ask her to give me five minutes, then have the Secret Service bring her in."

"Yes, sir."

Five minutes later, McDonald is escorted into the Oval Office. The Secret Service agent closes the door quietly behind her.

The president gestures to one of the couches. The director of the CIA suspects she knows what the president has on his mind, though she has no idea how he will deal with it. Egan wastes no time getting to the issue.

"Allison, I want your special team to bring our reporter from the Post to the White House—tonight."

"Tonight? Like what time tonight, Mr. President?"

"You tell me when he can be here. I don't plan on doing much sleeping this evening so when hardly matters. I want to speak with him."

"Sir, what we've already done is quite extraordinary. If I may ask, what are you planning on doing? If you're going to do what I think you're going to do—I don't know, sir. This could be a disaster in the making. Don't forget he's a reporter, Mr. President."

"I know he's a reporter, Allison. However, before I decide how to deal with Pat and Maria, I have to speak with him."

"Do you want me or my ops man with you?"

"No. I don't think that'll be necessary. However, someone should stick around, to take him back where he wants to go."

"Well, sir, I guess this is the craziest thing I've ever agreed to, but I'll have him here. I just need to have the team find him first."

"No problem. I have all night."

McDonald rises and starts for the door, then turns back. "Mr. President, I'm only willing to do this because I believe in you. Please don't go overboard and get killed politically—we need men like you in leadership."

"Thank you, Allison. And you have my word, I don't plan to torture him. I just want to talk with him. I'm only going to use the intelligence you've provided me with to get him to work with us."

"No problem, sir—so long as he doesn't realize we are not the FBI."

"I always loved a good double negative, Allison. Let's just say he can realize what he wants to realize. If he thinks he's in the hands of the FBI, I have no intention of disabusing him of that notion."

"No sir, I know better of you. I just wonder what happens if tomorrow he gets second thoughts and starts shooting off his mouth—or his pen."

"I have my ways, Allison, trust me."

Chapter Ninety-Two

End of October

Rear Admiral Joseph DeMello, commander of the U.S. Sixth Fleet, signs for the two messages the radioman messenger hands him. He reads first the message sent him by Fleet Admiral Robert Smith. After reviewing the two top secret messages, he asks his staff, "What's the status of the Kilo we've been dogging?"

"The Kilo's on a slow run continuing towards Israel," the operations officer replies.

"We've just received orders that the U.S. has moved to Condition Red. We are at war with the nation of Iran. Each military group will be receiving its orders. Our orders are to take out the Kilo. I want to do this without a great deal of fanfare. We don't need to advertise that we have just gone to war. Do we have any boomers following the Kilo?"

"Sir, we have two LA-class boomers ahead of the Kilo at ten thousand yards," the operations officer speaks up again. "We've been anticipating orders of this nature."

"Instruct them to plot courses to take him out," the fleet commander says with grim determination. "I want him totaled."

"What about survivors, sir?"

"If you heard me correctly, you know there will be no survivors."

"Yes, sir," the operations officer said.

*

TO USS MANCHESTER FROM SIXTH FLEET COMMAND * BREAK * ALONG WITH THE USS PORTLAND YOU ARE TO COORDINATE ATTACK ON KILO YOU HAVE BEEN TRACKING * BREAK * AS SENIOR CAPTAIN YOU ARE TO CREATE THE PLOT * BREAK * COMMAND INSTRUCTS YOU TOTAL THE KILO * BREAK *

*

Aboard the Manchester her captain looks at the message. *Good God almighty. We've just gone to war with Iran.* He knows what he must do.

After doing some calculations, Captain Brian Donnelly of the Manchester sends a message to Captain Peter Doyle of the Portland.

TO USS PORTLAND FROM USS MANCHESTER * BREAK * UNDERSTAND YOU RECEIVED A COPY OF FLEET COMMAND'S RECENT ORDER * BREAK * SINCE I HAVE COMMAND THIS IS MY PLAN * BREAK * WE WILL LINE UP ON THE KILO AT FORTY-FIVE DEGREE ANGLES OFF HER BOW BOTH PORT AND STARBOARD SO WE ARE IN PLACE WHEN SHE REACHES SEVEN THOUSAND YARDS * BREAK * AT SIX THOUSAND YARDS I WILL FIRE A SALVO OF THREE MARK 60'S * BREAK * IF FOR SOME REASON THEY DO NOT CONNECT I EXPECT HER TO TURN IN THE OPPOSITE DIRECTION * BREAK * THEN THE REST IS UP TO YOU * BREAK

*

TO USS MANCHESTER FROM USS PORTLAND * BREAK * MESSAGE RECEIVED AGREE TO TACTIC * BREAK * WHICH SIDE DO YOU WISH TO MAINTAIN * BREAK *

Captain Donnelly of the Manchester looks at each of the boomers' positions and sends a message back to the Portland.

TO USS PORTLAND FROM USS MANCHESTER * BREAK * WE WILL HANDLE STARBOARD * BREAK * DON'T BELIEVE SHE REALIZES OUR PRESENCE * BREAK * LET'S KEEP IT THAT WAY * BREAK *

*

Kilo 101 maintains its course at three knots, headed for a point two hundred miles off of Israel's shore. Captain Ali has no idea that his sub is the subject of surveillance, both by air and sea. His dreams of glory, of being the captain who brought death and destruction to the state of Israel, is clouding his judgment.

"Navigator, what's our position at the moment?" asks Captain Ali.

"Sir, we are currently two hundred sixty nautical miles off of the Israeli coast. We'll be in position by 1200 hours tomorrow."

*

Captain Donnelly guides the Manchester into position.

"Range to target?"

"Eight thousand yards," is the reply from sonar.

"Load tubes one, two and three with MK 60s." The phone operator relays the message the torpedo room.

From the torpedo room word comes back, "Tubes are loaded. Wires connected."

"Range?"

"Seventy-five hundred yards."

"XO, are we at the correct angle for a forty-five degree shot?"

"Yes, sir."

"Range?"

"Seven thousand yards."

Each man aboard, from the captain on down, is beginning to sweat. Not one of them has been ever had to fire a live torpedo at an enemy. Tension builds. Many are asking themselves, *Will the Iranian sub manage to escape—and counterattack?*

"Range?"

"Sixty-five hundred yards, sir."

"Sonar, is the target showing any signs of realizing we're here?"

"No, sir. Target is on the same course as before at three hundred feet."

"Range?"

"Six thousand yards."

"Fire one"—three seconds—"fire two"—three seconds—"fire three."

The executive officer, Kent Haggerty, activates the firing switches with each command. *This may be the hardest thing I've ever done,*

Haggerty thinks during the first three-second break. During the second, his thoughts have turned 180 degrees. *The fucking bastards.*

"Torpedoes fired, sir, and running normal."

"Sonar, status on the torpedoes?"

"Torpedoes running passive search. Will begin to run active search at three thousand yards." "Continue controlling wires."

*

Inside Kilo 101, sonar suddenly reports. "Control room, sonar. Torpedo in the water, range six thousand yards off our starboard bow. No, wait, second torpedo. No, a third torpedo. We have three incoming fish running high speed."

Captain Ali shouts, "Ahead full, left full rudder. Drop decoys! Drop decoys! Sonar, do you have a contact?"

"No, sir, we have no contact."

As Kilo 101 strains to turn herself in a tight arc, the first of the MK 60s reaches three thousand yards and begins to identify with 101's acoustics. Its wire is cut. The torpedo now has a mind of its own.

"Who in Allah's name is firing at us?" yells Captain Ali.

"Maybe the Israelis have found us?" his first officer responds, his face whiter than the paper on the desk in front of him.

"Sonar, where are the torpedoes?"

"Captain, we have three torpedoes locked onto us. The hull will never take three hits at one time."

"Blow tanks! Surface!" screams Captain Ali.

The captain can feel new vibrations as air forces its way into 101's ballast tanks, displacing the sea water within. *The surface never seemed so far before.*

*

Inside the Manchester, Captain Donnelly barks, "What've you got, sonar?"

"All three of the MK 60s are running true, sir. Kilo is blowing ballast and trying to surface."

Just as sonar says the word 'surface,' the first MK connects at a point three feet from the tip of the bow. Moments later Kilo 101 is hit amidships. The third torpedo finds its stern.

The three explosions can be heard aboard both the Manchester and the Portland.

Captain Donnelly's heartbeat begins to slow. He and his crew have just experienced their first wartime action, and he is more than pleased with how well they performed. He also realizes that they just sent a number of fellow human beings—fellow submariners—to watery graves.

"Radio room, send a message to the Portland. They can stand down from general quarters. Mission accomplished."

Within minutes, Captain Doyle sends a message of congratulations to Captain Donnelly.

Captain Donnelly goes to the radio room and dictates a message to be sent to Rear Admiral Joseph DeMello, commander of the U.S. Sixth Fleet.

*

Aboard Admiral DeMello's flag vessel, he receives the report that Kilo 101 has been totaled as ordered.

DeMello turns to his operations officer. "Send a copy of this report to Admiral Smith in Washington," he tells him.

*

In the Situation Room, deep in the bowels of the White House, Admiral Smith receives the communiqué from Admiral DeMello and quickly reads it. The news brings with it only a small degree of relief. *One down, four to go.*

Admiral Smith picks up the phone nearest him, asks to be connected to the president and is put right through. "We've taken care of the sub in the Mediterranean," he reports. "Now we can focus on those coming to our shores."

"Yes," says the president, surprised to be suddenly experiencing mixed emotions. *You can't go soft. This is war,* he lectures himself. "Your men did a great job, Bob. I'll call the prime minister and let him know the threat he faced from the sea no longer exists."

Chapter Ninety-Three

Same Day in D.C.

Janet White calls into the Oval Office. "Sir, the main gate just called. They say they have a Mr. Scott Brubaker from the Post. He's saying that you want to meet with him?"

The president smiles. *This idiot thinks he has the upper hand and can control the situation by just dropping in.* "Yes, I do want to meet with him. I must say, I did expect that he'd call for an appointment."

"What shall I tell the guards at the gate, sir?"

"Have him escorted in and—Janet, let him cool his heels outside your office for about fifteen minutes while I finish up some things."

"Yes, sir."

President Egan needs the time to decide how he's going to handle Brubaker.

*

Twenty minutes later, Scott Brubaker is escorted in the Oval Office by the Secret Service. As he enters, the president stands, then comes around his desk and offers him his hand. "Greetings Mr. Brubaker. I appreciate your coming on such short notice. Let's take seats over here," he says, ushering Brubaker to a pair of chairs off to one side of the office.

"Well, sir, when the president calls, I don't normally say no," Brubaker replies when seated.

"Good point, Scott. May I call you Scott?"

"Please do, sir. I have to say, I'm rather curious as to why you wanted to see me."

President Egan knows one thing: he doesn't want this conversation to get too personal. "As president," he says, choosing his words with care, "I'm interested in knowing how the Post obtained rumors that we're planning to go to war with Iran?"

"Sir, as originator of those pieces, I can only tell you that my sources are confidential. I'm sure you know that I cannot reveal them."

"I understand the normal process of protecting your sources, Scott. Yet do you not think, as a reporter, that you have an obligation to make sure the facts you're printing are true? Did you at anytime make any attempt to verify your rumors, as you call them, with me or with anyone in my administration?"

Brubaker stops for a moment. *Where's this going? I doubt I've been called in just to get my hand slapped.*

"Scott, I'm a very busy man, and I have no time for mind games. I'm going to ask you one time and one time only to divulge your source or sources."

"Sir, I understand that, as the president, you are concerned with national interest. However, as a reporter, I cannot function without the trust of my sources. They have to know that they will never be revealed. Otherwise there goes one of the basic tenets of democracy: freedom of the press. My sources must be able to trust in their anonymity."

With a straight face the president continues, "Freedom of the press. Trust. Good choice of words. As an American citizen, can I trust you not to consort with our nation's enemies?"

"What are you implying, sir?" Brubaker's face appears genuinely puzzled.

"I'm not implying anything. I asked you a question."

"Why would I be consorting with agents of our enemies?"

"Interesting you chose the word 'agent,' Scott. What do you know about your friend and occasional lover Melanie Jacobs?"

Brubaker's reaction to this question is much as the president expected: a pro, his expression is immobile, his face as responsive as if it had been carved from granite.

He doesn't know how to respond, the president thinks. "Take your time Scott, because it better be good. You only get one shot at this."

"I don't know what you're insinuating, Mr. President. We're good friends and, yes, sometimes lovers when she's in town. Last I heard that isn't a crime."

"You're right. It isn't—unless she happens to be an agent of a foreign nation."

"What? What are you talking about?"

"Well, Scott, it appears that your friend, or lover, or whatever you choose to call her, is an Iranian agent. We have retrieved materials that implicate you as the source of information which she has passed on to her government."

"This is bullshit," Brubaker blurts out. "I don't buy any of this."

"And I'm not selling, Scott—I'm telling. Now, I really don't care who you've screwed. I just want to know who your sources are that caused Ms. Jacobs to take such an interest in you. If you continue on playing the role of the knight in shining armor for your sources, then I have no other choice but to implicate you in crimes against the United States. Am I making myself clear, Scott?"

The Post reporter who had so confidently walked through the Oval Office door now finds himself facing charges of treason. Brubaker's mind springs into action. *Whoa. Why should I protect the chief of staff and the vice president? They're the traitors, not me. I really don't have much of a choice here.*

"What are you offering me, sir?" Brubaker asks. "Am I correct that if I divulge my sources you won't prosecute me for dealing with a woman who, honest to God, I had no idea was an Iranian agent?"

"Scott, you have my word."

"Sir, my source is your chief of staff, Maria Sterling. She told me that she and the vice president wanted the public to know that you're leading the country into war. They don't want to see a repeat of what happened with Iraq."

"Did she tell you that any information she had on Iran was top secret and not to be divulged?"

"Yes, sir, she did, which was why their names were never connected with my articles."

"Thank you, Scott. You have just confirmed what I imagined happened. Your reputation is safe with me. However, because of what I'll be doing in the immediate future, I must insist that you take a week's vacation."

"A week's vacation? I have deadlines to meet, sir!"

"Not this week, you don't. This vacation's mandatory, and we're not talking Club Med. You'll be staying as the guest of the government at a safe house, so we can guarantee your complete protection."

"You mean, my life may be in danger?"

"I don't know and, frankly, I really don't care, Brubaker. Right now, I need to be sure that you can do nothing with what we've discussed. Do I make myself clear?"

"Yes, sir," Brubaker responds glumly.

"Fine. I have two gentlemen waiting outside who will take you to the safe house. Enjoy your week's stay at the taxpayers' expense."

That said, the president stands and leads Brubaker to the door. When he opens it for him, he introduces Brubaker, first to Tony Romano, and then to Jim Stewart, who is standing beside Romano.

Brubaker recognizes Jim Stewart immediately. "Oh, now I get it. I never forget a face—or the name that goes with it. Wilson. Don Wilson, right? Oh, yeah, it's all coming back to me. Mister congressional committee guy," Brubaker says insolently. *Goddammit. Shut the fuck up, you idiot. You should be thanking your lucky stars—obviously they can't let this play out in the public eye. I'm getting off easy.*

*

From the Gaza Strip, multitudes of Palestinians, males of all ages, are on the march towards the Israeli border, firing weapons in the air and proclaiming death to the Jews. On the northern border of Israel, Hezbollah is in the process of creating an identical crisis.

Inside the prime minister's office, Yaakov Brumwell and his chief of staff, Jacob Rabinowitz, realize that the attacks have begun just as predicted, the diversions planned to kick off a full attack launched from Iran.

"How much time do we have, Yaakov?"

"Jacob, only God knows for sure. Egan said the diversions are meant to last three days. I just received a call from him. He had the Kilo in the Mediterranean destroyed, to save us from an attack from the sea—that threat no longer exists. It's our eastern borders we need to watch, not for Hezbollah and Hamas—for missiles."

"For missiles?" Rabinowitz physically shudders at the thought.

"I assume that's what he meant. We need to prepare our Arrow batteries and those few Patriot batteries we have left to fire at any incoming missiles."

"The anti-missile batteries have been repositioned for a week now," Rabinowitz says. "Our forces are on full alert. But what are we going to do with the borders of Gaza and Lebanon?"

"We are going to do as we have already discussed," Brumwell answers calmly. "They cannot be allowed to fire at our troops directly, but we must only respond with a small counter force, as if we just consider this a nuisance. However, should this become a major confrontation, I want the air force to attack both borders with deadly force simultaneously."

"When do we decide when and if that should happen, Yaakov?"

"I expect we'll reach that point near the end of the three days. For now, I refuse to buy into their plan."

*

On the second day the number of foot soldiers for Hamas in Gaza and the West Bank and the number of Hezbollah fighters putting pressure on Israel from Lebanon have increased. Rockets are being fired into settlements along the borders.

Jewish settlers living near the borders are fleeing, and as they go, they scream for their government to counter attack so they can return to their homes. So far the accuracy of the rocket attacks is poor and, fortunately, there have been few injuries.

*

President Egan now faces the toughest period of his presidency to date. Not only has he gone to war because it is absolutely necessary and unavoidable, but he now faces having to deal with two members of his cabinet who have violated his trust. He also fears that those leaks may have caused the Kilos to set sail earlier than originally scheduled, thereby changing the whole time table for Iran.

A rogue nation with a convoluted and carefully timed plan is bad enough, he thinks. *A rogue nation that's tossed its timetable out the window and is throwing together massive assaults on the fly is unimaginable.*

Chapter Ninety-Four

Dealing with the Vice President

President Egan sighs, then picks up his phone and asks Janet to have the chief of staff come to his office.

From the moment she walks through the door, Maria Sterling senses that something is not quite right. "Have a seat, Maria," the president says gravely. "I need to discuss some things with you before I go down to the Situation Room."

"Do you want me to go with you after we speak?"

"No, I don't."

"Mr. President, may I speak freely?"

"Go ahead. I intend to."

This is beginning to sound worse every time he opens his mouth, Sterling realizes.

"Maria, I selected you as my chief of staff because I saw in you a dynamic woman with the ability to get things done. Where did I go wrong?"

"I beg your pardon, sir?"

"I'm not in the mood for pussy-footing around. I want to know why you leaked information that ended up in two press releases to Scott Brubaker."

"Who said I leaked something to the Post?"

"Scott Brubaker did." The president stares intently at Sterling. "I want to know why you did what you did?"

Oh my God, the asshole couldn't keep his mouth shut. Sterling's response is nothing short of confrontational. "You want the contrite version or what I really feel?"

"Well, Maria, since the cat's out of the bag anyway, why don't you just go for the real thing."

"The way I see it, you're determined to destroy what our party has worked so long and hard to create, and in the process, throw away any hopes for winning the presidency for future candidates. Besides, your ass-kissing with Israel is making me sick."

The president refuses to respond in anger. "Well, I'm sorry to say it never occurred to me that your political ambitions were so high that you'd knowingly place the country in danger. And as for Israel, I'm sorry you're such a bigot. I guess there's no need for any further discussion, is there?"

"Then if you're done with me, I'll just go back to my office."

"Oh, I don't think so, Maria. Your office has been secured by the Secret Service, and you're being placed under temporary arrest until I file formal charges with the attorney general's office. I meant what I said when I said no leaks."

President Egan turns and picks up the phone. "Janet, send in the two women waiting outside your office, would you, please?" Jane St. John and her associate Maureen Hughes enter the Oval Office.

"Maria Sterling, I'd like you to meet your security detail. Jane, you already know where to put her up. Get her out of here."

"Yes, sir," replies St. John.

*

President Egan heads back down to the Situation Room to review the status of what all has been laid out on the screens in his absence. Dean Hargrove, Admiral Smith and General Bradley are busy plotting the trail of the four Kilos and the positions of all U.S. military units that are now on the offensive.

"Any major changes I should be aware of?" the president asks as he comes through the door.

"No, sir. Nothing's really changed much in the last few hours," Hargrove responds, "other than what we're already aware of. A number of confrontations along the borders in Israel, as you see. It appears that Iran's plan has begun."

"I'm going back up to the Oval Office. I need to meet with the vice president. Let me know if there are any changes, Dean."

"Will do, Mr. President."

As the president leaves all three men glance at each other but no one says a word.

*

On the way back, President Egan stops into Janet's office and asks her to have the vice president come to the Oval Office.

"Sir, I saw him leave the White House not ten minutes ago, without saying a word. I don't know where he's headed. I can call his office to check."

"Go ahead, then let me know how long he'll be gone."

Janet calls the vice president's secretary, who has no clue where he's gone or when she can expect him back. "I have to say, it's strange behavior for a man who's always let me know his itinerary," his secretary mentions.

Janet immediately calls the president. "Sir, Sarah has no idea where he was headed or when he's due back."

The president thinks for a moment before responding. *Shit. He must have seen or heard that something was going on with Maria, or that her office was under surveillance.* "Janet, who's the head Secret Service agent on White House duty right now?"

"That'd be DeWayne Richards, sir."

"Have him come in to see me, please."

"Yes, sir."

DeWayne Richards, senior Secret Service agent on watch, knocks on the Oval Office door. The president tells him to enter. "DeWayne, please have a seat."

"Yes, sir." Richards appears unsure of himself. *Uh-oh. Is one of my agents in trouble? Am I in trouble?*

"Relax, DeWayne," says the president, recognizing his concern. "None of your watch has screwed up."

Immediately, DeWayne begins to relax.

Joe Smiga

"DeWayne, this is very uncomfortable for me to even say. However, you and your people will need to be involved with what I'm planning to do. It appears that the vice president has left the White House, bound for parts unknown, even to his staff. It's imperative that I see him today. I want you to contact his security detail and have them bring him back to this office."

"Sir, am I correct in the assumption that you think he might not want to return?"

"You are a very perceptive young man, DeWayne. You're right. I'm ordering your people to bring him back."

Holy shit, what in the hell is going on. "Yes, sir.

*

As the president and DeWayne are conferring in the Oval Office, the vice president and his Secret Service detail pull up in front of the Devonshire residence. "Wait for me out here. I just need to get some things packed and you can run me to the airport."

Pat Devonshire has told his security team that the president has ordered him to be on the next flight to Columbia, for a special meeting dealing with the drug cartels. Further, he told them that security was going to be handled there for him, so there was no need for them to arrange for a Secret Service detail to come along. *Thank God the wife and kids aren't going to be home. Lord knows, I don't want to be answering questions while I pack. I'll get in touch with her when I'm somewhere safe and have had time to think.*

Coming out of his closet, he finds two of his security detail standing in the doorway.

"Sir, we've been ordered by the president to return you to the White House," the taller of the two says. "We ask you not to make this any more difficult than it is."

Like a man with the wind knocked out of him, Devonshire drops onto the edge of the bed, then starts shaking his head.

"Don't worry. I won't make this difficult. Just let me use the bathroom before we go."

The same man responds, "We'll be right here when you come out, sir."

Inside the bathroom, Devonshire reaches into the back of the medicine chest and pulls out a bottle of sleeping pills, his wife's prescription. *Almost full. They aren't taking me alive, goddammit.*

Aggravated, he struggles with the childproof safety cap until he finally gets it open, but by now his hands are shaking like those of a ninety-year-old. In his agitation, he can only watch in horror as he spills the entire container of pills, which skitter away from him in all directions. Throwing himself to the floor, he tries to gather up enough to do the job, but the two Secret Service men outside the bathroom door hear the commotion and instantly shove it open, grab the vice president and wrestle him to the floor.

The shorter man yells into his mike, "VIP Team Two, get into the house. We need you upstairs. Now!"

The two remaining agents race up the front steps and up the two flights of stairs to the master bedroom. It takes all four to drag the vice president out of the bathroom. They force him to sit on the end of his bed, and three of them remain standing around him while the fourth walks to the window and calls DeWayne Richards at the White House. Richards, still in the Oval Office, raises a finger to the president and answers his phone on the first ring.

"DeWayne, we have the vice president and will be returning shortly. However, you and the president need to be aware that he just tried to swallow what I'm pretty sure are sleeping pills. He asked to use the bathroom before we left."

"Did he actually swallow any?"

"No, I don't believe so. However, in my opinion, when he visits with the president, a number of us should be in that room to protect the president, and Mr. Devonshire as well. I have no idea what he may pull next."

"I'll advise the president. We'll be ready for you when you get back."

*

Richards has time to advise the president as the vice president and his security team return to the White House. When they arrive, they are hurried through the gate and brought quickly to the Oval Office.

Once inside the building, Devonshire's belligerence evaporates. He has no desire to make a scene here. Regardless, Richards has decided that he and two others of his men will remain in the room while the president meets with the vice president.

Looking a little shell-shocked herself, Janet White walks out of her office and tells Richards that the president would like them to go in.

As the four men enter the Oval Office, Janet can only wonder. *My God, now what's going on? The vice president looks like he's seen a ghost, and the president never has Secret Service in the Oval Office when they talk together.*

The president directs them to two couches. He and Richards sit on one, the vice president, with agents on either side of him, sits opposite them.

"Pat, I wanted to talk with you this morning," President Egan says. "Then I hear that you've left the building without telling anyone where you were going. Then I'm told you attempted to take sleeping pills when you were directed to return to the Oval Office. Tell me what's going on, Pat."

Raising his head ever so slightly, the vice president says, "I found out you talked to Maria. I don't know what she told you, but I'm not taking the heat for what she wanted to do."

"What did she want to do, Pat?"

For a very naïve minute the vice president allows himself a glimmer of hope. *The president doesn't know.*

The president smiles and shakes his head. "Yes, Pat I know all about it. I'm sorry that your demons caused you to attempt suicide. However, this situation grieves me to no end. You have now made yourself a security risk for this government and a safety risk to yourself. Therefore, I've made arrangements for these gentlemen to take you to Bethesda Naval Hospital for evaluation and possible treatment. You can feel comfortable that you will be accorded the same security that your position requires." Egan looks Devonshire hard in the eyes. Devonshire drops his gaze.

"Gentlemen, take him away."

*

When the Oval Office is empty, the president calls Janet. "Janet, get the directors of the CIA and NSA to meet with me in thirty minutes. I'll be in the Situation Room awaiting their arrival. Have them shown down there as soon as they arrive."

"Yes, sir."

When Allison McDonald and John Walker walk in, the president asks everyone in the room to please take a seat. "I'm afraid this is going to come as every bit as much of a shock to you all as it did to me, but I need to report that the vice president is on his way to Bethesda Naval Hospital, to be evaluated for taking an attempted overdose of medication. The chief of staff is now sitting in a safe house awaiting charges that will be brought against her."

Most in the room look stunned, though a couple can't help looking pleased.

"I called you together so that you'll hear this first-hand from me. This situation evolved from the leaks to the Post. The reporter from the Post with some arm-twisting—metaphorical arm-twisting, I hasten to add—admitted to me who his sources were."

*

On the third day since the disturbances began, the intensity continues to build, as the crowds grow larger. Small arms fire observes no borders as it comes across into Israel. By midday long lines of angry invaders are stretched across Israel's borders, from the Gaza Strip and the West Bank and along its northern border with Lebanon.

Then all of a sudden, as if an alarm clock had just rung, both sections of Israel's borders became a mass of hysteria and shootings. Wave after wave of Hamas and Hezbollah run, shooting and screaming, "Death to all Jews."

At that moment the IDF forces retreat to hundreds of yards from the border. For a couple of moments the attackers think they have the Israelis on the run.

Suddenly they hear first, then see jets screaming in at them from above. Squadron after squadron of fighter planes drop a combination of cluster bombs and incendiary bombs on those aiming to cross the borders. Even after their bomb loads are spent, the planes continue to make numerous diving attacks, strafing those who remain standing.

Within fifteen minutes, the borders look like the war zones they truly are, bodies strewn all around, on either side of the border. Most of those who have survived are wounded.

Joe Smiga

As soon as the planes returned safely to their bases, Prime Minister Yaakov Brumwell and Chief of Staff Jacob Rabinowitz review the damage assessments coming to them from the borders.

"Yaakov, the timing was perfect," Rabinowitz congratulates him. "We've taken minimal damage while causing both Hamas and Hezbollah a world of trouble."

"Jacob, this is the easy part, nerve-wracking as it may be. Our true test may yet come in the form of Shahab-3s, armed with nuclear warheads."

"Yaakov, remember God is on our side. We will handle it, trust me."

*

Inside Iran, at precisely 2130 of the third day, the Ayatollah Fadil Ahmajid, the Supreme Leader, gives the order for two Shahab-3 missiles with nuclear warheads to be fired into Israel.

Within minutes the two missiles have been launched and are headed towards the small state made up of Jews whose only wish is to live in peace.

As the missiles enter the earth's atmosphere, satellites from both the United States and Israel detect the launches. Panicked messages fly within both countries. In Israel, air raid sirens begin to wail. It is still early in the evening. Dinners are being eaten, or have just been finished. Shoppers are in the malls. The streets are congested. Fear and uncertainty instantly overtake Israel's population. Those who are not near family try desperately to get home. Everyone is ordered into shelters, no matter where they are.

Both missiles are halfway into their journey now, their trajectories controlled by onboard computers. One is headed for Tel Aviv, the second for Haifa.

Inside IDF, which houses Arrow II, Israel's most modern anti-missile defense system, both of these deadly vehicles moving to annihilate their country and its people are being tracked. As the missiles begin their descent over Jordanian territory, towards their targets, an officer standing over the man with his finger on the button says quietly, "Let me know when the targets have entered our parameters."

"Affirmative, sir." The controller is sweating so hard he feels like he's in a sauna.

"Anything?"

"Not quite there, sir." A full five minutes go by like this.

Finally, the controller is able to say, with both panic and relief, "Targets inside of our parameters."

"Fire unit one and unit four." The officer sits down and looks up to the heavens.

"Anti-missile units fired and on course toward targets," says a junior officer.

"Units looking good for intercept." The controller, who in effect controls the destiny of his country, cannot control the hint of glee that comes with his report.

"Now, we just hope and pray," says the officer as he thinks of his family.

Chapter Ninety-Five

Third Night of the Uprisings

At night on the third day of the diversions against Israel's borders, Iran's regular night patrol vessels clear their moorings by 2015 and the base is secured for the remainder of the night. It all seems strange to the sailors, who have noted among themselves that the Kilos have been at sea for much longer than usual. Otherwise, everything else appears normal.

*

President Egan has the five members of the Senate Armed Services Committee come to the Oval Office. Senators Daniel McGraw from Montana, Theresa Redding from Texas, Douglas Shaffer from Kansas, Timothy Dasher from New York and Mark Lozano from California appear at the appointed hour of noon.

"Senators I hate to impose on your lunchtime. However, it's vital that we speak at this very moment."

"Why, may I ask?" Theresa Redding seems more than a bit put out. The president chooses to ignore her confrontational tone.

"For months now, the United States has been fortunate enough to be able to read all communications coming out of and within Iran." The president pauses for effect.

Mark Lozano asks, "How were we able to do that? Were we able to break their codes?"

Everyone suddenly seems to sense where this meeting is going. Doug Shaffer glares at the president and states, "You mean to tell us that you had first-hand knowledge of that country's possible intentions of war and you never told us?"

"That's exactly what I'm telling you now. What we learned was so vital that we couldn't afford any leaks whatsoever, anything which might cause the Iranians to alter their code."

"Mr. President, are you telling us you don't trust this committee?" Tim Dasher says point-blank in frustration.

"No, Tim, that's not at all what I'm saying. However, I am saying that telling you might have allowed a leak."

Theresa Redding goes on the offensive again. "So the rumors in the Post were leaks, then?"

"Yes, Theresa. Now do you understand what I'm trying to say?"

"I'm sure you feel embarrassed, sir, but you didn't call this meeting to tell us you're embarrassed. What's going on?"

President Egan has always liked the no-nonsense side of Theresa Redding. She has a way of getting right to the point, pushing aside any and all bullshit in the way. He hesitates a moment before he answers her.

"What I'm about to tell all of you is two-fold. First, as we sit here, we are attacking the nation of Iran with both our naval and our air forces. Secondly, and you must keep this totally confidential, Iran has purchased four Russian Kilo submarines which are carrying cruise missiles—and they are headed for our shores. News of this could start a national panic."

"Do you have any idea where these subs are right now?" Dasher asks nervously.

"Approximately. We've located all of them since they left Iran. Our military is acting right now only because we were recently able to obtain definite proof that Iran had plans in play to use them to attack Israel and the United States."

The five senators sit back, speechless for the moment.

"Why aren't we taking out the Kilos instead of attacking the sovereign nation of Iran, Mr. President?" Shaffer asks pointedly.

"Our plan is to take out the Kilos, handling each situation to the best of our ability. However," Egan says vehemently, "we need to deal with the problem, not just the symptoms."

"Where are these Kilos headed—and is there any chance that they have nuclear capability?" Redding asks nervously.

"First, the Kilos are currently heading for Washington, New York, Los Angeles and San Francisco. And, yes," the president says slowly, "we have reason to believe their missiles are carrying nuclear warheads."

The five senators appear paralyzed by this news. "Oh, my God." Theresa Redding says what the rest are thinking.

"What are you going to tell the public?" asks Lozano.

"I plan to tell them about the verified nuclear threat from Iran and that we are currently undertaking a mission to eliminate that threat. I'm not going to cause a national panic, because that could be almost as bad as the problems we're already facing. We hope we can end this quickly."

"Mr. President," asks Dan McGraw, "when are you going to leave the city?"

"Not until the Secret Service forces me to, Dan."

"Then, sir—what do you want us to do?" asks Redding.

"Actually, nothing at the moment. I feel I owe you this. I believe in our form of government. However there are times that circumstances give us no choice but to sidestep normal policies. This is definitely one of those times."

*

At 2130 Iranian time, on the third day of the diversions, the USS Teddy Roosevelt, a Seawolf-class submarine, begins laying one hundred mines inside the mouth of the harbor of Bandar Abbas.

*

At 2330, fifty miles apart from each other, the USS North Dakota and the USS Vermont, both Ohio-class subs, begin to launch a total of forty-eight Trident D-5 missiles towards their designated targets at a range of fifteen hundred miles from Iran. As each Trident rises into the atmosphere, its fiery tail lights up the dark sky.

Each of the twelve facilities dedicated to enriched uranium processing and the thirteenth to plutonium reprocessing will receive two hits apiece. While one missile should be sufficient with a D 5 payload, the president is taking no chances. His goal is long-term destruction. The naval base at Bandar Abbas will be receiving two as well. The remaining twenty will be targeted for the five major air bases around the country and the fifteen known surface-to-air missiles sites.

*

Each of the three Los Angeles-class subs monitoring the Iranian nighttime patrols have received their instructions from Fleet Admiral Robert Smith. They are to take out the six vessels as soon as the first Trident hits at 0045. No vessel is to be allowed to enter the Persian Gulf.

*

At 0045 Trident D-5 missiles begin falling from the heavens over Iran.

*

Unit One and Unit Four from Israel's Arrow II system both detonate their targets at high altitudes. Arrow II has much higher altitude and range capabilities than the U.S. manufactured Patriot missiles. They destroy their targets over Jordan.

Unfortunately, Iran's attempt to destroy Israel is now causing radioactive waste to fall onto the nation of Jordan. The winds will eventually carry some of that radioactivity over to Iraq and Syria.

*

Within Israel, prayers are being said as the only homeland for the Jewish people is once again safe. Most will never know the degree of peril they faced. What most of them are asking themselves as they make their way home after the sirens have been silenced is, *How many times must we go through this?*

Jacob Rabinowitz, chief of staff of the IDF, can't stop smiling at the prime minister, he is so relieved. "Didn't I tell you to trust, Yaakov? You know that God has promised us this land. No one is going to take it away from us."

Yaakov returns a weary smile, glad that his friend has such strong faith. *Personally, mine has its ups and downs at times.* "Jacob, I need to let President Egan know that for now we are safe. I know he must have his hands full, but I need to tell him. Maybe just so I can truly believe it myself."

"Go ahead, Yaakov. That's what good prime ministers are for."

*

In an hour and fifteen minutes after the first Trident launch, the gates of hell have opened in the nation of Iran.

The first Trident falls on the eastern sector of the naval base at Bandar Abbas, taking out Chinese missiles sites and four naval vessels tied up to piers on that side of the base. The explosion is so intense that buildings on the base collapse, crumbling to pieces as the shock wave passes out onto the city of Bandar Abbas. People in the city are shaken awake by the blast, assume there's been an explosion of some sort at the base, turn over and try to get back to sleep.

Ten minutes after the first Trident hits, a second Trident comes down on the western side of the naval base, with similar results. Both missiles generate multiple fires that quickly engulf the military installation. By now, everyone in the city of Bandar Abbas is at their windows, witnesses to a raging inferno along the waterfront.

Untouched, fourteen naval vessels try desperately to get underway in case of further bombardment. Those that do manage to head out into the harbor soon come upon the many mines that await them. Ship after ship turns into a huge fireball, their crews jumping into the water, hoping to make it back to shore—and terrified to find what awaits them there.

Just yesterday these waters were clear of any obstructions. Now sinking hulks are creating a blockade that will close the channel for many years to come. Expert planning, thanks to accurate satellite intelligence, insures that the explosions cause minimal injury to the city's civilian population.

*

The planning for the enrichment and reprocessing plants is not the same; the goal for these is nothing short of total destruction, with no consideration for anyone inside the facilities. The military assumes that anyone there is performing duties contrary to the safety of the United States, even if they are foreign nationals.

Each of the thirteen facilities on the list is struck by its first missile, then after a short span, a second missile follows, insuring maximum destruction. Iran will spend decades just trying to clean up these sites.

The fifteen Russian and Chinese SAM missile sites, purchased and installed to provide protection for the facilities, are hit in similar fashion. The ability of the Trident to enter the outer atmosphere, then come down on top of its target, gives them no warning. Their own armaments only add to the destruction of the explosions from the Tridents. The devastation is so severe that nothing remains standing within a radius of three miles around each site.

As the first missiles begin to hit the enrichment plants, all five air force bases are bombarded with Tridents as well. These missiles are targeted so that their explosive force will both decimate planes on the ground and render runways inoperable.

Chapter Ninety-Six

Iran Ablaze

President Mahmoud Khasanjani's private security detail comes to wake him, but explosions already have. He brain is trying to make sense of what he hears as he jumps out of bed and pulls some clothing on. "Call the Ayatollah Ahmajid," he yells out to anyone within hearing range while he dresses. Air raid sirens start wailing. The sound is deafening. *What in Allah's name could be happening? Is Israel retaliating?*

Khasanjani stayed up late enough to know that the Shahab-3 missiles that his forces had fired at Israel have been intercepted by their Arrow II anti-missile system. *Damn Jews, their technology always seems to be two steps ahead of us.* Yet, he somehow doubts this to be a Jewish counter-attack, not this quickly. His ears refuse to make sense of what he's hearing.

Fully dressed, he stumbles out of his bedroom and runs right into his wife, who is trying desperately to keep the children quiet and assured that they are safe. "That's right. Listen to your mother," their father says, then pushes right past her.

"Doesn't anyone know what the hell is going on here?" he yells to the only guard in sight. "Get me my driver. I have to get to my office and find out what's happening."

Likewise, on the opposite side of the city, the Ayatollah Ahmajid is running like a madman down the stairs of his home, taking two at a time, his head bare—as is his scalp. He hears the sirens, but cannot imagine what's happening. *Israel cannot reach us with their planes and still be able to return safely home from this great a distance. This must be something else, but what?*

Ahmajid receives Khasanjani's third attempt to reach him by phone. "Fadil, what's happening? The Jews cannot be reacting this quickly to our firing two rockets at them," Khasanjani shouts into the phone over the noise in the streets. "They would have to have a plan in place. And even if they were planning a strike, it would take time to put into action."

"I agree, Mahmoud. Calm down. I don't know anything for sure yet. Maybe this is a reaction to something else altogether. I'm going to try and find out. Call an emergency meeting of the council. I will see what I can learn. Tell them we'll convene in thirty minutes."

The Ayatollah runs to the rooftop of his home, and looks about him in all directions. Practically deafened by the sound of ongoing explosions, he realizes that the explosions and fire are all coming from the west. Then it hits him. *It is coming from one of our enrichment plants. Has there been a catastrophe at the plant? Is that what we are dealing with?*

Turning he sees another source of explosions, fire and smoke considerably off in the distance. *One catastrophe is possible. Two is too much of a coincidence. We are under attack, but by whom? It can't be the Americans. We won't be off their shores for another twenty-four hours.*

Ahmajid runs down from the rooftop, stops momentarily in his bedroom to grab a scarf, and meets his driver in front of his home. "We need to be at the Council center, now," he barks.

Slamming the door after the Ayatollah enters the car; the driver almost trips and falls as he rushes to get into the driver's seat. He throws the car in gear and leaves rubber as he pulls away from the curb.

As the car fights its way through traffic snarled with panic, Ahmajid takes advantage of the delay to tie his turban. By the time they reach the Council building, he looks presentable—and notices that the air raid sirens are ceasing their shrill blaring. *Thank Allah for that, at least. I cannot think what could be happening. Who could be doing this?*

Ahmajid notices that the lights on the top floor are on as his driver pulls up to the front of the building and lets the Ayatollah off. Ahmajid rushes inside. Shunning the elevator for safety's sake, he rushes up the seven floors to meet with the others. By the time he arrives at the conference room, he's quite out of breath and can already see the others are not in a receptive mood.

Farook speaks first. "Who is attacking us? It can't be the damn Jews; it's too early for them to be reacting."

Abbas jumps in. "Does anyone know if this is the handiwork of the American Satan?"

"Right now, we do not know who is responsible nor how much damage they have done. I will put together a list of phone calls we need to make, to find out the damage and where that damage is."

"Agreed," says Givon. "We will wait here while you put the list together, then all of us can start calling to assess our damages."

Ahmajid and Kahsanjani race downstairs to the Ayatollah's offices one floor below and hurriedly do a quick inventory of bases and facilities to call. When the Supreme Leader returns to the conference room with the lists, he tells the Imans, "Mahmoud is pulling telephones from other offices so that we can all work together from here."

The president returns with five phones. They each hook up to one of the many phone jacks around the room, then each of them takes a portion of the list of calls to make.

The Supreme Leader's first call is to Bandar Abbas. No one answers. This is not a good sign.

The president's first call is to the enrichment site at Ardekan. No answer. He keeps letting the phone ring. Then, for some reason he would prefer not to contemplate, the line goes dead.

All of the Imams are having the same luck making their calls.

*

Twenty-five thousand feet above Iran, three squadrons of American stealth bombers approach their targets. Ten of the twelve are headed for military installations and terrorist training camps. Two have a special mission.

As the two B2 A bombers approach Tehran, they veer apart to move onto their intended targets. They will rejoin after they release their bomb loads. Dropping down to fifteen thousand feet, they approach the city. Each bombardier spots the lasers they will use to guide their bombs.

As each plane releases one of its half-ton bombs, the laser guides it precisely to its target. There are no mishaps, no unintended damage to other buildings in the vicinity.

The presidential offices, a block away from Council headquarters, receive the first bomb, reducing the enormous building to a pile of stone and dust.

Seconds later the president of Iran, the leader of the Guardian Council and his fellow council members realize that what they are hearing is the destruction of the presidential offices. They have hardly had time to process that thought when the second bomb reduces the council building, where they are still frantically placing phone calls, to rubble.

Chapter Ninety-Seven

Mission Accomplished

Gaping at the explosions they can see decimating the naval base at Bandar Abbas, five of the surface vessels on night patrol draw to a complete halt, which has the unintended effect of making the job of the three L.A.—class submarines stalking them that much easier; obtaining bearings and ranges to their targets has just became a far simpler task.

As the sailors stare transfixed by the explosions and mayhem, four of the vessels are torpedoed before anyone realizes what's going on around them. The fifth vessel is hit amidships and the sixth vessel, which is still moving, reverses its course and attempts to head back to Bandar Abbas. The captain of this small destroyer is doing his best to save his ship and crew, but they are no match for a U.S. submarine. Within five minutes of trying to escape, the last of the night patrol is sunk and six vessels float aflame in the Arabian Sea.

*

Following the Air Force bombardment, the NSA's satellites seek to assess the damages caused by American missiles and bombers.

Each pass of the three satellites covering Iran shows Bandar Abbas's naval base in a complete state of havoc. The missiles fired into the base have caused tremendous damage to the naval base itself but limited damage to nearby areas with civilian populations. Each of the known sites of enriching uranium or reprocessing plutonium has suffered catastrophic damage. Planes on the runways of Iranian air bases have been reduced to smoldering wrecks. The air bases themselves will be unusable for a long time to come. Training camps that were targeted are aflame.

John Walker personally views the images of the results from bombing the presidential offices and the Guardian Council building. Each building is totally destroyed. Earlier photos of the Guardian Council building indicate lights on at the very top floor. Since the Council members regularly met there, it is assumed they were there during the bombing run.

John Walker calls the president in the Situation Room. "Mr. Pres'dent, accordin' to what we're seein' over heah, I'd say we've achieved our objective. The devastation appears to be significant."

"Thank you, John," says the president, allowing himself to feel a measure of relief. "Now all we have to do is take out those Kilos."

"Would y'all like me to come to the Situation Room, suh?"

"No, John, there's not much the NSA can do at this point. Go home and get some rest."

*

The captain of the USS Thomas Jefferson, the attack carrier heading up this task force, receives word from his crew that all forty-eight Trident missiles hit their targets. The Seawolf's mines have successfully repelled those surface vessels that survived the initial attack, sinking them as they tried to escape. The three Los Angeles-class subs report eliminating their targets as well. Captain Dennis Roy launches three squadrons of F-18 fighters to patrol the Persian Gulf to insure the security of any merchant shipping passing through. He suspects it may not be necessary, but he'd rather be safe than sorry.

*

All twelve B2 A stealth bombers return safely to Diego Garcia. Aerial photos of their mission attest to the accuracy of their bombing runs. The pilots will be debriefed as soon as they change out of their flight gear.

*

Inside the safe house where he's being held, Scott Brubaker sits glued to the television, watching the footage Al-Jazeera has sent on to CNN in Atlanta. The headlines read: Israel attacks the nation of Iran. Iran fires missiles in retaliation. Brubaker so wishes he could tell the world what's really going on. He knows this is standard issue Arabian bullshit.

The more he thinks about what he's been through recently, and how people in times of stress tend to behave, the more he wonders if he wouldn't be happier in a different career.

*

The major newscasts, with access to everything on the airwaves, want to know why Israel is possibly out to start World War III. Talking heads begin to insist that the administration must put political pressure on Israel to get this thing resolved before it gets out of control and we become victims of what they are now referring to as Israel's foolhardiness.

Peter Boyle, the president's press secretary, calls him in the Situation Room. "Sir, the press is howling."

"I know, Pete, but you're going to have to tell them to leave me the hell alone for the next forty-eight hours and let me do my job."

Shocked, Boyle handily rephrases Egan's words for media consumption. "The president is sorting out what has really happened between Israel and Iran. He says he'll have a statement for you in forty-eight hours."

Needless to say, the media are far from happy with that response. Quickly, they set to work spinning their own versions of what might have happened, based as always on their own particular political biases.

*

The United Nations Secretary General calls the White House, demanding to know what the United States is going to do to resolve this situation.

Boyle again interrupts the president. "Sir, the Secretary General of the U.N. is on the phone and demands to speak with you."

"Pete, for the last time, I'm too busy to be bothered with politics. Tell her to come up with some possible solutions herself. After all, she's top dog at the U.N."

Admiral Smith and General Bradley smile in sympathy as they watch the president deal with the combined stresses of the situation and his position. "I wouldn't want that man's job for even a single day," the general says to the admiral.

When the president hangs up, he vents his frustrations on those assembled, "These people are a fucking disaster waiting to happen. Sometimes I wonder how we made it this far as a country. And these global assholes think they rule the world, when in fact, they don't have a fucking clue as to what's really going on."

"Sir, I've never heard you say 'fuck' before," Admiral Smith observes dryly, "and you just managed to say it twice in anger. Welcome to the real world."

"You're right," Egan says. "These third-world countries are constantly looking for handouts and somebody to make their world better. They think they can do it by putting constant political pressure on us. Speaking for myself, I've had enough of this crap."

The president stops and looks at Admiral Smith. "About the cursing—I apologize," he says, chagrinned.

"For what, being human? Damn it, Mr. President, you're only trying to save this country. If that bitch at the U.N. knew she could be nuked out of office, well . . ."

Chapter Ninety-Eight

Kilos Arrive

It is the fourth day since the beginning of the uprisings on Israel's borders. The communiqué sent from Iran to the Kilos instructed them to fire their missiles at 2400 hours GMT on the fourth day from a distance of three hundred kilometers from their targets. They were told to only fire one missile, provided the launch was successful. Their instructions explicitly told them not to assess the missile in flight or its impact, just to move out of the area immediately, and of course, they are not to attempt communications until they are two thousand miles from the enemy's shores. They are to protect the Kilos at all costs. None of the captains know their missiles carry nuclear warheads.

Admiral Smith is conferring with Vice-Admiral Dan Peterson, Commander of the Atlantic Fleet, and Vice-Admiral Kevin O'Rourke, Commander of the Pacific Fleet, from the Situation Room.

Looking at each other on screens providing satellite visuals, Admiral Smith says, "Admirals, what do you know at this point about the locations of the Kilos?"

Admiral Peterson replies first. "Sir, knowing that they will be somewhere two hundred miles off shore from their targets, we've created a box maneuver. We have two boomers coming in from the northern edge of where that two hundred miles begins, and two boomers coming in from the southern edge. One line of boomers is operating at one hundred ninety miles. The second line is coming in at two hundred ten miles. All four are operating on passive search so as not to give their own positions away, and will come together in the center of the box. A classic wolf-pack type operation, with a search spread of approximately forty miles from side to side."

"Sir, we're operating likewise," says Admiral O'Rourke, 'and both of us are using P3 Orions overhead to aid in the search. The problem we're facing is that the two-hundred-mile diameter still gives them a great deal of water to hide in. Though I have to think, looking at the amount of time left until 2400 GMT, I'd say those subs are darn near where they want to be. SOSUS can only give us approximations. What kind of readings are we getting from the system?"

"As you say, Kevin," Admiral Smith answers, "the Sound Surveillance System can only give us approximations and now that they're between hydrophone sensors, we can't tell what they're doing until they cross another one."

"We could use some surface vessels to try and get them to move or panic," suggest Peterson.

"I doubt that you could make these captains overreact and miss the opportunity of shooting at the United States—not likely. The boomers have to find them. I assume you've both laid out the inner screens we discussed, using our frigates and destroyers to provide surface-to-air missile cover if the Kilos fire the way we expect they will."

"Yes, sir," says Peterson. "Mine are laid out exactly as you ordered. I assume that Kevin's done so likewise?"

"Yes, my screens are laid out at one hundred and one hundred fifty miles," O'Rourke confirms.

"Good," Smith says. "That gives us two walls of surface-to-air missile interception capability before we have to resort to shore-based batteries to stop them. Gentlemen, I want your crews at battle stations alert until this whole thing is over and done with."

"Mine have been since the subs were three hundred miles out," O'Rourke says.

"Ditto," Peterson says.

*

The USS Nevada SSN 802, a Los Angeles-class sub, is operating one hundred-ninety miles off of Washington, D.C.

"Control, sonar. We have faint readings of a possible Kilo at twelve thousand yards, turning two knots. She seems to be circling to remain on station."

"Sonar, are you sure of that data?" asks the OOD.

"Sir, as sure as I can be. Our equipment says that the target is emitting transients identical to a Kilo."

"I have the conn," announces Captain Henry Turcott. "Sonar, give me a bearing and range to the target."

"Bearing is 085 degrees. Range is still twelve thousand yards."

"XO, give me a firing sequence to the target. Make it a three-fish spread."

"Aye aye, captain."

Inside Kilo 105 off the D.C. coastline, the presence of the Los Angeles-class submarine is suddenly noticed.

"Sonar, are you sure of your contact?" Anxiety builds quickly.

"Yes, captain, our computers say the sonar contact is definitely a Los Angeles-class U.S. submarine."

"Is there any reason to think he's identified us yet?"

"Not sure, sir. He's still twelve thousand yards away."

Captain Emir is sweating to such extent that his shirt is soaked. Looking over at his ship's clocks, and knowing full well that, by his orders, it's still thirty minutes before he was told to fire, he makes a battlefield decision. "Number one, make the missile ready for launch."

"You're going to fire early, sir?" questions the first officer.

"I cannot allow that sub to get closer and prevent us from firing. Status, number one?"

"Captain, the missile is ready to launch. It just needs final computer input. We should get closer to the surface and at the proper incline to fire."

"Rise to one hundred meters depth."

"Rising to one hundred meters. One hundred meters depth, sir."

"Incline the bow up thirty degrees. Open the outer door."

"Inclining the bow. Outer door is open."

No crew member makes eye contact with any of his mates. Dead silence fills the air.

*

Inside the Nevada, sonar contacts Captain Turcott. "Captain, sonar. The Kilo is rising."

"What the hell? From our intel, she isn't scheduled to fire for another thirty minutes."

"Captain, sonar. She's at three hundred thirty feet and is inclining her bow."

"XO, range and bearing to the target?"

"Target now bearing 087, range twelve thousand five hundred yards."

*

Kilo 105 launches its missile.

"Close the outer door. Now dive! Dive!" shouts Captain Emir.

*

"That son of a bitch spotted us. He's fired early. Sonar, tell me what that sub's doing. We're gonna have him for lunch."

*

Almost simultaneously, Captain Kadir of Kilo 104 is trying to avoid contact off New York by staying at three hundred meters.

Nervously, the first officer says, "Captain, we have twenty minutes to fire the missile."

"I know, number one. However, if those damned Americans identify us, we may never get to launch. My motto is better to be a little late then not at all. Or in this case, a little early."

"The Council will be upset, sir. You know how they are."

"Number one, the Council is not here trying to save their asses and do our job for them at the same time. Sonar, do you have any contacts?"

"No, sir. We are clear out to fourteen thousand yards right now."

"Number one, prepare to fire the missile."

"Come up to one hundred meters."

"One hundred meters, aye."

"Level at one hundred meters. Open the outer door. Incline the bow upward thirty degrees."

"Outer door open. Bow up thirty degrees."

The captain looks at the clock, which still reads 2351 GMT time." He looks at the firing board. All lights are green.

"Fire the missile."

The first officer hits the firing switch and the modified Shahib-3 heads out of the tube.

"Missile has launched successfully," reports the first officer.

"Now, let's get the hell out of here," says the captain.

*

Two Los Angeles-class subs, who are searching the area, record the missile launch and head for that position.

*

Two hundred miles off of the coast of Los Angeles, Kilo 103 holds at two hundred meters and raises its bow to get into firing position.

Captain Hafiz says to his men, "We are on a mission for Allah. Allah Akbar, God is Great. Death to the infidels. After today, the world will respect the nation of Iran. Number one, I will take the conn."

"Yes, captain."

"Bring us up to one hundred meters, and open the outer door."

"Rising to one hundred meters," says the planes operator.

"Firing board indicates outer door is open," says the first officer.

Captain Hafiz looks at the clock on the panel. It reads 2359 GMT. He glances at the firing board. All lights are green. "Fire the missile."

The first officer hits the firing switch and the missile's props begin to turn. Almost immediately, a tremendous, earsplitting noise screeches through the entire length of the submarine.

"What is *that*?" the first officer screams.

"The outer door must not be fully open," the captain bellows. "The missile is trying to get out of the tube and cannot."

The noise is deafening and the heat build-up inside of the tube is rapidly becoming intense as the missile tries to do the only thing it is programmed to do: escape and launch. The inevitable happens. The heat causes the warhead to explode inside of the torpedo tube. Within moments, the bow of Kilo 103 is blown wide open. The submarine immediately begins to flood.

"Captain, we need to get aft and seal the watertight compartments," yells the first officer.

"You go ahead, and take as many of the men that you can. I'll see if we have any survivors up forward."

The Kilo's design has six watertight compartments, separated by transverse bulkheads within a pressurized double hull. The explosion caused by the missile is sufficiently devastating that the first two compartments are simply gone. Water is pouring into the vessel at a rate faster than the remaining watertight doors can be closed and the pumps can handle.

The captain and any crew who were in the rear four compartments die trapped.

*

The missile's explosion bursts through the surface, sending up a spectacular column of over-heated water nearly fifty feet into the air, and shock waves over an area of thirty miles.

The first surface vessel hit by the shock wave is the USS Samuel Jones FFG 66, a guided missile frigate. Rolling fifteen degrees off center from the impact, the whole crew has to pick themselves up off her decks.

*

Captain Mukhtar, commanding officer of Kilo 102, has been exceptionally careful to avoid any vessels of the U.S. Navy. He arrived on station twenty-four hours ago and floated his vessel just below what the specifications say is the maximum depth for the Kilo design. He and his crew have played games of cat-and-mouse with one nuclear submarine and two surface vessels, none of which has detected his boat.

Now he is ready to launch his surprise on the United States mainland. Gleefully he says, "Bring her up to one hundred meters. Open the outer door. First officer, prepare the final sequences."

"Aye, aye, captain."

"We are at one hundred meters," states the planes operator.

"Incline her bow thirty degrees."

"Outer door is open," reports the first officer.

Planes operator says, "Bow is up thirty degrees."

Captain Mukhtar, the perfectionist, looks at the firing board. Its green lights give him great pleasure. He looks at the clock, which reads 2400 GMT. "Fire the missile. Then close the outer door and turn to course 270 degrees."

"Missile launched successfully," says the first officer, appearing very proud of himself. Their missile is on course to wipe out the city of San Francisco.

*

Admiral Robert Smith immediately telephones the president. "Sir, you need to come to the Situation Room. We have three missiles inbound."

"I'll be right down, Bob." *Christ.*

Chapter Ninety-Nine

Missiles Airborne

Everyone stands as, once again, the president enters the Situation Room. President Egan is in no mood for formalities. "Goddammit, sit down, everybody. Admiral, Dean, what have we got?"

Dean Hargrove replies, "We've got missiles fired and above the surface inbound on Washington, New York, and San Francisco."

"What about L.A.?"

"Our vessels reported a major explosion below the surface approximately where we suspected the Kilo to be. We're assuming some sort of internal explosion."

The president hesitates before asking the obvious question. "What are our chances of taking those missiles down?"

Before anyone can answer, a Secret Service detail headed by DeWayne Richards comes into the Situation Room. "Sir, my orders are to remove you immediately to a safe location."

"I understand. Where's the first lady?"

"Sir, she's aboard Marine Two and on her way to the same location."

"Gentlemen, I have no choice but to burden you with finishing this for me and for everyone else out there. God be with us all. Let's go, DeWayne."

The words of his chairman of the joint chiefs echo in Egan's mind as he hurriedly leaves the room. "We will, sir. Be safe."

Joe Smiga

*

DDG-88, the USS Thomas Edison, is stationed one hundred fifty miles offshore of Washington, D.C. The Combat Information Center, the tactical heart of this Flight IIA Arleigh Burke-class guided missile destroyer, is just receiving data of a missile launch from below the surface.

"CIC to Fire Control, we have a missile launch heading due west on 270 degrees, range ninety-eight miles. Data is being transferred to your computers for firing solutions."

"Fire Control, aye."

Inside the Fire Control Center, sailors and officers alike man the computers, sonar and satellite screens that will distill incoming information and fire the latest version of the AIM/RIM-7P Sparrow missile, a medium range, all-weather guided missile manufactured by Raytheon. Not only does the P include the all the features of the improved seeker capability of the M design, it also has reprogrammable digital capabilities to eliminate enemy countermeasures.

"CIC, Fire Control. We have the missile locked on and ready to fire."

The Edison's captain gives the order. "Fire."

The 12-foot, 7-inch Sparrow leaps from its launch tube and heads out to intercept the cruise missile coming in from the Iranian Kilo submarine.

*

Kilo 105 dives after firing their missile. "How many tubes are loaded with torpedoes?" Captain Emir asks

His number one officer replies, "Five tubes loaded, sir."

"What direction is that sub from us?"

"Sir, it's on a heading of 265 degrees, range 10,000 meters."

"I want a spread of three torpedoes with a five degree separation. Do not connect guide wires. Then immediately reload all tubes."

The first officer sets up the firing switches, then looks up at his captain, knowing that none of the torpedoes will probably connect. *He's trying to buy time to get out of here.*

"Ready to fire, sir."

"Fire."

The sub the torpedoes are seeking is the USS Nevada.

*

"Control, sonar. Three torpedoes are in the water, coming towards us at high speed."

"Predictable bastard," Captain Turcott says to his XO. "He's trying to buy time to get away. Deploy decoys and dive to six hundred feet."

"Captain, you're not going to change course?" asks the XO.

"No. I bet he's got an angle on those two outer fish. He's counting on us to change course and get in a lucky hit. It'll also take us more time to recover if we do. I'm sure he's running scared, and I guarantee you he hasn't wasted a moment putting guidance wires on those torpedoes. It's a crap shoot. If I'm right, the decoys will be our protection."

As the torpedoes approach, their propellers become audible throughout the sub. Each man begins to sweat, knowing that if they connect, the Nevada will become their coffin.

"Sonar, Captain. When will the torpedoes reach us?"

"Two minutes, sir." Faces ashen, the officers and crew can only wait and pray that the captain's hunches are right.

In two minutes' time they both hear and feel the shock wave from two explosions. Two of the torpedoes have hit decoys.

"Control, sonar. The third fish is running straight and true. It should run out of fuel in about five more minutes. Right now we're in the clear."

"Bring her up to four hundred feet," says the captain, "and let's go hunting. Sonar, do you hear anything out there."

"Negative, sir."

"Okay, people. He's gone quiet, hoping to slip away. Since he knows we're here, it's useless to stay on passive sonar. Sonar go active and start to ping."

"Sonar, aye."

In two minutes the pinging gets results. "Captain, we have a sonar contact at 100 degrees, range 15,000 yards. I'm sure he's heard the ping, sir."

"I'm sure he has. XO, work me a firing solution to take this asshole out."

"Aye, captain."

"XO, I want four fish in the water on this one. He may be used to the usual tactics of three. The fourth one may be his undoing."

"Ready to fire, captain."

"Fire one—fire two—fire three—fire four. Reload tubes."

"Torpedoes in the water, running fast and smooth," the XO reports.

*

Aboard the 105, the ping vibrates throughout the entire vessel. "How the hell did they find us so fast?" Captain Emir's question goes unanswered.

"Captain, sonar. We have three torpedoes headed in our direction." In his agitation, sonar, who expects to see a textbook attack of three torpedoes maximum, fails to look for the fourth.

The first three torpedoes have locked onto their target. Their wires released, they are on their own to attack. The fourth torpedo is still wire-guided, to see how it should handle any changes the target might make.

Captain Emir knows that the speed of the torpedoes is greater than the maximum speed he can generate from his submarine. Their only chance is to also discharge decoys, and hope that by turning and diving, they can minimize the threat.

The first two torpedoes are fooled by decoys. The third hits Kilo 105 in the stern and opens up the aft part of the vessel. The unanticipated torpedo number four hits them amidships as they maneuver the turn the captain has called for, exploding through their double hull and destroying their control center, splitting the sub in two.

*

Above the surface, the cruise missile fired by 105 is intercepted by the Sparrow twenty miles from the USS Thomas Edison. The explosion is enormous and the shock wave hits the vessel with great ferocity. Officers and sailors are bounced around the ships decks as if they are nothing but a crew of rag dolls.

Above the surface, off the coast of New York, Kilo 104's cruise missile, streaking upwards to gain altitude, is spotted by a squadron of F/A 18 Super Hornet strike fighters.

"Red Dog One, Red Dog One. Red Dog Two. Missile just launched from below the surface and is climbing to gain altitude. Over."

"I see it, Two. Three, mark this lock and load, and pass it on to command. Over."

As the missile reaches an altitude of two thousand feet, the squadron leader makes his decision. "Three and Four, fly to the port side, twenty miles parallel to the missile. Two and I will intercept. If something goes wrong, it's up to the two of you. Over." Red Dog Three and Four both key their mikes in response to their squadron leaders instruction.

"Two, Red Dog One. Stay off my left wing and ten miles ahead of me. I am going to fire one of my AMRAAMs at it. If it misses, you are to fire one of yours before it passes. We will intercept from ten miles away. Now let's head down and to take this baby out. Over."

The two F/A 18s head out to intercept. The missile is at a low altitude and heading on a straight course for New York City. They turn on their after burners and race to get a substantial distance ahead to line up their attack.

Squadron leader Red Dog One has the missile coming across on his radar screen, from right to left. His AMRAAM is energized to launch from under his right wing. Watching his fire control screen, he keys in the necessary data to the missile guidance system to intercept. He fires.

The twelve-foot, seven-inch diameter air-to-air missile is now controlled by its own radar guidance system. Its forty-five pound warhead will ignite as soon as contact is made with the cruise missile. Red Dog One watches as the medium-range missile streaks towards the Iranian missile.

In two minutes the sky explodes, and Red Dog One and Two are both flung upward and backward from the force of the explosion. Both pilots scramble to gain control as the G-force from the explosion tosses them about like paper airplanes.

The two pilots located further out are astonished at the size of the fireball created by the merging of the two missiles. They both share concern for their fellow squadron members.

Chapter One Hundred

Missile Mishap

Red Dog Three reports to Red Dog Squadron's command center the longitude and latitude of the approximate position the cruise missile emerged from the ocean's depths. A P3 Orion is the closest plane available to seek and destroy enemy submarines, and one of the best to do the job. The Orion is at the given coordinates within ten minutes after the cruise missile's destruction.

On site, the P3 confirms the longitude and latitude with command and begins an easterly track dropping sonar buoys every five hundred yards, hoping to pick up a signal. She begins by dropping passive sonar searches. When she has an active signal, she will start dropping active searches.

Two miles from the L & L, the P3 Orion gets an active signal. Having a full compliment of weapons and just beginning her patrol, the Orion is ready to take on whatever waits for her below the surface.

*

"Control, sonar. We're getting noises as if something's being dropped into the water.'

"Shit," says the captain. "We have an aircraft overhead dropping sonar buoys. Bring her down to three hundred meters. Proceed at two knots."

Just as the captain says this, one of the sonar buoys picks up their signal. The P3 then drops an active sonar buoy. "There he is, as big as life itself," the P3's pilot tells his crew. "I'm going to make a circle here to drop more active buoys. I want you to prepare the MK 46 torpedoes. Time to kiss this sucker goodbye."

As the P3 creates a circle, the submarine goes deep. For a while, the active buoys lose him up. Then, by sheer good fortune, three of the buoys pick up sounds that translate to submarine contact, allowing the P3 to triangulate its position according to heading, speed and, most importantly of all, its depth. The Kilo appears to be trying to escape, at the maximum depth for Kilos.

The pilot thinks, *Well, tough shit, buddy. You delivered a present to our door. Now you get one in return.* Then the P3 Orion drops four MK 46 torpedoes at thirty second intervals. Each torpedo has its own guidance system to seek and destroy. The systems aboard the P3 indicate all four torpedoes are running normal.

Two of the four identify their target and head for 104.

As the P3 makes a couple more passes around the area, two large eruptions spout skyward, followed almost immediately by oil and various debris rising to the surface. Their radar guidance system confirms that they have just earned a kill.

*

Action on the east coast has not met with any weather problems. The west coast is another story. Above the surface, heavy winds and drenching rains cover the entire northwest, from Canada all the way south to central California.

Naval vessels trying to maintain the vigilant watch they've been assigned are bouncing about like corks in a pond. Aircraft flying over the given parameters have their own set of problems.

The USS Hawkeye DDG 94 is maintaining her station on the most northern point of the picket line. Her radar picks up the launching of a cruise missile from Kilo 102.

Captain Jesse Meyers runs from the bridge down to the combat information center.

"Missile launch identified," he says, keeping his voice as controlled as possible, under the circumstances. "Get fire control ready to create a solution."

"Aye, sir," responds the watch officer.

"Fire Control, CIC. We have a missile launched from below the surface at 325 degrees, range fifty miles."

Fire control officers and sailors work feverishly to create a firing solution on the radar blip they have just identified as a cruise missile heading inbound toward San Francisco.

As the turret for the Sparrow missiles begins to turn, a complete systems failure occurs. The control officer tries three more times. Each time, the turret fails to respond.

"Captain, we have a systems failure on the Sparrow launcher," yells the Fire Control officer from the other end of the CIC.

"What do you mean, systems failure?"

"Everything just shut down, sir. We don't know why yet. Someone else better back us up for this shot."

"There's an emergency restart on that system. Have you tried that?"

"Yes sir. Three times."

"I want a report from your crew on my desk as soon as you find the problem."

The captain grabs a phone which allows him to communicate via satellite with Pacific Command directly.

The phone rings three times, which feels like a lifetime to the frustrated captain. Finally the secretary for Vice-Admiral Kevin O'Rourke answers it.

"This is an emergency. I need the admiral, right now. This is Captain Jesse Meyers of the USS Hawkeye."

"Yes, sir."

Almost immediately, the admiral is on the phone. "Captain, this is Admiral O'Rourke."

"Sir, we've detected a missile launch, heading for San Francisco. We are the northernmost vessel of our group and our Sparrow system has failed to operate. Notify land-based command to use their surface-launched ground-to-air missiles to take this thing out."

"Your current coordinates for the missile, Captain?"

The captain has the watch officer give him the coordinates, which he relays quickly and clearly to the admiral.

"Captain, I want a report from you on why that Sparrow system failed to function."

"Yes, sir. I do too. You'll have it, as soon as I do."
The captain and the admiral hurriedly hang up.

*

The army base command closest to San Francisco receives Admiral O'Rourke's phone call. The National Guard unit on station has two surface-to-air launchers located just north of the city. Their launch crews quickly realize the seriousness of the situation as their commander tells them what they need to do. These men are trained on this equipment, but have never fired a missile at an enemy. Up until now, it's been a shift like any other shift. The tension and fear that comes with impending combat takes each of the four-member crew by surprise.

At fifty miles out, the missile is targeted and they fire one of their medium-range surface-launched missiles. As it rises to intercept, it heads directly out to meet the Iranian cruise missile. To insure success, the team fires a second missile two minutes after the first launch. As they track their launches, they are horrified when they see the first of their missiles explode prematurely. Both the second launch and the cruise missile are thrown off their courses from the ensuing shock wave, each going in different directions.

"Dear God," the base commander cries, "that missile is going to hit the city."

The Iranian missile intended for San Francisco has been knocked slightly off course, coming down instead in the adjacent community of Oakland, just across San Francisco Bay. Landing almost dead center of a city of roughly 400,000, it detonates with nuclear fury. An American city is destroyed in a fraction of the time it takes the bomb's attendant mushroom cloud to rise over the entire San Francisco basin.

As soon as Admiral O'Rourke gets off the phone with the army, he places a satellite call to a squadron in his fleet.

BLACK ANGUS, MAINSTAY. OVER.

BLACK ANGUS. GO AHEAD.

PIRATE JUST SIGHTED MISSILE LAUNCHED NEAR HIS COORDINATES. HOWEVER HE HAD SYSTEM FAILURE WITH HIS SPARROW. HOW FAR ARE YOU FROM HIS LOCATION? OVER.

The OOD checks his radar to compare their position to where the Hawkeye is estimated to be. MAINSTAY, BLACK ANGUS. OUR LOCATION IS TWENTY MILES SOUTH OF PIRATE. OVER.

BLACK ANGUS, COORDINATE WITH PIRATE. HAVE YOUR SQUADRON JOIN UP WITH HIM TO TAKE OUT THAT KILO. HE CAN KEEP WATCH WHILE YOU GET THERE. OVER.

MAINSTAY, BLACK ANGUS. WHAT ABOUT THE MISSILE? OVER.

BLACK ANGUS, THE MISSILE IS NOW THE ARMY'S RESPONSIBILITY. OVER.

*

Captain Jesse Meyers cannot be angrier that their Sparrow system failed them when it was needed most. *There's one thing I can do besides cry in my beer,* he lectures himself. *We can terminate that sub.*

Vice-Admiral O'Rourke calls Captain Meyers on the satellite phone system and advises him that he has a squadron of destroyers and frigates coming to aid him in finding and taking out the Kilo. "They will communicate with you when they are within five miles," the Admiral tells him. "Your job is to keep monitoring the Kilo."

Chapter One Hundred One

Three Down—One To Go

Below the surface in Kilo 102, Captain Mukhtar cannot stand the anxiety of not knowing if his missile was successful or not. He decides to rise to periscope depth and trail his antenna wire to see if he can pick up any communications from the Americans.

Aboard the Hawkeye, CIC is contacting the captain. "Bridge, sonar contact. Range 10,000 yards bearing 300 degrees. He's close to the surface."

"This is the captain. I have the conn."

"All stop. Left ten degrees rudder. Steer course 300."

"CIC, I want the torpedo hatches open and ready to fire."

"CIC, aye."

"Sonar. Where is he now?"

"Sir, he's still at 300, range 9,500 yards."

"Tubes ready to be launched, Captain."

"Sonar, this is your ballgame. I want you to work out the fire solution. We will be making no turns to stay as quiet as possible."

The chief petty officer in sonar looks at his men. "You heard the captain. We're going to get this bastard."

"I want the helo in the air right now," says the captain. "Stay to our stern until I advise otherwise."

CIC responds, "Helo warming up and will be airborne in five minutes, sir."

"Sonar, are you ready?"

"Sir, he appears to be heading in a northwesterly direction along 300 degrees, traveling at two knots. He may be recharging his batteries. We don't believe he knows we are here. We recommend firing four fish, two coming in on him from starboard, and two from port."

"XO, do you concur with sonar?"

"Yes, captain. I'd also suggest torpedo depths at different levels so we can catch him as he dives once he hears the fish coming."

"Fire all four torpedoes, XO."

"Torpedoes in the water running smooth and clear, sir," the XO reports after all four tubes are clear.

"CIC to captain. Helo just left the deck, sir."

*

On board Kilo 102, the first officer, who understands and speaks passable English, is trying to make out a jumble of overlapping messages. He wants to hear whether their missile launch was a success or failure. The amount of radio traffic seems to be substantial, the tone of communications animated. He's having a hard time making sense of it all.

Then he hears, loud and clear, that a nuclear-armed cruise missile landed in the middle of Oakland, California. He stops. *That cannot be.* He listens again for further transmission. The first officer starts to radio the captain but finds himself speechless. *I can't have heard correctly. Nuclear weapons?* Instead, slowly, mechanically, he crosses from the radio room to the control room, seeking out the captain.

"Our launch was successful, Captain," he reports, his voice hollow. He pauses.

The captain looks up at him with nervous irritation. "Is there something else to report, number one?"

"Did—anyone tell you that the missile we fired was carrying a nuclear warhead, sir?"

"What are you saying? There was nothing in my orders about nuclear warheads. We were supposed to be firing conventional weapons. Certainly we would have been told . . ."

"Sir, what I have heard—and confirmed—is that there was a nuclear explosion in Oakland, California."

"But, number one, that has to be an error—we were firing at San Francisco."

"Oakland is directly next to San Francisco, sir. Perhaps the missile wandered off course for some reason."

"Will Allah forgive us?" the captain says with overwhelming guilt. His eyes turn to the heavens, above the upper hull of his submarine, above the water, above the world. "We may have, quite possibly, started World War III," he whispers.

The word of the successful launch travels throughout the submarine like wildfire. Close on its heels comes the fact that it carried a nuclear warhead, the thought of which quickly sickens the majority of the crew. As much as they all thought they would rejoice to see the United States, the American Satan, wounded, it had never entered their minds that they were taking part in delivering devastation such as this. They wonder if any of the other vessels know.

While the crew is hypnotized by this news, four torpedoes from the Hawkeye are closing in on them. Mid-sentence, one of the sonar operators happens to glance at his screen. To his horror he sees destruction headed their way.

"Captain, sonar. Four torpedoes in the water coming straight at us. Fast."

"Bring in the wire and take her down quickly to one hundred meters."

As the wire is being retrieved, the group of four torpedoes separates into two groups of two, each pair taking a side of the submarine.

"All stop! Eject decoys!" yells the captain, but he is too late. Three of the four MK 60s have already targeted the Kilo and will follow it wherever it runs, until they either connect or run out of fuel. All three torpedoes find their mark. The eruption of the torpedoes as they destroy the submarine produce three large spouts of water at the surface. The last of the Kilos is heading for the bottom of the ocean.

"CIC. Have the helo fly over the spot where we saw the eruptions. I want confirmation that this is a kill."

"Aye, aye, sir."

Within minutes the helo reports back to the ship that there are bodies, debris and slicks of diesel fuel floating on the surface."

"CIC, have the helo return to the ship and make turns for ten knots. OOD, you have the conn. I am calling Black Angus to tell him the Kilo's been eliminated."

Captain Meyers walks into CIC and picks up the satellite phone to call Admiral O'Rourke. When he has him on the phone, he simply says, "Meyers here. Our Kilo is history."

"Great work, Jesse."

"Thank you, sir. But I wish we could have gotten him before he fired. Were the land-based units able to take it out?"

"Captain, they tried, but apparently after firing two missiles at it, the first exploded prematurely and threw both the second launch and the cruise missile itself off course. The missile landed in Oakland."

"Jesus Christ, sir," Captain Meyers says quietly. "Oakland."

"Jesse, it was nuclear."

"Jesus H. Christ. How many lost, sir?"

"We have no idea yet, but it's bad."

Chapter One Hundred Two

The President Addresses The Nation

As the president is being flown back to Washington from the secure location where he'd been taken, he receives word of the Oakland disaster from Dean Hargrove. "I'm truly sorry sir," Hargrove says, his voice drained and weary. "Everyone did their utmost not to let this happen."

"I know, Dean, I know. Please have everyone, including NSA and CIA, meet me in twenty minutes in the Situation Room."

*

Melanie Jacobs is on assignment in London for her company. When she hears the news she collapses in front of a group of executives to whom she is making a presentation.

When she is revived, she explains haltingly that her parents live in Oakland and she is worried about them. Everyone around her tries to give her some comfort and the offer of any help in finding out if they survived.

Survived? Survived! What are these people, nuts? Even if they are alive, the rest of their lives will be a living hell from the radioactivity.

She feels the need to do something. *But what?*

*

The president is escorted to the Situation Room. The CIA director, the secretary of defense, the NSA director, the chairman of the joint chiefs as well as Admiral Smith and Generals James Bradley and Victor Sanford are on their feet, expecting him.

"Please, everyone take a seat." He sits, but barely on the edge of his seat. "First of all, I want to thank each and every one of you. I know this has been a terrible ordeal. We didn't come out of it one hundred percent, but it could have been so, so much worse. Secondly, I will be speaking to the American people tonight at 8:00." Once he has this much off his mind, he sags visibly.

"Now we have to get back to work. I need as much information about the whole picture as you can give me. I know that we're going to take flack on this because of what happened in Oakland. But I believe that the people will understand at some level that we did our best. Right now, that's all I have to say. I'll excuse myself to put my thoughts together for tonight."

*

Sitting in the Oval Office in front of cameras from all of the major networks, President Egan addresses the nation.

"My fellow countrymen and women, today America has suffered a great tragedy. A cruise missile, armed with a nuclear warhead, was fired at the city of San Francisco. It landed off course in Oakland, because one of our own interception missiles exploded prematurely.

"Tonight you need to hear the whole story. For a number of years now we've been at odds with the nation of Iran regarding their program for the enrichment of uranium. They have lied to us about their true intentions. Through effective intelligence and satellite spy coverage, we were finally able to learn what their true intentions were. They persisted with their strategy of labeling us as paranoid, telling anyone who would listen that we just want to colonize the Middle East.

"Six weeks ago, five Kilo submarines set sail from Iran. One was spotted in the Mediterranean, headed for Israel. The other four, which were heading for our coastlines, were followed by our underwater sonar systems. The Israelis took out the Kilo approaching their country." The president looks down momentarily, finding he cannot look the country in the eye, so to speak, telling this diplomatically necessary falsehood.

"Trying not to be the aggressors," he continues, "we followed the four coming to our shores until we could confirm through intelligence that they had orders to strike four U.S. cities: Washington, New York, Los Angeles and San Francisco. While looking for submarines is not the easiest thing to do in vast oceans, our military forces and intelligence agencies worked seamlessly together to find these vessels before they could launch their deadly payloads.

"Yesterday, at seven o'clock p.m. eastern time, one Kilo launched a missile at Washington. Another Kilo attacked New York, the third Los Angeles and the fourth San Francisco. Our Navy was able to intercept a missile heading for Washington. The Air Force, likewise, took out the one heading for New York. For some reason the third Kilo had internal problems and self-destructed while trying to fire its missile. However, it is the most painful thing I know I will ever have to say that the fourth missile landed in Oakland as we were attempting to destroy it.

"How bad is the damage? I do not have an accurate assessment at this point. I refuse to speculate, but I do promise to keep you informed. I do want you to know that the three Kilos that successfully fired missiles at Washington, New York and Los Angeles have been destroyed by our armed forces.

"I also want you to be aware that while the Kilos were crossing oceans to attack the United States, we took the battle to Iran, destroying its nuclear enrichment programs, a major part of its military and the heads of its government who plotted to declare war on the United States of America. Civilian casualties, which we wish could have been held to zero, were held to a regrettable minimum."

"I ask all of you for your prayers, especially for those we have lost and those who are suffering through this monumental rein of terror. Tonight, as your president, I close with a heavy heart."

*

First thing the next morning, Janet White knocks on the Oval Office door and asks to come in. "Janet, you look like you just saw a ghost," the president observes.

"Sir, I just got off of the phone with Bethesda Naval Hospital. They want you to call them as soon as possible. Something has happened to the vice president."

"Like what?" President Egan asks. *As if I didn't know.*

"I don't know, sir. They wouldn't tell me."

"Get whomever you talked to on the line for me."

"Yes, sir," she replies as she closes the door behind her.

President Egan waits for the director of operations at the hospital to come on the line. "Mr. President, Dr. Hillston. We have a serious problem, sir."

"What kind of a problem?" Suddenly, the president grows tense. Something in the doctor's voice . . .

"The vice president's body was found ten minutes ago. On the ground, just below his sixth-story window. It appears he has committed suicide."

Holy shit! "How many people know about this right now?" asks the president, trying to steady his voice.

"Right now—just our security force and the staff that retrieved the body. He was taken to the morgue immediately."

"Doctor, is there any chance there was foul play involved in this, something having to do with the Oakland bombing?"

"I doubt it, sir. He did have access to television, as do all the patients on that floor. They know about the bombing."

"Then I'll want the FBI to do a full investigation. I'll turn this over to them. Doctor, thank you for your professionalism."

The president picks up his phone. "Janet, I need you to call the director of the FBI, but before you do that, please come into my office."

As Janet enters she can read an even deeper level of gloom on the president's face than that with which he started this difficult day. "Please sit down," he says, then proceeds to tell her what he just learned from the hospital. "I'm sure I don't need to tell you not to let anyone know of this before it becomes public knowledge, Janet."

"I understand, sir."

Janet rises and leaves the Oval Office to make the call to the FBI.

*

President Egan picks up his phone and calls Allison McDonald on her private line. "Allison, I just received word that the vice president has probably committed suicide. I say probably because I don't know for sure yet—I'm having the FBI investigate. I want you to have Scott Brubaker call me this morning, and then I want you to have him released from the safe house he's in. I'm thinking of doing the same with Maria."

"You aren't going to prosecute her, sir?"

"Right now, I'm going to live up to my promise to Brubaker. I told him I'd work with him on a feature story if he worked with me. I also feel that the country doesn't need to have the administration dragged through a court hearing on a security leak, even if that leak was the cause of those Kilos departing Iran earlier than they'd planned."

"The people have been through an awful lot in the last couple of days," Allison agrees.

"I'm thinking that your special team has one more assignment for me, though."

"And what might that be, sir?"

"Accidents happen. I want to read about it in the paper."

Allison is stunned. She sits back in her chair, realizing that the president of the United States has just ordered one of her teams to assassinate an American citizen. "Sir, are you thinking this thing through clearly? Maybe in a day or two you'll change your mind about this?"

The president sighs and closes his eyes momentarily. "You're right, Allison. I have a lot of anger about what happened in Oakland, not just the leak. Let me give some more thought to what I just said. Allison—thank you."

*

After speaking with the director of the FBI, the president realizes that he's having a hard time focusing his mind on all he has before him.

Then Janet calls. "Sir, I have a woman on the phone. Her name is Melanie Jacobs. She says she's from Oakland, and that she has to speak to you and you only."

"What? How the hell is she able to call?"

"She says that she was in London, and that she's on her way to Washington right now. She says it's imperative that she speak with the president."

Just then the name Melanie Jacobs rings a bell. "Janet, as soon as she arrives have her brought to the Oval Office. Get me the director of the FBI again."

Chapter One Hundred Three

Aftermath of Destruction

"My fellow Americans, it's been seventy-two hours since I last spoke with you. I waited this long, not to increase your anxiety, but to try and lessen it. Most of what you've heard in the media is accurate. We've gone overboard not to hide anything from you. The good news is that the amount of nuclear material used in the Iranian missile had a comparably small yield-strength to it—in plain English, the radioactive fallout out is lower than what we expected.

"The bad news, of course, is that to date we estimate we have sustained over one-hundred fifty thousand deaths, and more that two hundred fifty thousand casualties. The cost of the physical devastation cannot begin to be calculated as yet. It will surely be in the billions of dollars.

"I will be speaking with the Iranian people just as I'm speaking with you tonight. I wish to relay to them that we understand those who created this havoc are no longer living, to the best of our knowledge, and that we would like to be able to work with a new government towards a future peaceful coexistence.

"I will also be addressing the United Nations three days from now, explaining what happened to us and to the nation of Iran. The world needs to hear firsthand that we cannot continue to betray each other if this world wishes to survive.

"Again, I leave you with a heavy heart, but one that says we will overcome this tragedy."

*

FBI Director Mark Richardson sits inside the Oval Office but sitting out of camera range, watching the president make his speech, having been called there by the president to discuss some matters after the speech is completed. Witnessing it firsthand, he is astounded at how calmly the president is able to handle all of this.

Once the president's address is finished and his office is cleared of camera equipment, Richardson and the president find themselves alone.

"Mark, we need to find out how we can identify the kinds and amount of nuclear material it takes to produce the amounts of radiation we're finding. The CIA has intel on a Russian mafiya transaction, to persons we believe were Iranian agents posing as Pakistanis. I want to see if we can't sidestep some of the worldwide bullshit that allows terrorists toys they shouldn't have."

"Will the CIA be working with the agency on this, sir?"

"Yes. I've already instructed Allison to do so, and she's more than willing."

"Good. I'll put a team right on it. We'll look at whatever's been found so far, and get you an analysis for comparisons so we can decide where we need to go with it."

"That's what I want to hear, Mark. How is the investigation going regarding the vice president's death?" The president really hates to ask.

"In all honesty, sir, it's looking like a clear case of suicide. We're not going to sign off on it until we've done more tests to see if anything's been overlooked, but I doubt we'll find anything."

"I have to make a public announcement regarding his death," the president says. "I'm hoping I can make it simple and straightforward. We don't want people to panic, thinking their leaders are falling apart on them. I also don't want his family suffering any more than they are already."

"I understand, sir. You'll have a final report hopefully tomorrow, two days tops."

*

At eight the following morning, the president's guest is sitting across from him in the Oval Office. Melanie Jacobs comes across as very professional—and very attractive. Looking her straight in the eye, he asks, "Okay, Ms. Jacobs, why are you here?"

"Mr. President, I'm sure by now you know that I've been acting as an agent for my native country. Yes, when asked to do certain things, such as confirming or providing information, I did so gladly, out of the belief that my country was struggling in a world that looked down on her as a third-world nation. I know America calls her a terrorist state, but many of us want much more for her future. I thought I was doing the right thing. I never realized the government was planning to attack the United States, much less use nuclear weapons."

"So why are you sitting in front of me? Are you planning on trading information for fear of our apprehending you, or are you seeking vengeance since I understand your parents are from Oakland?" President Egan avoids the subject of whether they have survived the attack.

Jacobs shudders, then pauses for a moment and considers what he just said. "Maybe a little bit of both, sir. I have learned that my parents—no longer exist." *It's easier to say that than to say that they died in the bombing.* "They never did anything wrong. They were good people who loved me. I feel terrible guilt."

"I'm sorry, Ms. Jacobs. Truly, I am. But again, I have to ask, what are you looking for from the United States?"

"When I read Scott Brubaker's feature article about the attack, I knew he had to have an inside track into what happened. Scott is a good writer, but there was so much he could never have known on his own. It was clear that someone was feeding him that information."

"You're correct. I did." The president's gaze doesn't falter.

Amazed Jacobs replies, "What did Scott do to deserve that kind of treatment?"

"That's not a matter for discussion. Right now I want to know how you can help the United States."

"I can offer you people who'd be willing to do what it would take to put Iran on a saner footing, who in time might be able to develop a working partnership between our two countries. I can also give you names and locations of a number of Iranian agents living in this country."

Somewhat amazed, the president studies the woman before continuing. Finally, he says "I'm going to turn you over to the FBI and have them advise me as to the value of what you have to offer."

"You're going to arrest me?"

"For the moment, you aren't under arrest. You will, however, be in protective custody. If your information is helpful, we'll release you and you can go wherever you wish."

The president reaches for his phone and calls Janet. "Get the director of the FBI on the line for me." Then he hangs up.

The president and Melanie Jacobs sit in silence looking at each other until the phone rings. On the other end is the director of the FBI.

"Mark, the person I spoke with you about is sitting here in the Oval Office. Please send down a team to escort her to your office."

"I'll have a team on the way as soon as I hang up, sir."

"Ms. Jacobs, I need for you to wait in the sitting room. A Secret Service agent will escort you there and stay with you while you wait for the FBI to arrive."

*

Upon notification that the radioactive fallout is relatively low, the governor of California boards a helicopter to survey the destruction.

Flying along the perimeter of the blast before going to its center, he thinks back to cities he read about in school that were bombed in World War II. Visually he estimates buildings were either totally destroyed or nearly so within a radius of ten miles from the center of the blast, due to the explosion itself or the shockwave that followed.

The National Guard is posted on the perimeter of the blast wearing protective clothing to minimize the effect of radioactivity. They will also be well prepared to handle crowd control, the president having promised the governor that Washington will rush 'Silent Guardians,' also known as 'active denial systems,' a joystick and computer screen innovation from Raytheon that employs wave technology to repel individuals without causing injury. *That's one thing I don't want more of—injury*, the governor thinks as he surveys the carnage. *The people of California have suffered enough merely for the crime of being Americans.*

One thing he is pleased about is that the president has agreed to back up his order that looters will be shot on sight. Every television station and radio station is broadcasting that information every half hour. *If some jerk misses it, tough shit.*

Joe Smiga

After twenty minutes over Oakland and part of San Francisco, the governor directs the pilot to return to his base. He is sickened by all he has seen, and now faces the biggest effort of his political career.

*

Through the efforts of the British Broadcasting Corporation, the president is going to be transmitting from the Oval Office via England into Iran, at noon in Washington, eight p.m., prime time in Iran. His greatest concern—and hope—is that the Iranian people believe him. The BBC is interpreting the president's message to insure Washington that it is being translated correctly.

He begins, "As President of the United States I wish to speak directly to the citizens of Iran. Seven weeks ago, the government of Iran sent five Kilo submarines on a mission of death and destruction. Through intelligence and high technology, the United States learned that four of the five submarines were headed for four major cities on our country's shores. The fifth submarine was headed for the nation of Israel.

"Today, the city of Oakland, California, is in ruins, having suffered the nuclear explosion of a cruise missile fired from one of the four Kilos. At the moment we estimate one hundred and fifty thousand dead and over two hundred and fifty thousand injured. The nuclear missile caused major destruction across a ten mile radius. We will have to deal with this disaster for decades to come, between the radioactive fallout and the devastation it left in its wake.

"Why am I speaking with you? You need to understand why the United States launched attacks on your country. You need to hear it from us, not some extremist within your midst. When we decided to deploy our forces against you, we did a number of things. First, we convinced Israel *not* to attack your nation. I credit them for the restraint they have used. Our forces attacked military installations, uranium enrichment facilities and lastly those in your government who engineered and brought about this tragedy. We did our best to minimize any civilian casualties and we did not use nuclear technology.

"None of us can undo what has happened, but we can come together for a better future. From sources inside of your great nation, we are aware that there are many individuals who would be willing to work towards creating a government that would seek peace and prosperity for you, instead of war and destruction.

"My offer, in good faith to you as a nation, is this: that the United States will assist your new government, *if* it chooses to coexist in peace, by helping you rebuild and also by protecting your sovereignty from outside forces while you are in the rebuilding process.

"We await a response from your nation."

Chapter One Hundred Four

At the United Nations

Mary Johnsen, Secretary General of the United Nations, stands at the podium waiting for everyone to take their seats. The gathering begins to settle down. "I wish to thank you for taking the time for this special meeting of the General Assembly," she says into her microphone, then waits her audience out for silence.

When the ambassadors have reached an acceptable level of attention, she continues, "Members of the General Assembly of the United Nations, to maintain effective communication regarding what truly transpired here in this, our host country, over the past few days, I have asked the President of the United States to address this body. Mr. President, you have the floor."

As the president rises to speak, the Iranian ambassador stands and shouts, "You war monger, you have decimated my country, and now you are here to give us excuses."

Mary Johnsen rises from her seat. Controlling her temper, she calls a halt to the Iranian's rant. "Mr. Ambassador, you may have the floor after the president is through," she says through clenched teeth.

The ambassador sits back down, angrily jamming on his head set to hear the simultaneous translation of the president's speech into Farsi. When the president reaches the podium, he repositions the microphone and looks around until he has everyone's full attention. Once he feels he has, he begins, "Members of the General Assembly, it is my duty to inform this world body about everything that has transpired in the

Middle East and in the Western Hemisphere over the last few months, and particularly over the last week.

"I am sure you are all aware that United States' military forces have attacked the nation of Iran. Our Navy and Air Force undertook this combined effort in an attempt to counter the threat of Iranian military forces attacking the United States.

"Seven and a half weeks ago, we know that five Kilo submarines left their berths at Bandar Abbas, in the Persian Gulf. Their mission was to have four of them attack cities in the United States. One was to attack the sovereign nation of Israel.

"The Israelis have taken steps to neutralize the threat to their nation. However, the submarines headed for our shores were harder to locate. Intelligence sources gave us forewarning of this plot. We waited until it was completely clear that the Kilos approaching the United States were really intent on their mission.

"Four days ago, nuclear warheads—I repeat, *nuclear* warheads were fired at the cities of New York, Washington, Los Angeles and San Francisco. Fortunately for us three of the cities escaped being hit, due to the efforts of our military. One missile, the one headed for San Francisco, was affected by a missile of ours that blew up prematurely. The Iranian missile was knocked off course, landing in the adjacent city of Oakland. At last count, Oakland and San Francisco have over one hundred fifty thousand dead, and over a quarter million injured. While we know the nuclear yield of the missile was relatively small, the explosive force destroyed a large section of Oakland.

"Yes, we did attack Iran. The United States will not stand by and be terrorized by anyone who wishes to destroy our way of life and our people. Our mission's plan was to decimate the nuclear enrichment and processing facilities of Iran, the naval base at Bandar Abbas, and Iran's air force. As I stand before you, I wish to also advise you that, on my orders, the government creating this catastrophe was eliminated. We will never have to deal with them again. I have personally made a plea to the next elected government in Iran, stating clearly that the United States will work to help them rebuild a government that is interested in peace and prosperity.

"Mr. Ambassador, you stated that I would give excuses to this world body. Every word I have just spoken can be verified as fact. On the other hand, based on sources we now have, I wish to inform you, before this world body, that we have evidence that you personally are an agent for the Iranian secret police. As such, you and two other members of your staff will be arrested. As this meeting concludes and all of you leave this chamber, I wish for everyone to be aware that the FBI will be arresting the ambassador for deportation, as he falls under the rules of diplomatic immunity. However, his staff members, who are being taken into custody as we speak, will face charges of espionage. At this very moment, we are also arresting twelve other Iranian agents around the country."

The ambassador looks around him and sees that teams of agents are moving in on him. His face a mask, he takes off his head set, reaches into his jacket pocket, removes a pill, and places it between his teeth, then bites down. His body reacts almost immediately; before the FBI can reach him, the ambassador from Iran drops from his seat, dead, to the floor. The entire general assembly first reacts with shock, then yelling and shouting breaks out.

Mary Johnsen moves to the podium alongside President Egan and starts shouting into the microphone for quiet, then calls a short recess. "Everyone please remain in their seats." Staff security come quickly to check the status of ambassador. Confirming that he is indeed dead, they call for a stretcher, lift his body onto it and wheel him from the auditorium.

When order is resumed President Egan continues with his prepared speech. "I deeply regretted having to make the decision to go to war. No American president will ever—can ever—allow this to happen to our country. For that reason, I do not regret the decision I made.

"We have also learned that the nuclear yield strength of the cruise missile that destroyed Oakland is similar to that of conventional battlefield artillery weapons, though of course, the fact that it was nuclear bomb made its impact so deadly. Our FBI and CIA are working jointly to compare intelligence to find where those nuclear components came from.

"At this point, I have nothing further to say and am not taking questions." President Egan leaves the podium and heads over to the Dave Gates, the American ambassador.

Mary Johnsen asks, "Are there any other statements to be made by any other member of the assembly?" With no hands showing, she adjourns the meeting.

When the president reaches Gates, he says, "Dave, you know what I want you to do."

"Yes sir, it will be taken care of."

As the assembly room is vacating, Gates looks over to his Russian counterpart and signals to for him to wait for him.

As Gates approaches, Mikhail Milodanovich says, "That was some show your president just put on."

"Misha, this is no show. The man knows how to take the bull by the horns and run with it."

"So what do you want from me, Dave?".

"We have intelligence that your mafiya sold nuclear materials to some Iranians who were posing as Pakistanis."

"Nonsense. You can't get that stuff on the black market."

"Misha, either you believe your government's propaganda—or you're lying through your teeth," Gates says flatly.

"Why would I lie to you, Dave?"

"Who knows," Gates replies blandly. "I certainly don't. I'm just passing along a message for you to pass along. We have reason to believe that the missiles destined to take out four major American cities carried materials from Russian warheads. It's up to your government to find out and take care of it."

"And if we don't?"

"You have thirty days to get back to us that you have taken care of the source. If not, then we will take care of it ourselves."

"You have no jurisdiction on Russian soil, Dave."

"Just remember, Misha, accidents happen. Thirty days and no more."

With a curt nod, Ambassador Gates heads for the exit, leaving the Russian standing alone. Glancing back, he sees concern on Milodanovich's face. If he could read the Russian's thoughts, he would find him thinking, *After witnessing what the U.S. just did in Iran, it's clear this president is not just a man of words. I best get back to the embassy and send a message quickly.*

The president's speech has gone out live on all of the major networks and, even though the nation has suffered its worst tragedy in its relatively brief history, the public take solace in knowing they have a man in the White House who will not sit back and only react.

*

Back at the Russian embassy, Milodanovich dictates a letter to his president. Briefly outlining Gates' demands, he ends by making it clear that the United States is not bluffing. The letter is encrypted and sent via satellite.

*

Inside Iran, groups of individuals are gathering, trying to assess what is really going on. They are aware that the presidential offices and the Guardian Council building are no longer standing. No one has seen the Supreme Leader, the president or any members of the council since the attack took place. Can it be that they are free to form a new government? And do they have the will to change from the ways of the past which brought such calamity upon them?

Chapter One Hundred Five

Epilog

The president stands at the podium in the chamber of the House of Representatives, addressing a joint meeting of the Congress, giving them a detailed report on what led up to the declaration of war and why it was so vital to keep those decisions under wraps. He does not tell them, however, that the NSA has broken Iran's military codes. Nor does he tell them of Sterling and Devonshire's leak to the Post. *Too many lips would make sure that story got out.*

He gives an up-date on all that's happening in California. "Members of the House and Senate, over one hundred decontamination teams from all over the country have volunteered to aid Oakland and the region as step one in the rebuilding process. The process is slow but is moving in the right direction.

"Countless volunteer groups are willing to go to the disaster area as soon as we say it is clear for them to do so. We also need to build enough relief housing for those forced to remain away from their homes and their jobs. Life for the survivors of this attack should be at the very least tolerable, not further punishment. Our people did not ask for this to happen.

"Insurance commissions are saying that, as an act of war, they are not responsible for coverage, which is, unfortunately, within their contractual rights. In light of this, I would like to see Congress step in and immediately draft a bill to aid the victims with interest-free loans. I will gladly sign such a bill as soon as it arrives on my desk—just so long as it comes to me with no—I repeat, no pork-belly or private interest amendments." He looks across the audience, taking note of both smiles of approval and grimaces of disapproval for this comment.

"I am starting to hear from groups active in Iran about the rebuilding of their country and their government. This, too, will not be an overnight process, but I think we can work something out that will, in the long run, be mutually beneficial. I would like a bi-partisan committee to work with me on this.

"I am open to questions."

The junior senator from California stands to ask, "Sir, right now, how long do you think it will take to recover from this disaster?"

"Senator, right now, I honestly have to say I don't know. If I gave you a date, I'd be lying. America has never suffered a nuclear blast. We're all learning as we go. I don't care what textbooks tell you, this is real life. What I will tell you, though, is that we pledge to do our very best to make things happen, and to get it right the first time."

Getting ready to wrap up his address, he grows somber once again. "I am asking each and every one of you to make a pledge of your own, to play your part in the recovery from this tragic event. This is our country. Those victims out there are our people. We need to take care of them. And, by God, we will."

*

As he heads for the Oval Office, the president tells his secretary that he needs to talk with Allison McDonald.

"In person, sir?" asks Janet, "or is a phone call sufficient?"

William Egan has been a tower of strength, running on adrenaline for what feels like half a lifetime, from the day McDonald first came to him with the intelligence that has driven the past ten months. He finally has to admit he's exhausted with it all. He tells Janet, "Have her call me. That'll be sufficient."

When the director of the CIA calls, the president gets right to the point. "Are you getting any feedback from our Russian friends, Allison?"

"No, sir, I'm not. My guess is they don't believe you're serious. Or you may be stepping on toes, upsetting somebody's blackmail or extortion scheme, or any number of other kinds of creative deal-making their bureaucracy seems to spawn on a daily basis. I'm sure they don't give a hoot about what happened here."

"You're probably right, Allison. Just remind me when it is thirty days." Allison can hear the weariness in his voice.

"I will sir, I promise. By the way, Mr. President, you should know that you've made the prime minister of Israel your trusted friend for life. His words."

"Well, at least I made somebody happy."

"More people than you realize, sir."

*

Allison McDonald makes the president aware when the thirty day period for the Russians to respond has expired. "There's still been no comment from the Russian government," she reports.

"Allison, I am going to wait fifteen more days. That should give them enough rope to hang themselves. In the meantime, I want to know everything your people can find out about that operation."

"I've been gathering that information for weeks. I figured we'd need it."

The president smiles. *This lady's so damn good at what she does. She's always a couple steps ahead of me.*

Fifteen days later, McDonald calls again. "What would you like us to do, sir?"

"You already know what to do. Just do it."

"Yes, sir. With pleasure."

*

On a very snowy day in Aspen, Colorado, Maria Sterling is skiing down towards the base lodge after having spent a full six hours on the slope. Tired, she can't wait to get home, in part because she has a new gentleman caller. Tonight will be their first real date, her first real date since she left the White House, in fact. She pulls out of the parking lot and heads south.

On the way back to her condo, Sterling is negotiating the mountain road a little too fast for the conditions and for safety's sake. All of a sudden, a large black Suburban crosses over the median in the middle of a curve. Having no where to go, reflex takes over. She pulls to the right, crashes through the guard rail, and drops nearly a thousand feet to the bottom of a ravine.

The accident isn't found until late the next morning, after state police notice the broken guard rail. No one can get down to where her car came to rest. The decision is made to wait for heavy-duty rescue equipment to arrive before attempting anything.

It's almost sunset before Maria Sterling is found dead inside of the wreckage of her car.

*

Forty-five days have gone by since Ambassador Gates had his brief exchange with the Russian ambassador.

Dimitri Kostovich is headed down the highway, to a dinner meeting with several associates. Vicktor is at the wheel of his favorite of his boss's vehicles, the silver 300S Mercedes sedan. Dimitri's bodyguard sits in the passenger seat.

Coming around a curve, they find the road blocked by an accident which appears to involve two trucks and a car. Two Russian police officers wave them to a halt and approach the Mercedes. Vicktor rolls down his window and one of the officers, looking in at all the passengers, advises them to park where they are. The road will need to be cleared before any traffic can proceed.

"Count yourself lucky," the second officer says, jovially. "At least you are first in line."

Vicktor throws the transmission into park, then glances in the rearview mirror. "First and last in line," he responds, just as both men pull out silenced automatic weapons and shoot Vicktor and his passengers. Afterwards, they clear away blood and neatly glue small figurines of bald eagles to the foreheads of each victim, then saunter away from the scene as if they had never been there.

Late that night, the Russian mafiya is advised of the deaths of their members, and about the bald eagles on their foreheads, just about the same time that Kostovich's office and all five of his warehouses, full of his stock in trade, just happen to catch fire and burn to the ground.

*

Hearing of the deaths of three upstanding Russian citizens, Aleksi Zheldak, the Russian president, flies into a rage. "Those fucking Americans think they can waltz in here and do anything they want. I'll show them."

Fedor Klopov, his vice president, says, "What will you show them? They gave you a chance to straighten it out. You've fucked up big time." This last comes out with an audible sneer, which only serves to make Zheldak even more furious. "You showed them how little support you would give them. Maybe your ego is bigger than your job."

"Don't talk to me that way. I am the president."

"Blow it out your ass, 'Mr. President.' Your title doesn't mean shit. Now you better get to work figuring out how you're going to do damage control with the Americans. Or the council will replace you. I will take care of that myself, personally.'

"What would you have me do?"

Klopov laughs dismissively. "You're the president—you think of something. Maybe it's about time you realized what's going on in the world around us."

*

In the weekend edition of the Washington Post, an obituary describes the accident that took Maria Sterling's life. After detailing her many accomplishments, it finishes with the fact that President Egan's chief of staff was on vacation at the time.